**More praise for the novels of
Jack DuBrul**

Pandora's Curse

"A rare treat—a thriller that blends some of modern history's most vexing enigmas with a hostile, perfectly realized setting. This is one thriller that really delivers: great characters combined with a breakneck pace and almost unbearable suspense."
—Douglas Preston and Lincoln Child,
coauthors of *The Ice Limit* and *Relic*

"Combining plenty of thrills and a touch of romance, DuBrul's action-packed contemporary adventure zips along like an out-of-control locomotive. . . . A well-researched foundation of facts and details grounds the reader in this frosty setting. . . . Mercer's love interest . . . is his fitting counterpart and a strong heroine, and their romance adds a degree of warmth to this swift, sensational tale. Those who enjoy a good adrenaline rush will find plenty here to satisfy."
—*Publishers Weekly*

"Have you been casually looking for a new thriller writer in the tradition of Clive Cussler? Would the idea of a touch of Jack Higgins intrigue you? Do you like your reading to move quickly, have a great plot, and the good guy gets the girl? Browse no more! Jack DuBrul is here. . . . *Pandora's Curse* hits all the buttons. Read it and run to your favorite bookstore for the others . . . a dandy read."
—*News & Ci̶t̶i̶z̶e̶n̶ (̶M̶o̶r̶r̶i̶s̶v̶ille, VT)

continued . . .

"The writing here is good, the pace very fast, the characters believable . . . a welcome addition to the ranks of thriller writers."—*Sullivan County Democrat* (NY)

"A fun thriller."   —*The Daily Oklahoman*

"An intricate tale filled with action and intrigue where the stakes are high. Mercer is an action character with a brain, a penchant for beautiful women, and the ability to think fast and inspire respect and trust. . . . A fast-paced story well told by an upcoming new talent in the spy thriller genre. DuBrul has earned an avid fan."   —*Cape Coral Daily Breeze*

Charon's Landing

"A pleasure . . . a densely detailed and well-paced thinking man's melodrama."   —*Kirkus Reviews*

"Jack DuBrul has to be the finest adventure writer on the scene today. Romance, violence, technology are superbly blended by a master storyteller. DuBrul creates a fast-moving odyssey that is second to none."
          —Clive Cussler

"DuBrul's well-calculated debts to Fleming, Cussler, Easterman, and Lustbader, his technological, political, and ecological research, and his natural gift for storytelling bode well."   —*Publishers Weekly*

DEEP FIRE
RISING

Jack Du Brul

AN ONYX BOOK

ONYX
Published by New American Library, a division of
Penguin Group (USA) Inc., 375 Hudson Street,
New York, New York 10014, U.S.A.
Penguin Books Ltd, 80 Strand,
London WC2R 0RL, England
Penguin Books Australia Ltd, 250 Camberwell Road,
Camberwell, Victoria 3124, Australia
Penguin Books Canada Ltd, 10 Alcorn Avenue,
Toronto, Ontario, Canada M4V 3B2
Penguin Books (N.Z.) Ltd, Cnr Rosedale and Airborne Roads,
Albany, Auckland 1310, New Zealand

Penguin Books Ltd, Registered Offices:
80 Strand, London WC2R 0RL, England

Published by Onyx, an imprint of New American Library,
a division of Penguin Group (USA) Inc.

First Printing, December 2003
10 9 8 7 6 5 4 3 2 1

PUBLISHER'S NOTE
This is a work of fiction. Names, characters, places, and incidents either are
the product of the author's imagination or are used fictitiously, and any resem-
blance to actual persons, living or dead, business establishments, events, or
locales is entirely coincidental.

To Jack D., Todd M., and Bob D.—
the first three links in the chain of my career.

ACKNOWLEDGMENTS

As always, I have to thank my wife, Debbie. The past year has been the most tumultuous in my life and I wouldn't have gotten through it without her. I also must thank my editor at NAL, Doug Grad, for his understanding and infinite patience. In the post–September 11 world, I've found sources more reluctant to discuss technical matters, even though my books are fiction. Those that do lend their expertise tend to wish to remain anonymous. I suspect other authors have seen this as well. Rest assured there are dozens of people who helped me in writing this novel and it certainly wouldn't have been possible without them.

I am very excited about *Deep Fire Rising*. This book went in a slightly different direction from my previous efforts and I'd like to know how you, the reader, felt about it. When you finish, please drop me a line at www.jackdubrul.com and let me know. I won't be able to respond to everyone, but I'll answer as many as I can. Now sit back, relax, and let me tell you a story.

Standing at the rail of the mail steamer *Loudon*, the watcher spat into the clear sea and cursed his stupidity as the tropical town of Anjer receded behind the ship. The tower of the Fourth Point lighthouse already resembled a spindle on the horizon.

He should have taken his chances ashore on Java Island when the ship made an unscheduled stop on its way from the Dutch Indies capital of Batavia to Padang on the west coast of Sumatra. Now he was trapped in a race across the Sunda Strait with six hundred other souls, and he alone knew what was coming, what the black clouds roiling on the skyline would bring.

Had he stayed on Java, maybe he could have moved far enough inland to survive the coming days. But he had decided to remain with the ship as it dashed to the Sumatran town of Telok Betong at the head of Lampong Bay. Over the past weeks he had cached food and water in the hills overlooking the bay to witness the approaching cataclysm. That was his job— what he'd been sent to the Dutch East Indies to do— to chronicle what he knew was going to be the greatest natural disaster in recorded history.

Ignoring the heat of the tropics, the man traveling under the name Han was dressed for his mountain homeland in wool trousers and a wool shirt. His boots reached almost to his knees and showed tufts where he'd cut away their yak-fur trim. Tucked into the satchel he carried was a simple cloak made of leather and embroidered by his wife many winters ago.

He was shorter than the Europeans aboard the 212-foot ship but taller than the 300 native convicts shackled in the forecastle under guard by 160 Dutch soldiers. He had a compact build, broader across the chest and shoulders than the Chinese laborers the ship had picked up at Anjer. His face was walnut brown and his dark eyes peeked out from pouches of wrinkles that partially obscured their Asian cast.

From a pants pocket he pulled one of his prized possessions, a gold watch on an ornate chain. He had set it this morning against the government clock in Batavia. It was three o'clock. They should reach Telok Betong in four hours.

He was certain they wouldn't.

The watcher turned from where the island of Java receded in the distance and peered over the port rail. The black clouds continued to build in the west, towering ever higher, flattening on top like an anvil. Even at this range the dark mass dominated the sky, an angry, burning column as evil as anything he had ever seen. It looked as if night had ripped a hole in the daylight and was pouring through. In the two hours since it appeared, the cloud had grown many times higher than Chomolungma, the tallest peak in the watcher's native Himalaya Mountains. And already it was starting to come down to earth.

He brushed his fingers along the burnished teak railing and felt a layer of fine grit. Not the seedlike granular discharge from the *Loudon*'s coal-fired boiler, but a powder so light that it vanished in the breeze of the vessel's six-knot speed.

The ship's master, Captain T. H. Lindemann, must have had an inkling of what was happening because he soon ordered deckhands up the rigging to set sails on the *Loudon*'s two masts to augment her single fixed screw. Soon she was making a respectable eight knots, sailing as close to the wind as she could.

Earlier in the summer, the *Loudon* had been taking sightseers into the Sunda Strait to witness the island that was slowly blowing itself into the atmosphere. And then just a few weeks ago, Lindemann had returned to the island to land a party of scientists, only to be driven back by ash and the burning heat exploding from the earth's core. At the time, the scientists had assured the captain that the eruption would soon come to a sputtering halt. With more than one hundred active volcanoes in the East Indies to learn from, Lindemann had no reason to doubt their opinion. Now, like the enigmatic watcher clutching the port rail, he felt that the scientists might be wrong. He gave the island a wide berth.

Creeping into the wide mouth of Lampong Bay brought no relief to the ship. Ash continued to rain down, even though the *Loudon* was forty kilometers from its source. Those crewmen not up in the masts were ordered to sweep the fine powder overboard. Lindemann had his steward, an old Chinese seaman named Ping, constantly wiping at the bridge windows with a dry cloth to keep them clear.

The sea had grown eerily still under the weight of ash, a surging mantle that parted reluctantly at the *Loudon*'s steel bows and closed immediately at the stern. The layer of ash was at least two feet thick and deepened steadily, like snow in a New England blizzard. Only this snow was pulverized rock that floated and remained warm to the touch long after it had been ejected from within the earth.

The chained prisoners in the forecastle moaned pitiably with each fresh gout of ash and at the increasing rattle of fist-sized pumice stones that peppered the ship's hull and deck.

At five p.m. it was as if the sky had been swallowed.

No light reached the ship, not the setting sun nor the first blush of the moon that had been near full the night before. There would be no stars. The bizarre atmospheric conditions made transmission on the newly installed wireless telegraph impossible. The *Loudon* was alone.

Two hours later they approached the town of Telok Betong. The lookout in the forward masthead could see nothing of the town. Ash had covered it completely and smothered the lights of a population of five thousand. Cautiously Lindemann dropped anchor in six fathoms of water. Nearby lay the side-wheeled *Berouw*, a small gunboat that regularly patrolled these waters for pirates. Lindemann ordered the *Loudon*'s sails lowered but had the chief engineer keep a head of steam in her boiler. He waited an hour for the lighters from shore to transfer the Chinese laborers he'd picked up at Anjer.

When he'd left his mountain village Han's orders had been explicit as to location and time, but vague when it came to the reason for his mission. He'd simply been told to find a place a suitable distance above sea level at the head of Lampong Bay and await what was to occur on the morning of August 27. He was to write down everything he observed in the ancient journal he'd been provided.

Shortly after his arrival in the Dutch East Indies in late July, he'd understood what he was there to witness. Unimaginable death and destruction. The island volcano churning in the middle of Sunda Strait had been erupting since the morning of May 20. That had been his first startling discovery since leaving his homeland. The second shock came when he realized he'd left Tibet a full week *before* the volcano first rumbled to life. He'd been told by the priests who'd sent him that they guarded a powerful oracle, but he couldn't understand how the prophecy about an event many thousands of leagues from their home could be so accurate. What was apparent was that they expected an even worse explosion in—he checked his pocket watch—seven hours.

His most strict order from the oracle's priests forbade him from interfering with the natural development of events. He was a witness only, a watcher prohibited from warning any who were going to be caught up in the inevitable catastrophe. Han had followed that mandate implicitly. But knowing the danger he was facing dispelled his obligation to this mission. It was bad enough they hadn't fully prepared him for what he'd been asked to observe. Now he feared he was going to become a victim. He'd made his travel arrangements from Batavia to Lampong Bay unaware that the *Loudon* would take the five-hour detour to Anjer. That delay was going to cost him his life if he didn't do something.

Han was not a fanatic, like some of the older watchers. He wanted to survive what was coming and the rules be damned. He rationalized his decision by convincing himself that the destruction of the steamship was not preordained. It was possible that the ship would survive even if he said nothing, though he wouldn't trust luck alone. He had to get a warning to the captain. They had to get away from shore if they were to stand even the slimmest chance.

Han squinted against the flakes of ash drifting from the night sky. He couldn't communicate with any of the crew. He didn't speak Dutch. Yet he had been on this ship several times when searching for the best vantage to watch the eruption and had befriended the captain's steward, Ping. Han's Cantonese was fluent enough for them to understand each other. He searched for the old seaman and spotted his skinny figure wiping the bridge windows with a filthy rag.

Moving so he stood directly below the steward, Han

cleared his throat to catch the man's attention. Ping ignored him and continued his fruitless work. "Old father," Han said respectfully, for the steward was many years his senior. "I would not interrupt you if it wasn't important."

"You should be below with the other passengers," Ping said, a little frightened by the mysterious traveler who he recognized had come from Tibet, a land populated by wizards.

"We have spoken over several trips together, but I have not told you the true reason I left my distant homeland. It is time to tell you that I am here to witness what is about to unfold."

Ping laughed nervously. "About to unfold? Look around you, man. It's already happened."

"This is just the beginning." Han spoke calmly, so Ping wouldn't think he was as panicked as the natives and laborers huddled in the crowded forecastle. "There will be another explosion, many times what happened today."

Ping stopped his wiping. The people of the Himalayas were said to have special gifts that allowed them to survive the harsh climate so close to the top of the world. He'd heard some fanciful stories about the mountain dwellers in his youth and had seen such unexplainable wonders in his time since that he had no reason to doubt them. The Tibetan standing so stolidly amid the swirling ash seemed so sure of himself that Ping wouldn't be surprised if he really did know something kept from normal men. It didn't hurt that he himself felt that the volcano over the horizon wasn't finished yet.

Han continued, "Tomorrow morning the mountain will explode again. When it does, it will destroy everything in the Sunda Strait."

Ping covered his astonishment with a skeptical look. "How do you know?"

"The same way I knew months ago that it would erupt at all. That is why I am here."

"The volcano has been erupting for months," Ping said. "Maybe you heard of this and came to see for yourself."

The watcher reached into his bag, careful to knock ash from its cover so as not to spoil what was nestled inside. The book he held in the corona of the *Loudon*'s running lights was many decades old. Its once blood-dyed cover had turned black, and the brass clasps that held it together were tarnished to the patina of old iron. "I can show you in this journal that I left my village a week before the first eruption to get here in time."

Han didn't add exactly how long ago the oracle had known this eruption was coming. It was bad enough he was trying to save the people on the ship in order to save his own life. He would not give up any more secrets than necessary.

"You may have heard that in my lands the rock speaks to us," Han said, feeding the steward's superstitions. "The great mountains told us that one of their brothers in the Indies was angry and that it would speak this weekend. They asked me to come to hear what was said and report back." On one level, the watcher wasn't lying, only he didn't know it. The rocks had spoken to the oracle, only not the way he and the old sailor imagined. "If you do not convince the captain to back away from shore, we will all die and the Himalayas will not know what upset their brother."

Han saw the transformation in the steward. Ping's doubt turned to interest. It didn't matter whether he believed the superstitious tales told about Tibetans or that his own seaman's senses were telling him that the calamities were far from over.

"You must get the captain to move us to shore," Han pleaded. "Or if not to shore then farther out to sea so we can weather whatever comes."

As agile as a monkey, the old steward swung around the railing in front of the bridge and lowered himself down a small ladder so he stood next to Han. The two men eyed each other, occasionally brushing flakes that settled on eyelashes and brows. Ping touched the dagger tucked into the rope he used as a belt. "If you are wrong about this, mountain wizard, I will gut you like a fish."

Han ignored the threat for what it was, an expression of fear. "Do you believe I'm wrong?"

Ping glanced over the stern railing. Because the ash had thinned, he could see an unworldly orange glow clinging to the horizon many miles away. "No. Come with me, the captain might want to speak with you."

Lindemann had just returned from the head. He'd splashed water on his face and the stray drops had cut channels of mud on his uniform. He paused when he saw his cabin boy with one of the passengers at the entrance to the small bridge. "Ping, you lazy savage, get out there and clean the windscreens."

"My captain," Ping said in rough Dutch. He waved to Han. "This man is a learned scientist from China. He is renowned in my country for his knowledge of the ways of the earth. He has traveled—"

"Do you have a point?" Lindemann snapped. "The seas are running hard and if the wind picks up we're going to be buried under ash."

"Yes, my captain," Ping groveled. "This scientist has traveled here to study the volcano and it is his scholarly opinion that it will erupt again. He believes that we must get everyone ashore." Ping turned to the watcher. "Say something so I can pretend to translate. Make it sound that you are sure of what you're talking about."

"But I am sure. Does the captain believe you?"

"What's he saying, Ping?" Lindemann's deep voice cut across their conversation.

"He says that sometime after dawn the mountain will explode like a million cannons," Ping began, embellishing his tale. "He says that the waves from so much force will fill Lampong Bay. He even knows what the Japanese call such waves. Tsunami."

"Those monster waves are just myths, Ping, like sea serpents and the kraken. Stories told by experienced sailors to frighten the new boys. Surely you don't believe in them."

"Captain Lindemann." The first mate had been listening to the conversation, a clean bandage on the back of his neck where a piece of scalding pumice had landed. "I don't believe in tsunamis either, but it wouldn't hurt if we backed off a few cable lengths. The chop is getting worse and the tide's coming in in a couple hours."

The veteran ship's master looked from Han to his mate and then to Ping and was about to speak when the largest wave yet surged up Lampong Bay. The men on the bridge scrambled to clutch handholds, and a lamp attached to the roof in a floating gimbal swung against the ceiling and shattered. The helmsman stripped off his shirt to smother the burning pool of kerosene before it could do much damage.

Lindemann made his decision. "Mate, prepare to raise anchor." He rang the engine-room bell to alert the engineer that he was going to require speed. "Mr. Van Den Bosch." A young officer drew himself to attention. "Get on the signal lamp. Alert the captain of the gunboat *Berouw* that we recommend he gives himself a bit more sea room."

"Yes, sir." The subaltern saluted.

"Ping, escort the passenger back to the forecastle and get yourself busy on the bridge glass."

Han paused at the hatchway coaming. Captain Lindemann was looking at him oddly. The big Dutchman nodded his head, as if to say the warning was just the last nudge he needed to enact the plan he'd already been contemplating.

The chorus of frightened cries from the enclosed forecastle masked the sound of the heavy anchor chains grinding up the hawsepipe while ash obscured the thick smoke pumping from the *Loudon*'s squat funnel. The man who called himself Han waited at the ship's rail to see if the nearby gunboat would reply to Captain Lindemann's warning. He was unable to spot the small craft in the darkness, nor could he see the flash of her signal lamp. In fact, the beam from the *Loudon*'s light couldn't cut more than a few dozen yards into the swirling storm of ash.

A few minutes later, the steamship began to swing around in a wide arc, her rigging creaking against the wind while her boiler kept the bronze prop thrashing the ash-choked water.

For the rest of the night the *Loudon* held station two miles from the town, where the chart said she had seventy feet of water under her keel. She rattled against her anchor chain while the engine-room crew fed coal into her boilers to keep up the steam. The winds were increasing by the minute, stripping the top layer of ash from the sea like desert sand blown from a dune.

Dawn arrived as a weak wash of light obscured by a raging maelstrom of soot and ash. Han had spent a miserable night huddled with the terrified prisoners and their equally frightened Dutch guards. The Europeans in the first-class cabins in the midships superstructure couldn't have fared much better than the mass of humanity in the forward spaces. Four times during the night massive waves passed under the *Loudon,* lifting her so savagely that those not holding on to a bulkhead floated in space when she dropped abruptly into the trough.

Even the washed-out dawn and sulfur-leaden air was a relief from the claustrophobic confines of the forecastle, which reeked of vomit and loose bowels.

The watcher was the first passenger on deck and he noticed immediately that the temperature had dropped more than twenty degrees from the previous day. Captain Lindemann stood on the small wing jutting off the bridge, a long spyglass to his eye. Han had been given a smaller collapsible telescope and retrieved it from his bag, paying no heed to the six-inch layer of hot ash that slowly cooked his feet. He peered through the glass in the direction Lindemann was looking.

At first he wasn't sure what he was seeing. And then the image became clear. The side-wheeler *Berouw* was no longer at her anchorage. She was gone. Han scanned the quiet town of Telok Betong. A layer of soot covered everything, dulling the buildings to a uniform gray as lifeless as the surface of the moon. Many of the natives' huts on the outskirts of town had toppled under the weight of ash. Only a few ragged figures lurched through the ruins.

Panning the spyglass across the once-thriving waterfront, Han found the gunboat and his hands began to tremble. He turned back to see the captain had been watching him looking at the town. Their eyes locked, assuring each other that they had seen the same thing.

At the end of a street Han didn't recall from his previous visits sat the *Berouw*. What Han had thought was a street was in fact the path the thousand-ton ship had plowed as the sea heaved it inland. A dozen stone buildings had been flattened by the tumbling vessel. Countless more rattan and thatch huts were destroyed. The tidal waves' equally fearsome withdrawal had scoured away the debris, including the dead.

Han plunged his hand into his pocket for his watch. From numerous readings of his journal he knew that the mountain would erupt again very soon. The original journal entries were written in an archaic language the watcher couldn't decipher, but translations had been inked into the margins, detailing the exact location and time. Comparing his watch to the journal and factoring how long it would take the noise of the eruption to reach the bay, Han saw he had a few more minutes. He prayed that somehow the oracle would be wrong.

He steadied the book against the railing and retrieved a calligrapher's inkpot and a quill from his bag. The scribes in Tibet had given the geographic location of the island: six degrees ten seconds south by one hundred and five degrees forty-two seconds east. What they couldn't possibly have known when they wrote the tome so long ago was the local name of the mountain. He took a moment to write it in now.

Krakatoa.

The smaller eruption the day before had thrown nine cubic miles of ash into the air and undermined a subterranean dome. The dome finally collapsed at a little past seven on the morning of the twenty-seventh in a titanic avalanche of rock and sea. The thermal shock of billions of tons of water vaporizing against the magma below the dome split the air in a crack that could be heard in Australia, two thousand miles away. The sound was the loudest heard in human history. Six-hundred-ton boulders were thrown forty miles or more, burning missiles that caused forest fires that would rage for days. The catastrophic eruption threw a fresh column of ash and debris into the upper atmosphere that would eventually envelop the earth. Average temperatures in Europe and America would plunge five degrees for the next several years. The concussion wave would circle the globe seven times before finally dissipating.

Although the term would not be coined for several decades, the force of the eruption would measure in the thousands of megatons. The island of Krakatoa was split into three pieces and parts of it were obliterated altogether.

As furious as the eruption was, it wasn't what would kill the thirty-six thousand victims of the disaster. What took them lurked moments behind the shock wave and traveled at half the speed of sound.

For a full minute after the blast, the watcher remained on the decking where he'd been thrown. It had been like standing in the largest bell ever built while giants assaulted it with sledgehammers. He could see crewmen frantically hoisting the anchor, but their voices were lost in the ringing that echoed in his head. The vibration of the *Loudon*'s engine blurred with the palsylike trembling in his limbs.

He knew that when the tsunami struck the ship, no place would be safe. Either all would die or all would survive, so he remained on deck to await the wave's attack down Lampong Bay. The horizon had been sliced in two by the ash cloud, but soon another phenomenon began to blur the line between sea and sky.

The tsunami raced at the vessel at three hundred miles per hour and grew in height as it roared up the shallows. From a small hump far in the distance, the wave piled on itself, growing like a snake rearing its head, its crest frothing while still a mile away. The sound was a thousand cyclones confined in Han's skull.

At the last moment, his courage failed him. He dashed into the superstructure as the *Loudon* was lifted thirty feet up the wave's leading edge. It was as if the ship had been thrown vertical. And just as quickly the wave passed under the steamer and she dropped straight down, her keel flexing like a bow. She buried her prow in the trough and would have gone under had the captain not put on a burst of speed to meet the monster head-on.

Once again the watcher picked himself up from where he'd been tossed and staggered out to see the wave continuing its relentless journey.

The wall of water was thirty feet tall when it passed under the *Loudon* and had doubled by the time Han reached the rail. It doubled again in the last seconds before it struck land, forced ever higher by the sloping beach. From Han's vantage it seemed the tsunami had already swallowed the land. In the seconds before it toppled, the wave completely hid the hills behind Telok Betong.

The surge was so powerful that it didn't pause when it hit nor slow as it drove over the town, leveling everything in its path. It raged up the shore, snapping trees like matchsticks and ripping buildings from their foundations. The rubble was tossed a mile into the foothills. The wave destroyed two hundred years of careful colonial rule and hundreds of acres of cultivated land. It flattened some hills and built new ones with the rubble. It disinterred countless coffins from the Dutch cemetery and spilled their grisly contents into the bay. It wiped five thousand people off the face of the earth.

Like a demon claiming its prize, the receding wave seized nearly all evidence that the town had ever existed and dragged it into the sea. All except the *Berouw*. The little gunboat was left stranded two miles from shore along the bank of a river.

Because there was no hope of survivors in town, Captain Lindemann decided his duty lay in returning to Anjer so he could report the calamity. The ship plodded out of Lampong Bay, cutting through a carpet of ash, torn trees, the remnants of huts and thousands of mutilated corpses.

The eruption had whipped the winds to a hurricane pitch, and the ashfall became so severe that Lindemann ordered the soldiers and their prisoners to the deck to help keep the *Loudon* from foundering under its weight. A miserable rain soon started to fall, mixing with the ash so that large clots of mud pummeled the ship. Soon strings of gray ooze hung from the rigging and drooled from the scuppers. The *Loudon* resembled a ghost ship adorned with tattered funeral shrouds.

When the first bolt of lightning struck, it jumped across the rigging as it sought ground, splitting into fingers of blue fire that blew mud from the ship like shrapnel. The native prisoners screamed in terror as a ball of St. Elmo's fire danced over their heads. The felons were still chained in groups of ten. An arc of electricity coursed through the shackles of one group, killing two men outright and burning the other eight so severely that none would survive the hour.

By ten thirty in the morning, daylight was gone and the deck was buried under two feet of muddy soot despite the best efforts of the passengers and crew. They worked under the driving rain while dodging chunks of pumice that continued to shoot from the sky.

At noon, the sea was too rough for work. Lindemann ordered everyone belowdecks and the hatches secured. He would have to risk capsizing under the load of ash. He had himself lashed to the ship's wheel and the chief engineer secured to his station.

The *Loudon* slowly emerged from Lampong Bay like an icebreaker cleaving pack ice. At the head of the bay, the crust of ash was seven feet thick, too much for the ship's overworked boiler. She could barely make headway and the captain feared she'd sink if she stopped.

They retreated west around Sebesi Island to circle far around the still-erupting volcano. And for the next eighteen hours, the plucky steamer fought the waves and wind, the rippling tsunamis that continued to radiate from the epicenter, and the ash that didn't so much as fall from the sky but seemed launched directly at the ship.

The sun remained hidden by a pall of soot. The darkness was more complete than any night, darker than any cave. It was as if Monday, August 27, 1883, never came to the Sunda Strait.

Six more times the ship was struck by lightning, and once more she would battle a killer wave as Krakatoa erupted the last time. That final collapse of the caldera was the weakened rock at the rim of the volcano plummeting into the half-mile-deep crater, finally sealing the aperture into the earth's heart.

The day before it had taken the *Loudon* four hours to travel from Anjer to Telok Betong. The return trip took twenty. Approaching the Java coast south of Anjer, the steamer ran parallel to the shore amid a sea of flotsam—ash, ripped-up trees and more bodies than anyone could count. The coast, once verdant jungle and productive plantations, resembled a desert. The scattering of villages had all been wiped away and those few survivors had yet to return from the hills where they'd fled.

If anything the damage to Java was worse than what they had witnessed on Sumatra. The city of Anjer, home to ten thousand people, was gone.

Han wrote furiously in his journal as the ship plowed through the morass. Wherever he looked, bodies poked through the undulating blanket of ash, most stripped naked by the tsunami, some burned horribly by the near-molten pumice.

The only thing keeping him from being driven mad was the physical act of writing. His quill flew across the pages as if the speed of his hand would allow the image to flow from his eyes to the page and not seep into his memory. Yet when he closed his eyes the glistening wall of water hovered in his consciousness, poised to overwhelm him.

Han had never seen the oracle himself—that honor was reserved for the high priests—so he didn't know how such an accurate prediction as this could have been made. Some of the retired watchers said the oracle was a woman rumored to be two hundred years old. Others speculated that the oracle was an intricate machine that could detect the earth's faintest tremble. Priests somehow interpreted this information to foretell the future. Still others believed it was a gift of prophecy bestowed on a succession of children, like the reincarnated spirit of a lama.

Han didn't care to know the truth. He had witnessed the oracle's precision and would never do so again. He understood human nature enough to know that even if he had warned the inhabitants of the Sunda Strait only a handful of people would have been able to save themselves. Still, the burden of seeing the death and destruction was too much. He would let some other watcher complete the journal he carried.

It was titled *Pacific Basin 1850–1910*. Understanding that the oracle foretold this cataclysm thirty-plus years ago sent a chill through Han's body worse than the deepest frost of winter. He prayed this was an aberration, that the oracle had been right just this one time. It had just been his bad luck. That was all. The next prophecy would doubtless be wrong. It had to be. Nothing could predict calamity.

In the front of the ledger were a series of letters sealed in wax. Nine of the ten envelopes had been opened; he had opened the latest one when he left for Batavia four months ago. That meant there was one more great disaster coming in the next twenty-three years.

He was prohibited from breaking the wax seals that hid the time and location of the next disaster. Watchers only opened the envelopes for the events they themselves were to witness. The last envelope was to be opened on January 1, 1906, which would presumably give a future watcher enough time to reach his destination. With a jerk Han snapped the wax seal and read the yellowed text.

The date was meaningless. Just a day, a month, and a year. April 18, 1906. The coordinates meant nothing either. More numbers. But some resourceful cartographer had written in the name of the town that stood at the epicenter of what would be one of the worst earthquakes in history: a city called San Francisco, California.

Mercer woke with one thought on his mind. Seven uninterrupted days. He'd been working without a break for six and a half weeks. And in the past seven months he'd managed just one four-day weekend and a few stray days to himself. This was going to be his first real vacation in over a year. His second thought was that when it was over, he'd be returning to the Canadian Arctic, where he'd spent the past month and a half. He was facing at least another four weeks at an isolated mining camp thirteen hundred miles north of Montana. De Beers was looking to invest a further half billion dollars in the newly discovered diamond fields and was waiting for Mercer's final test results and geologic report.

He'd been able to wrangle the time away because the rotary blast drill used for boring test holes had been so damaged by the brutal cold that Ingersoll-Rand was sending a team of mechanics to repair it. The hard reality of working in the Arctic was that while men could be insulated from the weather, steel became as brittle as glass. They'd been lucky no one had been injured when a main bearing detonated like a grenade.

It wasn't unusual for Mercer to be away from home for months at a time, trotting around the globe prospecting, assaying, and troubleshooting for different mining companies. His expertise in geology had made him wealthy, although the price was very little time to enjoy it. So when he could string together enough consecutive days for a vacation, he liked to maximize every moment. Still, he procrastinated for another half hour under a feather duvet before swinging his legs out of bed.

The tan he enjoyed from a scuba-diving weekend in the Bahamas had long since faded. His lean body was as pale as a marble statue, the result of the Arctic's twenty-two-hour nights and the exhaustion of continuous fifteen-hour work shifts. The only color came from his hands and forearms, which were darkened by ingrained dirt that wouldn't wash out, and a dense bruise on his shoulder where a twenty-foot length of drill string had caught him.

Mercer's home was a three-story brick rowhouse in one of the few sections of Arlington not yet turned into high-rise office buildings. He'd bought the building years ago and converted the six apartments it once contained into one home; it was difficult to see the extent of the remodeling from the outside because he'd left the original façade untouched. His bedroom was located on the third floor and overlooked an atrium that took up the front third of the house. On the second floor were two guest bedrooms, the family room, which was actually a bar modeled after an English gentlemen's club, and an open space he used as a library. On the ground floor was a little-used kitchen, the dining room, where he kept a billiard table, and his home office. A spiral staircase restored by an architectural salvage firm in Connecticut connected the three levels.

The town house's eclectic style and decoration reflected its owner, and because of his travel schedule Mercer had made certain it had become the anchor his life needed. He considered it one of his only real indulgences.

He'd arrived home from Canada at four in the morning and had been asleep for ten straight hours. Afternoon light spilled through the skylight above his bed and drifted over the balcony at the edge of the mezzanine. Mercer threw on a clean pair of jeans and an old Colorado School of Mines sweatshirt. His luggage lay stacked at the foot of his bed.

He'd remembered to set the automatic coffeemaker behind the bar before collapsing but had planned on waking at noon. The two-hour-old brew was as thick as tar. Perfect.

Since he rarely used the kitchen, he kept some groceries in the cabinets under the back bar and set about making a bowl of cereal. He didn't think about the expiration date on the milk until the first cottage-cheese-thick curd landed in the bowl. Gagging at the smell, he poured the mess down the bar sink and cursed his house sitter. The orange juice in the rebuilt lock-lever refrigerator he stocked with beer and mixers was just as old.

Harry White, Mercer's eighty-year-old best friend and the man who Mercer was convinced put the crotch in crotchety, knew he'd be home today and was supposed to have done the shopping. Harry tended to treat Mercer's town house as his own, which wasn't necessarily a good thing. He had the domestic skills of a rabid wolverine. In the trash can were a dozen empty Jack Daniel's bottles and about ten cartons' worth of cigarette butts.

Mercer had been gone six weeks and felt it could have been worse. At least Harry had gotten his mail and had taken his phone calls. There was only one message on the answering machine. He hit the PLAY button. "Dr. Mercer, this is Cindy from Dr. Cryan's office." Mercer's dentist. "I'm just calling to remind you of your cleaning appointment Wednesday at ten."

He ran his tongue around his mouth and decided his teeth weren't in immediate danger of falling out.

He'd reschedule for when he got back from Canada next month.

Sipping his coffee and thumbing through the stacks of mail, Mercer was grateful that Harry hadn't repeated last year's trick of putting him on a handful of pornographic mailing lists. He hadn't been able to look his mailman in the eye until that mess had been straightened out. Delving deeper into his pile, he realized Harry's distorted sense of humor had been in full swing after all.

Not only had he brought over junk mail from a half dozen of his cronies, he'd meticulously shuffled Mercer's important stuff in with wads of credit-card solicitations and other garbage. The trade magazines were hidden inside catalogues for companies Mercer had never heard of. It would take an hour just to separate out his own stuff.

The phone rang. "Hello."

"Hey, Mercer. You're finally out of bed." Harry's voice, the result of sixty years of chain-smoking and hard drinking, grated like a diesel engine on a cold morning.

"Yeah, I didn't get home until four. Wait, how'd you know I was asleep? Where the hell are you?"

"I came by a couple hours ago when you were sacked out," Harry breezed, a lungful of smoke hissing past his lips. "I came back a little after noon. I'm downstairs in your office on line two."

Mercer checked his phone and saw the light for the fax line was on. "I should call the cops and have you arrested as a Peeping Tom. Why didn't you get milk, you bastard? You knew I was coming home today."

"I did buy milk," Harry protested. "To save time I got it two weeks ago and brought it over yesterday. It's right in your fridge with the OJ you wanted."

"And it was lumpier than my cereal."

"Gripe, gripe, gripe." Harry pitched his voice as

high as he could. It still rumbled like a longshore-man's. "This milk is too sour. This milk is too lumpy. Jesus, you're worse than Goldilocks. Hold on. I'm coming up. I need a drink if I have to listen to you bitch about every little thing."

Mercer was smiling as he set the cordless on the bar. In the ten years since they'd met, he couldn't recall a single nice word between them. Nor could he recall a denied favor either. Harry was the other an-chor in Mercer's nomadic life, an unlikely friend who meant more to him than anyone he'd ever known. That one was more than twice the age of the other had never had a bearing on their relationship. Both had recognized early on that their personalities ran parallel and seamlessly transcended the generations. Mercer was very much the man Harry had been forty years ago and Mercer supposed, and occasionally dreaded, that in a few decades he'd be like Harry White.

In the moments it took Harry to climb the antique staircase that coiled up to the library adjoining the bar, Mercer had a Jack Daniel's and ginger ale waiting.

The two men were the same height and roughly the same build, although gravity was shifting the breadth of Harry's shoulders into a potbelly. Where Mercer's eyes were sharp gray, Harry's were a sarcastic blue. His face was as lined as a topographic map and his silver hair remained as stiff and full as a shoeshine brush.

Harry sported his traditional uniform of baggy pants, an overlaundered white oxford that showed the outline of the T-shirt underneath, and sneakers. A mid-March chill forced him into a light windbreaker.

"Welcome home," Harry greeted, taking a seat at the bar in front of his drink. He hooked the sword cane Mercer had given him for his last birthday on

the brass handrail. Although he'd lost a leg decades
ago, the walking stick was still more of an ornament
than a necessity. "Jesus, you look like the main course
at a vampire convention. When was the last time you
saw some sun?"

"I knew I should have gone on another diving trip
rather than stay home and take your abuse—" Mercer
paused. He heard a strange sound that seemed to be
climbing the spiral staircase. A sort of click, click,
shuffle, wheeze.

The clicking stopped while the wheezing continued.
It sounded like something had reached the top of the
wooden stairs and was moving slowly across the carpet
in the library. Mercer looked to Harry. Harry swiveled
to look through the French doors that separated the
bar from the reading room.

"Come on, boy," he rasped. "It's okay."

A moment later, Mercer's eyes widened. "What the
hell is that?"

"A dog, for Christ's sake. What do you think it is?"

"If I had to guess I'd say an overstuffed sausage."

The basset hound seemed to understand he was the
center of attention. His tail gave a feeble wag before
drooping back to the floor. He was as long and round
as an old canister vacuum cleaner and so bowlegged
his belly rubbed the floor. His frayed ears dragged like
neglected laundry as he tottered into the room. The
old hound's bloodshot eyes complemented the gray
fur on his muzzle and the silver string of drool coming
from his slack lips. Mercer put the dog's age somewhere between fifteen and fifty. "They say that people
look like their pets, Harry. That poor thing's gonna
have to get a lot uglier if you two are gonna be twins.
Where did you get him?"

"He was rooting in the Dumpster behind Tiny's."
Tiny's was a neighborhood bar run by a former jockey,
Paul Gordon. Harry was as much a fixture there as

the horse-racing pictures on the walls. "No tags, no collar. Tiny wanted to call the Humane Society, but I figured no one was going to adopt him so I took him home. That was just after you left for Canada."

"My God. A kind gesture. From you?"

"Up yours," Harry growled, but couldn't hide his self-satisfaction.

"Have you named him?" The dog heaved himself onto one of the leather sofas.

" 'Cause the damned thing never wants to go for a walk, I call him Drag."

The basset heard his name, let loose a long bawl and collapsed in exhaustion. He was snoring in an instant.

Mercer smiled. Harry had spent a great many nights passed out on the very same couch. "You two are more alike than I first realized."

"At least I still have my balls."

"Even if you don't need them," Mercer teased.

Harry downed the last of his drink and lit a fresh cigarette. "Viagra, baby. Viagra."

Shuddering at the image that conjured, Mercer mixed Harry another whiskey. Mercer had been awake for less than an hour, but with nothing to do for the next five days, he poured himself a vodka gimlet and turned on the commercial air purifier. The cigarette smoke was already becoming a noxious cloud.

"You sure you don't want to go diving or something?"

"I'm sticking around," Mercer replied cautiously. Harry's tone put him on alert.

"In that case, I guess I have to invite you to the party I'm throwing here on Saturday."

"Mighty nice of you."

"Don't mention it," Harry demurred. "Least I can do."

An hour later, Harry was on his fourth drink and Mercer his second when Harry hauled himself to his feet. "If I've got to pump ship, I'm sure Drag does too." He had the dog's leash in his jacket pocket. He clipped it to Drag's collar and tugged gently to wake him. The basset snored on. "Come on, you mangy beast."

Drag's skin twitched like a horse shooing flies and he woofed in annoyance. It took Harry a minute to coax him down the stairs. Mercer went to the library balcony to watch the tug-of-war. True to his name, Drag slid onto his belly when he reached the tiled foyer, forcing Harry to pull him by his leash until he realized stubbornness wouldn't get him out of the walk.

Harry looked up. "Told you so."

The doorbell rang an instant before his hand touched the knob.

The two men standing on the doorstep were dressed in off-the-rack suits that screamed government employee. Their muscular builds, overly short hair, and expressionless faces narrowed the field to law enforcement or military. Startled that the door had opened so quickly, both reached inside their jackets. They stopped from drawing their concealed weapons a second before the pistols were shown, but there was no disguising what they'd almost done.

"Are you Dr. Philip Mercer?" The taller of the two men made it sound like an accusation.

"Yes, I am," Harry replied automatically.

The shorter of the pair stepped closer, pushing Harry back a couple paces. He was a few years older than his partner and appeared to be the leader. He looked Harry in the eye so there could be no misunderstanding when he said, "Omega ninety-nine temple. Counter?"

Harry had been a merchant-marine officer during

World War Two and recognized a code when he heard one. He said the first thing that came to mind. "The rain in Spain falls mainly on the plain."

Standing above them, Mercer hadn't heard the exchange nor did he see the play of confusion turning to anger. He had no idea who the men were or what they wanted. Didn't particularly care either. He was on vacation. And then Harry called up to him, "Does omega ninety-nine temple mean anything to you?"

The jolt of adrenaline hit like an electric shock. He'd been given the recognition code at a White House briefing three months earlier by the deputy national security advisor, Admiral Ira Lasko, USN (ret.). These men were Secret Service agents, doubtlessly part of the president's detail. The counter code flashed in his mind. He yelled down, "Caravan eleven solstice."

The lead agent shot a furious glance up to where Mercer stood above them. "You're Mercer?"

"Yes."

Although Mercer didn't know the specifics, he knew why the agents were here and it was his own fault. It had to do with his past accomplishments.

Long ago Mercer had realized there were two ways to look at the distribution of the earth's mineral wealth. Either Mother Nature had deliberately hidden her treasures in some of the world's most turbulent political hot spots, which seemed rather unlikely, or the presence of mineral reserves turned indigenous people on each other in order to control the resources. Mercer knew it was the latter. He'd seen it firsthand too many times not to.

The illicit diamond trade and the need to control the gem-producing regions funded nearly all of Africa's recent civil wars. Colombia's rebel groups, FARC and others, had been fighting for thirty years, buying their weapons with illegally mined emeralds. And the

Middle East wouldn't be able to export its particular brand of aggressive fundamentalism without the oil deposits to pay for it. It came as no surprise to him that the increased levels of rebel activity in Indonesia came shortly after the opening of an enormous gold mine on the island of Irian Jaya.

The truth of it all was that wealth generated greed in some and jealousy in others and eventually the two sides would fight for dominance. The banners they rallied behind, the causes they claimed, were contrived disguises to hide the ugly truth of this most basic of human conflicts.

Mercer's career had embroiled him in all of it: the terror, the massacres, the unbelievable savagery. He'd been in the middle of a half dozen low-grade wars, ethnic conflicts, and revolutionary coups. It wasn't in his nature to remain passive in situations like that, or to turn tail as many foreign workers tended to do. Often, Mercer stayed behind and through his direct involvement had been instrumental in saving countless lives.

Because of Mercer's record for success, he had come to the attention of military and intelligence circles as someone with unique professional credentials and terror-related experience. Ira Lasko had approached Mercer last year with an offer to join his staff. He wanted to create a post specifically for him as special science advisor. The job went far beyond the purview of the chief executive's regular scientific personnel. They focused on forming national policy. Mercer was to be a consultant and sometime field agent for when the worlds of science and terror collided, a fresh perspective on problems that no one else could solve.

Mercer spiraled down the stairs and crossed the foyer. The easy banter from the past hour had evaporated, and his anticipation for his first vacation in a year was gone. Ira wouldn't send two agents unless he absolutely had to. Something was up. Something big. "Why don't you gentlemen come in," he said. "Harry, take your time walking Drag."

"Right you are." The octogenarian smiled at the agents. "Sorry about my little joke. No hard feelings."

The shorter agent flashed his Secret Service credentials to Mercer. He was Special Agent Michael Thayer. "Who was that man?"

"A friend who knows about my position with Ira Lasko. Relax."

Thayer remained terse. "Admiral Lasko sent us to deliver you to Andrews Air Force Base, where an aircraft is standing by. He said you should pack for a week."

At least Ira's expecting me to return, Mercer thought. He asked one of the more practical questions swirling in his head. "Do you know where I'm going? I need to know what to bring."

"We weren't told," the second agent said.

"All right, give me a few minutes." He went back to the stairs. At the balcony, Mercer saw neither of the agents had moved from near the front door. "The old man and his dog will be back in a few minutes. Tell him I'm in my bedroom packing."

Mercer hadn't unpacked from Canada, so he dumped the dirty clothes from his suitcases into the hamper and tossed the empty luggage on his bed. An aircraft waiting at Andrews could mean a thirty-minute helicopter ride or a C-5 Galaxy cargo jet that could take him to the other side of the planet. No sense trying to guess what he'd need. He stuffed a week's worth of socks and underwear into a bag along with his toiletry kit. A pair of jeans went next, a couple of casual shirts, a pair of slacks and a sports jacket. He added one dress shirt, one tie and a pair of heavy-duty miner's coveralls with reinforced patches at the knees and elbows.

Before throwing a metal hard hat on top of the pile,

he grabbed the Beretta 92 semiautomatic from his nightstand. The weapon was coolly familiar in his hands. There was no need to check if the magazine was full; he could tell by its weight. He slid it into the helmet's liner and zipped it into the leather bag. Work boots and loafers went into outside pockets.

He checked his watch. Three minutes and forty seconds from the time the bag hit the bed until he was done. Not bad.

He heard Harry's voice from downstairs and peered over the balcony. "Don't bother coming up. I'm leaving."

"You think I care what you do?" Harry retorted. "I left a full drink on the bar."

They met at the library landing, and Mercer followed Harry into the dark oak-and-brass barroom. He downed the last of his gimlet. "I'll be gone a week, or so they tell me. Who knows." Mercer peeled two hundred-dollar bills from his wallet. "For your party."

"Thanks." Harry left the money untouched.

"Hire someone to clean up when you're done. Last time there were enough pizza boxes lying around to corner the world cardboard market." Mercer smiled. "See you, Harry."

"Yeah, see you." Harry shot him a good-natured scowl, trying not to show his disappointment.

Drag rewarded Mercer with a sloppy kiss when he scratched behind the basset's ears. Then he ambled off to lie at his master's feet.

Mercer pulled a bomber jacket from the coat closet next to the front door and followed Thayer and his partner to a dark Chevy Suburban parked in front of his town house. Traffic to Andrews was a snarl so it took more than an hour to reach the base. No one in the SUV said a word, which suited Mercer just fine.

These were the first moments to think about what was happening and he found he resented the unnecessary secrecy. Ira could have easily called to tell him why he was needed. Mercer would have gone. Lasko didn't have to send two goons to virtually kidnap him and rush him off for some clandestine flight. Typical government zealotry, Mercer thought, the kind he detested.

Once past a series of checkpoints, Thayer guided the Suburban through the sprawling air force base and onto an access road behind the flight line. A KC-135 tanker was just taking off. Its engine shriek split the air while the four black smears of exhaust looked like claw marks on the otherwise bright sky. The Suburban pulled in toward an enormous hangar and drove through its side door. Thayer braked next to the only aircraft in the cavernous space, a Gulfstream IV executive jet painted in U.S. Air Force livery. Standing next to the open hatch was a soldier in camouflage fatigues. The dark insignia on his collar showed him to be a captain

Without preamble, the muscular African American asked Thayer, "You got my passenger?"

Mercer unlimbered himself from the SUV holding his bag in one hand.

The soldier eyed him. "Mercer?" Mercer nodded. "I'm Sykes. Omega ninety-nine temple."

"Caravan eleven solstice."

"Good enough for me. Get aboard."

Even before Mercer got to his seat, the jet's tail-mounted engines spooled to life and the nimble plane was towed through the hangar doors facing the complex of runways. Noticing that all the shades had been pulled over the windows, he reached to open the one nearest him. Captain Sykes leaned back in the seat in front of Mercer and closed the shade again.

"Sorry, Doc. Think of it as blackout conditions." Sykes had a wad of tobacco in the corner of his mouth and appeared to be swallowing the juice.

"Any idea how long the flight will be?"

"Long enough for you and I to play a whole lot of gin."

This was just getting better and better. "Do you know Admiral Lasko?"

"I know he authorized this flight," Sykes replied, "but I've never met the man. Way above my pay grade."

"If you happen to meet him before I see him again"—Mercer settled deeper in his seat, stretching out his six-foot frame and closing his eyes—"tell him he's a dead man."

"So, no cards, Doc?"

"Try solitaire." Mercer felt the plane leap from the tarmac a few minutes later. There was no sense speculating about their destination. The same went for trying to guess what Ira wanted him for. Instead of frustrating himself further with mental gymnastics, he allowed his mind to slip into a balance between sleep and consciousness. If this was going to be a long flight, the least he could do was tune out most of it.

Hurtling into the unknown. It was a phrase that just popped into his head and immediately reminded him of the first time he'd been involved with a mine rescue. The visions came back to him with a dreamy quality, a kind of hyperreality where Mercer seemed to be standing still while the events rushed past him. He was twenty-seven at the time, on one of his first consulting jobs. A fire had broken out eleven hundred feet below ground at a West Virginia coal mine where he'd been plotting the best way to extract a newly discovered vein. As the only miner there who'd trained with South Africa's famed Proto Team, the world's best subterranean rescue group, Mercer had been the first volunteer to go down into the mine. He led four other men into the elevator cage after it had been verified that not all the men who'd gone down on their shift had returned when the mine was evacuated.

Mounted above the cage was a crude sign: THIS MINE HAS OPERATED FOR 203 ACCIDENT-FREE DAYS. Not anymore.

Smoke billowed up the shaft like pollution from a factory's chimney, so thick that their lanterns were reduced to pinpricks. Smudge built up on their full-face oxygen masks and simply smeared when they tried to clean them. Fear caused Mercer's breathing to come in sharp gulps.

The elevator dropped—hurtling into the unknown—past ten levels and deeper into the smoke. As it approached eleven the heat was brutal, radiating from the rock like an oven. But none of the men were willing to stop. Not until they knew what had happened to the twenty-six unaccounted miners caught up in the conflagration.

The scene when the cage doors opened was worse than the most gruesome image of Hades. The walls, ceiling and floor smoldered with the residual energy of the fire's overflash. Anything combustible was a searing pocket of flame—men mostly, horrible twisted shapes of char. Almost worse was that some of them were still alive. The rescuers used portable fire extinguishers to shoot out jets of foam to smother the flames. As the sound of the fires waned, the pitiable cries of the dying grew.

The first explosion had exhausted most of the mine's supply of air, but even with the industrial fans on the surface shut down, it was drawing in more like a flue. The blaze would reignite the swirling eddies of coal dust as soon as enough oxygen had been drawn down. Mercer understood that he and his team had minutes. They dragged the wounded into the skip hoist. Two of the rescue workers wanted to stay down and look for others, but Mercer wouldn't let them. The mine was too hot. The risks they were taking already bordered on suicidal.

The second explosion, as violent as the first, rocked

the hoist when they were fifty feet from the surface. Without the protection of their retardant suits, the overpressure wave would have scalded them to death. They used their bodies as human shields to protect their fallen comrades until the hoist reached the top. Scrambling amid a hellish torrent of smoke, they carried the seven men they'd saved clear of the heat. A triage station had already been established. Topside workers carried the wounded to the building as Mercer and his men stripped out of their scorched suits. By the time Mercer staggered into the first-aid station, only one of the men was still alive, and even he didn't survive long enough to make it to the nearest hospital. The mine continued to burn for twelve days. After the bodies were recovered, level eleven had never reopened.

Of all the mine rescues Mercer had been involved with, that one struck the deepest in his mind. Not because it was the first, but because it was the only one where he hadn't saved at least one miner who survived long enough to be found.

Mercer shook his head as if to dislodge the images. His memory was so full of such horrors that he tried not to revisit them. He blamed his uncharacteristic dark mood on the fact that this whole situation had him on edge. The unknown was perhaps his most feared adversary. As soon as he knew what was happening, the mood would pass.

A little over four hours later, the engine's steady drone changed in pitch. They were beginning their descent. Guessing the aircraft cruised at five hundred knots, Mercer estimated they'd covered about twenty-four hundred miles. But not knowing their direction could put them anywhere in a circle large enough to touch on South America, the Azore Islands, the tip of Greenland and as far west as . . .

It couldn't be.

Maybe it could. There was one easy way to find out. Sykes wasn't exactly asleep, but he hadn't turned the page of the book he was reading for the past fifteen minutes. Before his escort became aware the plane had left her cruising altitude, Mercer inched open his window shade. The darkness outside the aircraft was absolute. They could be over the Atlantic as far as he knew, but he doubted that very much.

The bright moon played against the underside of the clouds above the Gulfstream, and when Mercer pressed a hand to the Plexiglas to cut the glare from the cabin lights, he caught the dark reflection of mountains running off to the horizon.

The plane made a gentle turn and a riot of light erupted from the ground. It was a garish display, an unworldly sight like no place on earth. It was Las Vegas.

And Mercer knew of only one place near Vegas that was secret enough to warrant the level of security he'd endured. It was a remote section of desert euphemistically called Dreamland, but known more widely by its designation on an old Department of Energy map.

Area 51.

AREA 51, NEVADA

Knowing his destination only deepened the mystery surrounding Mercer's clandestine trip.

What little he knew about Area 51 came from cable television. The secluded facility, along with Nellis Air Force Base and the Yucca Flats Atomic Test Range, encompassed a territory larger than Switzerland and had first been used for flight testing the U-2 spy plane in the 1950s. Since then most of America's premier aircraft had gone through flight trials at Groom Lake, the massive dry lake bed on which Area 51 was built. The SR-71, the F-117 Stealth, the B-2 Spirit bomber and the F-22 Raptor had all first taken flight here. Rumors persisted that they were currently developing a hypersonic spy plane to replace the Blackbird, called Aurora, and that it was stationed at Dreamland. While the military continued to deny the existence of the base, these were the most acknowledged facts about Area 51.

Mostly, however, the legend of Area 51 grew from the myth that a flying saucer, which reportedly crashed in Roswell, New Mexico, in 1947, had been transported to this isolated desert facility for study. Conspiracy theorists took the government's denial as proof it really had happened. They strung together reports of strange lights, the testimony of charlatans and crackpots, and their own paranoia into a fantastic story of reverse engineering on the ships and bizarre medical experiments on the crew.

Mercer didn't believe a word of it. Area 51 was simply the place where the military developed our next-generation aircraft in secret. Disregarding the absurdity that an advanced civilization was clumsy enough to crash on earth, the idea that the military could keep such a secret for half a century defied belief.

The one part of the story he did believe, however, was that the security forces at Area 51 were authorized to use deadly force. He had no idea if this directive had ever been needed, but he'd heard of cases where backpackers and aircraft watchers were escorted from the region by hard-looking well-armed men they'd derisively dubbed Cammo Dudes.

The window shade snapped closed like a guillotine. When Mercer looked up, Captain Sykes's eyes held equal measures of displeasure and resignation. "You shouldn't have done that, Doc."

Before Sykes could say anything further, the copilot emerged from the cockpit. "Captain, a word."

Sykes joined him at the front of the cabin and listened for several seconds. He nodded once then returned to his seat. The copilot closed the cockpit door behind himself.

Before sitting, Sykes reached into an overhead storage bin. He retrieved a helmet and tossed it onto Mercer's lap. It resembled a welder's helmet, but the face shield was completely opaque. With it on Mercer wouldn't be able to see a thing. "You're going to have to put that on when we land," Sykes said.

"Captain, I know where we are. Is this really necessary?"

"If you pretend you don't know where we're landing, I don't have to pretend to fill out a ton of useless reports. Call it a favor. Seems we've hit a bit of headwind on our way here. Usually we'd land and you'd be transferred to a blacked-out van. But we've missed our schedule, and in about ten minutes a Russian spy satellite will be passing overhead. We're going to be landing normally, but we'll taxi straight into one of the hangars." Sykes's voice took on an earnest tone. "Security at this installation is the tightest in the world, Doc. Standing orders are to shoot first and don't worry about the questions afterward. You reading me?"

"Yes."

"I'm telling you this to save your life. When we get off this aircraft, I'll guide you along. Do not remove that helmet. You do and they won't just pull a gun on you. They'll drop you where you stand."

Mercer let a sarcastic retort die on his lips. Sykes was telling him this for his own good. He twisted the clumsy-looking helmet on his lap. "Just tell me when to put it on."

The plane continued its descent, leaving the glare of Las Vegas a hundred miles astern, and made its approach on the longest runway in the world, a strip of reinforced concrete more than twice the length needed to accommodate the space shuttle. The Gulfstream touched down more gently than any commercial flight Mercer had ever been on. In a race to hide from the spy satellite coming over the horizon, her engines barely seemed to slow as the pilot looped them across the apron for a distant hangar.

The sudden deceleration when the aircraft reached its destination chirped rubber from the tires and jolted Mercer in his seat. The executive jet seesawed on its landing gear as the engines wound to silence.

"Okay, Doc, might as well get that face shield on," Sykes suggested. "I'll take care of your bag."

Mercer slipped into his jacket and settled the helmet on his head. His world went gray. The lack of vision was momentarily disorienting. Not until he tipped his head back could he see the tops of his shoes and the plush carpet. "Feels like we're going to play a bizarre game of pin the tail on the donkey."

Sykes laughed. "So long as the guards don't play pin the nine millimeter on the geologist. Okay, come toward my voice. There's enough headroom so you don't need to duck. That's good. All right, turn here. You're almost at the boarding stairs. There's four of them to the tarmac."

Sensing a change in lighting as he neared the exit, Mercer paused, gave Sykes's warning a half second's consideration, and pulled the helmet from his head.

What he saw took his breath away.

The hangar was several orders of magnitude larger than the one at Andrews, lit with powerful lights recessed in the ceiling ten stories over his head. The huge doors, easily large enough to accommodate a commercial airliner, had already closed behind the Gulfstream. It wasn't the building's multiacre dimensions that caught his attention; they barely made an impression. Nor did the matte-black snout of a B-2 Stealth bomber as it loomed like some nightmare creature, its knife-edge silhouette interrupted only by the integrated engine nacelles and her two-man cockpit.

What drew his attention was the saucer-shaped aircraft hovering a short distance to his left. The craft floated soundlessly a couple feet above the concrete floor. It was just there, impossibly hanging in space. The saucer was roughly thirty feet in diameter and maybe eight feet tall, composed of a silvery material with a sleek texture.

Then Mercer did a double take and burst out laughing even as Sykes came bundling up behind him. What he thought was alien writing on the side of the aircraft was actually a very stylized font that spelled out ACME SAUCER COMPANY. The hovering disc was an elaborate model, some technician's idea of a joke. The cables suspending it from the ceiling became apparent when Mercer looked for them.

There was no sign of the armed security Sykes had warned him about.

Who was waiting there made Mercer do his second double take. Ira Lasko stood off to the side with a woman in a white lab coat. They were beyond easy conversation range, so Mercer turned his head to address Sykes. "Thought you'd never met Ira."

Sykes shrugged. "Hell, I'm not really your escort either. Admiral Lasko sent me to D.C. yesterday and I just happened to catch this flight back."

Mercer descended the boarding stairs and crossed the fifty feet to Ira. The deputy national security advisor was in his mid-fifties, painfully thin, but with unbelievable strength for his size. He kept his head completely shaved in a tactical retreat from pattern baldness. It leant him a determined air that augmented his pugnacious jaw and penetrating mind. His eyes were a watchful brown under silvering brows. He wasn't particularly tall at five feet seven, but his authority was not in doubt.

Ira wore khaki pants, a matching shirt and a Navy bomber jacket. The temperature in the hangar barely reached fifty degrees. Despite its desert location, Area 51 lay nearly five thousand feet above sea level.

"I told the security chief that you wouldn't wear the helmet if the plane had to park in here." Ira waved toward the far side of the hangar, where futuristic-looking shapes—aircraft, no doubt—were hidden under large tarps. "That's why the really interesting stuff was covered up."

Mercer's anger at the tactics to get him here had been replaced by a sense of awe. He was being granted a peek at the innermost sanctum of government secrecy. If the conspiracy nuts were correct, things went on here even the president didn't know about. Still, he wouldn't give Ira the satisfaction of showing that the surroundings had shaken his composure. He took Ira's proffered hand. "Are you going to explain why you felt it necessary to have me shanghaied? A phone call and a plane ticket to Vegas would have sufficed."

"I've been calling your place for two days," Ira replied. "I didn't leave a message because Harry kept answering the phone." He and Harry had swapped war stories on several occasions. Ira had spent his early naval career aboard submarines, and Harry had spent his dodging them in the Pacific. "You think if I let on that you were coming here that he wouldn't be on the next plane out?"

Mercer couldn't deny that possibility, no, inevitability. "Maybe he should be out here. Don't forget, he saved my ass in Panama last fall."

"And ran up about six grand in gambling debts on your credit card."

Mercer's smile turned to a frown. Ten thousand was closer to the truth.

"Besides," Ira continued, "you won't need him watching your back. You're out here for a straightforward job. Nothing fancy, but something you're eminently qualified for. A job that we consider vital."

Mercer cocked an eyebrow. "We?"

Ira turned to the woman standing at his side. "This is Dr. Briana Marie. She's heading the project. She'll explain everything."

"Pleasure to meet you, Doctor." Mercer shook the petite brunette's hand. She wore no makeup; her girl-next-door appeal didn't need any. He laughed to himself when she used her left hand to unnecessarily wipe at the lapel of her lab coat. Her wedding ring flashed in the bright light. Then he considered the situation from her perspective. There were probably a hundred men for every woman here and an early declaration of her marital status must have become habit. "Are you an M.D.?"

"Nuclear physicist," she replied in a remarkably deep voice.

The answer surprised Mercer. He looked to Ira.

"A lot more than testing aircraft takes place here," the admiral explained. "All of it under complete compartmentalization. Hell, I only know a few things under development and I'm on the president's staff."

"A case of the right hand not knowing what the left is up to?" Mercer joked.

"The personnel here don't even know there is a left hand," Dr. Marie deadpanned.

"Even with your top secret clearance," Ira went on, "I had to pull some strings so you'd know the details of this operation. The men you'll be working with have no idea."

Mercer got a sudden chill that had nothing to do with the weather. He'd spent enough time with Ira to fairly judge his moods. The stress lines around his eyes and on his forehead hadn't been there the last time they'd shared a drink at Tiny's. And his pallor went far beyond a normal end-of-winter hue. "What's going on here, Ira?"

Briana Marie answered, "There's been an accident. People are dead. We need you to carry on with their work."

The whistle of wind beyond the hangar doors sounded like a mourning dirge.

Mercer learned he'd be spending the night at the main complex. Tomorrow he'd be taken to an even more secret base on the Area 51 grounds, a place Ira called DS-Two. Ira asked Captain Sykes to show him to his billet in a building behind the hangar. A metal roof covered the walkway, presumably to hide foot traffic from orbital observation.

The room was like any hotel Mercer had ever stayed at, only the door locked from the outside. To leave, he had to buzz a uniformed staffer seated in the barracks' reception area. He took his first shower since Canada, thirty-six hours and roughly five thousand air miles ago. Returning west had fortunately nullified his jet lag. As the scalding water sluiced across his body, he thought of the old joke about a harried tourist on a package tour. "Oh, it's Monday. Then this must be Rome."

By the time he'd toweled dry, he'd figured out what Dr. Marie was working on. With Yucca Mountain only a short distance away, the answer was obvious.

Sykes was waiting for him at the reception desk when the corporal on duty allowed him out of his room.

"Is this your regular posting?" Mercer asked as Sykes led him across the facility.

"Nah," Sykes drawled. "Me and my team have been here a month."

"Team?"

"Delta Force." This was the army's elite hostage rescue team. "If you don't mind a little free advice, Doc, I've learned you get along better out here if you don't ask too many questions."

Despite their awkward introduction, Mercer found he liked the soldier. He'd already realized his slow demeanor wasn't laziness. Rather, Sykes possessed a cool deliberation, as if he knew when he woke each morning every action his body would take and every word he'd need to speak. It was only a matter of doling them out at the right time.

"And let me guess," Mercer commented, "one question is too many?"

Sykes grinned. "You're catching on."

Sykes led him to a nondescript building, a slab-sided office cube with the architectural flair of a Soviet apartment house. Most of the base had been built in the 1960s and substantially expanded in the '80s, yet it retained the Cold War sterility of its roots. The buildings Mercer could see were laid out in geometric blocs. There was no ornamentation, no landscaping and certainly no streetlights.

Nor, he noticed, were there any people. It was like walking around a postapocalyptic ghost town.

"Kinda creepy, huh?" Sykes seemed to be reading Mercer's thoughts as they reached the building's door. "I guess the isolation really gets to some of the people out here, having to live under cover all the time. A couple days after I got here, a bunch of the younger soldiers were given permission to put on a show for a Chinese spy satellite."

"What'd they do?" Mercer followed Sykes to a flight of stairs. The building's interior was as drab as the outside.

"They laid themselves out on the runway in nothing but their birthday suits. They used their bodies to spell out 'Up yours, Mao.' "

Mercer laughed. "Would the Chinese be able to see it?"

"Shit, they've stolen enough of our technology to be able to tell which ones were circumcised."

At the head of the stairs, Sykes opened a paneled door into a conference room, then told Mercer that Ira would escort him back to his room. The two men shook hands at their parting.

Heavy drapes were drawn over the room's picture window, and banker's lamps reflected puddles of cherry light off the burnished table. Along one wall were photographs of the U-2 spy plane. Ira sat at the head of the table, his jacket draped over his chair. He'd had the foresight to bring a bottle of his favorite Scotch and a bucket of ice.

Mercer accepted a glass gratefully. Though not a Scotch drinker, this had shaped up to be one of those days. Dr. Marie, on Ira's left, drank from a bottle of water.

Sitting opposite the physicist, Mercer saluted them

both with his drink, knocked it back in two quick swallows then shredded their veil of secrecy with his accurate hypothesis. "You're building a subterranean repository for undocumented nuclear waste, like what the Department of Energy is constructing at Yucca Mountain."

The silence had the weight of lead.

Dr. Marie finally managed to stammer, "How did you . . . ," before her voice failed her.

Ira merely laughed.

For half a century America's nuclear power plants had been splitting untold tons of radioactive material to extract its energy. The result was a vastly more concentrated product than what went into the reactors, a deadly waste that wouldn't lose its lethality for millennia. The short-term solution had been to store this waste in cooling pools at the plants. The only viable long-term disposal method was to find a suitable place to bury it and hope to God that they could put a heavy enough cork on it to keep the nuclear genie in its bottle.

Work was currently under way to construct a pair of fourteen-mile tunnels a thousand feet below Yucca Mountain. The waste would be stored in rooms excavated off these tunnels. Even with the water table lying a further thousand feet below the repository, extraordinary measures were to be taken to prevent seepage from coming into contact with the impenetrable casks that would contain the radioactive materials.

The forty thousand tons of nuclear waste currently stockpiled would be moved to the facility over the next two decades. When the repository reached its seventy-seven-thousand-ton capacity, there would be a century of additional monitoring before the complex was completely sealed in 2116.

Mercer gave Dr. Marie an ironic smile. "To answer your almost asked question, it's the only thing that makes sense. We're maybe forty miles from Yucca Mountain, you're a nuclear engineer and my principal job is digging tunnels. That adds up to only one thing. Throwing Ira's presence into the mix just gives this situation the right touch of subterfuge."

"I resent that defamation of my character," Ira grumbled without malice. "And your assessment is a bit off. The waste we plan to store here is documented. What we want to do is bring in most of the really nasty stuff before anyone knows it's on the move."

"By nasty you mean the waste left over from our weapons program and by anyone you mean terrorists?"

"Exactly." Ira recharged Mercer's glass. "We want to do the same thing they did when they transported the Hope Diamond."

Mercer knew that story well. The last time the fabled diamond was moved from its home at the Smithsonian to New York City for a thorough examination and cleaning the security had been unprecedented—armored cars, police escorts and a large contingent of guards. Yet when they arrived at Harry Winston's Jewelers in Manhattan, the box containing the fabulous gem was empty. What no one knew, not the guards, not the media or the public, was that the security entourage had been a ruse to throw off potential thieves. The stone had actually been sent in a nondescript package through the regular mail.

Dr. Marie leaned forward in her chair. "We'll use standard shipping casks and all the regular safety devices, but we want to avoid the media attention that would tip off terrorists or anyone else who wants to derail the operation. By shipping material in secret, we eliminate the temptation."

"How long do you plan to keep the waste here?" Mercer asked.

"It'll be moved into the permanent repository over time. Because of the heat generated by the material we'll be storing here, it has to be spread out all through the Yucca Mountain facility."

"What we're looking to build," Ira interrupted, "is a temporary holding area away from media attention and out of reach of terrorists. Nothing will remain here by the time the main site is sealed."

Leaning back, Mercer digested what he'd learned. He grasped the need for what Ira wanted to do. He knew that a great deal of nuclear policy was based on emotion rather than science, although he didn't discount the horror if there ever was a major catastrophe, or even a minor one. By moving the worst of the waste before anyone knew it was happening, Dr. Marie felt she could cut the nation's anxiety levels as well as better protect the shipments. It made sense because one way or the other the material *would* be transported.

He understood the need for secrecy. What they hadn't explained is the urgency, and he was willing to wait for hours before asking that question. While it was Ira's nature not to divulge any more than necessary, Mercer wouldn't agree to help until he knew the whole truth. He didn't take it personally. It was the price he paid for his friendship with a professional spy.

Neither Ira nor Mercer showed the least discomfort sitting next to each other in silence. Dr. Marie, however, felt the urge to fill the lull. "We had an accident two days ago. A cave-in. We've been running twenty-four hours a day in three shifts, ten men per shift. The collapse occurred during a shift change. Fifteen men, including two shift supervisors, were killed."

"The other five?" Mercer asked.

"Escaped unharmed," she replied. "For security reasons, we don't want to bring in any more miners. However, we all felt that we needed a second engineer. When our request reached Admiral Lasko, he said he had the right person. You're a mine engineer who already has a high enough security clearance to work here."

Again, Mercer noticed, nothing was said about the urgency.

"Listen, Mercer." Ira's voice deepened. "We're already two months behind schedule. The tunnels should already be done and contractors brought in to handle water seepage problems. The first load of waste will be arriving in one hundred twenty-one days."

"Why so precise?"

"Because a storage pool at Oak Ridge won't be able to take any more spent fuel rods and they're scheduled to replace the current fuel assemblies in an experimental fast-breeder reactor in a hundred twenty-one days. We want to bring what's in the pool here rather than shuffle it to another facility."

Satisfied with the answer, Mercer asked the next question that was bothering him. "I was told I'd be here for a week. Obviously that's bull. I'm in the middle of a contract with De Beers. How long do I have to put them off? Am I here for the two months you said you're behind?"

Marie shook her head. "Our remaining shift boss says we're no more than two weeks from breaking into the subterranean chamber we're planning on using. It's a natural pocket in the rock. Our original geologic survey said it's a hollow space left behind after an intrusive magma dike subsided."

That's where the seepage Ira mentioned came into play, Mercer thought. Though not common, such a dike—basically a tongue of molten rock injected into the surrounding strata—can drain back into the central magma chamber that spawned it. In this situation, it leaves an empty cavity in the earth that often fills with water. Once they got the hydrology handled, it made sense to use this natural chamber for their short-term repository.

"Who did the original survey?" he asked, doubting they'd found a drained dike. It was more likely a sill or laccolith, which ran with the grain of sedimentary layering rather than against it.

"Gregor Hood."

Mercer nodded. "I know him. He takes a while, but he's good. What about the other shift supervisor? Who have you got?"

"Donald Randall, he's a professional miner from Kentucky."

It took a moment for the name to sink in. "Donny Randall?"

"He prefers Donald," Dr. Marie said primly, as if maintaining such niceties could somehow lessen the feeling of loathing Randall created.

Mercer's eyes bored into Ira's. His voice went flint-hard and accusatory. "You hired Randall the Handle? Do you know what an effing psychopath he is?"

Ira looked away. "We've had some complaints about him, but it's too late. He's already here and we can't bring in anyone else."

Donny Randall, Randall the Handle, got his nick-name in South Africa before the end of apartheid. He'd gone there because his reputation for quick violence had gotten him booted from the United Mine Workers and blackballed from every mine in the States. South Africa became a perfect place for him. It wasn't so much that he was racist, he was simply sadistic. Back then the black miners had no way to redress labor issues so he could be as brutal as he wanted without fear of retribution.

Standing six feet six, with a build to match, Randall delighted in fighting any man who challenged him, though he preferred to use the handle of a pickax rather than his fists, thus his moniker. Mercer had

heard that he'd killed at least six men in the mines
around Johannesburg and had beaten dozens more. It
was also in South Africa that Randall had found another application for his two-inch-diameter piece of
hardened hickory. He'd use it to sodomize workers
too young or too small to defend themselves. Because
of the permissive attitude of the courts, he hadn't been
tried for any of his acts. He'd left the country when
Nelson Mandela assumed the presidency. Some said
he was asked to go, but Mercer believed the story that
he'd fled from a mob of black miners who'd wanted
to give him a Soweto necklace—a burning tire around
his neck.

His name had come up from time to time in the
years since, but Mercer hadn't known Randall had
returned to the States. The last he'd heard, Donny
was in a Russian prison following an attempt to steal
diamonds from the Mir mine in northern Siberia.

Mercer finally stopped staring at the top of Ira's
bald head and allowed his eyes to sweep across Dr.
Marie. If she thought all mine engineers were like
Randall, no wonder she'd been chilly toward him. "I'll
help with your project," he said, and Ira looked up,
"on the condition that I can square things with De
Beers—"

"We'll take care of that."

"—and that you make sure Randall knows I'm in
charge. You've got enough men for two shifts working
eight- to ten-hour days. Once we're settled I don't
even want to see that son of a bitch."

Ira and Briana Marie realized the emotion in Mercer's voice wasn't fear of Don Randall. It was fear
he'd kill him.

"Thank you, Dr. Mercer," Briana said. "You don't
know what this means to us."

"I knew I could count on you," Ira added, a couple
of the tension lines in his forehead subsiding. This

time he filled three tumblers with Scotch and they toasted each other.

The following morning, Mercer and Ira boarded a Chevy Suburban identical to the one that had taken him to Andrews Air Force Base. He idly hoped the government received a volume discount on the massive SUVs.

There was one difference, he quickly discovered. This vehicle had heavy curtains drawn over the windows and an opaque screen dividing them from the driver. Despite what he'd seen the evening before, it was obvious he wasn't cleared to view other parts of Area 51. Then he thought that maybe Ira wasn't cleared either. An interesting notion.

When he asked about Dr. Marie, Ira explained that she now worked out of Washington and had only come to Nevada for the briefing the night before. She wouldn't be needed at the secret repository until well after the tunnel had been excavated. As the darkened truck rolled away from the base the two men passed the time drinking a thermos of coffee and reminiscing about their first meeting in Greenland almost a year ago.

Once the van reached an area beyond the immediate perimeter of Groom Lake, the unseen driver lowered the partition so they could see out the windshield and Ira drew back the curtains.

The mountains held a distant chill even if last night hadn't been cold enough for frost. The few plants, cactus, yucca, and sage mostly, were stunted by their harsh environment as though life in the barren stretches was an experiment that was slowly failing. This was a land of rock in a thousand shades that changed and shifted as the sun rose higher. The dome of sky hinted that it stretched far beyond the horizon but seemed contained by the jagged hills.

Their destination was two hours from the main base, tucked at the end of a box canyon. Mercer recognized that the mounds of tailings, the material excavated from a mine shaft, had been spread evenly along the canyon floor to disguise that any work was taking place. The camp was nothing more than several battered mobile homes situated close to the towering canyon walls. An overhang of rock at the canyon's lip kept the facility in perpetual shadow and hid it from aerial observation.

The camp was as forlorn as a West Texas trailer park, Mercer thought, although he'd worked in much, much worse. A tumbleweed skittered from between two trailers, whirled in a crosscurrent of wind, then dashed past the SUV like a frightened animal.

Then he spotted a natural cave at the end of the canyon. It was at least seventy feet wide and nearly half as tall. It appeared to stretch a hundred feet or more into the mountain. Powerful arc lights mounted on scaffolds lit the interior and highlighted the machinery at the top of a twenty-foot-square hole driven into the living rock. The two-story hoist allowed overburden to be dumped directly into trucks that spread it on the desert floor. Nearby were massive ventilator ducts to keep fresh air circulating underground and several box trailers for storage. Near the mouth of the cave were two large generators for power and the massive outlet of a down-hole water pump to handle drainage.

Mercer was impressed with the security as well as the efficiency of what Ira had created here. "Put in a golf course and some condos and you'd have a nice spot for a retirement community."

"Hell Hollow Home for the Aged?"

Mercer laughed, grateful that the Ira he knew was coming back. "I was thinking Desolate Digs for the Near-Dead. Harry could be your spokesman."

The Suburban braked at the first of the trailers. Ira stepped to the dusty ground as the trailer door swung open. The man standing at the threshold in jeans, cowboy boots, and a white T-shirt seemed as apropos as the tumbleweed that had crossed their path. As dried and tough as a piece of beef jerky, he squinted at Mercer and then nodded when he recognized Ira. "Howdy, Mr. Lasko. This our new boss?"

"Hey, Red." What little showed of Red's hair from under his hat was brown. "This is Mercer."

"I heard of ya." Red's voice twanged like an untuned guitar. "You're that fella what found a new diamond mine in Africa a couple years back."

They shook hands while Ira continued the introductions. "Red Harding was the number-two man on the shift that lost half the crew during the cave-in."

"You didn't want to take over?" Mercer asked, needing to know now if this guy resented him for taking a job he felt he might have deserved.

"Hell, son"—Red was perhaps fifteen years older than Mercer, although it wouldn't come as a surprise if he had fathered some children in his mid-teens— "comes a time in a man's life where he don't wanta give the orders no more. It's a piece easier just takin' 'em."

"Tell me what happened?" Mercer invited.

Red paused, giving the question thought despite the days he'd already had to consider the cause of the cave-in. "A chunk of hanging wall that had no reason to crack loose cracked loose. Came down in a flat piece about eight feet thick that spanned the entire drive. Crushed everyone under it. Fifteen men."

Mercer got the sense that Red wasn't comfortable with this vague description of the accident. Not that he was holding anything back. It was just that there was something about it he didn't understand. "You hadn't bolted the hanging wall?" Hanging wall was mining parlance for the roof of a tunnel. Bolting was what it sounded like, screwing long bolts into the ceiling to help stabilize the rock.

"No need. We're boring through some serious hardrock. No water seepage, no fissures, nothing."

"They're bolting it now," Ira offered.

Mercer expected no less.

After being shown his room in one of the trailers, Mercer changed into his miner's coveralls while Ira was loaned a spare set by Red Harding. With no place to hide his pistol in the utilitarian room, Mercer decided he'd keep it with him. He tucked it against the small of his back under the coveralls and planted his helmet on his head.

Ira had to keep his baseball cap on to prevent the helmet Red had given him from slipping across his hairless scalp. He suffered the ignominy in silence.

The cavern was markedly cooler than the canyon, even with the excess heat generated by the diesel-powered equipment.

As they waited for the personnel lift to trundle up from underground, Mercer examined a fist-sized chunk of rock that had spilled from the ore shoot. He always marveled at the fact that in the millions, or even billions, of years since this innocuous lump of stone had solidified in the earth's crust, not one human had ever seen it. He was the first to give it any thought at all. It made him feel like a Golden Age explorer peering at a newly discovered continent. He'd worked in mines since his teenage years in the granite quarries of Vermont, and that thrill had never left him.

The cage hoist arrived with a clang of bells and the three men stepped into the roomy car. The small scope of the project meant that one mine shaft could be used for hauling material from the depths as well as transporting the men to and from work and provide forced air ventilation through enormous ducts secured to the side of the hole.

The bells rang again and the bottom fell out from under them.

Ira clutched at a safety rail while Red and Mercer suppressed knowing smiles. The first descent into a mine was a terrifying experience that many could never repeat. Lasko finally released his grip on the railing when he'd regained his equilibrium.

"And I thought commuting to work around Washington was bad," he said to cover his apprehension. "Is it always like that?"

Red shook his head. "The horizontal tunnel we bored off this shaft is eight hundred feet below us. In South Africa, some of the men work ten times deeper. To get them there quickly, you damn near free-fall the whole way."

"Hell of a way to make a living," Ira remarked as they dropped into impenetrable darkness.

Mercer ignored the sarcasm. "It sure is."

Several minutes later, the rattling car slowed and a yellowish glow seeped up from around the elevator's edges. They were nearing where men drilled and blasted toward the subterranean cavity the Department of Energy planned to use as their temporary storehouse.

Red threw open the gate when the car stopped bouncing at the end of its eight-hundred-foot tether. The chamber was the size of a railway tunnel and well lit. They were that much closer to the earth's core, so the workings were appreciably warmer too, though not uncomfortably so. In ultradeep mines, ventilated air was forced through massive refrigeration units just to maintain a temperature of one hundred degrees. Littering the antechamber were hydraulic compressors for the drills, mechanical scrapers and other specialty equipment designed to operate in the claustrophobic confines of the tunnel.

At the far end of the room was the main tunnel, lit by a string of bulbs that vanished far into the distance. "How long is the drive?" Mercer asked.

"Twelve hundred feet," Red said as he stepped over snaking coils of hydraulic lines and power cords as thick as his wrist. "The lab coats who told us where to dig wanted the access shaft sunk fifteen hundred feet from the pocket."

"What about the sump under the hoist?"

"The shaft bottoms out three hundred feet below this level."

Meaning they could store more than a hundred thousand cubic feet of water below the level of the drive. "Why so deep?"

"The lab coats again. They say we're blasting toward an underground lake. When we cut through they want to keep as much water as possible. Some sort of irrigation project, right, Mr. Lasko?"

"That's right, Red." Ira gave Mercer a significant look. Red didn't know the details of the project. Mercer cut short his questioning.

Once they stepped out of the well-lit antechamber, the three men switched on flashlights and continued deeper into the guts of the mountain. The ceiling was a roomy eight feet and the passage was fifteen feet wide. Mercer assumed it was sized to accommodate the nuclear containment casks. Under the beam of his light, the stone was a featureless gray.

Ira asked about the puddles of dirty water on the floor.

"You use water to cool and lubricate the drill bits. Nothing to worry about," Mercer replied, then added, "It's when you see clear water that you should be concerned. This far down any sediment in the water has been distilled as it percolates through the rock. Clean water means seepage."

A thousand feet down the tunnel, they came to where part of the hanging wall had let go. The debris and the bodies had been removed so the area looked sanitized. The only evidence of the tragedy was that the ceiling was double its normal height. The break where the stone had split appeared clean, as if the section that collapsed had been a separate piece of rock waiting for eons for its support to be taken away.

Mercer looked at Red.

"Like I said," the Texan drawled, "weirdest damned thing."

The bolt heads recently shot into the stone were silver bright.

They continued deeper into the tunnel. Heavy beams supported on timber balks had been placed every twenty feet. They used wooden columns because the fibers made popping sounds long before they collapsed, giving workers plenty of time to reshore the area or, if need be, to clear out entirely.

As they neared the working face, the sound of mine work became a teeth-shattering combination of steel on stone and the grind of heavy equipment. They passed several small mechanical shovels and a string of ore cars mounted on solid wheels. The awkward train, with its low-slung electric tractor, resembled a metallic centipede. Nearby was an even stranger insectlike machine, a four-drill drifter. The drifter was a platform mounted on crawler treads that could precisely position four of the heavy rock drills. The drills themselves were roughly the same size as machine guns and had the same wicked appearance. Hydraulic cables snaked from the machine like arteries.

The men at the tunnel's limit worked in pairs using slightly smaller hammer drills to bore more holes into the stone. Rock chips and lubricating water spewed from the hundred-pound tools in a stinging rain. Sullen rainbows caught in the lights seemed to resent being caged in this stygian realm.

Mining had come a long way from the days when men hand-packed sticks of dynamite into drill holes and hoped for the best. Advances in explosives and techniques meant miners could peel rock with near-surgical precision. Here the men used the drifter to drill out the larger holes at the center of an expanding spiral pattern. The rest of the holes were hand-drilled using notes on depth and angle determined by the shift boss. This intricate arrangement allowed the explosives in the middle to core out a void in the rock face. Timed with microsecond delays, the next ring of charges blew debris laterally into the cavity, expanding it and creating space for the rubble from still more shots. The explosions corkscrewed out like a blooming flower and gave the men unprecedented control over how much material they excavated with each shot.

Red broke away from Mercer and Ira to tap the shift boss on the shoulder. With the drillers working full out, it was impossible to hear over the din.

Even before he turned, Mercer recognized Donny Randall just from his size and the slope of his wide shoulders. His blocky head made his helmet look like a finger bowl.

They'd met once in Botswana, at a retirement party for the underground manager of the Orapa mine. Donny had been at the stylish affair because an incentive contest gave an invitation to the shift boss whose gang held the monthly record for most ore removed. He'd basically brutalized his way in. As he partied that night, one of his men was in a hospital bed recovering from a slenectomy while another was learning to eat without front teeth, all thanks to Donny's pick handle.

Mercer had learned about this and some of his earlier exploits in South Africa later, although even then he could sense Donny's brute stupidity and elemental savagery. As one of the only Americans there, Donny had tried to speak with Mercer. He'd been drunk when he'd arrived at the hotel ballroom and could only slur his words.

The incident was one of the few times Mercer's memory had failed him and for this he was grateful. He couldn't recall what was said during their minute-long conversation, but he did remember that Donny had been thrown out of the hotel by a half dozen guards, most of whom went home with bruises or black eyes as souvenirs.

Randall had a brutal face, heavy brows and a mouth perpetually twisted into a smirk. His nose looked so often broken and reset there was little cartilage remaining. His hair was dyed jet-black and he sported sideburns like a latter-day Elvis. His eyes were dark and disturbing. It wasn't their shade that was so unsettling, it was their feral quickness. They twitched from person to person as though he was a cornered animal seeking escape, or a liar waiting to be found out.

Mercer knew him to be both.

Randall's eyes finally settled on Ira and he gave a mock salute. The fact that Admiral Lasko signed the paychecks did little to impress him. Red indicated that they should move back down the drive to get away from the din.

"What are you doing back here?" Donny demanded of Ira. Like many paranoids, he never understood that his brusque suspicion contributed to the cycle of animosity he encountered.

Ira let the lack of respect slide. "I'm here with the new shift boss to replace Gordon and Kadanski. This is Mercer."

Donny made no move to shake hands, nor did it appear he recognized the name or Mercer's face.

"We're down to sixteen men, including him." Randall tossed his head in Mercer's direction. His voice was a strange combination of menace and petulance.

"Because you won't get more miners you can't expect me to make your schedule."

"I've seen the progress reports," Ira replied evenly. "Even when you had three shifts you guys weren't making three shots a day."

"That wasn't my fault. Gordon and Kadanski didn't know what they were doing. Hell, if I hadn't picked up their slack we wouldn't have moved ten feet from the main shaft."

Red Harding's derisive cough wasn't necessary. Mercer knew Donny was blaming the dead men to cover his failure.

It had taken only moments, but Ira had had enough, remarkable since Mercer had rarely known him to get upset. Randall had that effect on people. Ira stiffened, his bearing becoming that of a thirty-year naval veteran dressing down a subordinate. "Mercer will be in charge from now on, so you don't need to worry about my schedule. All you have to do is work where and how he says or you're through. Are we clear?"

Donny Randall muttered something unintelligible.

"What was that?" Ira snapped.

"I said yeah."

"You will say, yes, sir."

Donny's defiance lasted a fraction of a second. It was a murderous spark that blazed behind his eyes, a savage glimpse into his capacity for rage. It vanished as abruptly as a cage door slamming. His expression shifted to an empty smile. "Yes, sir." He stepped closer to Mercer to shake hands. "Welcome aboard. Good to meet you."

"Likewise," Mercer choked.

Fifteen hours later, Ira had returned to the main Area 51 complex for his flight back to Washington. Mercer had his crew working nights, leaving the day shift to Donny Randall.

The night sky was suffused with a blur of stars so startlingly close they appeared to hang just overhead. The air was still, timeless. Moonlight electrified the drab landscape, highlighting features with its silvery glow while outlining others in deepest shadow.

Don Randall gave no indication he saw the ephemeral beauty, let alone gave it any consideration. He strode across the desert with the single-minded determination of a migrating animal, driven by instinct rather than intellect.

He'd created elaborate excuses for the hour-long walks he took every couple of nights, although none of the men had shown the slightest interest in his activities. He took their silence as respect for his privacy, never considering they were glad for anything that got him out of the communal recreation hall.

His boots dug deep into the loose scree as he panted his way up a hillock two miles from camp. At the top of the hill he checked the loose piles of boulders he'd stacked around his cache. None of the tells he'd left appeared disturbed, nor were there any footprints that didn't match his size-thirteen feet. He grunted his satisfaction and tore into the pile, heaving fifty-pound rocks as though they weighed no more than bricks.

Ten minutes after beginning his work, his fingers closed around the plastic handle of an armored suitcase and with one jerk he freed the case. He was careful to dust off the lid before opening it.

While the electronics within the case were state-of-the-art microminiaturization, the banks of batteries gave the crate its size and considerable weight. Also nestled inside the case was a compass. He set the box on the ground and rotated it until the retractable antenna pointed ten degrees east of due south, as he'd been taught. When he switched on the electronics he was greeted by a series of green indicator lights and the machine emitted a high-pitched tone. It had found the satellite hanging twenty-two thousand miles from Earth.

The complexities of the heavily encrypted satellite phone were beyond him. All he knew was what direction to point it and how to turn it on. He'd tried using it once to dial a phone sex service, but the machine wouldn't access the number. It could only reach the people who'd paid him to make reports about the mine.

He snatched the handset from its cradle, hit a button that activated the phone and waited for a single ring for an electronically muffled voice to answer.

"Go."

Donny licked his dry lips. The voice had always given him an uncomfortable feeling, like there was nothing human behind it, like he was taking orders from a machine. "We've got a problem."

"What is it?"

"The replacement for Gordon and Kadanski is here."

"We expected there would be one. You know what to do."

"It ain't that easy. The new guy—it's Philip Mercer."

For the first time in all his conversations, the person/machine paused. "Very well. Do nothing for now. We will deal with him when the time comes."

"Okay," Donny replied, but the connection had already been cut.

The floor of the box canyon was in shadow long before sunset, making it easier for Mercer to pretend it was almost dawn rather than a few minutes until dusk. Just one of the tricks he used when working a graveyard shift. The other mental games he played weren't doing much to alleviate the tension cramping his shoulders, the nagging pain in his lower back or the gritty, red rims around his eyes. He hadn't spent as much time at the mine as the others, yet he'd pushed himself so hard he felt the deep exhaustion infecting them all. The work pace had been brutal and he hadn't yet recovered from Canada.

In the command trailer he stooped over the seismograph, his attention focused on the steady line of ink trailing across the revolving drum of paper. The stylus remained motionless but wouldn't for long. Although it meant reporting to work an hour before his shift, he'd gotten in the habit of watching the results of Donny Randall's blasts.

Red Harding stepped into the trailer where they kept the seismograph and several other pieces of scientific equipment. He placed a cup of coffee at Mercer's elbow. Mercer acknowledged with a nod. Observing the seismograph had become a "morning" ritual for both men.

"Still haven't figured it out, huh?" Red sipped from the Pepsi that gave him his jolt of caffeine.

Outside, the men of Donny's team made their way past the trailer on their way toward their rooms for showers, dinner in the mess, and bed. The schedule left most too tired to bother with the satellite television, pool table or other amenities in the rec hall.

"Not yet," Mercer said absently. The big clock on the wall showed that a minute remained before Donny would fire the charges his men had just planted.

Harding scratched his sunburned bald spot. "He has a different technique is all."

Mercer had noticed the anomaly over the course of the ten days he'd been on-site. Both work shifts removed similar amounts of rock with each blast, although Donny used slightly more explosives. What tickled the back of Mercer's mind was that the seismograph readings indicated Donny's shots were slightly smaller than Mercer's. Somehow Randall managed to reduce the amount of seismic shock from the charges he laid, creating less stress in the surrounding strata, something miners strove for. Mercer had watched him working but had found nothing to indicate how he was doing it.

It was ego driving him to find the answer, he knew. He didn't want to admit the possibility that Randall the Handle was the better blaster.

"And if you average out our teams," Red added, "we have cleared six feet more tunnel than he has. He ain't better than us. He's just overpacking his holes after he places his 'splosives. That accounts for the damping effect."

"You're probably right," Mercer replied, not wholly satisfied with the answer but unable to find another.

The earth and the stylus jumped at the same instant. The bump at the soles of their feet was much less dramatic than what happened on the seismograph. The steel needle traced a jagged line on the paper like an EKG recording a heart attack. A moment later the shock waves dissipated and the machine flat-lined as if the patient had died. On an adjoining computer Mercer brought up comparison patterns from previous blasts. Like before, Donny's shot showed a two percent decrease in shock waves from what Mercer's team managed. The six additional feet that his men had excavated wasn't enough to make up that difference.

Mercer's mouth turned down at the corners.

The trailer door crashed open. Randall loomed at the entrance, his face and clothes covered in dirt. Pomade and dust turned his hair into a shiny helmet that clung to his skull. The dye he used to keep his hair unnaturally black bled down his forehead in gray streaks of sweat. "How'd I do?" His voice crashed unnecessarily loud.

"Three point two," Red mumbled, as if betraying his supervisor with the answer.

"Hah," Donny sneered. "I hot-loaded that shot with ten extra cartridges of Tovex. Had you made that shot, the graph would've spiked at four-oh, minimum." He walked away without waiting for a reply.

"As if we needed another reason to think he's a jerk," Red commented to Mercer.

Mercer said nothing. What could he say? He checked the sensors monitoring ventilation for fume and dust concentrates. It would take a half hour for the massive fans to clear the workings of the choking mixture. Next he called up the video feed from a shielded and stabilized camera placed just back from the end of the tunnel.

It took a second for his eyes to adjust to the swirling clouds of dust blocking the camera's view. It looked like a furious sandstorm. He sipped his coffee while the ventilators drew the smog to the surface. After a few minutes he could see rubble strewn on the floor of the tunnel, the debris blasted from the rock face by Donny's charges, and then the end of the tunnel resolved itself from the haze. The stone was remarkably uniform considering the explosive onslaught it had just endured. Donny's blast had been clean.

Mercer was just turning away so he could get ready for his shift when a shadow on the rock wall caught his attention. He almost ignored it, figuring the blemish was the result of the camera's low resolution, but he sat back down and studied the mark.

Red sensed his sudden tension. "What is it?"

"Not sure," he said. "Nothing probably." Mercer watched for another minute. The stain remained unchanged. And still he felt a premonition. The geologic reports said they were roughly thirty feet from the subterranean reservoir, so it couldn't be water, but what was it?

He made a quick decision. From a wall rack he grabbed a portable air cylinder and a mask with an integrated intercom. "Stay here and keep an eye on the camera. I'm going below."

"Sure you don't want me down there with you?"

"Positive. If that spot on the wall changes, tell me."

"What do you think it is?"

"Probably an inclusion in the rock, but I don't want anyone going down until I'm sure." Mercer grabbed his hard hat and jogged from the trailer.

The elevator operator was just climbing from his control booth when Mercer entered the cave. "Mike, fire up the skip and don't leave your station. I might need you to haul me out fast."

"What's up?" the worker asked even as he swung himself back into his elevated chair.

"Possible pressure seepage." Mercer slammed the cage doors closed and barely heard the warning bells before the car dropped away. He fitted the oxygen tank onto his back and checked his communications link with Harding. "You reading me, Red?"

"Loud and clear."

"Any change?"

"Nothing yet. You think the report was wrong and that we've already hit the water, don't you?"

"Maybe." The motes of dust swirling in the beam of his light were like a snow flurry that became a full-blown blizzard as he plunged into the depths. His visibility was down to thirty feet by the time the elevator reached the substation eight hundred feet below ground.

The geologic reports said they were well back from the underground lake, but he couldn't discount that the blemish really was water seeping through the earth's crust. The pressure behind it would be unimaginable, and the rock dam between the water and the tunnel could withstand only so much. If it was water, the next set of drill holes could easily cross that threshold and the whole thing would let go in a catastrophic flood. It was possible that even now the rock was breaking up and would explode.

Mercer couldn't risk sending his men down here until he was sure. The fear of drilling into an undetected aquifer was one more on the long list of mining dangers, one very few survived to talk about. More than cave-ins or fire, miners feared a flood in the shafts. He recalled the long three days he'd spent in Somerset County, Pennsylvania, consulting with local experts to rescue six trapped workers caught in an unexpected flood. Getting them out safely had been one of the closest calls he could remember.

His emotions were torn between urgency and caution, but like so many times in his life, he let his dedication to his job push him on. He ran down the drive, his boots splashing through puddles and echoing dully in the tunnel's confines. His breath hissed behind his face mask. The beam from his helmet lamp danced with each long stride.

If they had hit water, he'd have to keep men out of the mine for a minimum of thirty-six to forty-eight hours to monitor the seepage rate. Then they would have to change their blasting techniques. Finding seepage this soon would slow them down dramatically.

The vent fans were doing a good job clearing the air. As he approached the working face, his visibility had increased slightly. He stepped past the camera.

"I see you, Mercer," Red called over the radio.

"How's my butt look?" he joked to ease the strain in Red's voice.

"Your overalls make your ass look big," Red teased back. "The spot hasn't changed."

"I'm looking at it now."

From a tool locker built into one of the small electric bulldozers, Mercer grabbed a six-foot steel pry bar. The ground was a jumble of rocks, some as large as car engines, others reduced to pebbles by the explosives. Although the ceiling looked pretty good, he tested some fissures with the pry bar to make sure none of it would collapse on to him. He jimmied loose a few stones, dodging aside as they crashed to the floor. It took him a further ten minutes to safely approach the blemish. Red called down to tell him the air was cleared enough to breathe. Mercer removed his face mask and unlimbered the air tank.

The beam of his light slashed across the spot and reflected off its slick surface. It looked like water *had* seeped from the reservoir through microfissures in the rock.

Mercer bent closer. The rock itself wasn't exactly wet to the touch. It almost felt like a snake's skin, merely hinting at moisture. He returned to the toolbox to get a piece of chalk and traced the perimeter of the two-foot stain. The outline would give him a reference if more water filtered into the tunnel.

Sitting back on his heels, he studied the spot, breathing slowly through his mouth because dust continued to flow past on the ventilation currents. For five minutes his concentration didn't waver as he watched to see if the mark was growing. Had it expanded even a fraction of an inch he would have run from the mine as fast as he could.

Red's voice on the intercom finally drew his attention. "It's water, isn't it?"

"Yes, but I think it's stable." Mercer stood. "There's no indication of continued flow."

"You want us down there?"

"Not yet. Give me a few more minutes."

Mercer turned his attention to the mounds of rubble displaced by Donny's last explosive blast. The wet spot was low down on the left side of the tunnel so Mercer concentrated there, using the pry bar to pick through the debris. He was looking for evidence of how deeply they'd already mined into the waterlogged rock. Unwilling to risk any other men in the tunnel, he strained to roll some of the larger boulders by himself. His body was soon bathed in sweat.

It took ten minutes to find the first chunk of stone showing water saturation. It was darker than the surrounding material, almost oily to the touch. Once he knew the appearance of the hydrostatically altered rock, he found several more farther down the drive. It became clear that Randall had ignored the evidence of seepage when he drilled the shot holes for his last charges. With the crews generally blasting three times during their shift, he wondered how many times Randall had knowingly risked his men by drilling into the dangerous formation.

Mercer felt his body grow taut with rage. "Red," he called into his comm link, his voice cracking like a whip. "It looks like Donny drilled his last shot holes knowing he'd hit seepage. Get a team together to check the overburden he sent up during his shift. I want to know if any of it shows further saturation."

"Roger. Anything else?"

"Yeah. I don't want anyone else coming down without my express order. Get a portable seismograph ready. I want to take direct measurements of the working face. It looks like it's holding, but there could be tremors I can't feel."

"Okay."

"And find the Handle." Mercer had returned to the rock face so he could move the camera closer to the damp spot.

The water stain hadn't expanded beyond the chalk outline he'd drawn. By releasing the counterpressure of rock against the water, it didn't appear they'd increased the flow rate. Mercer was relieved and thankful. He bent close once again, moving so his face was an inch from the shiny stone. He deliberately stuck out his tongue to lick the grainy surface.

And he recoiled at the alkaline taste.

"What the . . .?" He licked another spot just to make sure of what his senses had just told him. The water percolating from deep inside the earth was salty. After being filtered through untold hundreds of feet of rock it should have been as clear as a mountain spring.

"Not just salty," he said aloud, baffled. "It has the exact salinity of seawater."

Mercer had everyone working straight out for the next three hours. Ignoring Ira's prohibition to draw attention to themselves, he had every light at the facility blazing away as sweep lines of men scoured the tailings recently excavated from the mine. With each empty pass his anger ebbed slightly.

Sleep-dazed and pissed off when he'd been roused from bed, Donny Randall insisted he hadn't seen any water when his men drilled the last holes on their shift, and it appeared evidence supported his claim of innocence. None of the overburden pulled out prior to the final blast showed that water had seeped past.

Randall's curses had evolved into snide comments by the time Mercer admitted that he'd been wrong about Donny putting his men in jeopardy.

Randall sat in the command trailer wearing sweatpants, heavy boots, and a leather jacket over his bare chest. The trailer was only slightly warmer than the desert night. He was picking at his fingernails with a folding knife when Mercer entered. Randall's dyed hair shimmered like·an oil slick under the fluorescent lights. He dropped his feet off the desk when he saw Mercer. "Since you didn't find shit, I'm going back to bed." He stood over Mercer in an attempt to intimidate him. "I guess your Ph.D. and your thousand-dollar-an-hour consulting fee and the fact that Ira Lasko thinks the sun shines out your ass don't mean much, huh?"

Mercer recoiled. He hadn't realized that Randall did indeed know who he was.

Donny laughed, misunderstanding Mercer's movement. "Next time you want a lesson on mining, you come and ask me and I'll tell you how it's done." The animal hatred flashed in his eyes once more and he poked a hardened finger into Mercer's chest. "And the next time you question my ability you'd damn well better be right, because if you're wrong again I'm going to beat you to an inch of your life. You hearing me?"

Mercer didn't consider the eighty pounds of weight or six inches of height he was giving to Randall. That wasn't even a factor. The only thing keeping him from snapping Donny's finger was that the move would only anger the larger man and the subsequent fight would likely end up destroying the trailer.

"I didn't think you were as tough as I'd heard," Donny scoffed with a dismissive toss of his pomaded hair. He was almost out the door when Mercer's comment stopped him dead:

"I was wrong about you, Donny. I apologize."

"That's more like it." Randall laughed.

Mercer's face remained expressionless. "You're not only the dumbest son of a bitch I've ever known, but I've watched you checking out the other men here and realized you used a pick handle on those boys in Africa because you're also the most sexually confused."

Randall blinked, the nature of the insult taking a few seconds to register. To Mercer it was almost as if he could watch the thoughts ricochet in his mind like a pinball bouncing from bumper to bumper. Just as his eyes widened in comprehension, Red Harding and a half dozen other men stepped into the trailer. They'd just completed their last sweep of the mine tailings and had no idea what they'd walked in on.

Randall paused for another heartbeat before deciding to let this drop, but he gave Mercer a murderous look. As if Mercer didn't already know it wouldn't end there. He almost smiled at Donny's transparency.

"What was that all about?" Red asked after Donny had skulked into the night.

"Just Donny expressing his disappointment about how I sullied his character."

"Come again?"

Mercer chuckled. "Randall was just trying to prove he can piss farther than me."

"Gotcha," the wiry Texan said. "We're ready to place the remote seismograph. You're going to need a hand." He pointed at the monitor showing the camera's view of the water stain. "The spot hasn't grown since we first saw it, so I think we'll be okay for a quick trip down."

The fact that water wasn't continuing to seep through the rock quelled only part of Mercer's uneasiness. He was more bothered now by the nature of the water, although he hadn't said anything about it. He was going to stick by his original decision to keep men out of the mine for at least a day.

"All right. You coming?"

"Damn straight."

Mercer nodded his appreciation. "Get one other man. Meet me at the skip in ten minutes."

"You going to call Admiral Lasko?"

Mercer reached for the encrypted satellite phone on the desk. "That's next on my list." He waited until the men had left the trailer before placing the call.

"Lasko."

"Ira, Mercer. We hit water."

A stunned moment, then, "How bad?"

"It just looks like a small patch of saturation. It's not growing, nor is any water wicking through."

A sudden realization hit the deputy security advisor. "You guys haven't broken into the chamber, have you?"

"No. It looks like we're still some twenty-eight feet shy, but the water seems to have expanded past its cavity, at least in this one patch."

"Ah, is this common?"

"Hard to tell," Mercer said after a moment. "It all depends on the water pressure, the permeability of the rock, how long the water's been there—"

"Why would that have anything to do with it?" Ira asked sharply.

"Given a few million years water will seep through just about anything. Knowing how long ago the void in the earth was filled would give me an idea how fast the water's moving."

"Oh, right."

"I've got a camera monitoring the damp spot, and we're about to place a portable seismograph to judge the rock's stability."

"Good. How many men are down there now?"

"None," Mercer replied. "That's one of the reasons

I called. Until I get a better handle on this, I don't want anyone working at the face."

Mercer expected a protest, but Ira agreed instead. "Good idea. For how long do you think? A couple of days?"

"At least. The plug separating the tunnel from the reservoir is under strain, and until I can determine how safe it is, we can't risk the men."

"Hold on a second, Mercer." It sounded like Ira had clamped his hand over the phone's receiver to speak with someone in his office.

It was nine o'clock in D.C. Mercer wondered why Ira was working so late.

"Okay, I'm back. There's no sense you guys hanging around for two days, so I'm organizing helos to get you to the Area 51 air base. They'll hold their regular personnel flight to Vegas for you. I've got someone working on getting you hotel rooms."

Mercer was grateful, and somewhat surprised Ira had had the same thought as he did earlier. Then again Ira was a master administrator and knew how to maintain peak performance from those under him. Forty-eight hours in Vegas was exactly what his men needed after months of continuous work. He laughed. "Just great. A few minutes ago the men thought I was the hero for giving them a few days off. No way I can top you sending them to Sin City."

"When you're there," Ira joked back, "you can pick up the tab at the strip joints they will no doubt visit."

The teasing tone evaporated on Mercer's lips. "I'm not going with them. I want to stay and monitor the mine."

Ira's reply carried the same seriousness. "You are going with them."

"Forget it," Mercer said. "No offense to your hydrologists, but I'm the one in charge out here and I'm the one who has to be satisfied the tunnel is safe."

Ira's smile resonated in his voice. "That's why you and I are friends, Mercer. You'll take responsibility even when you don't need to. I've done that my entire life. Go to Vegas, for Christ's sake. You can study the hydrology reports when you get back. You were hired to dig the tunnel, not oversee the entire project. Besides, I won't be able to get Dr. Hood or Dr. Marie there until the day after tomorrow at the earliest."

"I don't want anyone going into that mine," Mercer cautioned. While his work made him an expert in hydrology, he conceded that Gregor Hood knew this area much better. Until his arrival, there wasn't much for him to do except stare at computer monitors. And whether he was at the mine or in Las Vegas, nothing could stop water from bursting through the rock plug if it was already unstable.

"I'll order some guards to the site. No one goes in or out. Take a couple of days off. If we're that close to the underground cavern, you guys have earned it."

"All right." Mercer felt himself relaxing. "You win."

"Choppers will be there in half an hour. Only takes fifteen minutes by jet to fly from Area 51 to Vegas. Hold on." Ira again clamped a hand over the phone to speak with someone in his office. "Okay, thanks. Mercer, you're booked in the Luxor Hotel. Sorry it's not a suite, but you're traveling on the government's nickel. I'll try to get away from Washington and meet you when Drs. Hood and Marie arrive."

"Okay. I'll see you in a couple days." Mercer paused. "And if you tell Harry I'm in Vegas for two days, I will kill you." On Harry White's list of life's priorities, he ranked gambling below smoking and drinking but above eating and showering. Mercer was already planning on calling him from his hotel to rub it in.

Ira laughed. "There are practical jokes, and then

there's downright cruelty. Your presence there is considered a national secret. You're safe."

Mercer swiveled off his chair and started for the mine head. He remembered he wanted to tell Ira about the salinity in the water deposit, but figured it could wait until he talked it over with Gregor Hood. More than likely it meant nothing and he'd find the hydrologist had experience with similar abnormalities during his previous evaluation.

Red was waiting with another miner, Ken Porter. At their feet was the seventy-pound armored case for the seismograph and its batteries. They heaved it by the handles and followed Mercer into the cage lift. No one spoke as the elevator dropped into the gloom. Normally miners whiled away the commute with jokes or games of dice on deeper shafts. For this descent they remained grim-faced and tense. They all understood the risks.

At the substation, Red and Ken set the seismograph on a utility tractor as Mercer got into the low-slung bucket seat and engaged the electric drive. He continued a dialogue with the topside safety monitor, who was watching the camera for any changes at the working face. He stopped the tractor well before they reached the end of the tunnel, knowing that the slight vibration of the heavy tires on the rough ground could trigger a catastrophic collapse. From this point on, they moved with the careful deliberation of demolition experts defusing a bomb.

Red and Ken lugged the seismograph, heads down under their burden. Mercer twisted his head in a steady rhythm so his lamp flashed on the floor, ceiling and walls. Their boots crunched on the debris-strewn tunnel.

At the face, Mercer went straight to the damp spot, satisfying himself that the camera hadn't lied. The stain seemed safely contained by his chalk outline.

"Let's get it planted and get out," he said, straightening. He pointed to where he wanted the unit set.

He and Red began the laborious process of calibrating the seismograph and jacking it into the same data cable carrying the camera images to the surface. Ken Porter spent the time scouring the rock for additional water spots that Mercer might have missed.

"Son of a bitch!" he shouted suddenly, scrambling away from the working face.

Mercer looked up. "What is it?"

"UXB."

Mercer's body went cold. UXB was an old term for unexploded bomb. Ken had found an explosive charge that hadn't gone off with the others. He pointed to one of the two-inch holes Donny Randall's team had drilled into the stone. At this angle Mercer couldn't see into it, so he couldn't tell that it was nearly ten feet deep. Ken had been right in front of it and had flashed his lamp down its length and saw the blue wrapper of the Tovex explosive.

"Back away nice and easy," Mercer cautioned in an even voice. Tovex was one of the most stable demolition charges on the market, but he wasn't going to take any chances.

Ken took several steps back, his face ashen, his eyes glued to the black hole in the dark stone. He angled away from the mouth of the hole to get out of the potential blast radius and was twelve feet away when the charge blew.

Because the drill hole hadn't been repacked to contain the blast, the explosion came out like the exhaust of a rocket engine, a seething plasma of gas and flame that shot down the tunnel in an expanding plume. Ken had just gotten himself clear yet was still thrown a dozen feet by the concussion.

Mercer and Red too were tossed back by the blast, neither able to hear the warning shouts of the other because their hearing had been nullified by the overwhelming detonation. Mercer was the first to get to his feet, swaying against the ringing in his ears. He began to rush to where Ken lay like a limp doll and pulled up short. What he saw in the wavering light of his helmet lamp defied description.

Like a spreading pool of spilled ink, the area around the smoking hole darkened as he watched. Water under tremendous pressure was filling microvoids in the rock, oozing out almost like sweat from pores. At first the surface appeared merely damp and then began to glisten. In seconds, drops of water formed and began to trickle from the stone.

The primitive part of his brain told him to forget the others and flee, but he fought the temptation. Keeping one eye on the impending flood he reached for Ken Porter, shouldering the unconscious miner in a fireman's carry. Red Harding was up, staring at the water now spurting from the solid rock.

"Let's go!" Mercer screamed at the top of his lungs. His voice was deadened even in his own head.

Red finally saw Mercer lurching toward him, shook himself of the shock and started loping down the tunnel. Behind them the water tore at the stone from behind, exploiting the tiniest cracks until it found the weakest spot. Like a liquid laser, a shaft of water shot from the drill hole, a two-inch diameter spear that hit the seismograph machine. For a moment the water exploded around the armored case in a roiling froth, but its power was too great to be deterred by such a puny obstacle. The heavy case began to slide across the floor, slowly at first, then accelerating. Red had a fifty-foot head start on the tumbling crate and it nearly bowled him over as the water jet propelled it like a projectile down the tunnel.

The noise began to swell as the hole widened and more water gushed through. It was more powerful than any fire hose. Mercer knew if it somehow touched him the least that would happen was it would knock him flat. More likely, he realized as he ran, it would tear away whatever limb it encountered.

They raced on, pursued by the relentless flood. The water level rose and waves pulsed down the drive so that two hundred feet from the working face they kicked up spray with every pace. After five hundred feet the water was up to their knees. Red looked at Mercer, reading in his eyes the determination to fight on despite the lengthening odds.

Far behind them billions of tons of water tore at the rock, seeking release from its subterranean reservoir. The hole widened, allowing the flood to come through with such force that the stream remained airborne for fifty feet before the water column hit the tunnel floor. It swept past the utility tractor like a raging river, boiling around the four-ton vehicle until it too was dragged along in the torrent.

With Ken slung over his shoulder, Mercer could barely keep up with Red, and yet the loyal Texan didn't leave him behind. They ran in step, fighting side by side as water climbed up to their waists. The speed of the water pulled them along and threatened to tear their legs out from under them. Both knew that to fall was to die.

After what seemed like an hour but was only eight minutes, Mercer saw the lights of the substation. He could even hear the water as it cascaded into the deep sump, a thunderous sound that shook the earth. He began to hope. If they could reach the skip, maybe they could be pulled out before whatever rock still damming the underground lake failed completely.

It wouldn't happen.

There was just too much water, too much pressure. Rather than collapse in sections, the entire span of the tunnel, from floor to ceiling, failed at the same

time. The wall of water hurtling down the tunnel filled
every square inch of space, a solid barrier moving at
forty miles an hour.

Because water cannot be compressed, the collapse
formed a pressure bulge that shot through the flood.
Mercer and Red were caught totally unaware.

Like a tsunami, the wave rushed over them in a
near-solid sheet that left both men tumbling in its
backwash. Mercer lost his grip on Ken Porter when
he smashed against the wall, the precious last gulp of
air he'd taken exploding from his lungs at the blow.

He managed to right himself in the tumult and came
up gasping. The black water settled to its earlier level
and he staggered to his feet, knowing the massive
surge had been a preview. Red surfaced a short distance away. His breathing was labored and he couldn't
focus his eyes. This time Mercer couldn't deny his
instincts. Searching for Ken meant he'd lose Harding
for sure.

He grabbed the smaller man by the back of his
overalls to keep his head clear and charged down the
tunnel like a rampaging animal. The flood had taken
one man and he wouldn't let it take another. He'd
lost his helmet and its precious lamp in the swell so
he focused on the distant constellation of lights ringing
the substation. A fierce wind howled past his shoulders, driven to hurricane force by the wall of water
bearing down on him.

Had the floor of the skip elevator not been an open
mesh that allowed the water to vanish into the sump,
the tunnel would have already flooded to the ceiling.
However, this reprieve was double-edged. If Mercer
and Red were caught in the cage when the main wave
hit, their bodies would be diced against the heavy-
gauge wire like cheese through a grater.

He staggered the last steps into the substation and
allowed the torrent to sweep him off his feet so that

he and Red were carried into the elevator and pinned to the floor. From there, Mercer clawed his way to his knees, his throat aching from swallowing so much water, his eyes stinging from the salt. He slapped his palm against the UP button and fell back so he was facing the tunnel. The car began to lift, water sieving through the floor. Mercer barely noticed. Far down the drive, he saw the lights strung along the walls begin to wink out as they vanished behind the rampaging flood. Two hundred feet. One hundred. Fifty.

The elevator had risen only three-quarters of the way above the tunnel.

The tidal wave exploded into the wider substation, filling every corner as it sought freedom. As if sensing an outlet, the wall surged toward the elevator shaft. The carriage had just climbed clear when the water hit the back of the vertical passageway and geysered through the floor. Mercer and Red were lifted bodily, slammed against the mesh roof and pinned there for many long seconds until the elevator lifted them clear of the water's grip. Both dropped to the floor, lying in pitiable heaps, bruised and dripping and unable to believe they were alive.

Below them water thundered into the sump in a solid curtain that ran clear and green. A subterranean Niagara Falls.

"You okay?" Mercer asked through labored gasps.

Red needed a moment to answer. "Cracked my head, busted some ribs and I think my wrist is too. Yeah, I'm fine. Ken?"

Mercer needed a moment to come to grips with losing one of his men. As much as he hated it, Ken Porter wasn't the first he'd lost underground, and as long as he stayed in the business he probably wouldn't be the last either. That was the nature of the work. "He's paying the butcher's bill."

Red held up two fingers and then three and then

gave a thumbs-up. Two out of three was damn good considering what they'd just endured. "Question for you," he said, palming water from his hair. "You notice this tastes exactly like seawater?"

Mercer nodded in the darkness, then answered when he realized Red couldn't see him. "Yeah, I noticed."

"You got an explanation?"

This time Mercer just shook his head as the elevator climbed for the surface.

Because everything had to be trucked to the mining camp, including fresh water, showers had been strictly regulated to five minutes under a limp drizzle. So for the first time in nearly two weeks, Mercer relaxed under a pounding spray in his tiled bathroom, the steady beat of the near-scalding water working into his shoulders and back, loosening knots deep in the muscle. He'd already gone through the complimentary shampoo and lathered himself so much that only a sliver of soap remained.

His image in the vanity mirror opposite the shower stall was merely a watery outline hidden in banks of steam.

An hour after emerging from the flooded mine, Ira's promised helicopters had arrived. One took off immediately with Red Harding, whose injuries were a lot worse than he'd led Mercer to believe. The crack he'd taken to his head had left a fist-sized depression in his skull. And while most of the men, including Mercer, had been ferried to one of the Boeing 737-200s the government used to shuttle workers between Area 51 and Las Vegas, two additional Blackhawks were dispatched to the mine area to search for Donny Randall. He had returned to the command trailer while Mercer and his team had gone to place the seismograph, but no one had seen him since. Most of his clothes were still in his room, but enough were missing to make it clear he'd made a run for it. Not that Mercer needed this further evidence to be convinced of the link between Randall and the misfiring of the explosives that caused the flood. He also now understood why Donny had used more explosives while working. He'd been hoarding the Tovex to flood the mine.

It took a second call from Ira Lasko to order Mercer away from the site. He'd wanted to assist in the search. Ira assured him that the infrared detectors placed all around Area 51 would pick up a lone man in the desert on the first pass. Randall would be in a cell inside of eight hours.

Unsatisfied, but with no choice, Mercer agreed to go only after getting Ira's promise that he could be there when Donny was first questioned. Ira relented and told Mercer he'd be at Area 51 in thirty-six hours and they'd interview Randall the Handle together.

He had sat by himself on the flight from the secret base to Las Vegas, trying to think through why Donny had done what he'd done. There was no way he could have anticipated that Randall was planning on a murder in the mine, so he no longer blamed himself for what happened. For now he focused on his anger. The short trip gave Mercer no time to find answers. Nor did he have much time when they landed because the secure terminal used by Area 51 employees at McCarran Airport was a stone's throw from the Egyptian-inspired Luxor Hotel.

Mercer's last visit to Las Vegas had been during the spring break of his first year at the Colorado School of Mines. He'd known the city had grown significantly in the years since, but he wasn't prepared for the scale of the changes. All the hotels were massive, designed upon various themes to entice gamblers, and more recently, entire families. There were fantasy castles and circus big tops, reproductions of New York City and a hotel designed to evoke Venice, Italy. The Luxor, with over four thousand rooms, was one of the largest hotels in the world, and its pyramid design made it the city's most distinctive. Atop the three-hundred-fifty-foot black-glass structure was the brightest spotlight ever built, at three hundred thousand watts and forty billion candlepower.

While smaller than Egypt's Great Pyramid, the design and execution of the building stunned Mercer. He became even more impressed when he entered the lobby and realized the hotel was just a shell for an atrium large enough to hold ten wide-body jets.

The statuary, carvings and faux temples could not distract from the hotel's real attraction. From the lobby, it was just a few paces to the casino floor, where the staccato chime of coins falling into hoppers and the ringing of slot machine bells lured gamblers by the thousands.

A few of the workers made plans to meet at the craps tables as soon as they'd stowed their meager luggage. Mercer's first interest was a couple of room service drinks and a thirty-minute shower, preferably enjoying both at the same time.

Mercer reached into the soap dish for his vodka gimlet. It was his second drink and a third waited on the nightstand for when he was dressing. He checked the time on his TAG Heuer, assessed the puckered skin on his fingers, and gave himself another five minutes before shutting off the taps.

He dialed his home phone with a towel wrapped around his waist. He gazed out the window overlooking the azure swimming pools a hundred thirty feet below his room. Two workers were cleaning the area and stacking lounge chairs. Beyond, the city glittered almost to the horizon in a thousand shades of neon. The phone rang four times before his machine picked up. He cut the connection and dialed Tiny's.

"Forget it," a voice sneered.

"Nice way to answer the phone," Mercer said to Paul Gordon.

"Hey, Mercer! Sorry about that. I've got caller ID," Tiny explained. "I recognized the seven-oh-two area code but not the number. I figured you were a Vegas bookie looking to give me odds." Apart from owning the tavern, Gordon ran a rather lucrative illegal sports book. "What are you doing out there? Harry said you were kidnapped by some government types for a job."

"I was. Is he there?" Talking with Harry always lightened Mercer's spirits and cleared his head.

"Yeah, hold on."

Mercer could hear Tiny speaking to Harry and mentioning that he was in Las Vegas.

"You son of a bitch," Harry rasped when he got on the line. "Why didn't you tell me where they were sending you?"

"I didn't know myself," Mercer said quickly.

"How long are you staying?"

Mercer could sense the wheels already turning in Harry's head. "Just the night," he lied, knowing if he'd said two Harry would be on the next plane. He was dressing as he spoke: black slacks, a white oxford and an unstructured sports coat.

"Goddamn it. You just called to yank my chain, didn't you?"

"Harry. I can't believe you'd think that of me," Mercer said innocently. "I thought that maybe you were worried and would like to know I was all right."

"Screw you and your all right. You called to bust my balls about being in Vegas."

"I would have called even if Ira had sent me to West Podunk, Wisconsin."

"And I would've said you deserved to be sent there, you bastard." Harry softened a little. "Where are you staying?"

"Luxor."

"Do me a favor."

"You want a shot glass?"

"Why? I steal yours. From the balcony outside your room you look right over the casino. See if you can take the phone out so at least I can hear it."

Mercer laughed. "Are you that desperate?"

"I haven't gambled since Tiny and I swiped your Jag to go to Atlantic City."

"That happened last summer. Are you forgetting you hit the tables pretty hard when we were in Panama?"

Cackling, Harry said, "Last summer? Hell, we took your Jag again a couple weeks ago when you were in Canada."

Mercer shook his head. He should have known. "Hold on, let me see if the cord will reach." He slipped his feet into rubber-soled leather moccasins. "Also, I'm on the eleventh floor so I don't know if you'll hear much."

After untangling the long cord from where it coiled behind the bed, Mercer crossed to the door. "Almost there, Harry."

Because the Luxor's rooms overlooked the casino floor and sound echoed in the enormous atrium, the doors were soundproofed. When closed the room was silent, but as soon as Mercer swung it open, he was hit by a wall of sound from a few thousand gamblers, the music from a lounge, and the insistent chorus from the slots. "Here you go, buddy," he said and held the handset over the balcony so that maybe Harry could hear the infectious din.

The scream should have come from down below, the joyous shout of a lucky winner at a roulette wheel or slot machine. But it came from Mercer's right, down the long corridor that terminated in a corner of the pyramid near one of the hotel's elevators, called inclinators because they rose at thirty-nine-degree angles. And the scream was an expression of horror, not excitement.

In a rush, three men dressed in matching suits raced from the elevator alcove. The woman who'd screamed tried to run away from them, toward Mercer, but in her high heels she was overtaken in a few paces. Two of the men cradled machine pistols with curved magazines and long silencers. The third appeared unarmed. As they reached her, the unarmed man casually shoved her in the shoulder, flinging her into the waist-high railing. Her scream rose in pitch as momentum tumbled her over the rail. She was gone in a swirl of her orange skirt.

Mercer turned to run, only to see another pair of gunmen emerge from the elevator alcove in the opposite direction. Harry's voice scratched from the forgotten phone.

The woman's shriek suddenly cut out.

Without knowing how he knew, Mercer was sure the men were coming for him—to finish the job Donny Randall had failed. He launched himself back into his room, the only direction open to him. The move bought him a little time but also meant he was trapped. There were no connecting doors between the hotel rooms.

Mercer dropped the phone and ran to the bed, where his bag lay open. The Beretta 92 lay nestled atop a polo shirt. He snatched it up along with the spare clip and racked a round into the chamber.

Pandemonium would be erupting down in the lobby. The horror over the woman's death would spread through the casino, but it would take precious minutes for the hotel's security staff to figure how and from where she'd fallen. Mercer had just seconds before the assassins reached his room and forced their way in. Even the thickest soundproofed door would eventually fail under the onslaught of so many automatic weapons. The casual brutality of the woman being pushed over the balcony began sinking into his gut. He didn't notice his hand tightening on his pistol until the knuckles turned white and his wrist shook.

The phone wasn't an option. It would take too long. The concierge was trained to deal with lost luggage and ticket requests, not a report about armed men gunning for one of their guests. Mercer's eyes swept the room. He broke his problem down to its component parts, examined them individually, and built it up again to give him his only solution.

He snatched a book of matches from a table and leapt onto the bed. His hands remained steady even as his heart fought to escape his chest. He struck a match and touched off the whole book, sending a sulfurous cloud directly into a smoke detector. The hardwired unit began screaming at once.

Mercer then reached across to where a sprinkler head poked from the wall. He worked under the assumption that water wouldn't erupt from the pipe if a guest smashed off the head through stupidity or rage. By triggering the fire-control computer with an activated smoke detector, he hoped the system would discharge water and alert those in charge of security. This way whoever was sent rushing to his room would know they were facing an emergency.

He made sure his weapon was on safe and the barrel pointed away before smashing it into the steel sprinkler head. Compressed air began to hiss through the torn metal and he hit it again, breaking off the head. A second later, a gush of rust-stained water blasted from the pipe in a jet that nearly reached the sloped windows on the far side of the room.

Twenty seconds had passed since he'd jumped back into his room. He figured it was enough time for the gunmen to . . .

The buzz-saw whir of an automatic weapon muted

by a silencer was further quieted by the thick door,
but the subsonic bullets had little trouble chiseling
through the wood.

Mercer dropped to the floor and fired two careful
shots on each side of the door, anticipating the shooter
was flanked by his two backups. His 9mm sounded
like a cannon compared to the silenced weapon, and
his bullets punched much larger holes through the
hardboard and soundproofing material. He heard a
grunt of pain and fired twice more, aiming lower, as he
expected the hidden gunman to be falling to the floor.

The auto-fire stopped for a moment.

Mercer aimed farther from the door, punching four
successive holes in the wall, trying to use his sup-
pressing fire to herd the assassins away from his room.

Keeping low, Mercer dashed across his room, snapping out his empty magazine and slamming home his
only spare. Numbers swirled in his head as he looked
out and down the building's flank. The hotel was three
hundred fifty feet tall and about six hundred feet wide
at the base. His room was on the eleventh floor. That
put him a hundred twenty feet off the ground and
roughly one hundred sixty feet back from the outer
edge of the pyramid. The slope was thirty-nine degrees, too steep to slide down without special equipment, and Mercer had no such gear.

Before the assassins regrouped again, Mercer fired
at the door several times, hoping to keep them from
destroying the weakened lock with a concentrated
burst. The center window on the western side of his
room had a stencil that read BREAK AWAY GLASS. FIRE
DEPT. USE ONLY. He pumped two shots into the window, but the double pane refused to shatter until he
heaved a desk chair through it. The desert heat swirled
into the room, sucking the stench of gunpowder and
fear from the air. Far below stood the well-lit pool
and beyond was a parking structure. While Mercer

had never been bothered by heights, knowing what he was about to attempt made his vision swim.

He fired again at the wall adjacent to the front door. The sprinkler had pumped hundreds of gallons into the room, soaking everything. Mercer stripped off the bedspread and blanket and tore away the saturated top sheet. One of the gunmen threw himself at the mangled front door. Mercer triggered off two quick rounds before the man could try to break through again. His ears ached from the booming concussions. Like a washerwoman hanging laundry to dry, Mercer took the wet sheet to the smashed window and unfurled it as high up the side of the building as he could. He pressed it smooth against the glass. The lower edge ran with water.

The only way he could survive the drop down the side of the pyramid was to slow his descent. His shoes wouldn't provide nearly enough drag against the windows so he had to improvise. His desperate plan was to expand on the simple childhood experiment of sticking a wet washcloth to the side of a bathtub. Hydrostatic pressure made it cling to a flat, clean surface, often requiring surprising force to dislodge it. If the sheet he'd unrolled was large enough, the drag of the cloth against the building would save him from tumbling down the slope and smashing into the ground at near-terminal velocity.

Standing at the angled window, it took all of his discipline to fire off the last rounds in lengthening intervals, hoping that when he emptied the magazine, the assassins would pause for the moments he would need to make his drastic slide down the building.

Who the hell are they? he wondered, then shook the question from his mind. It didn't matter. Not until he was well away from the hotel.

Eight, nine, ten. He gave it one more second, took a deep breath, and fired his last shot.

He dropped the Beretta and jumped onto the windowsill, keeping one hand on the metal frame to steady himself as his equilibrium seemed to dissolve. The wind chilled his still-wet hair. Details on the ground that appeared crisp when the window was intact now looked indistinct, rendered vague by the height. A hundred and twenty feet was nothing when seen horizontally, yet viewed vertically, from the top down, it seemed to drop forever. The half-million-gallon pools looked as small as puddles, the cars atop the garage like toys.

Mercer put it all out of his mind. He had to lean awkwardly to grasp the closest downslope corner of the sheet. The far corner was a further six feet away. Clamping one corner of the sheet in his right hand, he threw himself out the window. Automatic fire erupted outside his room and was answered by the unsilenced blast of a security guard's side arm. Mercer twisted as he flew, landing flat on his back against the pyramid and immediately began sliding down the slick sheet. His fingers worked frantically to grip the far edge of the material. He just managed to grab a handful before he slipped entirely free.

And then nothing happened.

Mercer dangled from a soaking three-hundred-thread-count sheet on the side of the Luxor Hotel with his arms stretched wide as if he were being crucified. The sheet remained stuck to the glass as though glued. Far from slowing his descent, the queen-sized swatch of cotton arrested it completely. His weight couldn't overcome the viscous bond between the sheet and the windows. A dark hundred-forty-foot void sucked at his feet.

"You've got to be kidding me."

He heard several more earsplitting shots from inside the hotel, followed by a muted fusillade from the unknown assassins. The corridor outside his room had turned into a pitched battle while he was pasted to the side of the building like an insect on flypaper. He had no illusions that the undergunned security guards could prevent the assassins from eventually swatting him off.

Mercer jerked his arms, trying to unstick a little of the sheet. He slid a few inches before the bedding became glued again. The strain of holding the material sent pain pulsing from his shoulders. He next tried to shimmy his hips, wriggling back and forth. He gained another foot and this time the sheet didn't stop fully. It continued to ooze down the building, but at a snail's pace.

A moan of frustration and mounting agony escaped his lips. He jerked the material again as a gust of wind worried at the top edge of the sheet, finding and expanding a small wrinkle until a square foot of the cloth had lifted from the glass. Mercer's pace doubled, then doubled again. The fear of the entire sheet peeling away from the glass made him dig his rubber-soled shoes into the window. His heel caught a rubber gasket separating two of the enormous panes. The wrinkle settled when the wind died again and he stopped dead. He'd slid eight feet. The top of the sheet was a mere foot below his own shattered window.

He hadn't heard a guard's weapon in ten seconds or more.

As insane as the stunt he was trying to pull off was, he knew it wouldn't be enough. He was helpless and the gunmen would be in his room in moments. It would take no time for them to figure where he'd gone and blow him from the building with a burst from a machine pistol.

There was only one way to increase his speed and that was to diminish the hydrostatic pressure on the glass. Because he couldn't reduce his weight, he had to reduce the area of cotton. And once he did, there'd be no going back.

"As if I can go back now," he muttered and hunched his shoulders, peeling the lower third of the sheet from the window.

Mercer accelerated like a skier bursting from knee-high powder onto an icy patch of trail. In a fraction of a second he knew he'd never recover. He felt he was already hurtling down the building too fast, and every foot he dropped stripped more of the sheet from the glass and sped his plunge.

Wind rushed past his ears as he struggled to flatten the sheet again by stretching his arms as far as they would go. The effort made his upper body tremble. He spread his feet wide, hoping his wet slacks would give him a measure of control. His heart beat in his throat and he hadn't taken a breath for what felt like hours.

He didn't dare look down, but as soon as the thought popped into his head, he did. He'd slid eight of the eleven stories and could judge how quickly the ground was rushing up to meet him by the expressions on the two pool workers staring up at him. Their mouths widened the farther he plummeted. Yet it didn't appear he was going as fast as he thought. He'd slowed and the impact wouldn't be too . . .

A window exploded to his right, razor shards cutting his side and outer thigh. Another burst blew a pane of glass above him and caught him in an avalanche of deadly fragments. He didn't need to look up to know at least one of the gunmen stood in his window firing down the building's sloped flank. The next burst would likely spike through the top of his skull.

He was a story and a half from the ground when he released his grip on the sheet.

At the last second before he hit the ground, he cocked his knees and launched himself from the building, vectoring the impact so that he crashed onto a neatly trimmed bank of shrubs with his shoulder and back. He rolled hard, tumbling to the lawn before slamming into a stack of lounge chairs. His entire body had gone numb for a blessed second until pain exploded in his shoulders and right leg from hip to ankle.

"Dude, I have always wanted to try something like that!" The teenage workers had rushed to his side.

"That was awesome," the other said. "What was it like?"

Nine-millimeter rounds rained from above. The first teen went down with the back of his thigh ripped wide open. The other caught a bullet in the top of his shoulder and dropped as if poleaxed, his arm barely attached to his body.

Mercer staggered to his feet, trying to get the youths out of the line of fire—trying to save himself. Chips of concrete burst from a statue of a sphinx as more bullets peppered the pool area, some forming tiny geysers where they hit the still water. Hobbled by his deadened leg, Mercer zigzagged around palm trees and garish statues. Because the hotel was fashioned out of black glass, it was easy to see the light streaming from his shattered window and the silhouette of the gunman who'd realized his quarry had escaped. In the dying glare of the setting sun, Mercer couldn't hope to identify the assassin, but he'd be glad to meet him again under different circumstances.

Mercer threw an ironic wave he was sure the gunman saw.

He reached the decorative wall separating the pool area from Luxor Drive and was just about to scramble over when a group of men, wearing the same suits as the gunmen upstairs, appeared at the hotel's back entrance. One shouted something indecipherable and reached inside his jacket for a weapon. As best he could, Mercer launched himself over the wall, falling in an untidy tangle on the sidewalk below.

There was no traffic on the two-lane road and the

cover afforded by the parking garage was far out of reach. He looked up and down the half-mile street, as trapped here as he had been in his room. Only this time there were no crazy options. The gunmen had seen him and would be over the wall before Mercer could cover twenty yards. He arbitrarily turned to his left and began running, further punishing his injured leg.

The sweep of headlights blinded him and the squeal of brakes sounded unnaturally loud. The car was a new silver BMW Z3, one of the more exotic vehicles a tourist could rent in the city. The driver slid the car into a controlled four-wheeled skid so that it pointed in the direction it had come. The engine snarled. Although the top was up, the passenger window was down. The driver remained hidden in the car's interior.

"Dr. Mercer," a woman called. He caught a glimpse of her dark hair glittering like obsidian. "If you want to live, come with me."

Mercer lurched toward the car as she swung open the long door.

"I've waited a lifetime to meet you, Doctor," she said, pressing the gas even before he was fully in the car. "It's too bad I came too late."

"I'd say you were just in time," he panted.

She spoke from the driver's-side shadows. "I'm sorry, but I am. You see, you're going to die anyway."

Before Mercer could react to her statement, she cranked the nimble little car onto Mandalay Bay Road and then onto Las Vegas Boulevard, the casino-lined stretch of highway known around the world as the Strip. She blew through a red light and accelerated away from the traffic snarl she'd created.

"I didn't mean that the way it sounded, Doctor."

Mercer struggled to find his mental equilibrium in the wake of what had just happened. As the adrenaline wore off, his legs and shoulder throbbed in time with his still-pounding heart. His breathing came in deep gasps. "Exactly how many ways are there to interpret 'you're going to die anyway'?"

"What I meant was that they will keep coming after you," she said from the shadows. "They want you dead."

As they tore past one of the Strip's more garish neon signs, a wash of pink and teal light flooded the dim interior of the BMW. Mercer finally got to see his rescuer.

She was in profile, her mouth held taut in concentration, and the lights played against her smooth skin, kaleidoscoping in the planes and angles, at once making her beautiful and demonic. Her hair was shimmering black, cropped short around her head and curling in tendrils down her slender neck. She looked at him at that moment.

She wore black-framed designer glasses that gave her a no-nonsense air. Her large eyes were almond shaped and wide spaced belying some Asian ancestry. Above them, her brows were saucy arcs. Had he not just escaped his second assassination attempt in four hours, he would have found her attractive. Stunning, actually.

And then he looked closer at her eyes and saw what drew him so quickly. It was the eyes themselves that he would know forever and how her beauty made the pain in them that much more difficult to witness. In them he saw a despair that seemed to drop into infinity, as if she'd seen horrors no person should ever see. It was like looking into the suffering eyes of a refugee child. Or those of a mother who'd just lost one. Whatever had led her to this moment had so haunted her that it looked as if she'd never come back.

Mercer had to fight himself to put aside the upwelling of empathy she evoked and concentrate on what had just happened. He asked the most obvious question. "Not that I'm not grateful, but I know you didn't happen along at the right moment, so do you mind telling me who you are, who those gunmen were and why they want me dead?"

"My name is Tisa Nguyen." Her last name was a common Vietnamese surname, but her first, which rhymed with Melissa, was one Mercer had never heard before. "And those men were sent to kill you because of your work at Area 51."

That she used the name of America's premier research facility wasn't a surprise. After all, it was one of the best known secrets in the world. What startled him was that it seemed everyone and their sister knew he was working there. Ira Lasko was in for a shock if Mercer somehow survived long enough to tell him.

He noted that she hadn't given the assassins' identity.

Tisa guided the car onto a cross street and then rocketed up a ramp onto I-15 heading north. Commuter traffic was thick but she seemed immune to it, exploiting the tiniest opening and using deft touches on the accelerator and brake to keep them rolling at a steady eighty miles per hour. She handled the car like a professional race driver.

"I can't tell you who the gunmen were. I'm sorry. But please know that my saving you tonight is an indication of my sincerity." She paused. "I didn't think it right that you should suffer for something out of your control."

"Lady," Mercer flared, "the past twenty minutes has been about as out of control as things can get. Since you knew where I was staying and what was about to happen, don't you think you could have just called to warn me?" She tried to interrupt, but Mercer overrode her protests. "Thanks for your help, but why don't you just pull off at the next exit and let me out?"

"I tried calling," Tisa snapped. She spoke English with an accent, French and something else. "Several times. You never picked up and then just before they were to hit your room, the line was busy."

Mercer opened his mouth and let it close. What she said was plausible. He'd been in the shower for a half hour and then dialed Harry almost immediately after he toweled off. Maybe she had tried to warn him. That still didn't negate the fact that she knew exactly what time the gunmen were making the hit. Meaning? Meaning either she'd been tracking them or she was part of their team. He chose his next words carefully. "You know they killed at least one woman that I saw." He kept his voice mild to heighten the barbarism. "Probably got two or three security guards too."

His hoped-for reaction of guilt never came. Tisa barely blinked at the news. "It could have been worse," she finally said.

"Worse? I just told you innocent people are dead

and you say it could have been worse. I think you could have saved them. I think you could have stopped them by warning the hotel or something. Don't you realize their blood is on your hands?"

"Theirs isn't the first, Dr. Mercer," she said matter-of-factly. "And it certainly won't be the last."

A tense minute went by. Mercer studied her profile, conflicted by her beauty and seeming indifference.

"I was too late to stop them from attacking your room," she said at last. "But I could try to save you if they failed. I've put my life at risk just by helping you, though it doesn't really matter."

"What doesn't matter? That innocent people are dead or that you may be next?"

"Actually, none of it." They sped up to ninety miles per hour as traffic thinned.

Mercer had heard enough. He hadn't needed Tisa to figure out that the attack concerned Area 51. He was thankful for his rescue, but he wasn't going to put up with her nonanswers. He would know the truth after he and Ira grilled Donny Randall, who no doubt had some connection to the gunmen. And the truth, he knew, had nothing to do with Ira's bogus cover about a nuclear repository. Terrorists didn't assassinate miners for digging a waste dump. They'd attack the nuclear materials en route or hit the site after it was full.

He put his hand on the gear shift lever. "In ten seconds I am going to jam the transmission into neutral."

Tisa glanced at him, then returned her eyes to the road.

"Unless you're armed you can't stop me, so why don't you just pull over."

"I'm not armed," she admitted.

"Then stop the goddamned car."

Tisa ignored his demand. She spoke confidently.

"Four months ago there was a seismic disturbance that was triangulated to a remote spot at Area 51."

"One."

"The epicenter was eight hundred feet below the surface."

The exact depth Mercer and his men had tunneled off the main shaft. "Two."

"Looking through U.S. Geologic Survey records, there's no evidence of a fault in this location, certainly not that shallow. It is the first such earthquake there."

This part of Nevada was riddled with microfaults; many of which hadn't been discovered. Mercer was unimpressed. "Three."

"The problem is that it wasn't an earthquake at all."

Tisa paused and Mercer had to remind himself of his countdown. "Four."

"The closest analogy is that a bubble erupted inside solid rock. One second everything was normal and the next, seismographs showed a tremendous displacement of simultaneous P and S waves. As quickly as it happened, everything went back to normal. Almost like a contained nuclear explosion that only lasted for a moment."

"How big?" Mercer asked, despite himself.

"Five."

"On the Richter scale?"

"No. Your ultimatum. You're up to number five. On the Richter it registered a single spike of three-point-one."

"Duration?"

"Like I said, one second."

"That's not possible," Mercer stated. "What about foreshocks or aftershocks?"

"Just the one spike."

While Mercer had never heard of anything like this, an unusual earthquake was no reason to have him assassinated. He asked her why.

"What about your countdown?" Tisa asked with a little lift to her lip. Despite his palpable anger, she was teasing him.

"I'm keeping it going in my head," he growled, although a smile was trying to tug at the corners of his mouth. "Why would someone want me dead for working near an undiscovered fault?"

"Because it wasn't a fault. They believe it was a weapon test of some kind. I don't know the details. I . . . I'm not part of the group that ordered your murder. When I learned what was going to happen, I flew to Las Vegas to save you. You're a pawn in this. Innocent. I didn't want to see you hurt."

"Why?"

She looked at him for the first time in several miles. Her eyes went soft while her mouth remained defiant. The shock of the attack had worn to the point Mercer could admit to himself that she was achingly beautiful. "The reasons are my own. That's all I'll tell you."

"Can you at least tell me how you knew I was involved with Area 51?" He himself hadn't known about the job until being stuffed into a government SUV.

She laughed. "I never expected modesty from you, Doctor. It's charming."

"I'm not being modest," Mercer said.

"In some circles, you are one of the most famous people in the world. You are perhaps the greatest prospecting geologist working today. You've found or been instrumental in the development of dozens of successful mines. Opals in Australia. Diamonds in Canada and Africa. The Ghuatra ruby mine in India. It's been estimated that you alone are responsible for having one hundred million cubic yards of earth shifted in just the past eight years."

Mercer understood then. The way she'd been talking, with a kind of reverent fatalism, it should have been obvious. She belonged to an environmental group, one with a radical arm that decided to forgo passive protesting and turn to violence. Like some fringe right-to-life groups whose members began to gun down abortion doctors, it was inevitable that extremist environmentalists would eventually target those they considered the ecosystem's worst enemies. He still carried the scars from dealing with a similar group in Alaska a few years earlier.

"So your people think I'm Earth's enemy number one and that by killing me a few acres of desert will remain unspoiled for future generations to ignore?"

She considered his accusation for a second. "Quite the opposite, actually. I do belong to a group, called the Order, and we do strive to protect the planet, but not in the way you think. We don't chain ourselves to trees or chase whaling ships in rubber boats. Our work is more"—she searched for the right word— "consequential."

Mercer scoffed. "And you consider me consequential enough to kill?"

"I never wanted you killed," Tisa said fiercely. "But others do."

"Because I'm a successful mining engineer," Mercer interrupted. "And you think my work damages the environment?"

Tisa eyed him again. "With the exception of a few extreme cases, Doctor, one person cannot affect the environment in any appreciable way. You should stick to being modest. It suits you better. Very little of what you've accomplished has required any kind of adjustments on our part."

Mercer had no idea what she meant by adjustments. He was about to ask when she continued.

"I'm afraid you were targeted because you stand in the way of certain people learning what happened four months ago deep under Area 51. Until they, no, I should say we—in a way I am part of this—until we learn the nature of what happened, people within the Order feel there is a tremendous risk."

"I have no idea what you're talking about."

She nodded. "You don't have any idea how much you don't know. And I'm afraid I don't have time to explain it to you. Well, I have the time, but you would never believe me."

He was beginning to think his rescuer was more than a little insane. Nothing she said made sense.

"And I do want you to believe me." Her eyes caught his, held them in the dim glow from the dashboard. The anguish had faded, but there remained a gentle sadness, a sort of pervading melancholy that softened her features. He saw that her words were an intimate confession. "By saving you I hope I've demonstrated that you can trust me, at least a little bit. Had I known their plans earlier, I would have gotten a warning to you, I swear. I am sorry about that hotel guest you mentioned. What time is it?"

"I'm sorry?"

"The time?"

"Oh." Mercer glanced at his watch, noting that the dash contained a digital clock. "Eight thirty. Why? Is something going to happen?"

"No," she said absently. "I just don't wear a watch. I saved you because I thought it was time for someone to take a stand. Our group never started out this way. Using violence, I mean. This has only come about recently and I'm afraid it's going to get worse."

"Why haven't you gone to the authorities?"

"That's just what I'm doing. I've come to you. You have the experience and understanding to grasp what I will show you and hopefully the influence to prevent it."

Mercer's senses went on alert. "Prevent what? A terrorist attack?"

"Nothing so simple, I'm afraid. I'm going to rely on a little of that trust I hope you feel and say that I can't tell you yet, but I can give you a demonstration." She looked at him sideways. "You must understand that what I'm about to tell you breaks a code of secrecy dating back more than a hundred fifty years."

She took a breath. Mercer was at a loss to explain who she was or what her group wanted, but it was clear she was fighting a battle of conscience. She seemed more reluctant to break her vow than she did to endanger her life by rescuing him.

"Can you meet me on the Greek island of Santorini on the twenty-seventh?"

"I suppose," he said cautiously.

"There's a tramway that carries people from the harbor up to the town. I will meet you at the upper terminal at five in the evening."

"Tisa, I'm sorry, but you haven't given me any reason not to think that this is all an elaborate setup of some kind."

"And there's nothing I can say or do until the twenty-seventh," she countered, then reversed herself with a yelp. "Wait! Yes, I can."

Such was the transformation that to Mercer it seemed like another person was driving the car. Her eyes, far from being dim and haunted, came alive.

"Something is going to happen in the Pacific Ocean in a couple of days. I'm sorry I don't know what, only that it's some kind of natural phenomenon that's never happened before. Whatever it is, I'm sure you will recognize it. If it happens, will you meet me?" She was almost pleading.

"This something, it has to do with your group, what did you call them, the Order?"

"Yes."

"But not a part you're involved with?"

"No. It's . . . it's the same faction that attacked you tonight."

"If I meet you, will you finally explain who you really are?"

"Once you see the demonstration, you'll understand." She paused again, as enigmatic as ever, but beguiling in way that Mercer knew he shouldn't trust. "People call you Mercer right, not Phil or Philip?"

"Yes."

"May I call you Mercer, too."

"If we're to meet again on one of the most romantic islands in the world, I think it's the least you could do."

Her facial muscles contorted as she fought to contain a smile. "Mercer," she said softly, as if trying out the name for the first time.

Tisa suddenly brought the car to a stop. "Here we are," she announced.

They'd left the highway at least an hour ago. A milky moon silhouetted the barren mountains to the east while overhead the stars burned cold and indifferent. Nearby, tall utility poles marched to the horizon like stick-figure soldiers. For as far as they could see there wasn't any other evidence of human habitation, no lights, no buildings, nothing.

"You call this place a 'here'?"

"Not exactly the Gare du Nord at rush hour, but this is your stop." Tisa noticed Mercer tense and reached over to place a hand on his arm. Her fingers were long and slim. She said nothing for a second, just studied the pale outline of her skin against the dark material of Mercer's sports coat. "Relax. We're on an access road that leads into Area 51. About a hundred yards farther up is the perimeter. Once you pass the marker, security cameras and heat-tracking devices will detect you. It should take base security only a couple of minutes to find you. It may take a bit longer for you to establish your identity, but I think you'll be all right."

"What about you?" Mercer asked, more concerned than he thought he'd be. "Are you going to be all right?"

"So long as you meet me in a couple of weeks in Santorini, everything will be fine."

"What about . . .?"

"The—what should I call them, the rogue faction? They won't dare touch me. Don't worry."

He stepped from the car and closed the door, finding no context in what had just transpired. If asked to explain the past hours, he couldn't. As the taillights disappeared around a bend, he realized there were two ideas he could cling to. One was that Ira Lasko had better have some answers for him when they met. And the second was that despite the skepticism he'd shown Tisa, he didn't doubt her sanity. Too much had happened for him to think there wasn't something much larger going on. The explosion in the mine, Donny Randall's disappearance, the attack at the Luxor. There was a connection, but he had no idea what and wouldn't allow himself to speculate. That would come later. For now he drew his damp jacket tighter across his shoulders and began his trudge up the chilly road. A third idea came to him and he glanced over his shoulder to where the wind had swallowed the sound of Tisa's car. He felt certain that whatever she knew, or thought she knew, it was worth pursuing.

Mercer spent twenty tense minutes convincing two camouflaged security guards who'd materialized out of the desert that he shouldn't be run immediately to the local sheriff as a trespasser. What followed was a two-hour ride in the back of a Jeep Cherokee, a further hours-long wait in an isolated building while his identity was checked and rechecked, and then a quick hop in a windowless Blackhawk helicopter to the main complex.

He was escorted to the same spartan room he'd been given his first night at Area 51. Five minutes after stepping from the shower and into some dry clothes left by the soldier at the reception desk there was a knock on the door.

"Omega ninety-nine temple." Even muffled by the door, Mercer had no problem recognizing the deep voice.

He returned the countersign. "Caravan eleven solstice."

The door swung open to reveal Captain Booker T. Sykes, his escort from the flight from Washington. The big African American held a six-pack of beer in one hand and a deck of playing cards in the other. He was dressed in desert fatigue pants with a black T-shirt stretched across his chest. An unlit cigar jutted from between his even teeth. "Heard you blew back into town."

Mercer grinned. "This place has better shampoo samples than the hotel in Vegas."

Sykes stripped two beers from the six-pack and handed one over. "Cheaper room service, too." He took a seat at the small table under the window and began shuffling the cards. "Rumor has it base security picked you up wandering in from Highway 375 near the town of Rachel."

"I got lost looking for a hot craps table."

Sykes shook his head. "Didn't figure you'd tell me what was up. Admiral Lasko's due to arrive in a couple hours for your debrief. I figured you could use a few beers more than the sleep."

"You could say that." Mercer took a long pull from his beer and checked the cards Sykes had dealt him. "Did your rumor source say if they caught Donny Randall, the miner that skipped out from my project?"

"The guy vanished into thin air. Knowing me and my Delta team were here, security even called us in to help on the search. We had his tracks running south from DS-Two for eleven miles and then they vanished. No sign a chopper landed to pick him up, no sign of anything."

"Thermal scans?"

"Lots of jackrabbits, a few coyotes but no missing miner. Even if he'd died out there, his corpse would stay warm enough for us to detect. My men are still searching. I came back when I heard you're here to see if you have any explanations."

"I have no idea how he disappeared. I don't even know why except someone must have gotten to him, bought him off or something. That explosion was deliberate. He tried to kill me and a couple others. I believe he also caused a cave-in before I came here that killed a dozen men."

"I bet you don't believe the admiral's story anymore, huh?"

"About a nuclear waste dump? Not anymore. Hey,

I thought this was supposed to be compartmentalized. How do you know so much?"

"Lasko. We talked yesterday after you and your men were sent to Vegas. We've been reassigned as special security for his project. He figured the explosion and Randall are the beginning of something bigger."

"Me too," Mercer agreed, dropping his cards to reveal a quick win in their first game of gin. "Since we're going to be spending some time together, does this mean you can tell me what it is you've been doing out here?"

"Ah." Sykes lit his cigar with a gold Zippo. "Let me tell you about Project Monkey Bomb."

Three hours and several dozen games of gin later, the telephone on the nightstand rang. "Morning, Ira," Mercer answered, knowing who would be calling. The sun was just starting to outline the mountains outside his room.

"Tell Sykes to bring you to the conference room in five minutes."

The line went dead.

Startled by his friend's brusque tone, Mercer replaced the handset and cocked an eyebrow at Sykes. "I think I'm in some deep shit."

The captain got to his feet. "Yeah, actually you are."

Ira wore a suit only slightly darker than the bags under his eyes. He'd shaved hastily, probably on the plane, leaving patches of silvery stubble and several raw cuts. A carafe of coffee and four cups were on the conference table. Dr. Briana Marie sat on his left wearing her ubiquitous lab coat over a red blouse. The deputy national security advisor didn't look up when Mercer and Booker Sykes entered the room and he continued to thumb through a folder as the two men poured themselves coffee.

Mercer took a seat, slurping at his cup for a full minute. No one spoke, no one moved. Dr. Marie looked like she wasn't even breathing. Ira finally closed the file and pulled off his reading glasses. He looked at Mercer as though he were a stranger. Or an adversary.

"How did you get from the Luxor to where the guards picked you up?"

Mercer couldn't explain why he lied, but it came without hesitation. "Hitchhiked. I got lucky. A couple of college kids picked me up. They were headed to Rachel because they heard the UFOs fly just before dawn and wanted to be in position near Freedom Ridge."

"Freedom Ridge has been closed to the public since 1995," Dr. Marie said sharply.

"I said they were college kids. They probably didn't know. I'd never even heard of Freedom Ridge." Mercer knew of the bluff overlooking a corner of the base from a television special.

"So what happened at the Luxor?" Ira hefted the file. "This is a preliminary police report. One dead tourist, one slightly injured security guard, two severely wounded pool cleaners and two unknown subjects found dead outside your room when security chased away three other unsubs."

Mercer was surprised. And impressed. He thought his indiscriminate cover fire would have maybe injured one of the assassins, not kill two of them. There was something to be said for luck, because firing through walls required no skill. He told the story as accurately as he remembered it, his conversation with Harry, the woman being pushed to her death and his headlong plunge down the sloping glass wall. He omitted nothing except his rescue and subsequent conversation with Tisa Nguyen. He wasn't going to give her up until he knew what Ira and Dr. Marie were really doing at the DS-Two site.

"And what about Donny Randall and the explosion?" Ira prompted "Any theories?"

"The same ones you have," Mercer answered. "That the accident that killed those men and prompted you to call me in wasn't an accident. Donny arranged that as well, expecting to be named overall boss of the project in hopes you'd tell him what was really happening out there. When that didn't happen, whoever was controlling him decided to cut their losses. Randall was told to kill me and disappear. The charge he planted would have done the job had Ken not spotted the explosives. Donny was in the command trailer and would have seen us on the camera. He remote detonated them an instant too late. He didn't stick around to see if we drowned and obviously had help getting out of Area 51. Because Sykes's men didn't find vehicle tracks, and I assume radar coverage here would have detected a helicopter at even treetop height, you might want to consider a two-man hovercraft met him in the deep desert and took him away. Everyone at the mine knew we were headed to the Luxor, so the killers had a backup team waiting in case Randall failed. Is that about how you read it?"

Ira took a breath. "Everything but the hovercraft," he admitted. "Hadn't thought of that."

"I've been square with you." Mercer's expression was one of ill-disguised anger. "Don't you think it's time you're square with me? What's going on out there, Ira? A lot of people are dead and it's not over a secret nuclear waste dump."

"It's not, but I can't tell you any more. I'm sorry. I'll understand if you want out of the project as long as you promise not to discuss anything that's happened in the past two weeks."

"I don't even *know* what's happened in the past two weeks," Mercer said with frustration.

"It's best that way," Briana said gravely.

Mercer could take Ira's deal now, walk away, and there'd be no hard feelings. He'd probably even keep his job as special science advisor. But he'd never learn the truth, and to Mercer that wasn't an option. Ira had dangled a mystery in front of him, baiting him with just enough information to keep him interested. He was being played. He knew it, Ira knew it. And both knew Mercer wasn't going to back down. This offer was more about keeping the guise of secrecy rather than any real secret.

"I'll stick it out with the promise that I get ten minutes alone with Randall the Handle when you finally catch him."

Ira grunted. "I'll hold the son of a bitch down for you."

"So what do you have on the gunmen?"

"No ID. Their clothes had all the labels removed but looked like they could have come from any Sears store in the country. The cops are checking all the cars in the surrounding parking lots, but with a hundred thousand tourists in town at any moment I doubt they'll find anything. The weapons are on their way to the FBI lab. We'll probably find they were bought at a gun show from a guy with an attitude toward the government and a real short memory. We haven't gotten anything on the men themselves, at least from the criminal databases. It'll take more time to search all the others. I'm not too optimistic."

"You don't think they're locals hired for the job?"

"Not unless the Vegas mob is hiring out Thai contract killers."

"Thai?" Mercer hadn't taken the time to look at the assassins' features so the revelation that they were Asian came as a shock. He immediately thought of Tisa Nguyen. And the group she belonged to.

"Thai, Laotian, Cambodian. Not sure which yet. We've got a physical anthropologist coming in to make a determination."

"There were five men who hit my room and more outside. Anything on them?"

"Nothing on the three that got away. The guards were too far away. They went down the emergency stairs and left the hotel in the confusion. According to a few eyewitnesses who saw the men rush into the pool area, they were tall, short, black, white, Hispanic, well dressed, wearing rags, carrying rifles, carrying pistols, and one guy was certain one of them was carrying a sword. All of which is pretty typical with panicked witnesses."

The room fell silent. It was clear that the hitmen were professionals. The evidence they left behind wouldn't amount to anything. The truth was, the assassins were gone. Donny Randall was gone. And in their wake were a whole lot of questions no one could answer.

"What's happening at the mine?" Mercer asked, pressing on.

"High-speed pumps are draining the shaft," Dr. Marie answered. "It might take a few days."

Mercer recalled the force of the deluge and knew it would be longer than a few days. He also recalled the water's strange salinity, how it had tasted and even foamed up like seawater. He decided against asking about it. Like Tisa's presence, he thought it best to keep a few things to himself. "Then I guess the only thing to do is wait for the pumps to do their work."

"And look around for an abandoned hovercraft," Sykes added.

The pumps were still going full blast, discharging a hundred thousand gallons an hour, when a patrol in a Jeep Cherokee found the truck-sized hovercraft a hundred miles southwest of the DS-Two site. It lay on its deflated rubber skirt next to a heavy-duty trailer. The fuel tank was near empty and Donny Randall's fingerprints were all over the passenger side of the open cockpit. Tire tracks matching those left by the government Jeeps continued on in the same direction. It was simple to figure out how they'd done it. The extraction team had trailered the hovercraft into Area 51 with a Jeep Cherokee like the guards used to arouse less suspicion. They'd unloaded the air cushion vehicle at its maximum range from where Randall waited at the rendezvous spot. Once they had their mole, they'd returned to the Jeep, abandoned the hovercraft and trailer, and simply drove away. A neat, well-executed operation.

It took just six hours to trace the hovercraft to its manufacturer in California and determine that the vehicle had been stolen a week earlier from the company's proving grounds. Dead end.

On Mercer's recommendation, half the miners assigned to the project were sent home with a fat bonus while the men from his shift remained in Las Vegas in case they were needed once the mine was drained. The only personnel left at the DS-Two site were a handful of engineers to monitor the pumps and Mercer himself. Ira and Dr. Marie remained at the main Area 51 complex and called in for daily updates.

He was sitting in the control trailer idly thumbing through a week-old news magazine, his feet on a counter, a cup of coffee at his elbow. He was contemplating getting lunch when a noise penetrated his lazy musings. Not a noise, but rather the lack of noise. For four days he'd heard the steady background roar of water rushing through the twelve-inch pipes from the pumps. It became one of those sounds, like traffic to a city dweller, that became so pervasive he had to concentrate to hear it. When it cut off suddenly, it took a moment to realize it was gone.

Several pairs of feet ran past the trailer as technicians raced to the mine head. Mercer launched himself out the door in their wake. The man overseeing the big cycloid pumps had already hit the master override so the diesel engines chugged in neutral and the pumps spooled to silence.

"What happened?" Mercer snapped, already taking command of the situation.

"Something's clogged the intake on pump number two," the air force staffer replied.

"Any increase in turbidity levels?"

"No, sir. Particle levels in the discharged water have remained constant. We're not sucking mud."

That eliminated Mercer's first idea, that the pump had been fouled with silt. "Have you tried reversing the pump to blow the intake clear?"

"The computer does that automatically whenever there's a jam. It didn't work. Whatever's in there is stuck solid."

Mercer went quiet for a moment. "Okay, what's the water depth at the intake?"

The sergeant checked a monitor slaved to the main pump station. "One hundred ten feet."

Not too deep that Mercer couldn't dive it. He knew from his conversations with Sykes the first night back from Vegas that his team had brought all their equipment to Area 51, including scuba gear. It would be quicker to dive to the clogged intake than wait for an underwater camera to be shipped in.

"Here's what I want," Mercer said, his plan in place. "Kill the diesels. I don't want either pump run up again. We can't risk the guts being torn out of them if whatever's down there gets into the other one. While they're down, make sure the second pump wasn't damaged. I trust the computer override, but only so far."

"Yes, sir. Anything else?"

"That should do it." Mercer returned to the command trailer and dialed Ira on a secure phone. "Ira, we've hit another snag."

"What happened?"

"Pump is fouled and we can't clear it. I want to dive down there with Sykes to take a look. Can you send him over with some scuba equipment?"

"Ah, hold a second." Ira must have clamped his hand over the mouthpiece because Mercer couldn't hear a thing. The pause stretched to a minute. "Ah, okay. Dr. Marie wants to know the water depth."

"A hundred ten feet. Shallow enough for Sykes and me to reach."

"Hold on again." This time Ira was away for over three minutes. "Yeah, I'll send him over, but I'm coming too. There are some things I need to brief you on. We'll chopper in within an hour."

Forty-eight minutes later, a Blackhawk landed a quarter mile from the mouth of the box canyon that hid the DS-Two mine at the edge of the shallow lake of water pumped from the tunnel. The lake was ringed with mud where its shores receded each day through evaporation, then expanded again at night as the pumps discharged their flow. Mercer dispatched a Humvee to pick up Ira, Sykes, and the dive equipment, then ordered everyone else from the cavern. Whatever Ira had to say in his briefing would likely be secret.

The Humvee backed into the cave and braked next to the elevator hoist. Sykes immediately began to heave the heavy dive bags from the back of the vehicle as though they were sacks of groceries. Mercer and the driver helped with the air tanks. Ira waited near the lift, peering down into the inky blackness of the shaft. The air held the tang of salty water, like a thin sea mist.

"I guessed at the size," Booker Sykes said as he peeled open the first bag. Inside was a black wet suit.

Mercer held it up. It looked about right. "I'm touched you noticed."

"Funny. So what's it like down there?"

"We'll take the elevator to the water's surface. There's a trapdoor on the bottom. From there it's a straightforward dive down to the pump intakes. They're forty feet below where we tunneled off the main shaft."

"Anything in the tunnel we should worry about?" Sykes continued to pull equipment from the bags: lights, regulators, weight belts.

"I doubt it. The way the water was blowing through there, any equipment would have been shoved down into the sump."

Sykes took a moment to visualize the dive and nodded to himself. "And what about you? Can you handle the dive?"

"I don't have your experience, but I should be all right. This isn't like diving into an unfamiliar cave. I know the shaft and we don't need to go into the tunnel."

"That's for sure," Ira interjected.

The two men looked up from their work.

"Under no circumstances are either of you to enter the tunnel." Ira's tone was harsh.

Mercer was about to ask why, caught the look in his friend's eyes, and let the question die on his lips. He'd always known Ira to have a great sense of humor and an understanding of how to supervise people. He rarely gave such a direct order unless there was a compelling reason. Mercer understood enough about the world Ira inhabited to know he would never tell him what that reason was. Ira held Mercer's glance for a moment, and Mercer let his focus drift away. It was as much of an acknowledgment as he would give.

"That's an order, Mercer," Ira said. "I don't give them very often, but when I do people had better listen. This one's for your protection, not mine. Do not leave the main shaft."

"Okay," Mercer finally said.

"Captain Sykes?" Ira directed his attention to the Delta Force operator.

"Sir."

"Mercer is not to leave your side and neither of you are to enter the tunnel. Go down, clear the intake, and come straight back up. Is that clear?"

Even on his knees, Sykes managed to look like he'd come to attention. "Yes, Admiral."

He's scared, Mercer realized. Ira's scared of whatever's down there. What the hell were he and Dr. Marie up to? What was it Tisa had said? A single seismic spike, like a bubble, had formed within the rock and then vanished. Her exact words were "a contained nuclear explosion." Maybe there had been a weapon test like her group believed. Something that got out of control?

From where he worked next to Booker, Mercer could see into the yawning mouth of the mine. It was uniformly square, darker and suddenly ominous. The damp air coming from it felt like an icy breath.

Fifteen minutes later, after Sykes ran through a number of safety procedures Mercer already knew, they were ready for the descent. Ira sent for a crane operator to work the hoist while Mercer and Sykes shuffled into the skip and settled themselves on the floor. Standing around for the minutes it would take to reach the water level was an uncomfortable option with fifty pounds of gear on their backs. Both men had various tools linked to their weight belts for when they reached the pump intake.

"Down and back," Ira said as he slammed the steel gate.

"Down and back," Mercer echoed.

The elevator fell from beneath them.

"Oh, one thing I forgot to tell you, Booker," Mercer said loud enough to be heard over the cage's rattle, "the water is highly saline."

"People call me Doc, and how salty?" Sykes asked in the darkness. Neither bothered to turn on their dive lights or the lights on the mining helmets.

"I'd say like seawater."

"We should be okay weightwise. Just don't need to add so much air to your buoyancy compensator."

The temperature plunged as they dropped, the heat sucked into the millions of gallons of water still flooding the mine. Again, Mercer was reminded of a chilly breath. The car began to slow and came to a gentle stop at seven hundred sixty feet. Mercer heaved open the trapdoor cut into the floor of the car and flashed his light into the depths. The still water reflected the beam like a black mirror. He reached for the telephone built into the side of the elevator and ordered them lowered another five feet. The water was now just inches below the steel mesh floor.

Doc Sykes reached down and brought a palmful of water to his mouth. He spat it immediately. "Shit! Tastes exactly like the ocean."

"Told you so." Mercer looked closer at the water. Tendrils of something floated on the surface. He snagged one with the tip of a pry bar and brought it into the elevator. It was green and stringy, like seaweed. He smelled it. It had the same decayed fishy odor too. But this was impossible. The subterranean reservoir had been cut off from the rest of the world for tens or hundreds of millions of years. There was no way seaweed could have evolved in this isolated lightless realm so far from any ocean. He showed it to Sykes. A troubled look passed between them.

"Let's just do this, okay?"

Mercer flicked the mess off the pry bar and re-clipped the tool to his belt. "Right," he said doubtfully.

Sykes went first. He slipped his regulator into his mouth, took a couple of breaths and eased himself

through the trapdoor. He treaded water until Mercer
was at his side. They took a minute to adjust their
buoyancy and let the water saturating their wet suits
warm against their bodies. Sykes gave Mercer the
okay sign with thumb and forefinger and sank from
view without a ripple.

Mercer was much less graceful but managed to claw
his way under the water, feeling it close over his body
and experiencing that momentary thrill of weight-
lessness. If not for their powerful lights, it would have
been easy to imagine they were floating in space.

Sykes maintained an easy pace, keeping one hand
on the foot-thick pipe that would lead to the clogged
intake. His fins moved lazily, more for steering control
than propulsion. Like any experienced diver he was
letting his weight belt do the work for him. They
passed the mouth of the tunnel. Sykes didn't even
flash his light toward it as they glided deeper into
the depths.

Mercer stayed five feet above the soldier, keeping
Sykes centered in the cone of light from his lamp. The
water was polluted with suspended particles too small
to identify but too large to be silt. He'd never seen
such contaminated artesian water. They should be
swimming through water clearer than crystal, not this
soup. Sykes didn't seem bothered by this, but Mercer
was troubled. Something was seriously, seriously
wrong. He was thinking about aborting the dive and
demanding answers from Ira when Sykes slowed his
descent.

Mercer checked his depth gauge. One hundred four
feet. Sykes was hovering just above the clogged intake,
blocking Mercer's view of the pipe. Mercer finned
down next to the soldier and trained his light on the
pipe's terminus.

The mouth of the intake was blocked by a circular
piece of white plastic about four feet in diameter,

something Mercer didn't recognize as being in the mine before the flood. In fact, he'd never seen it before. The tremendous suction from the topside pump had warped the plastic, extruding it into the coarse mesh that prevented debris from flowing up the line. The plastic was so deformed that reversing the pump had only lodged it tighter.

Sykes pulled out his board and a grease pencil and drew a sharp question mark.

Mercer shook his head. He had no idea what they were looking at. Both men levered their pry bars next to where the plastic had bent around the steel pipe, heaving in concert to peel an inch of the disk from the intake. They shifted the levers and repeated the maneuver, working their way around the pipe like they were opening a can. The intake mesh had gouged a waffle pattern into the plastic that locked the two like Velcro. It took several minutes of heavy work before the disk popped clear. It floated free, bobbing in the currents formed by their effort. As it slowly revolved, the side pressed into the intake danced into the beams of the lights. The lettering printed around the perimeter was perfectly legible: RYLANDER CRUISE LINES. THE HAPPY SHIPS.

The mysterious disk was a plastic tabletop, one of several dozen usually found arranged around the swimming pool on a cruise ship. An unremarkable artifact in and of itself, something that probably gets lost at sea quite often when the weather's rough, but how had it gotten stuck eight hundred feet under solid rock a good four hundred miles from the nearest ocean?

Sykes didn't need to redraw his question mark. The confusion was in his eyes.

Mercer grabbed his own board and wrote for a moment. *We're going down the tunnel to the working face. Calculate our air time.*

Sykes shook his head. Mercer jiggled the board, emphasizing his demand. Again, the commando shook his head. Mercer erased his message and wrote another.

I'm going with or without you.

Wasting just another second with silent defiance, Sykes checked Mercer's gauges and his own and typed the numbers into the dive computer strapped to his wrist. He read the numbers and wrote: *We've got forty minutes at this depth. More where the tunnel branches off.*

Mercer used a snap clip to attach an air bag to the tabletop and pulled the lanyard that inflated the rubber sphere. The table rose into the murk. They'd haul it onto the elevator when they finished the dive. He started for the tunnel, confident that Sykes was right behind him. At sixty-seven feet they reached the tunnel. Mercer twisted in and continued on, swimming in smooth strokes that pushed him through the water with minimal effort. He didn't even consider the last time he'd been in this tunnel was when the flood had claimed Ken Porter's life. He focused entirely on what lay beyond the dike they'd blasted through. There had never been a subterranean lake—at least not until four months ago. The water looked and tasted like seawater because that's exactly what it was. And the answer to how it got to the middle of the Nevada desert lay a quarter mile ahead.

He had to force himself not to rush. In his wake he left a steady trail of bubbles as he drew deep, even breaths. His light receded from him as he swam, like the corridor from a nightmare that never ends. It took seven minutes to reach the site of the explosion. All the debris from Donny Randall's final blast had been swept away in the flood. Most of the working face was gone too. Only jagged chunks of rock hanging from the ceiling and jutting from the floor like rotted teeth marked this as the spot where Ken had died.

Mercer didn't slow. But as he pushed through the shattered dike, his light vanished, the beam swallowed by an enormous chamber. Mercer stopped dead in the water, trying to adjust to the sudden change from the tunnel's claustrophobic confines. Sykes swam up next to him. He played his light around. The water was too deep to see the floor and the walls were lost from view. He flashed his beam upward and tapped Mercer on the shoulder.

The light bounced off the water's surface forty feet overhead. The pumps had drained the reservoir to the same level as the main shaft where the elevator waited.

They didn't need to confer to know what to do. Sykes watched his depth gauge and worked his computer to calculate decompression stops. No matter what they found, they had five minutes before they had to return to the elevator car.

A moment later they broke the surface. Mercer swept his beam around in a circle, the light penetrating much farther through air than the water. The chamber was at least five hundred feet across, and the ceiling was a dome lofting a hundred feet above them. The cave's walls were smooth and curved, like the interior of a stone sphere that had been polished to perfection.

All of this he saw in a quick glance, an impression more than an observation, because something else had caught his attention. As confused as he was about finding seaweed and as stunned as he was discovering the table, what he saw now defied all logic.

Even in the low light of a single dive lamp, the size and silhouette were unmistakable. Floating serenely in the middle of the underground lake was the dull gray shape of a submarine.

Charlie Williams didn't like his position one bit. In fact, he hated it. And to make matters worse it was his own fault. He hadn't noticed how his opponent had shifted pawns to open up his rook, and now the white castle was decimating his few remaining pieces. With his queen effectively pinned by the pair of table-hopping knights, it was inevitable that he'd lose the game. His only solace was that this was only the fifth game of chess he'd ever played and the ship's third officer, Jon Carlyle, had needed fifteen more moves to beat him than their last game.

Charlie's wife, Spirit, sensed her husband's frustration and looked up from the book she'd borrowed from the ship's small library, a biography of Alfred Watkins, the discoverer of England's purported geomagnetic ley lines. Besides the glow of instruments and the wash from Charlie's laptop where the game was being played out, her lamp was the only spot of illumination on the bridge of the *Sea Surveyor II*. Beyond the large windows, the night was starless and the ocean calm. The door to the bridge wing was open and a tropical breeze cut the ozone smell of electronics.

"C.W.," she called in a voice that could have made her a fortune as a phone sex operator, "I hate to say this, lover, but even if chess's most powerful piece is female, the game itself is based on misogynist ideas of class warfare in which the goal is to keep an impotent king alive while pieces get sacrificed with little regard to what they'd mean in the real world. I think it's good that you keep losing. It means you're enlightened."

"It means," C.W. answered back without taking his eyes off the computer game, "that I'm actually a died-in-the-wool monarchist who, if I were king, would think nothing of letting my queen get killed if it kept me in power for a few moments longer. What do you think, Jon?"

The watch officer was approaching fifty years old and had a daughter not much younger than Spirit Williams. He thought C.W. had gotten a handful when he married her. She was a deadly combination of hardened opinions, iron will and absolutely no patience. On the other hand, she was gypsy beautiful and obviously loved C.W. with every fiber of her being. Carlyle used the keyboard to deepen his attack on C.W.'s king by advancing his bishop two-thirds the way across the board. "I think that since you two apparently never sleep and don't mind keeping me company on the graveyard watch, I'll withhold an answer so you don't abandon me."

"Diplomacy from a chessboard warrior?" Spirit teased. "Maybe you're a little enlightened too."

"I'm many things"—the veteran seaman smiled across to her—"but you're the first to call me enlightened."

The research ship *Sea Surveyor II* was owned by a consortium of California universities and was used exclusively for hard science research on the world's oceans. While many who sailed aboard her were wide-eyed grad students who knew little beyond their specialties, her crew were all experienced sailors, many with military backgrounds, who enjoyed the relaxed pace of a ship at sea nearly ten months of every year.

This was Carlyle's fifth voyage and C.W.'s second, but for Spirit Williams, a second-year doctoral student studying the effects of global warming on deep-ocean currents, this was her first trip on the 238-foot ship. C.W. was a new member of the vessel's support staff and was responsible for the NewtSuits, high-tech one-person submersibles that resembled a combination suit of medieval armor and the cartoon Michelin Man. He was also rated to pilot *Bob*, the three-man submarine, stowed in a special garage over the *Sea Surveyor*'s fantail.

C.W. and Spirit had met a mere six months ago and married just four weeks later. He'd grown up in Southern California and retained the toned physique and tan of a lifetime surfer. His moppy hair was just starting to lose its sun-bleached brassy sheen and return to a more natural blond while the top of his nose remained lumpy and scarred by layers of precancerous skin. He was two years shy of thirty and had gotten into the field of deep-sea submersibles because his college roommate's father owned a company that designed and built them in a warehouse in Long Beach. During his schooling C.W. worked for him during summer vacations and was hired on full-time after graduating. Charlie had a relaxed live-and-let-live attitude, caring little beyond the immediate scope of his life. He had never voted, hadn't been in a church since he was a kid and harbored few deeply held opinions.

Spirit Williams was opposite in nearly every way. Her hair and eyes were dark, her skin pale. Like her name implied, she was deeply spiritual. She'd grown up in a commune outside of Monterey, raised by parents who'd never accepted that the sixties had ended. Her mother, a Wicca priestess and midwife, and her father, a so-called organic farmer who grew the most potent marijuana in the state, had schooled her in the ways of the natural world. She believed that the earth was Gaia, a living spirit, and that humankind was actually at the bottom of the world social order, not the top. Unlike her husband, Spirit firmly believed in a list of tenets. Environmentalism, feminism, animal rights, children's rights, Native American rights, prisoners' rights, and nearly every other liberal cause fell within her interest. At twenty-five, she'd already been arrested for smashing a Starbucks window in Seattle and was pepper-sprayed at a WHO summit in Washington, D.C.

"Since you don't know chess, I wonder, what kind of games did you play growing up?" Carlyle asked her.

Spirit marked her place in the book with an owl feather. "Your typical kid games. You know, like natives and oppressors."

"Cowboys and Indians?"

She nodded. "If you insist on using bigoted names. Um, there was hide from the pigs."

"Hide and seek."

Spirit smiled. "And when I was a teenager there was always medicine man."

It took Carlyle a second to translate that one. He was aghast at her impudence. "Doctor?"

"Like your daughter never played it."

"Maybe she did, but she had the sense not to tell me about it."

"I bet you were one of those fathers who didn't know when his little girl got her period, yet knew the exact day and time your son had his first hard-on."

Jon could have been offended but knew she meant nothing by her comment. It was just her way and he threw it right back at her. "It was June eighteenth, 1997, at seven twenty-one in the morning. He seemed mighty impressed with it as I recall."

She arched an eyebrow. "Maybe I should meet him someday."

Jon shot an uncomfortable look at C.W., but her husband was used to her flirtations and was studying the electronic chessboard to see if there was any hope of escape.

"All ships signify, all ships signify. This is the USS *Smithback*. Mayday, mayday, mayday." The voice from the speakers rang clear, and all three on the bridge could hear the fear in the sailor's voice.

Jon Carlyle grabbed up the radio handset. "*Smithback, Smithback, Smithback*, this is the MV *Sea Surveyor*. State your location and the nature of your emergency."

"*Sea Surveyor*, we've been authorized by Pacific Command to issue a mayday and ask for immediate assistance."

Carlyle imagined the scenario. A U.S. Navy ship was in trouble—from the tension in the radioman's voice, severe trouble—yet they still had to get permission to ask for help.

"*Smithback*, please state your location and the nature of your emergency," Carlyle asked smoothly. Over his shoulder he asked the Filipino helmsman to alert the ship's captain, Perry Jacobi, and have him summoned to the bridge.

"We've struck an iceberg. We are shipping water, but our pumps are keeping pace."

Jesus, Carlyle thought, he must be receiving an errant signal, a radio distress from Arctic or Antarctic waters that had bounced around the atmosphere, a not uncommon occurrence. That was how ham radio operators could talk to counterparts on the opposite side of the globe. He recognized, too, that it was unlikely the *Sea Surveyor* was the closest to render assistance. In fact, depending on where the navy vessel was located, it might be days before a rescue ship could reach them.

"We are at 21.21 degrees north by 173.32 west. . . ."

With an angry shake of his head Carlyle tuned out the rest of what he was hearing. This was a crank radio distress, the maritime version of yelling fire in a crowded theater. Some jerk with a powerful transceiver was pretending to be a sinking American ship, only he was too stupid to realize the coordinates put him in tropical waters a mere ninety miles from the *Sea Surveyor*. Struck an iceberg, my ass.

"This is *Sea Surveyor*," he said tautly. "You are in violation of maritime law and are liable for prosecution if you don't desist."

A new voice came over the airwaves, more assured than that of the crank radio operator. "*Sea Surveyor*, this is Commander Kenneth Galloway, captain of the USS *Smithback*. This is not a joke. We are a U.S. Navy cargo ship and we've struck an iceberg. It didn't show up on radar. It sort of popped out of the water just ahead of us. We didn't have time for evasive maneuvers. We first thought we'd hit a submarine, but now there are dozens of bergs around us."

Over the radio link Carlyle and the others could hear alarms wailing and the frantic voices of panicked men on the floundering ship. Carlyle got busy computing an intercept course.

"I'm sorry about the misunderstanding, Captain," Carlyle replied. "We are seven hours from your position and are getting under way now. What is your situation?"

"At first the damage didn't appear that severe. Our pumps can handle the inflow of seawater, and emergency crews already have the hole repaired with timbers and plates, but we still appear to be sinking. We're down four feet in the past thirty minutes. If this continues, your seven hours will be too late."

In the minute the *Surveyor*'s officer took to consider the situation, three other ships in the area—two container ships heading to Los Angeles from Japan and a small tanker ferrying gasoline to Wake Island—responded to the distress call. None was closer than the research ship, although their captains had ordered detours to offer assistance. A navy patrol plane from Midway Island was en route.

Carlyle didn't question the impossibility of what Galloway was telling him. If he said his ship was sinking despite effecting repairs, then that was exactly what was happening. He considered that they had missed another spot where their ship was holed, but it didn't seem likely. Repair teams on navy ships were well trained. They wouldn't make such an elemental mistake.

"What does this mean?" C.W. asked the officer. Spirit was at his side, holding his hand.

Carlyle had almost forgotten their presence. "I don't know."

"Mayday! Mayday! Mayday!" It was the radioman again and his voice was a shriek over the radio. "We're sinking fast. Down at the head. The bow's awash. This is the USS *Smithback*. Oh, Jesus, Mary, and Joseph. The sea. The sea is starting to burn."

A muffled explosion rumbled from the bridge speakers. Another scream and then the roar of water. And then silence.

For the six hours and forty minutes it took the *Sea Surveyor II* to reach the *Smithback*'s last known coordinates, Jon Carlyle continued to radio and received no replies. The P-3 Orion antisubmarine warfare plane out of Midway had already reported in by the time they reached the site. That had been an hour after the last call from the *Smithback*. The Orion found no wreckage, no debris, not even an oil slick.

It was as if the navy cargo ship had never been.

Ira Lasko wasn't waiting in the cave when Mercer and Sykes emerged from the flooded mine. He wasn't in the control van either. Mercer, still wearing his borrowed wet suit and oblivious to the sharp stones that cut into his bare feet as he searched the camp, found his friend in the rec hall. Dr. Briana Marie was with him, her lab coat tossed over a sofa as she and Ira conferred over a thick binder.

Both simply glanced up when he crashed through the door. Dr. Marie closed the file and leaned back in her chair. Ira ran a hand across his bald head. The only sound was a steady whir from an air conditioner and the drip of seawater off Mercer's body. He threw his flippers into a corner.

"Nuclear physicist?" he taunted Briana. "How about Harry fucking Houdini?"

"You were told not to enter the cavern," she snapped back.

"Easy, Doctor," Ira said.

"He isn't cleared for this project, Admiral. You assured me he could complete the tunnel to the cavern and not ask questions."

Ira shot her a hard look. "I don't like lying to my friends and I've done it long enough. It's over." He turned to Mercer. "I didn't have a choice. The orders came straight from the secretary of defense and the president's office."

Mercer heard the sincerity in Ira's voice, saw the shame in his eyes. This was the Ira he'd known and agreed to work for. The tension lines that had etched his face seemed to be relaxing with each passing second. Mercer unzipped his wet suit and used a handful of paper napkins stored in a sideboard to wipe water from his eyes and dry the hair on his chest. Whatever he was about to hear, he knew he'd need to sit for it. He'd probably need a drink too, but the camp was dry.

"That cavern," he said, "it's not natural, is it?"

"No," Ira replied, "it's not. It was formed when the submarine refocused."

"Refocused? What does that mean?"

Ira hesitated. "I think it's best if Dr. Marie explains it."

For a moment she seemed to struggle between the need to keep her project secret and the desire to brag about her work. And then it came in a rush of pride.

"How much do you know about quantum physics, Dr. Mercer?"

"It's the realm of the subatomic, where the rules we live by, like gravity and magnetism, no longer apply. Most everything I've read about it is so counterintuitive that I tend to ignore it."

She nodded. "A reasonable and honest answer. There are only a handful of scientists in the world who wouldn't give that exact same response. And yet what you don't know is that it is the branch of physics that will one day revolutionize the way we live our lives."

"I don't think the ability to move a submarine into a mountain is going to better my life any time soon," Mercer said sarcastically, still riled by all the lies he'd been told.

She didn't like his flippant comment and her tone became brusque. "Well, then how is this for counterintuitive, Doctor—we didn't move the submarine into the mountain. In fact, the sub never moved at all."

Mercer held up a supplicating hand. Antagonizing her wasn't going to get the answers he wanted. "Could you start from the beginning, please? In laymen's terms."

"All right. What is the fastest possible speed in the universe?"

"The speed of light. One hundred eighty-six thousand miles per second."

"Newton's second law of thermodynamics basically states that all systems decay into chaos, right?"

"I believe so."

"Does a tree falling in the forest make a sound?"

"What does this have to do with that submarine?"

"Please answer the question."

"Sure, why wouldn't it?"

"In the quantum world, you just gave three wrong answers. The study of the subatomic came about from the work of Niels Bohr and Werner Heisenberg. One of the principles all subsequent research has been based on is called the Heisenberg Uncertainty Principle. In the simplest terms it means that observing an event alters its outcome. Therefore nothing in the universe happens without direct observation. It sounds arrogant, I know, that we, the observers, make things happen by our very presence, but it has been proven in the lab dozens of times. That means the tree in the forest can't make a sound because it never fell.

"And in the world of the subatomic, both in time and in space, order can spontaneously arise from chaos. Albeit for fractions of a second, but even that short time span refutes Newton's second law."

"And the galactic speed limit?" Mercer pressed. "The speed of light?"

"What if I told you I've seen an experiment where a beam of laser light that was shot through a gas medium at extremely low temperatures actually came out the other side of the chamber *before* it was fired. Effect came before cause. Somehow in the quantum world, a message traveling faster than the speed of light was relayed to the detector that the laser beam was coming."

Mercer didn't doubt her claims. He was more aware than most that the immutable laws of the past were falling to scientific breakthroughs at an ever-accelerating pace. Yet he couldn't fully grasp the implications, or how this got a submarine weighing a thousand tons or more into a mountain hundreds of miles from the sea.

"Now, what if we take that experiment one step further? What if we could do it with particles? In one sense, that is what light is, a particle we call a photon."

"You'd have a particle existing at two places at once."

"And what if in the process of shooting the particle, the original you started with gets destroyed?"

"You'd end up with a duplicate particle on the other side of your super-cold gas chamber." The realization hit like a body blow. "You're talking about some kind of science fiction transporter system."

She gave him a pained grimace. "That isn't how it is. There's no 'Beam me up, Scotty'. The media keeps hyping the possibility, but in truth transporting a human being, while possible in the abstract, will never be practical."

"But is that what you wanted to do with the submarine? Transport it to Area 51?"

Her expression turned even more sour. "No, but we were afraid it might happen. You see, our aim was to make it invisible. We call it optoelectric camouflage. It's designed for surface ships and perhaps aircraft if we can scale down the necessary equipment and reduce the power consumption. We used a sub because there was a theoretical chance something like this could happen."

Ira interrupted. "It got away from them."

"It didn't get away from us," she said curtly. "The navy was told about this possibility. We built in the fail-safes."

"Tell me what happened."

"The system my team and I developed uses a bubble of intense magnetism to bend visible light into a toroid, a kind of doughnut shape. We observe an object because light is reflected off its surface. Some wavelengths get absorbed and the ones that bounce back give the object its color. Now, something that is black will absorb all the wavelengths, so we can't see it, yet we perceive its presence against a colored background. My theory was that if we could trap the light in a toroid so it couldn't escape, and then bend it around the object, the observer wouldn't see anything. It would be like how water bends light so a pencil looks disjointed if half of it sticks above the surface.

"And?" Mercer prompted, because while what she was saying sounded far-fetched, it wasn't an explanation for what he'd seen in the mine.

"We ran into the quantum world," she said as if that clarified everything.

"Meaning?"

"Meaning there was a consequence we had considered, took precautions against, but rejected as a real concern. The magnetic field bent visible light until it became a self-sustaining loop, a point in space in which light itself couldn't escape."

"Hold it, that sounds like a black hole."

"No. Black holes are the collapse of matter due to gravity. We were using magnetism."

"What's the difference?"

"The difference is that gravity hasn't been reconciled with the quantum world. It was what Einstein was working on when he died, a grand theory of everything—nuclear forces, magnetism and gravity."

"So you stumbled onto something new."

"Yet the consequences are the same."

"What consequences?"

"For lack of a better way of putting it, we stopped time. The magnetic pressure, like gravity at a black hole, created a bubble around the test submarine. As the light within that bubble became trapped, the Heisenburg Uncertainty Principle took over."

"So your experiment no longer had an observer?"

"And in the quantum world when there is no observer, nothing happens. That tree in the forest is still standing until someone goes out to look at it."

"What did that do to your sub?"

"In essence, for the submarine time stopped and the rest of the universe vanished. A couple of scientists on our team thought this could have happened. That's why we took precautions. We installed a trigger device using quantum entwining that would cut the power to the magnetic sphere around the submarine and return the normal flow of time. In theory it would reappear in our world."

"Only you missed and it came back in Nevada. Why?"

" 'Tide and time wait for no man,' " she quoted. "We didn't miss at all. The earth rotates at more than a thousand miles an hour and travels around the sun even faster. Factor in our solar system's rotation in the Milky Way and you can see we didn't do half bad just returning the sub back to our own planet. It could have just as easily refocused in orbit or on the far side of the moon. We couldn't bring it back in the ocean because we couldn't guarantee that the sub could come back above its crush depth, so it was decided to trigger its return at a remote secure facility on land. Area 51 was the perfect location."

"DS-Two?"

"Destination Site Two," Ira said. "The primary return coordinates were the area the sub first vanished off Jacksonville, Florida, the hope being that if it did fade out it would only be for an instant."

Ira's use of the word "fade" was what triggered the memory. It was one of the favorite stories told by UFO enthusiasts, conspiracy nuts and believers in the absurd.

"You're describing the Philadelphia Experiment," Mercer said.

"That story was what piqued my interest in physics," Dr. Marie admitted.

Though debunked by the very man who started the myth, the Philadelphia Experiment remained a popular topic in fringe Internet chat rooms. The legend centered around a navy vessel, the USS *Eldridge*. As the story goes, during World War Two a secret program, Project Rainbow, was initiated by Einstein and the famed inventor Nicola Tesla. They wanted to create a light-bending camouflage using enormous magnetic pressures to hide Allied ships from Nazi U-boats. A newly commissioned destroyer was outfitted with all sorts of scientific gear including massive electric generators. During the first experiments, everything seemed to go as planned. A green-blue fog grew around the vessel when the equipment was turned on and moments later the ship faded from view. It reappeared when the power was cut.

The experiment was repeated several times until August 1943. Some adjustments were made to the ship and when the system was activated again it faded into a fog, only this time it reappeared an instant later in Norfolk, Virginia. A few moments later it returned to Philadelphia and emerged from the unnatural mist. If this tale wasn't fantastic enough, a witness aboard a nearby cargo ship, the SS *Andrew Furuseth*, named Carlos Allende, reported seeing some members of her crew walking around in a daze, while others continued to fade in and out, as if they were ghosts. He claimed that still others were fused to the ship's deck, grotesque mannequins caught in poses of unimaginable agony.

"But that was bullshit!" Mercer exclaimed. "I remember reading that years later Allende himself admitted to making up the whole story. Besides which, it was proved the *Eldridge* was never in Philly and Einstein was busy working on the Manhattan Project."

Briana Marie smiled for the first time since Mercer had burst into the rec room. "Do you think the fact that it never really happened matters? Science is the melding of experimentation and inspiration. Where the ideas come from is irrelevant. There are countless examples of inventions being inspired by legends, myths, and science fiction. Dick Tracy's wrist radio was just a fantasy in the 1930s, but you don't question the cell phone. Jules Verne described an atomic-powered submarine almost a century before Admiral Rickover built the USS *Nautilus*, which he named after Verne's creation. Science fiction preceded the laser, radar, sonar, space travel, cloning, and hundreds of other technologies. Don't you think we scientists are influenced by what we read as children, thinking that someday we could make real what those authors only dreamed about?" She became heated.

"I've spent my professional life trying to realize the *bullshit* of the Philadelphia Experiment and you saw the goddamn proof."

"Okay," Mercer retreated. "I'll admit that I have read a little about quantum teleportation. But all that's ever been achieved is a couple thousand atoms, basically a ball of gas that was shot from one side of a lab to another. You're telling me you can move an entire submarine, composed of an incalculable number of atoms, and reassemble it exactly the way it was."

"This isn't quantum teleportation." She blew a

breath. "That word again. This is something new. I call it a magnetic sink. We didn't deconstruct the sub. We removed it from one of the four known dimensions—the three cardinal points and time. Remove any one dimension from an object and it ceases to be. A shadow is a perfect example. It is a two-dimensional facsimile of an object, but not the object itself. I proved that the same principle works with time. We took the sub out of our time and then brought it back.

"And even you can't be so naïve to think military research isn't years ahead of what gets published in the scientific journals. The military had supersonic flight thirty years before Concorde and GPS tracking decades before it became commercially available. The ball of gas experiment you mentioned was ancient history to my project team."

"How long was it gone?" Mercer asked, trying to get the conversation back from the abstract.

She looked at Ira, again seeking permission to divulge another secret.

He answered for her. "Almost twelve months."

They'd had to wait for the earth to nearly circle the sun before they could return the boat to—Mercer didn't know the right word—reality?

"The orbital calculations had to be unbelievably precise," Briana Marie added with pride. "We had to factor in longitude, latitude and altitude. Getting it to return to a secure location like Area 51 meant it would refocus deep underground. That is why we needed miners to tunnel an access shaft. A delay of even a few seconds would have seen the sub return outside of Bakersfield, California, at an altitude of eight thousand feet. A few seconds earlier and it would have come back eleven thousand feet under Lake Powell, Utah."

"Ah, how long ago did you bring it back?" Mercer asked, sensing he already knew.

Ira's cell phone rang. He pulled it from the inside pocket of his coat and pushed his rolling chair out of immediate earshot. Dr. Marie answered for him. "Four months ago."

Something happened out there, something not natural. It was Tisa's voice Mercer heard in his head. He'd earlier dismissed her comments. Now they sounded like a warning. *A bubble erupted in the earth, like a contained nuclear explosion that only lasted a second.* Her group had detected the submarine reemerging from wherever it had drifted for the past year.

A thought struck him. Why the hell would they care?

They should have assumed the seismic jolt was just an earthquake. Surely other seismograph stations had recorded it and just as quickly discounted it. Central Nevada was a jigsaw of shallow fault lines. Why were they so focused on this single event? Focused enough to try to sabotage the tunneling operation. Was there a leak in Dr. Marie's department, a whistleblower or a traitor who'd divulged the secret?

Mercer's head pounded from the shortened decompression stops he and Sykes had been forced to take. He'd seen the proof of Dr. Marie's work even if he couldn't grasp the science behind it. For now he'd put that out of his mind. The questions that needed answering were about Tisa Nguyen and her group. Mercer had deliberately withheld how she had rescued him from the Luxor Hotel, but he knew now he'd have to tell Ira. If Dr. Marie's team had a leak, it had to be plugged.

Ira had said little during his phone conversation. His expression was grim when he wheeled himself back to the table. "The navy just lost a ship in the Pacific, a cargo vessel. Preliminary search-and-rescue report no survivors. No debris either."

Wait, I can give you some evidence. Something un-

usual is about to happen in the Pacific Ocean. Something involving your group? Mercer had asked. *Yes,* Tisa had replied.

Mercer lost all interest in what Dr. Marie had been telling him. "What happened?" His voice cracked in the sudden silence.

"Unknown. A civilian research ship heard the mayday and is just reaching the last known position. Preliminary intel from Pacific Command reports the ship hit an iceberg, but they were in tropical waters. I'm betting she was rammed by a submarine coming to the surface or maybe a large cargo container that had washed off a freighter. Her last radio call said the ocean had caught fire. I think a container carrying volatile materials split open when the ship hit it and ignited somehow."

How do I convince you that the world is about to end? Again Mercer heard Tisa in his head. *Obviously me just blurting it out won't be enough, so I need to show you some kind of proof. And the only way to make that work is if I gain your trust through incremental steps. Are you with me so far?*

This had been late in their conversation. At the time, Mercer still wasn't sure what to make of the beguiling woman. She seemed rational and totally illogical at the same time. He supposed many mentally ill people sounded the same way. She was trying to convince him, yes, but she didn't sound as if her world revolved around convincing others of what she believed. Conspiracy addicts needed affirmation to keep themselves from thinking they were nuts. That's why they fed off each other so much and why the Internet was full of chat rooms concerning the paranormal. But Tisa wasn't like that. She wanted Mercer to believe her, not because she couldn't bear him disagreeing. More, it was like she wanted his help and the only way to gain it was to draw him into her world.

Tisa must have known this when she said something unusual was going to happen in the Pacific. By doling out information like breadcrumbs she could convince him to follow the trail to Santorini, where presumably he'd learn another truth, perhaps what she meant by "the world was about to end." One thing was clear. He had to be involved with the search for the ship if he was to learn anything further.

"There's another possibility," he said slowly, looking Ira in the eye. "I held back some information about my escape from the Luxor Hotel. Something rather critical."

It took fifteen minutes to fill in the details of how Tisa had rescued him, how she appeared to be on the run from her own organization and how she believed the end of the world was coming.

"I'm just as skeptical as you, Ira," Mercer concluded. "I wouldn't have even brought this up if too many coincidences hadn't already fallen into place." He ticked them off with his fingers. "The cave-in that killed most of your first work crew, which I suspect was Donny Randall's handiwork, considering his attempt on my life. The fact Tisa knew when the sub re—what was your word?—refocused at Area 51. The gunmen at my hotel. Tisa's well-timed rescue. And now a navy ship sinks in the Pacific under unusual circumstances.

"There are two ways to read this. Either someone on Dr. Marie's staff leaked information about their experiment and it somehow fell into the hands of a group that wants to stop it for some reason . . ." Mercer trailed off.

"Or?" Marie and Lasko said as one.

"Or they detected the sub refocusing, knew the seismic disturbance wasn't natural and sent a team to investigate. Judging by their organizational sophistication and logistical support, I don't think this is a new group formed as a result of your work here. They've been around for a while, only we've never done anything that put us in their sights."

"Why should my experiment 'put us in their sights,' as you say?"

Mercer leaned back in his chair. The wet suit was drying and his entire body itched. "I suspect the answer lies out there where the ship sank."

"And in Greece?" Ira asked.

Mercer thought about it, considered the pattern Tisa had set out for him. "No, I think there I'm only going to find more questions."

"You're still going." Ira made it sound like an order.

Mercer turned it into a bargaining chip. "Only if you get me to the Pacific to see for myself what happened to the navy's ship."

Ira didn't hesitate. This was exactly the kind of mission he'd expected Mercer to tackle as special science advisor. "I'll make the arrangements."

"What happens here?" Mercer asked.

"We'll finish pumping out the mine so Dr. Marie's people can get to the sub. I guess then they all head back to their drawing boards and the navy writes off a hundred million dollar mistake."

In the twenty hours since his conversation with Ira, Mercer bounced from Area 51 to Vegas for a commercial flight to Hawaii. From there he hitched a ride on an air force cargo plane headed to Guam. He was met there by navy aircraft carrying crew and mail to the carrier USS *Ronald Reagan*. An aged Sea King helicopter finished the last leg of his journey to the research vessel. Lasko's name and position carried considerable weight with the military and the transfers had gone off without a hitch.

From the air, the *Sea Surveyor* looked like any other scientific vessel, with her superstructure hunched over her bows, a long open deck at the rear and an A-frame derrick hanging from her stern. Two boxes the size of shipping containers ate some of her deck space. Mercer figured these housed science labs and the topside support facilities for the bright yellow submersible that sat below the crane. The ship's helipad jutted awkwardly from the back of the superstructure two levels above the main deck and required all the pilot's concentration to land. He held the chopper just long enough for Mercer to dodge out of the aircraft and catch his bag and some other gear from a crewman.

Gale-force rotor wash whipped Mercer as the long-range chopper eased away from the pad and thundered off to rejoin the *Reagan*. A moment later a man in his late forties appeared from a nearby door. He wore a white tropical-weight uniform with short sleeves and gold epaulets at the shoulder. He had a slender build and wasn't more than five feet seven, but his graying hair and the steadiness of his gaze gave him a strong physical presence.

"Philip Mercer?" he called a bit suspiciously, as if he was expecting someone else choppering out to the middle of the ocean. "I'm Jon Carlyle, third officer. Welcome aboard."

"Thank you." They shook hands and Carlyle led him into the superstructure. The air-conditioning beat back the humidity and heat.

"We were startled by the radio message this morning from the navy that they were flying you out. I'm sorry, but I wasn't expecting a civilian. You are a civilian, right?"

Mercer was still getting comfortable with using his title and the startled looks it invoked, but he needed to establish his credentials early. "Actually, I'm special science advisor to the president."

"Of the United States?" Carlyle was suitably impressed.

"That's the man. I'm here under the authority of Admiral Ira Lasko, the deputy national security advisor. Not only were you at the right place and time to monitor the sinking of the USS *Smithback*, but until the navy can get a salvage ship from San Diego, you're also the only one with the proper equipment to investigate the wreckage."

"Ah, we weren't told you'd commandeer our sub for a survey."

"Your captain—Jacobi, I think his name is—should be on the ship-to-shore right now getting orders to assist me in any way. And in case you're wondering, the government's picking up the tab."

"What exactly are we supposed to do?"

"You know the circumstances surrounding the *Smithback*'s sinking?"

"I was on watch when her distress call came through," Carlyle replied. "She said she hit an iceberg. At first I thought it was a crank, but now, well, I have a theory."

Mercer waited.

"It was the last words, about the sea catching fire. I think she hit a container that fell off a freighter and whatever was in it caused the blaze."

"That's our assumption too." Mercer had decided not to mention anything about Tisa Nguyen and her predictions and would have proposed the container theory had the third officer not thought of it already. He'd also created a plausible cover for the urgency of his mission. "However, the navy needs confirmation. There have been unspecified terrorist threats against our ships in the Pacific, and if this turns out to be something other than an accident . . ."

"They have to know right away so they can take appropriate steps," Carlyle finished for him. "I was in the navy for twenty-one years. I know how it goes and personally I'm glad we're here to help."

"Thank you, Mr. Carlyle."

"Jon."

"Jon. People just call me Mercer."

"Let's get you settled, Mercer, and come up with a plan to survey the wreck."

Mercer stowed his meager luggage in the cabin assigned to him and took a brief shower. He stepped from the tiny bathroom wearing only a towel and was about to toss that on the bed when he saw a raven-haired woman standing in his doorway. He recalled closing the door minutes earlier. She wore sandals, tight shorts, and a T-shirt that sweat kept plastered to her skin. It was obvious that she wasn't wearing a bra. She radiated an earthy sexuality that Mercer imagined would captivate most men.

She appraised him for a moment. "That was quite an entrance."

"The helicopter?"

"That, too." The flirtation went from her voice. Her eyes hardened. "I'm Spirit Williams, one of the scientists who's losing their opportunity to work because of you."

"I—"

"There's nothing you can say, so don't. I've spent a lifetime to get aboard this ship, and I wanted to say thanks for screwing it up for me." She wheeled away and was down the hall before Mercer fully grasped what she'd said.

He didn't go after her. It would be a waste of time. He knew the type. A scientist, probably still working toward her doctorate, so dedicated to her work that anything, no matter how serious or important, was a distraction she refused to tolerate. Such narrow-minded focus served scientists well in their own world, yet made many insufferable to the rest of society. He expected the rest of the science staff on the *Sea Surveyor* would treat him in a similar fashion. With any luck he'd complete his mission before seeing her or any of the others.

Ten minutes later, Mercer found the mess hall and saw his luck had already run out. Spirit Williams was in the mess hall with Jon Carlyle and a young blond man in diving trunks and a garish Hawaiian shirt. Her leg was pressed against his, and she was drinking orange juice from a glass in front of him. Noticing the ring on his hand, he assumed they were married, although she wore no jewelry.

"Ah, Mercer." Carlyle stood. "Let me introduce one of our sub drivers, Charlie Williams."

The tanned surfer stood. "Call me C.W. This is my wife, Spirit."

"I've had the pleasure." Mercer took the fourth chair at the table. A mess steward asked if he wanted anything. Mercer took coffee.

"I met Mr. Mercer earlier and told him I didn't appreciate his presence on the *Surveyor*," Spirit said acidly. "I suspect he's here as part of a government cover-up. The navy was probably doing some illegal research, killing whales with sonar like they did a few years ago off Long Beach, and something went wrong. Now he's going to hide the truth."

"He's here to find out why a lot of brave sailors died two nights ago," Jon retorted. He'd had his fill of Spirit's rancor. The vessel's crew had no real interest in what the ship did once she was at sea, but the researchers had tight funding and guarded their time on board jealously. Even a few days' delay was a colossal waste of their time and resources. They hadn't stopped griping since getting the news, and C.W.'s wife had been the most vocal.

"Their souls have crossed," Spirit replied. "They should be left to rest. Sending people down there to gloat over their remains is ghoulish."

"Mr. Mercer isn't here to gloat. He's here to get answers so more sailors aren't lost."

"They knew the risks when they joined the navy. Dying's part of their job."

Carlyle's face grew red. "Defending our country is their job."

"Oh, I see." She became even more sarcastic. "Dying is just a fringe benefit."

Mercer caught C.W.'s eye. The submersible operator showed no interest in restraining his wife. He'd heard her in action before and knew to stay out of the line of fire.

"Now, see here," the normally unflappable officer thundered. Since the loss of the *Smithback*, his admiration for the navy and its men had been rekindled. Before he could continue, four other men entered the mess room.

Carlyle glared at an unrepentant Spirit, wiped his

brow with a handkerchief and made the introductions. One of the newcomers was a second sub pilot. The other three headed the support staff.

"You'll have to go, sweet," C.W. told his wife.

Like flipping a switch, her temperament did a complete reversal. She smiled at the assembled men and gave C.W. a long kiss on the mouth. "Come get me at the lab if you're diving today. I want to be in the van. Love you."

"Love you, too."

If Jon expected C.W. to apologize for his wife's behavior, he had a long wait coming. The seconds grew.

Mercer realized no one would cut the silence, so he cleared his throat. "Okay, down to business. Jon may have told you I've been sent here to discover what happened to the *Smithback*. It seems we're all under the same impression that she struck a container that split and whatever was inside burned. The navy wants me to verify this hypothesis by physically inspecting the wreck. Have you pinpointed it on the seafloor?"

Jim McKenzie, who headed the team, spoke up. "We found her on side-scan sonar about ten hours after reaching the area. She's directly below us now in nine hundred eighty-eight feet of water."

"That seems kind of shallow," Mercer said. "We're in the middle of the Pacific Ocean."

"We're atop a subsea plateau that rises from the abyssal plane. Had the *Smithback* sunk fifty miles to the north, she'd be two miles down and unreachable by anything we have on board. *Bob*'s rated for two thousand feet, and our two ADSes can safely operate at one thousand. Just so you know, *Bob* is the name of our submersible. It's what she does when she resurfaces. Just bobs in the ocean."

Mercer smiled. "I have a friend who named his dog Drag because that's how he takes his walks. What's an ADS?"

"Atmospheric Diving Suit. Also called a NewtSuit. Think of it as a one-man submarine with arms and legs. It keeps the operator at sea-level pressure so we don't have to bother with decompression but gives a freedom of movement we can't get from a larger sub or even an ROV. C.W. helped in their development and is about the best operator in the world."

"Jim's exaggerating," C.W. said to Mercer. "In college I worked part-time in the factory watching a computer-controlled lathe form the suits' torsos out of aluminum blanks." He gave a lopsided grin. "But I am the best."

"How many men can *Bob* carry?"

"Three," McKenzie answered. "Pilot and two observers. We do have a problem. We fried one of *Bob*'s banks of lights doing a test a week ago. At this depth you can't see an inch beyond the porthole, and our ROVs operate with low-light cameras so they can't provide enough backup illumination."

"The solution," C.W. interrupted, "is that I go down with you in an ADS and use it as a mobile lighting platform."

"Are the ADSes autonomous?"

"They're tethered to the *Surveyor* by a lifting cable and communications lines but don't rely on the ship for air. Don't worry," C.W. added, "we've run the NewtSuit and sub together quite a few times."

Mercer turned to McKenzie. "How long before we can dive on the wreck?"

"Weather isn't a problem. No storms predicted for days. Batteries are all fully charged and we just replaced the CO_2 scrubbers. We need to fit new ballast plates and charge the O_2 tanks, then run a few tests. Say, five hours."

"Are you going to want to see the tower too?"

This was the first Mercer had heard of any tower. "What are you talking about?" he asked Carlyle.

"The underwater tower about a mile to the west of us. We found it on sonar when we were searching for the *Smithback*."

"What is it?"

"We're not sure," McKenzie answered. "It appears to be some kind of underwater oil- or gas-drilling platform. From its sonar image, it stands about eight hundred feet tall and is about a hundred wide at the base. It tapers as it rises. The top is about forty feet square."

"And it's completely underwater?"

McKenzie nodded. "The bottom there is deeper than here, about thirteen hundred feet. The top of the tower rests five hundred feet down."

Mercer had never heard of such a structure. He was familiar with deep-sea drilling even though he wasn't an oil geologist. An eight-hundred-foot platform wasn't all that unusual anymore. Some in the North Sea stood over a thousand feet, but all of them were serviced by modules constructed above sea level. What McKenzie and Carlyle were talking about was something entirely new. And as he thought about it further, something else came to mind. As far as he knew, there weren't any oil deposits within two thousand miles of their current position. One mystery at a time, Mercer decided. He was sure there was a connection between the enigmatic structure and the *Smithback* accident, but he wanted to see the ship before investigating the tower.

"Let's check the ship first. What's *Bob*'s range?"

"She can stay down for thirty hours or more, but at a top speed of three knots she isn't exactly mobile." This came from Alan Jervis, the submersible operator who would actually take Mercer down to the wreck. Jervis was about Mercer's age, with dark receding hair and gold-framed glasses. "If you want to remain on the bottom and reach the tower, it'll take us an hour or more because we'll be bucking a two-knot current the whole way."

"We'd have to move the *Surveyor*," Carlyle said. "C.W. will be tethered to us. To get him over there, we have to reel him up, steam over to the tower, then lower him down again."

"Is that a problem?"

"No. And with your slow speed, he'd be in position before you."

"Then that's what we'll do," Mercer announced. No one questioned his authority. "We'll drop down to the ship first and then check out this tower of yours."

Mercer tried to catch a nap after the meeting, but the strong coffee and a rattling air-conditioning fan kept him awake. After the first hour of staring at the ceiling, he admitted his insomnia had nothing to do with caffeine or noise. The image of Tisa Nguyen kept sleep out of his grasp. It was her eyes he kept seeing, their depth and their pain. He didn't believe it was personal trauma. That was something people kept better hidden, at least from strangers.

She reminded him of the subject of a religious painting, a Madonna and Child perhaps, where the beatific Mary looks lovingly at her infant yet in her eyes is the knowledge he would have to die for the world's sins. Did Tisa know of such sin? Was that why she was convinced the world was ending?

He wondered what she had witnessed to make her believe that. Hers wasn't general angst about the state of a world racked by wars, famines and other sundry catastrophes the media reported so cheerfully. He was convinced it was something specific, something she and her group alone knew had happened or was about to happen.

She'd all but admitted her group's involvement with the sinking of the *Smithback*. No, that wasn't true, he recalled. She'd only said that something unusual was going to happen in the Pacific.

He had never felt so unbalanced. He felt like he was walking through a minefield holding the wrong map. In the past weeks he'd been tossed a dozen lies, survived two murder attempts and met a woman he couldn't stop thinking about. Connecting all this was a fiber too thin for him to see, let alone grasp.

Did Tisa Nguyen know about the *Smithback* being in the vicinity of the tower? Had she not warned him in time and allowed it to sink the way she'd not prevented the death of the woman at the Luxor Hotel? Or was the sinking an unintended consequence? What if the *Smithback* had wandered into some type of experiment that her group was conducting. Did it have anything to do with Dr. Marie's experiment in optoelectric camouflage?

He could only hope that some of the answers lay a thousand feet below where he tossed on his bunk.

An hour later, bound by frustration, Mercer gave up on trying to sleep. He donned the coveralls Alan Jervis had provided earlier, used the head as the sub pilot had requested and made his way to the *Surveyor*'s fantail.

Bob sat in a cradle under the A-frame derrick. The submersible was painted bright yellow and its hull was studded with auxiliary oxygen tanks, small thruster nacelles and a pair of heavy-duty manipulator arms ending in wicked-looking pincers. Her bow was a single piece of curved Lexan six inches thick. Through the tough acrylic dome, Mercer could see the cramped cockpit. Alan would sit behind and a little above the two observer seats. The interior walls were covered with dials and banks of switches and several flat-screen computer monitors. The little sub was the pinnacle of high-tech deep-sea technology.

Nearby, C.W. worked on an even more unusual piece of equipment, the ADS. The suit was also painted yellow, and the twenty rotator joints made it look segmented, like the body of a corpulent caterpillar. The helmet had a wide faceplate for good visibility, and at the end of the arms were nimble three-finger grapplers.

"What do you think?" C.W. asked with obvious pride.

"Damn amazing. What does it weigh?"

"Over five hundred pounds empty, but the way the suit's balanced and the fluid in the joints work, it's almost weightless below thirty-five feet. It's the next best thing to scuba diving, provided you're not claustrophobic."

"How do you work it?"

"Nothing to it." C.W. snapped open the back of the suit. "I was about to do a systems check. You can do it with me. Hop in."

It was like stepping into a pair of steel pants. Mercer used a bar attached to the ADS's lifting cradle to heave himself through the opening. He lowered his feet down into the legs and thrust his arms into the appropriate openings. His head came up inside the domed helmet. When he was settled, he could feel large rocker switches under his feet and several control buttons and toggles next to his hands. The suit smelled of electronics and disinfectant with just a trace of the previous user's sweat.

"Do you feel the foot pads?" Even with the access hatch open, C.W.'s voice was muffled and distant.

"Yes."

"They control the thrusters. Put pressure on the back right and the suit moves backward. Try it now."

Mercer pressed down on his heel and a pair of thrusters attached to his shoulders began to whine.

"Press forward and you go forward."

He tried it and the small propellers stopped in an instant and began turning the opposite direction.

"Your left foot controls rotation," C.W. explained. "Back spins you right and forward spins you left."

Mercer applied pressure and other thrusters

mounted on the exoskeleton spooled up to a high-pitched buzz. He then tried out the arms. He'd had thousands of hours operating heavy mining equipment that used joysticks similar to those inside the suit's arms. It took him just a few minutes to get the feel of the ADS's controls.

"Shit, man, you're a natural," C.W. exclaimed when Mercer reversed himself out of the aluminum suit.

"The controls are pretty logical." Mercer was impressed. "And you said at thirty-five feet you don't even feel the mass?"

"It's amazingly flexible." C.W. patted the suit's metal hide. "Muscle power alone moves the arms and you can bend through forty-five degrees. NASA astronauts who've tried one of these say it's better than their space suits, and the pressures we work in are a hell of a lot stronger than the vacuum they experience. If you have the time while you're aboard, I'll let you try one on a test dive."

Mercer smiled. "I'd love to take you up on that, but I don't think it'll happen. I expect to be out of here as soon as possible."

C.W.'s normally easygoing expression faded. "What's really going on?" he asked. "Are you allowed to say? Was Spirit right about a government foul-up?"

"No, there isn't any kind of cover-up, though I doubt my word will convince your wife."

The former surfer chuckled. "It took me all of five minutes to learn that if she says the sky is green, I'm better off not debating her."

"You must be a slow learner," Mercer teased, comfortable with C.W.'s mellow demeanor. "I figured that out in five seconds."

"She is something, huh? I met her at a beach party. I had just convinced this other girl to go back to my place when Spirit walked up behind me. She said that I was a sexist pig and that I had no interest in the

other girl beyond her silicone boobs. I turned around
to call her a dyke or something, and man, I just
stopped cold. I think she felt it too. The only other
thing I remember about that night was later, we were
in bed and she said something like 'Better than silicone, aren't they?' "

Mercer smiled at the story, at some level envious
that Charlie had been able to transform lust into love.
He'd felt that momentary jolt of desire many times,
but for one reason or another nothing developed
much past a casual affair. Harry White had once told
him that getting married is equal parts the person and
the timing. One without the other just won't work. Of
course taking marital advice from an eighty-year-old
bachelor wasn't the best idea in the world, but Mercer
couldn't deny the truth in his words.

Many women had come into and out of his life. He
didn't think the problem was with them, so it had to
be the timing. Or with himself.

His atypical train of thought was interrupted by the
approach of Alan, the sub pilot, and Jim McKenzie,
the topside coordinator. Alan tossed a sweatshirt to
Mercer. "It gets cold at a thousand feet and we can't
afford the battery power for a heater."

As Mercer slipped into the garment, the three men
went over their predive checklists and made last-
minute adjustments with a team of hovering technicians. He noticed Spirit standing on the helipad above
the deck. If he wasn't mistaken, she was staring at him
and not her husband. Then their eyes met. Spirit shot
him a contemptuous look and retreated into the superstructure. The intensity of her anger was out of pro-
portion with the delay he was causing her research. It
felt almost personal.

"We're all set," McKenzie announced. "Let's get
you into the can and buttoned up."

Mercer climbed the ladder leaning against *Bob*'s

curved hull and carefully lowered himself through the hatch, mindful of the thick grease smeared around the coaming to help maintain a tight seal. He stepped first on the pilot's seat, then contorted himself all the way in so he slid into one of the cramped observers' positions. In front of him was an array of dials and switches Alan had assured him he needn't worry about. From his seat, the pilot could control everything except the manipulator arms. A moment later, Alan eased into the sub. He donned a headset and began another predive checklist with McKenzie, who'd already moved into the control van with a handful of others. To Mercer it was like listening to the arcane language of a pilot talking to the control tower, just a series of numbers and indecipherable acronyms.

"Okay," he announced. "Everything checks out. We're good to go. We'll launch first and then they'll send down C.W. in the NewtSuit."

"How long's the descent?"

"Shouldn't take more than twenty minutes. It's only a thousand feet. And just so you know, the pressure's something in the neighborhood of five hundred pounds per square inch."

"Remind me not to buy property in that neighborhood."

With a jolt, the A-frame lifted the eleven-ton submersible from its cradle and gently transferred it toward the fantail. Beyond the ship's stern, the sea was calm and a deep blue found only far from shore. The sky was cloudless. *Bob* was slowly lowered into the water. Mercer unconsciously took a deep breath when the first waves lapped against the Lexan bubble.

"Never been down like this before, huh?"

"Is it that obvious?"

"Not really," Alan replied. "Most first-timers are so nervous they don't stop talking. But no matter what, everyone takes a deep breath when the sub starts to sink." The pilot switched on his headset. "Jim, my board is clear, go ahead and release."

There was another jolt as the cables securing *Bob* to the cradle let go and the submersible floated free.

"And down we go," the pilot said.

Negatively buoyant because of the ton of iron plates attached to the underside of her hull, the sub slipped beneath the waves. Mercer craned his head to peer upward as water covered the top of the Lexan bubble. The surface of the ocean reflected a wavering mercury sheen. The surface receded from view as the submersible slipped into the depths. For many minutes there was enough light filtering from above to see the surrounding water. Food scraps dumped from the scullery had attracted schools of scavenger fish and the predators that preyed on them. A few of the braver ones paused long enough to determine if the submersible would be their next meal before disappearing into the thickening gloom.

The water acted as a prism the deeper they dropped, cutting the light's spectrum so that the colors began to separate and fade away. Yellows and oranges vanished first, then reds, until their view was a violet void. And even that faded to blue and finally to black.

"Think we're alone?" Alan asked after ten minutes.

"I would assume so," Mercer said, sensing he was being set up by the experienced pilot.

Alan hit a switch to turn on the working set of lights. The sea came alive. The water was far from clear. It almost looked like a snowstorm outside the sub's protective cocoon. The bodies of tens of millions of tiny creatures slowly drifted toward the abyssal plain where bottom feeders would eventually assimilate them back into the food chain. Fish that had kept their distance from the gawky interloper rushed at the lights. They were still shallow enough for Mercer to recognize the shape of the fish if not the species. The sea's truly bizarre creatures, the vampire squids, the gulpers, the angler fish, and the others, lived far below *Bob*'s crush depth.

"I've logged more than six thousand hours down here," Alan said with a trace of reverence. "I never tire of it." He killed the lights again. "Sorry, got to conserve batteries. I know this won't be a long dive, but it's SOP."

"Thanks for the glimpse. It's a hell of a place you work in."

"Depth is eight fifty," Alan called out, both for Mercer and the men anxiously watching their monitors on the *Surveyor*.

"C.W.'s on his way down," Jim McKenzie announced over the directed laser pulse communication set.

"Roger, Jim. We should be on the bottom in six minutes."

"Confirmed."

Jervis activated the bottom search sonar, a weak acoustical pulse that rang like an accelerating electronic chime the deeper they fell. Mercer's chest tightened in time with the tones. He was getting closer to an answer, he knew, only he wasn't sure what the question had been.

"Bottom in fifty feet," Alan murmured, his fingers flying over control knobs and switches as he began to trim the sub.

"We're showing you one hundred ninety feet due east of the wreck," McKenzie announced over the radio.

A drop of condensation dripped onto Mercer's face. He'd known to expect it—there was a sixty-degree temperature difference between *Bob* and the ocean— yet any water inside the sub with so much pressure against her steel hull made his heart jump.

Alan activated the forward thrusters and kicked on

the lights once again. Had they not been reduced to half capacity, they still couldn't have revealed much beyond twenty feet. The water appeared as dense as ink. Mercer peered into the murk, straining to be the first to spot the wreckage of the USS *Smithback*. The bottom was sandy and showed the undulating ripples of a steady current. It was also entirely featureless. The moon showed more topographic variance.

"There!" Alan said. Experienced in deep dives, he spotted the hulk a minute before Mercer could see the vessel emerge from the darkness.

The wreck of the *Smithback* rose from the seafloor like the ruins of a Moorish fort long abandoned in the Sahara. She'd sunk only days earlier yet looked decades old, forlorn, forgotten, haunted.

"Jesus. Look at her."

The USS *Smithback* had been a military sea-lift vessel, a boxy cargo ship with blunt bows and a square stern. Purchased from the Maersk Line following the Gulf War, the *Smithback*'s job was the rapid delivery of an entire armor task force of up to sixty M1A1 Abrams tanks. At more than six hundred feet long, she'd only needed a crew of forty-eight. Although Mercer and Jervis were limited to half illumination, they could see enough detail to know that whatever happened to the *Smithback* could not be explained away by a collision with a shipping container. Mercer couldn't understand what he was seeing.

The ship's hull and superstructure had been crushed flat by the impact with the seafloor. This phenomenon wasn't unusual. A falling vessel could approach twenty miles per hour by the time it reached the end of its plummet, and structural members weren't designed for that kind of force. Yet the damage to the *Smithback* was much more severe than either Mercer or Jervis anticipated.

It was as if a giant fist had ground the vessel's remains into the seafloor. The bow was buried deeply in the silt and her keel had fractured amidships. It was impossible to tell if she was listing because she had so completely collapsed. From the spec sheets Ira had had delivered to Mercer, he knew the *Smithback* had been ninety feet tall from keel to bridge. The hulk of twisted metal plates resting on the bottom of the Pacific looked no more than a quarter of that. She'd completely pancaked.

The light outside the submersible shifted as C.W. in his diving suit approached the wreck. "What happened to her?" he asked when he saw the extent of the damage.

"We're trying to figure that out," Mercer replied. "Let's start with the bow and work our way back."

"Roger."

The nimble NewtSuit lifted away from the hull and swooped toward the front of the ship. Alan maneuvered *Bob* into place so the combined lights bathed the wreckage in a diffused yellow light. The two sub drivers moved as one as they made their way down the vessel's length. The ship's steel skin had wrinkled like an accordion and crossbeams from within the hull had punched through the metal like fractured bones. When they reached the amidships superstructure, Mercer had Alan take them as close to the ship as he dared. Every one of the six decks in the blocky superstructure had been flattened into the one below. Glass from the wheelhouse had exploded out onto the deck and glittered like gemstones. Near the stern they found where bunker oil leached from the hull in dark bubbles. There were only a couple of spots where air pockets vented into the sea.

"What do you think?" C.W. asked after they finished their inspection.

"If I had to guess," Alan Jervis answered, "I'd say that she was fully laden when she sank and all the air escaped the hull as soon as she went under. That's the only way she could be going fast enough to cause this much damage. What's your take, Mercer?"

"Good theory but there's a problem." Mercer rubbed his jaw as he considered the implication of what he was about to say. "The *Smithback* was dead-heading back from Korea. She was empty. Her cargo decks encompassed more than a hundred thousand cubic feet. Even if her loading ramps had been somehow jarred open, it would take time to expel that much air. I think it was something else."

"Like what?" C.W. asked.

"I don't know, but I hope the answer's over at the tower your guys found. Jim, can you hear me up there?"

"We've been monitoring your comms," McKenzie said from the *Surveyor.*

"We're going to head over to the tower now. Haul in C.W. and we'll meet him there."

"Affirmative. Alan, make your heading two hundred sixty-five degrees. We'll correct your course for the crosscurrent en route."

"I hear you, Jim. Two hundred sixty-five." The pilot lifted the sub away from the wreck of the *Smithback* and killed the lights. The darkness became impenetrable once again as they moved steadily away from the ghostly hulk.

Alan turned on a portable tape player to drown out the incessant buzz of the forward thrusters. An up-tempo jazz song filled the cramped cockpit. "I've dived on about twenty wrecks," he said after a few minutes. "You see that kind of collapse on older ships. After corrosion eats through the steel, they implode. We found a World War One freighter once off the coast of France. She'd fallen apart like that. Nothing more than a sandwich of decks and rust. But I've never seen anything like what happened to the *Smithback.*"

"I can't explain it either."

"But you have an idea?"

"Maybe," was all Mercer said. Without at least a bit of evidence he wasn't about to voice his off-the-wall theory.

Jervis flew the little sub by her sophisticated suite of sensors and didn't seem bothered that he couldn't see more than a half inch outside the Lexan dome. Mercer had become comfortable in the disorienting environment and settled deeper into his seat. The temperature in the cabin was down to fifty-eight degrees and he was thankful for the sweatshirt. He kept his hands clamped between his legs and still they felt frozen. Part of his chill came from what he feared he'd find at the tower.

Forty-five minutes later, Jim McKenzie called a change in course and warned them they were a thousand yards from the tower. The sonar showed the seafloor was three hundred feet below *Bob*'s rounded hull. Jervis nosed the little sub downward as they approached the mysterious structure.

"We'll start at the base," he said, switching on the external lights. "C.W. can't dive this deep, so we're on our own for a while."

"Okay."

The first of the tower's massive legs came into view when they were fifteen feet out. The steel column was at least forty feet in diameter. There didn't appear to be any anchor mechanisms other than the structure's massive weight driving it into the seafloor. Fifty feet up from the bottom, bolted girders extended off the leg and presumably attached to other columns. Angled cross members completed the skeletal design. It was like finding the Eiffel Tower in thirteen hundred feet of water.

They circled the tower as they rose, spiraling upward while keeping the sub scant feet from the structure. When they were two hundred feet from the bottom and still a hundred feet below where C.W. could help them investigate, they found the first propeller. The massive five-bladed affair was stationary, but each vane was wickedly curved for maximum efficiency if it began to rotate. In the wavery light it was difficult to tell what the forty-foot propeller was made of, but it appeared to be some sort of flexible material. The navy used malleable props on its quietest submarines to reduce cavitation noises.

"What do you make of that?" Jervis asked without expecting an answer.

Nestled within the labyrinth of structural steel behind the propeller was a large enclosed capsule at least twice the size of the submersible. Mindful of the thruster nacelles attached to *Bob*, Alan nosed the sub between some of the larger struts to get a closer look at the strange construction. An axle ran from the propeller into the rounded box. From its bottom, several large pipes dropped into the gloom. Mercer and Alan hadn't noticed the pipes on their way up.

"It's like a giant windmill," Mercer said. "Notice how the blades face into the prevailing current. Water passing over the blades makes them turn."

"To do what? Does it pump something out of the ground, like oil?"

"I don't know. Back us out and let's see what's above us."

They found three more of the large propeller and housing assemblies as they ascended. At seven hundred feet below the surface, C.W. waited for them in the bulbous ADS.

"How many of these things are below us?" he asked through the comm link.

"Four."

"And there's two more above us."

"Did you find any kind of storage tanks?" Mercer inquired.

"Just the propellers and their support mechanisms. None of them are turning right now and I think they're all linked by pipes. One thing I did notice is the water's colder around the thinner of the pipes." Thinner was a relative term. The network of plumbing that connected the machines had a minimum diameter of five feet.

"How much colder?"

"Five to seven degrees, according to the suit's sensors."

Mercer felt he was on the trail of that first scrap of evidence he needed. "Can we check temperatures at the base of the tower?" he asked Jervis.

"No problem. Remember, *Bob*'s designed for scientific exploration. I can get temperature, pressure and salinity readings every fifteen seconds."

"C.W., stay here," Mercer ordered, gripped by excitement. He was pretty sure he knew what they'd found. There was a measure of risk staying this close to the tower, but he felt justified. "We're going to need you when we come up. I want to open up one of the propeller's housings to see what's inside."

"I'll work at it while you're down," C.W. said in his surfer drawl.

"No. Wait for us to come back."

"Oh, sure, man," he said, chastened by Mercer's sharp tone.

Alan Jervis eased the sub away from the tower and sent the craft toward the bottom again. "What are you thinking?" he asked after they'd sunk through a thousand feet.

"Turbines can be used for three things," Mercer said. "Pumping something up, injecting something down or generating electricity. There aren't any transmission lines so this rig isn't producing power. We didn't find any reservoirs to hold something being pumped from the seafloor. That leaves us something being pumped down into the ground."

"Makes sense, but wouldn't there be reservoirs of whatever was being injected?"

"Not if it were seawater. Or if the system was a closed loop."

"Which one do you think it is?"

"In a sense, both."

"You gonna explain that?"

"Ever wonder how they keep hockey rinks frozen?"

Jervis chuckled. "I grew up in Arizona. Hockey wasn't much of a priority."

"The Coyotes play in Phoenix," Mercer pointed out. "It's done by pumping salty water—brine—through a system of tubes under the ice. Because of the salt, the brine remains liquid below thirty-two degrees. The supercold pipes keep the ice frozen and voilà, slap shots in the desert."

"Hold on," Jervis interrupted, "we're coming up on the bottom. The water temperature's dropping faster than it should. It's down four degrees in just fifteen feet."

The lattice of struts and supports near the tower's base wouldn't allow them to get close to the pipes coming down from the turbine housings. Instead Mercer had Jervis circle the structure in ever-widening loops. Revealed under the lights, the bottom appeared featureless. The silt had a green cast in the artificial glow, and the blizzard of drifting organic material made it impossible to see more than a few feet. Still, Alan maneuvered the sub like an expert, keeping her nose scant feet above the abyssal plain.

"What's that?" he asked after a few moments. "A crater?"

"Not sure," Mercer said, but he was.

It took several minutes to cross over the crater from rim to rim. The bottom-profiling sonar showed it was a hundred feet deep. Mercer did the figures in his head. The crater had a volume of almost half a million cubic feet. He asked the pilot to hover at the edge of the large pit.

"What are we looking for?"

"Just hold it steady." Mercer took hold of the manipulator controls.

"Hey, you can't do that!" Jervis protested as the arms unfolded from their stowed position.

Mercer flexed them out straight, testing how his movements on the joysticks affected the joints and grapplers. "I'll pay for any damage."

In seconds he had the system figured. Like the controls for C.W.'s diving suit, *Bob*'s manipulator arms felt familiar because of his years working with mining equipment. Mercer returned one of the arms to its default attitude and moved the other closer to the crater's rim.

"What's going on down there?" McKenzie called over the comm.

"I want a soil sample," Mercer said.

He eased the grapple hand into the ooze, causing a small avalanche of mud to slide below the submersible. Although there was no feedback resistance on the joysticks, Mercer could tell the arm hit something solid. A silvery bubble burst from the mud, and in the cavity he'd excavated he could see a strange white mass.

"What is that?" Jervis asked.

"Ice."

"What? That's impossible."

Mercer turned to look at the pilot. "And yet there it is. The rig is a giant heat pump."

"What for? This thing doesn't make any sense."

"Hey, guys," C.W. called from above, his voice metallic from the echo within his suit. "Something's happening up here. The blades are starting to turn. Wow."

"What is it?" Alan asked quickly.

"Current can't be more than a knot or two, but this thing's spinning like it's in a freaking hurricane."

It took Mercer a second too long to digest what

C.W. had just said. He'd been looking at the tower one way, ignoring the implications of another point of view. As he realized his mistake, his eyes widened, and yet when he spoke his voice carried a steel edge. "C.W., secure yourself to something. Grab on to the tower. Jim, can you hear me up there?"

"I'm here, Mercer, what's going on?"

"We're sitting on top of a methane hydrate deposit. That's what sank the *Smithback*. You guys have got to get out of there."

"What are you talking about?"

"Methane hydrate. The last great source of fossil fuel on the planet. It's a gas kept locked in ice by the temperature and pressure on the seafloor. It's normally stable, but I think this tower's designed to cause the hydrates to melt. The gas is about one hundred fifty times the volume of its solid state. If the deposit is big enough, that much methane is going to cause the ocean to bubble up like champagne. If it's bad enough, it will reduce the water density and the *Surveyor*'s going to lose buoyancy. She'll sink like a stone."

"Is it erupting now?" McKenzie asked, understanding the danger.

"It's going to." Mercer's first assumption about the tower being a heat pump had been correct. Only now he realized it wasn't forcing cold brine into the soil to keep the hydrate stable, it was designed to draw it up in order to dissipate the chill in the warmer shallower water and trigger a gas burst.

The *Smithback* must have sailed through an eruption and struck an enormous chunk of hydrate ice that hadn't dissolved on its journey to the surface. But that damage hadn't caused her to sink. It was the change in water density. Ships stay afloat because they weigh less than the volume of water their hulls displace. In the case of the *Smithback*, the frothing mix of gas and water wasn't dense enough or didn't weigh enough to support the vessel's mass. She began to weigh more than the water she displaced and lost buoyancy. At some critical point she would have dropped from the surface so suddenly that no one could have saved themselves. The *Smithback* would have careened toward the seafloor much faster than normal. The ship could have been doing fifty or more miles per hour when she hit bottom. No wonder there wasn't much air escaping the hulk. It had blown from her when she impacted.

And the fire reported just before she sank? Methane hydrate, even in its ice form, was extremely flammable. The air around the ship would have been saturated with gas, and even the smallest spark would have set off a catastrophic explosion. Mercer purged the horrifying image from his mind, that of a vessel engulfed in flames while her crew vainly tried to understand why the small amount of damage from the impact was causing their ship to sink. He refocused his mind on his own impending predicament.

Over the comm link, Mercer could hear hurried orders being shouted in the topside control van. "We have to haul C.W. back aboard," McKenzie protested.

"I don't think you have time."

Mercer pointed to where he wanted Jervis to guide the sub, away from where he suspected the next gas eruption would take place. On a CRT screen, the bottom-profiling sonar had drawn a digital picture of the surrounding seafloor, and it looked as though the tower had been erected in the middle of a series of hills. One of the hills had already vanished in a gas explosion, leaving the deep crater in its wake.

"C.W., what's your status?" McKenzie asked.

"Stand by," the young Californian called back. "Ah, I think I'm okay. I can do an emergency cut on my tether as long as Alan knows to come pick me up."

"Temperature's up three degrees," Jervis warned.

Mercer keyed his mike. "C.W., when this deposit erupts, you're going to be right above it. Are you sure you can hold on?"

"Yeah, I've locked the arms around a strut. I'm not going anywhere."

Outside *Bob*'s cocoon of steel and composite materials, the water began to vibrate, and what little visibility they had vanished in a storm of fine silt. At first there was no sound, but quickly a bass tone built into a steady roar.

"Temp's up another three."

"Stay up-current of the tower and bring us to seven hundred feet," Mercer ordered, banking that the plume of gas about to explode from the seafloor would drift away from them.

"Affirmative."

With a suddenness no one expected, the ocean bottom vanished in a billowing smog that grew like the mushroom cloud of a nuclear detonation. The methane hydrate deposit, a massive pocket of frozen hydrocarbons, vaporized in a swelling cascade as warm water pumped from the top of the tower raised it to its boiling point. The leading edge of the gas raced for the surface, spinning in a maddened burst of energy like a giant tornado.

The sub was caught at the outer limit of the diffused eruption. Jervis had dumped ballast for the ascent and had the thrusters tilted down to help propel the craft toward the surface. Her rate of climb dropped once the frothy water engulfed the little sub.

"Damn," Alan spat and increased thrust, mindful of the electrical charge remaining in the batteries.

"C.W., you've got to cut your tether," Mercer shouted. "Jim, the deposit's erupting. Get the *Surveyor* away as fast as you can. Head west against the current, otherwise you'll be engulfed like the *Smithback*. Alan and I are trying to get into position if C.W. gets into trouble."

"Once I'm off the tether, I lose communications."

"I understand," Mercer said. "We're pushing *Bob* to reach your depth." Outside the sub's dome, the water surged and fizzed as though boiling.

"Rate of ascent down to fifty feet a minute and slowing," Alan said.

"Can you dump more ballast?" asked Mercer, hating that for the duration of the dive he was nothing more than a passenger.

"Not if we want to hover at seven hundred to help C.W."

"What about getting us farther from the main part of the gas plume?"

"If I change the vector on the thrusters, we'll probably start falling. I'm afraid we'll have to wait it out. Shit, we're at neutral buoyancy."

As hellish as the view from the sub was, what C.W. saw from inside the ADS was worse. The sub had been caught at the periphery of the eruption. He was right in the middle of it. So much methane had been released that at times he was engulfed in enormous sacs of the deadly gas. Stranded inside the bubbles, he could see water sluicing from his helmet like rain from a windshield. Then the bubble would pass and he'd be slammed again by the tremendous pressure of the sea. Several times he lost his footing and the suit's metal claws that were his hands scraped against the tower strut.

At the surface, the scene was no better. McKenzie had relayed Mercer's orders to the bridge with no time to spare. The helmsman had slammed the throttle handles to full ahead and twisted the ship with her dynamic positioning thrusters so she was pointed to the west, upstream from the tower. No sooner had she begun to move than the first hint of the gas reached the surface. It was just a mild disturbance of dirty water, a localized phenomenon that would have been overlooked as a downburst of wind disturbing the sea.

But then more and more methane broached. Seething geysers of water shot thirty, forty, fifty feet in the air. It was as though the sea was dissolving. A dive buoy that hadn't been retrieved during the emergency maneuver sank away as the water lost density. The *Surveyor* became sluggish. Gas pockets were displacing the seawater she needed to remain afloat. She squatted low, with swells running just a few feet from her gleaming rails. More and more gas appeared. And then the steady eastward current began to carry it away. The ship found clean water and floated higher, the red stripe of her Plimsoll line clearly showing along her flanks.

Mercer's quick warning had saved them from the same fate as the USS *Smithback*. For he and Alan, the dice were still rolling. And the plucky little submersible was falling deeper into the abyss.

The SoHo loft was on an upper story that allowed golden light to stream through the tall, arched, cast iron framed windows. The bright rays made the wooden floor look aflame. The walls were exposed brick and the furniture was kept to a minimum—a futon couch, a low table, several large pillows strewn haphazardly about. The loft was one large room. The bathroom, with its stand-up shower, was screened by swatches of fabric hanging from the high ceiling. The kitchen was little more than a nook smaller than the galley on a modest sailboat.

The figure posing in the middle of the room was covered in sweat. The thermostat was at maximum. She stood on a thin mat, her back arched until her fingertips brushed the floor behind her. She was completely nude, and her small breasts shifted as she stretched. She bent farther and could press her knuckles to the mat. She flexed the supple muscles in one leg and slowly raised it, shifting her weight to her hands. She balanced on her fingers, her body completely still, not a tremor or any other outward sign of exertion. After holding there for several seconds, she continued to slowly ease her leg around until it slid between her arms and she settled on the mat in a gymnast's split. She bent forward, resting her head on her slick thigh.

Her next move was to scissor her legs together, arch

herself once again and slowly somersault back to her feet, her cheek pressed to her knees. She'd been practicing for an hour, yet her sweat smelled clean and sweet.

She dropped back to a split, rotated her leg around so both were in front of her, then lifted her backside from the floor with her knuckles. When she had enough clearance, she tucked her legs against her chest and used the flat muscles of her stomach to rotate around her arms and press herself into another handstand. And then she scissored her legs in a violent maneuver at the same time she allowed her pose to collapse. She landed flat on the floor, both heels touching the back of her head, her body as taut as a finely drawn bow.

"I would almost think you were doing this for my benefit, Tisa."

She dropped with a start and quickly reached for the silk robe thrown over the futon. She hadn't heard him enter the apartment. She recognized the voice immediately, the softly affectionate tone. Her cheeks burned with shame. She stood facing away from him and pulled the robe tighter around her body She slipped her glasses from the pocket before turning to him. The man at the door was three years older than she but looked like her twin. Yet where her mouth was sensual, his looked petulant. Her wide eyes were inviting; on him they held an insolent cast. Where she was demure, he looked emboldened and arrogant. She would have preferred being spied on by a stranger rather than her half brother, Luc.

"I remember watching you practice when you were a child. The things you could make your little body do."

The way he spoke made Tisa's flesh crawl. His voice lacked the fraternal pride of an older brother. Instead it was tainted with the wistful lament of a former lover. In his eyes she saw he wasn't remembering her hours of yoga and contortion practice. Another memory lurked there, one that he brought up with disturbing frequency. Despite herself, her glance drifted down. His black slacks were made of thin material and did nothing to hide his arousal. He must have been watching her for some time.

When her eyes returned to his face, his smile was lupine. He took a cautious step toward her. "You think about it too, don't you?"

Tisa shuddered with disgust but refused to step back. "We were children, Luc."

"I knew what I was doing," he said tenderly. "I was fifteen. I compare every woman I've been with since to you. Just that one time together has spoiled them all for me."

They were living in Paris with her mother when it happened. Tisa's father hadn't protested the end of his second marriage or that she was taking their daughter and his teenage son. He had become obsessed with his work and wouldn't see his family for months at a time, even though they lived in the same isolated village in the Himalayas. Tisa's mother had come to the village of Rinpoche-La, Jewel Pass, from France, where she'd been recruited into the Order as a young woman. Though ostracized in Tibet for abandoning her husband, whom many saw as divine, she had enough family and friends in Paris to help support her return. They had settled in an airy apartment above a yoga studio on the Left Bank. The owner knew of Tisa and Luc's father and refused to accept payment for the apartment.

Tisa had always known of her father's importance in their village and in the ancient monastery that dominated the head of the isolated valley, but the landlord's donation had been the first time she knew of his influence so far from home. And it was her first taste of the scope of the organization she had been born to.

Looking back, Tisa realized her older brother had had a better understanding of the Order. He had quickly adjusted to their life in France, enjoying the entree his father's name gave within certain circles. In just a year he'd learned colloquial French, and begun to avail himself to some of the younger female disciples who'd taken to using the yoga studio as a meeting place. Although Luc had yet to be schooled in the full scope and intent of the Order, he knew enough to impress the naïve.

Tisa had been home alone one afternoon following school. Her mother was working as a translator at the time. Her children had inherited their ear for language from her. Tisa spoke three languages by then, Luc five and their mother seven. She'd been in her bedroom. It was summer and there was no breeze. In the sweltering heat, she wore panties and an overly large T-shirt emblazoned with the image of the latest teen pop sensation.

Luc came into the room and silently draped a damp towel across the back of Tisa's legs as she lay on the bed doing her homework. Startled at first, she allowed him to remain, grateful for the towel's cooling effect. This had been a week of record heat in the city, the highest temperatures either had ever experienced. His hand rested on her hip.

At first they talked about nothing in particular, but soon they returned to the topic that had fascinated them since her mother had taken them away: their father. They had spent hours speculating about the real nature of his work. They suspected he was some kind of freedom fighter who had come from Vietnam to Tibet to liberate the people from the Chinese. To spice their hypothesis were rumors about mystical powers he controlled. Neither knew where the tales had come from, but there had always been whispers about the things he could do.

So on that boiling afternoon, they talked again, embellishing stories they'd told each other a hundred times before, both secretly thrilled to be part of the legend they'd built around their father. After all, they were part of whatever destiny awaited him. Luc spoke about how they were different from the fringe members of the Order who gathered at the studio, and how everyone could sense it. People who visited often talked about how special they were. He asked if Tisa could sense it too. Ever since arriving in France she *had* felt people treated her with deference and respect she hadn't earned but had rather been born to. She and Luc were set apart from the rest, placed higher in a hierarchy no one really understood. His hand moved farther up her hip, almost to her buttocks.

They'd shared so much together, he'd said, recalling the one night they'd sneaked into the huge monastery rising from the cliffs above the ancient Tibetan town. There they'd seen the vault of old books with their embossed wax seals and overheard two monks talking about something they called the Navel of the World. He talked about how they'd swum as kids in the hot springs below the village, enveloped in fragrant steam with snowcapped mountains looming over them like gods. He reminded her how they'd named the mountains for animals. And he reminded her about the time she had come into his bed one night when a freak storm had settled in their secluded valley and thunder echoed so loudly she was sure the mountains were going to explode. He'd held her for hours, he said, drying her tears with the hem of his nightshirt.

He said he'd always been there for her, no matter what. Hadn't he made their move to France so much easier? His fingers were kneading her flesh by now. Tisa had remained still during the entire talk, aware of his hand, but so lonely for their village that his touch was a reminder of home. He seemed to know what she was thinking. He bent close. "I miss it too," he whispered in her ear, and allowed his mouth to linger near her neck.

The rest of the memory had been expunged from Tisa's mind. It had taken years, but she truly didn't remember how far they had gone that sultry afternoon. That deep and dangerous form of denial was the only way she saw she could get around the shame without telling anyone. And that was something she wouldn't, couldn't, do.

"What are you doing here, Luc?" Tisa stepped away from him.

His smile faded. "I should ask you the same question."

"I've got every right to use this apartment. It belongs to the Order."

"I'm not talking about the apartment. I'm talking about why you're even in the United States. I thought you were home."

"I haven't been there in months." Tisa moved behind the bathroom screen to slide into a pair of baggy sweatpants. She left the robe around her torso because the only top she had handy was a sports bra.

"In New York the whole time?" Luc asked. It sounded like he'd moved into the kitchen.

"I came through Los Angeles. I met with some of our people there to talk about the San Bernardino earthquake."

"That quake was months ago. What more could you possibly have to talk about?"

Tisa stepped out of the bathroom. Her body felt sticky with sweat and her muscles protested because she hadn't had a proper cooldown. "I wanted the revised fault slippage numbers. Our estimates were off by almost a meter, and if you paid attention to our real mission you'd know that the oracle's time retrogression has grown another eleven minutes across all of North America."

Luc acted as if he hadn't heard her. "And you came straight here? Didn't stop along the way?" He was roaming around the apartment like a caged animal, a sleek predatory cat. He moved lightly, possessing the effortlessness of a dancer.

Tisa tugged at her robe. He knew. "No, I came right here. I'm going to Greece in a couple of days and wanted to wait in New York rather than L.A."

"Because I was in Las Vegas with some of our people and someone swears they saw you at the wheel of a BMW with Philip Mercer."

"How could I do that?" she protested too quickly. "I've never even met him."

Luc laughed, all pretense of civility gone. "I think you have met him. I think you followed me to Las Vegas and helped him escape. I think if I could prove it, I'd have you killed for interference."

"Interference?" Tisa shot back, ignoring his empty threat. "Interference with what? You weren't authorized to go to Las Vegas in the first place."

"I don't need authorization."

"When you wear the Lama's blue robe, you can make decisions, Luc. Until then you are under his authority."

He threw himself onto the futon. "Screw the Lama. I don't need him anymore. None of us do. Watchers stuck on the sidelines. That's all he wants us to be. We should help shape the world. *That* is our true destiny."

"We are watchers. That is what we've been for a hundred and fifty years. Even you must see the consequences if we change our role."

"And you didn't try to change your passive role when you contacted Mercer in Las Vegas?"

"What were you doing there?" Tisa dodged.

"Investigating a seismic disturbance," he said smugly. "Same as you do all the time."

To confront her brother further, Tisa would be forced to admit her efforts at the Luxor Hotel. "You weren't supposed to be there," she said lamely. "We have chroniclers in California that could have gone to the epicenter."

"The epicenter was in the middle of a secure government facility, dear girl. They wouldn't have gotten close. This is one I had to do."

"Don't flatter yourself. And I'm not your 'dear girl.' "

"You were once."

"Stop it," she spat. Her hair was plastered to her head and her temperature was rising. She felt uncomfortable in her own skin. She wiped moisture from her glasses. "Tell me why you're here."

He stood, his tone turning sharp, his volatile temper showing through. "To give you a warning. You just reminded me about noninterference. I think you'd better take your own advice. I know it was you at the hotel. You had better not try to warn Mercer about what is going to happen. Not that there is anything he can do to stop it, but we've survived for a century and a half by not telling the world what we know. You don't have the right to do it now."

"And you have a right to try to kill him?" she shot back. Then softly, trying to calm him, she said, "That's not in our power." Her words only enraged him further.

"It will be!" He was screaming now, almost out of control. "That's what you and the rest never understood. We've watched the planet tear itself apart when we could have stepped in and prevented it. We have the power of life and death over billions of people, only we've been too timid to use it. No more. Very soon the world will know what we know, and they will

give us whatever we want to protect them. Millions are going to die, but afterward we will reveal the truth and how the survivors can be saved. Don't you understand? We will be the prophets of a new religion. We will be worshipped."

"Then we should tell them now," Tisa pleaded. "You want to be worshipped? Help me tell the world what's coming. We can prove it to them before so many die needlessly. You will be given all the power you want."

Luc dropped his head, his body rigid. Tisa could sense his indecision. He wasn't an evil person. He was simply torn between what they'd been taught and what they knew was right. He didn't want those people to die, but he needed a grand gesture so those left behind would believe him. He was acting out of fear that if there wasn't a significant demonstration he'd be ridiculed. It was the same reason she wanted Mercer with her on Santorini—so he could witness what she'd known for years.

"We can do it," she cajoled. "There are other ways, other scientists we can approach. We can show them our evidence, the chronicles. We can save millions of innocent people." She swallowed her revulsion. "You and I together, Luc, just like you've always wanted."

He looked up. She'd gone too far. She was trying to use his unnatural attraction to seduce his emotions and it had backfired.

His eyes burned. "Bitch."

"No, Luc, just your little sister."

This time he turned away. "It should have been, Tisa, but it's too late. I came to tell you to drop it. Don't contact Mercer again. I'm letting you live because I love you. I mean I really love you."

"If you loved me, you'd stop this."

"I can't. This is my destiny. I know that now. I alone understand the necessity of sacrifice. It's been my entire life."

"It's been *our* life. Don't you see that? We are in this together. We always have been." She was desperate, willing to try any lie to get her brother to stop.

He moved to the door. "I gave you a chance to be together. You rejected it. Now I give you a warning. Don't ignore it. I will crush you and anyone you ask for help." He paused. "When it is over, I will try to find you."

She held his gaze so he'd know she wasn't bluffing. "If it really does happen, Luc, I'll make sure I don't survive. There's no place for me in the world you want to create."

"That's what it is, isn't it? Creation."

He closed the door. Tisa collapsed onto her yoga mat. Creation, he called it. The single greatest calamity in human history and he saw it as an act of birth. She'd known for years her brother was unstable, but now she saw he was dangerously psychotic. She thought he wasn't evil, but she was wrong. He was and she could only pray she could stop him in time.

She slumped, burying her face in her hands.

Outside the apartment building, Donny Randall stood like a rock in the river of people negotiating the narrow sidewalk. With his thick arms crossed over his chest, he forced pedestrians to either skirt next to the building or step into the street, where traffic crawled bumper to bumper. He seemed to be enjoying the glares he received, but was disappointed no one tried to confront him. Luc walked past him without acknowledging the giant. Donny fell in step.

"What happened?" Randall asked after half a block.

"It was her, all right. I was upstairs when that car rescued Mercer at the Luxor. I never saw the driver, but Pran was certain it was her. I'm sure now too."

"Then we should go back and take care of her. Uh, unless you already did?"

"Shut up, you moron," Luc snapped. "She's not to be touched."

Donny bristled. Luc Nguyen was paying him more than he'd ever made working as a miner, but he didn't like the little half-breed and wasn't going to take his crap. "Watch who you're calling a moron. One phone call and I can blow your entire operation."

Luc didn't change his gait, didn't seem to do anything other than walk, but suddenly Donny was sprawled on the sidewalk, the impact with the cement absorbed by a suitcase set on legs where a grifter sold counterfeit Rolexes. The watches flew in one direction while the young Ethiopian immigrant went in the other.

Luc paused to help the big man regain his feet. "Sorry about that, Don. That was uncalled for on my part. I wasn't thinking."

Donny massaged the spot where his hip had hit the sidewalk, impressed rather than angry. "How did you . . . ? Never mind. Some of that kung fu stuff, huh?"

"Something like that, though it predates most martial arts by centuries. My father taught it to me when I was a boy."

They began to walk again. "Ah, listen," Donny said, now trying to impress his new employer with his towering intellect. "You know your sister can still be a problem. We don't have to kill her or nothing, but maybe we should be careful about her."

"Don't worry. I know where she's going. And I think I know who she's meeting." He liked the symmetry of being able to kill Mercer at the same time he took Tisa home to wait out the coming chaos.

What would come afterward sent a shiver through his body. In the world that followed, Tisa would soon recognize the need for the sacrifice about to occur and why he'd let it happen. She would then see his greatness as he worked to save the rest of humanity from the very planet they called home. She would slowly come to worship him. And then they would be together in the way he'd wanted since childhood.

The eruption of methane hydrate gas continued into its tenth minute. Despite Alan Jervis's expertise and coaxing, *Bob* still remained negatively buoyant and sank ever deeper. Even out of the direct path of the gas plume, the water barely maintained enough density to keep the submersible from plummeting like a stone.

"We have to drop the rest of the ballast," the pilot said grimly. Once they did, there would be no reserves. It was a make-or-break maneuver, and if C.W. got into trouble, they wouldn't be able to come to his aid.

"What's our rate of descent?"

"Almost a hundred feet a minute and accelerating."

"And our distance to the bottom?"

"Two hundred eighty feet."

"Can we survive the impact?"

"I don't know. It depends on bottom consistency. If we hit rock, we're finished. If we hit silt, maybe we'd be okay, but there's a chance we might get stuck."

"It's your call," Mercer said. "You know your boat, but if you dump the last iron plates, C.W. is as good as dead."

Jervis was quiet for a moment, watching his dials. "Rate's slowing. Eighty feet a minute. Damn. Okay, we'll ride it out."

"Provided we survive the impact, what's the best attitude to prevent us from getting stuck?"

"Optimist?"

Mercer smiled around his anxiety. "Always."

"Landing on our belly is standard procedure, but I've had a theory that if we hit on the bow at an angle, the sub would tip slowly and wrench the nose out of the mud. 'Course, if there's something on the bottom, a boulder, for example, we'd crack the dome."

"We'd never know until it was too late so let's give it a try. I'll extend the manipulator arms to cushion the blow."

"Blow? Why didn't I think of that? Mercer, you're a genius. There are lifting bags kept in a storage tray under the manipulators. They're filled by releasing high-pressure CO_2 from a cylinder. We use them to haul artifacts and samples to the surface while we remain below. They're not large enough to provide any buoyancy for us and they won't inflate even halfway at this depth, but they will act like air bags to protect the bubble."

"Tell me what to do."

Jervis talked Mercer through the necessary steps. Mercer's hands were sure on the manipulator controls—tension made him forget all about the chill in the little sub. He tried not to think about the pressure either—not the psychological stress, but the tons of water pressing against the craft's steel shell. At sea level there were fourteen pounds per square inch. That doubled at thirty-three feet, tripled at sixty-six. Quadrupled at . . . He forced himself not to run the numbers in his head.

"Six hundred fifty psi," he muttered without realizing he'd done the calculations.

He'd swiveled an exterior closed-circuit video camera so he could see the equipment tray under the sub's nose and eased one of the pincers into position to grab a deflated lift bag. It came out smoothly. The yellow balloon was neatly folded into a tight bundle. Attached to it were large clips for securing it to mesh baskets also stored in the tray. The gas cylinder was a foot long and had a lanyard that could be easily grasped with the other manipulator.

"What's our depth?" he asked.

"Don't worry," Alan replied. "You've got time. Nice and steady now. I'm about to put us on our nose."

He used attitude thrusters to raise the stern. Mercer was forced to brace his knees against a console to keep from sliding out of his seat.

"Okay, pull the cord."

Because of the gas still boiling out of the earth, the lanyard flapped like a pennant in a high wind. Mercer missed grabbing it with the left set of pincers on his first two tries and finally got it on the third. Next, he gently pulled the cord. They couldn't hear the gas release into the balloon, but they saw it begin to expand, swelling slowly as the CO_2 pushed against the crushing pressure of water. After a moment, it had filled as far as it would, about a quarter of its six-foot diameter. They wouldn't know if it offered enough protection until the sub hit the bottom.

"Forty feet. Our descent's still slowing."

Mercer maneuvered the arm so the half-inflated bag was in front of the Lexan view port. It blocked most of his view, which in a way wasn't a bad thing.

"Twenty feet." The roar of erupting methane hydrate faded as the pocket of gas was depleted.

"Ten feet."

Mercer willed his body to go slack. Either they would survive the impact or they'd be crushed instantly. He thought about the wall of water that had chased him through the DS-Two mine shaft. If the Lexan shattered, at least this time he'd never see it coming.

"Two feet."

At the last second, a corner of the lifting bag folded on itself. Through the turbid silt Mercer saw the bottom was flat and blessedly free of rock. The sub hit. A cloud of mud billowed from the seafloor, enveloping the small craft. *Bob* shuddered at the impact. A clipboard and a thermos clattered past Mercer and fell to the Lexan bubble. The sub continued to settle, but her stern refused to drop from its near vertical position.

"Come on, *Bob*," Alan whispered. "Fall, damn you, fall."

Her nose appeared buried. The impact had driven her too deep into the mud for her to right herself. Alan fought with the thrusters trying to get *Bob* to move, but nothing worked. He even dumped the last ballast plate, but at their angle, the chuck of pig iron wouldn't slip free. They'd gambled and lost, and rather than the quick death of an implosion, they were now trapped fifteen hundred feet from the surface facing the long agony of asphyxiation.

Jervis began to hyperventilate. "What are we going to do?"

"Stay calm," Mercer said. "I've got an idea."

"I know what you're thinking. Forget it," Alan panted. "The manipulators aren't strong enough to lift the sub clear. They won't even move."

Mercer ignored the dire prediction and tried anyway. But Jervis was right. Neither of the two manipulator arms would budge, trapped as they were between the bottom and the sub. He had only a little movement on the wrist actuator on the arm holding the lifting bag.

With the submersible pointed straight at the bottom, Mercer couldn't even lean back in his chair to rethink the situation. Above him in the pilot's seat, Alan used the thrusters to try to rock the sub free, slamming the lateral controls from lock to lock. His efforts did nothing but drain their precious battery reserves. After three fruitless minutes he gave up and shut down everything but the atmosphere scrubbers. He punched a console several times and kicked at another before jamming his knees against the back of Mercer's seat and sitting quietly. Mercer was thankful for the silence.

All but a tiny crescent wedge at the top of the Lexan dome was buried in silt, affording a narrow view of the black ocean beyond. Closer in, Mercer could see the half-inflated lifting bag wedged between *Bob* and the seafloor and the mechanical pincer still holding it tight. To the right of the bow, a single exterior lamp cast a sullen glow through the mud, like a flashlight through thick burlap. And then it faded as its circuit closed and the darkness became complete. A drop of condensation fell from the back of the sub and hit Mercer's ear. His heart tripped.

A few minutes later Alan asked, "Do you have a family?"

"No," Mercer said, knowing where this conversation was heading and not wanting any part of it.

"I've got two kids. They live with their mother. She left about six years ago. Said she couldn't stand me being away so much. She married her divorce lawyer about a year after she left me." He chuckled without humor. "I found out later they'd been together since before we split. But my kids are something else. Two girls. Twelve and eight. Karen is the captain of her soccer team and Ashley's learning to play the violin. She can—"

Mercer cut him off. "Alan, stop it. I know what you're doing and this isn't the time. We're not dead yet."

"What's the difference? Now or hours from now when the air becomes unbreathable, we're just as dead. And if you don't want to hear me talk about my kids, well, tough shit. I was about to say that Ashley can already play 'Twinkle Twinkle, Little Star.' "

"If you'll stop talking and give me a second I think I might have an idea."

"What?"

"I said I think I have an idea of how to get us out of here. Can you turn on that outside light again."

"Okay. Give me a second." Jervis powered up the sub's systems again. Consoles and display panels came alive. A moment later, Mercer saw the umber light diffused through the silt.

"It's like I remember. The air bag is trapped between us and the seafloor. It's only half inflated, but if I release what little air's in it, we should have a moment when the sub is unstable again."

"What do you need me to do?" Alan's professional tone had returned.

"The bag is sitting left of center. When I cut it I want you to hit the right-hand thrusters with everything they've got. With any luck, *Bob* will tip to the right enough to free us."

"Tell me when."

Mercer used the manipulator controls to open the pincer. Pressure forced the bag to shift and slide between the steel fingers. "Okay. Hit it."

The thrusters wound up to their maximum setting. The hull vibrated but remained stuck in the ooze. Mercer jammed the pincer closed. The serrated edges clamped tight onto the bag and he managed to twist the wrist a few degrees. The teeth bit into the rubber, tearing at it until the bag split. The gust of CO_2 spewed from the cut like champagne from a shaken bottle. The sub pitched slightly, just enough to break the vacuum seal it had formed with the silt. Slowly, slowly, the bow began to slide free of the mud as the stern dropped to the right. Silt oozed across the Lexan dome to settle once again on the seafloor.

"Holy shit. You did it."

"Resecure that ballast plate or we won't be able to help C.W.," Mercer warned.

"Done." Alan clamped the heavy plate in position and spooled up other thrusters to back the sub from the bottom. In seconds he had her righted and hovering five feet from the bottom, a few yards from the cloud of silt drifting slowly on the current. Smears of mud dribbled from the hull.

"That was the closest I've ever been," Jervis said after a minute. "I've never had a problem on a dive, never even been in a car accident. Jesus. How did you stay so . . . ? I mean, you've never been down before and I was about to piss my pants."

Mercer smiled over his shoulder. "Don't sweat it. If that trick didn't work I'd have joined you on the panic parade. Now, let's go see if C.W. needs help."

"Right."

The gas explosion had all but ended; only a few desultory bubbles drifted toward the surface, silvery balls that looked like enormous jellyfish in the weak light thrown from the sub. They backtracked to the tower and made a sweeping circle around the structure. Mercer didn't ask why Alan performed the maneuver. He knew the pilot was searching for the crushed remains of C.W.'s NewtSuit. Heartened they found nothing, they slowly began their ascent, keeping to the western side of the structure, where they'd left the diver clinging precariously to a stanchion.

And that's where they found him, only he was past precarious. During the eruption he must have lost his footing. He'd fallen only a few feet before banging into the tower and wedging an arm where two crossbeams joined. He hung there in a near horizontal position, like a flag in a stiff breeze.

C.W. had been forced to cut his cables to get free of the *Surveyor* so there was no way to communicate, but he must have seen the sub's lights because he began to bicycle his legs.

"What's your status down there?" The call came over the comm gear from the surface. It was Jim Mc-Kenzie. He'd been out of range when the *Surveyor* made her desperate race to avoid the eruption, but now he'd brought the ship back into position.

"Glad to hear your voice, Jim," Alan breathed.

"It was a close thing. I didn't think this old girl could move that fast. How are you guys?"

"Other than the bit of paint we scraped off *Bob*'s nose, we're okay. We're at the tower with C.W. His arm is wedged." Jervis swung the sub next to the diver as he spoke.

"Can you get him out?"

"We're working on it. What do you think, Mercer? Any more brilliant ideas?"

"Sorry, one per day's my limit. Are the manipulators strong enough to pull him free?"

"I doubt it. They're built for delicacy, not strength."

"All right. Then we'll have Jim send down the lifting cable and a welding rig and we'll put Humpty-Dumpty back together again."

"Pretty tricky job. Want me to handle it?"

Mercer shrugged. "I'd love for you to, only I can't fly this oversized septic tank. And you need to keep it steady against the current."

Alan switched on his microphone. "Jim, we've got a plan. Can you send down C.W.'s cable and some welding gear?"

"I think I know what you have in mind. Give us ten minutes."

They had the cable down to the sub in eight. Alan talked Mercer through the procedure and an hour later the cable was securely welded to the back of the NewtSuit. The trickiest part of the operation was directing the topside winch engineer. One false move, or an ocean swell hitting at the wrong time, could tear the arm from the suit, killing the diver inside. After several tense minutes, the suit came free and C.W. dangled at the end of the cable like a fish. They began to reel him in. Alan took up a position directly below C.W. as he was hauled to the surface in case the weld failed and the suit dropped free.

Nearing the surface, the sub peeled away, as Jim McKenzie had ordered several boats into the water to secure the Advanced Diving Suit. It took a further half hour for scuba divers to sling a net under the suit so C.W. could be safely hauled onto the *Sea Surveyor*. And only then did they lift the submersible from the sea.

When the hatch swung open and Mercer took his first breath of clean air in more than five hours, he realized how foul the atmosphere in the sub had become. The bright sunlight was painful to his eyes, but he turned his face toward it as if waiting for a long kiss.

Technicians had gotten the back of C.W.'s suit opened by the time he joined them. The lanky Californian eased himself from the armored rig. No one commented on the smell of urine. Spirit Williams pushed through the crowd, shouldering aside workers like a halfback, and crashed into her husband, almost knocking them both to the deck. She was laughing and crying at the same time and smothered his mouth with hers. The assembled men roared their approval.

With his wife clinging to his arm, C.W. shook first Alan's and then Mercer's hand. "Man, that was something, you two. I thought I was a goner when a gas burst knocked me off the tower. Then I got stuck, but the methane was blowing by so fast I was sure it'd knock me off again. When the gas finally stopped I thought you'd be right there, only you weren't. Dude, it's a good thing I lost communications 'cause I was cursing you something fierce."

"We ran into a little difficulty of our own," Alan deadpanned.

"It felt like an hour later when I saw *Bob*'s lights. Jesus, I've never been so relieved in my life. What took so long with the welds?"

"We had to use oxyacetylene," Mercer answered. "You weren't grounded so an electric arc welder would have fried you in the suit."

"Oh. Good thinking. Thanks."

Mercer and Alan exchanged a guilty glance. "Thank Jim. We hadn't even considered it. How are you feeling?"

He gave Spirit a quick squeeze. "Better now."

Spirit turned from her husband to Mercer. "I suspect you're waiting for me to thank you for saving him."

Jesus, she is one hard bitch, Mercer thought. "Not at all." He smiled.

"Well, I won't. Rather than thank you, I blame you. If you hadn't ordered him to dive today, none of this would have happened."

Jim McKenzie stepped up, saving Mercer from telling Spirit where she could shove her blame and how far up it could go. "Nice job. All three of you. That was one hell of a thing."

He didn't sound too overjoyed. In fact, to Mercer he sounded distracted, worried. They chatted for a few more minutes before Spirit led C.W. back to their cabin and Alan went to find a shower. Mercer and McKenzie were left alone at the rail looking out over the horizon. McKenzie's thin sandy hair rippled in the breeze.

A silent minute passed.

"You going to tell me what's on your mind, Jim?"

"You don't strike me as the kind of guy who believes in coincidences." McKenzie lit a cigar after offering one to Mercer, who refused.

"Like how that machine down there kicked on during our dive? Nope."

"Yeah, me either. While we were waiting to hear back from you, I double-checked our logs from radar, sonar, acoustical gear and every other piece of science gear we run twenty-four/seven."

Mercer's heart tightened. "And?"

"And I think we've stumbled onto something big."

Mercer didn't correct him that they hadn't stumbled onto anything. They'd been deliberately lured here by the sinking of the USS *Smithback*.

McKenzie continued, "We got a signal off the passive sonar suite a minute before C.W. reported the blades on the current turbines began to turn."

"What kind of signal?"

"A series of tones, something nonrandom. It only lasted a couple of seconds. If I'd have to guess it was an acoustical activation code sent to switch that thing on and release the gas. Someone was trying to sink us."

Or sabotage the dive, Mercer thought. "Could you tell where the signal came from?"

"It didn't last long enough to triangulate. The way sound travels through water, it could have been anywhere. Our radar coverage only goes out eighteen miles. There could be a ship sitting twenty miles away listening to everything we said when you were on the bottom. They could have transmitted an activation code at the critical moment."

Mercer scanned the horizon again, an unconscious check to see if they were being watched. Of course, there was nothing out there but what his imagination conjured. Tisa had said their organization was huge, numbering in the millions, though many didn't know they even belonged. It was a secret core that ran things, and within the inner circle was a faction that had gone rogue. Up until this moment he wasn't sure if he believed her. As far as he had seen, her group was just a handful of gunmen who had no compunction about murder. She could belong to any number of fringe groups with a couple of guns and an excess of hatred. But now he had proof of something else. And not just the tower itself, which was an expensive undertaking beyond the scope of all but the largest multinational companies. No, what he saw as proof was the activation signal sent from another ship. That meant they had access to an oceangoing vessel of some kind and a sophisticated network of informants to let them know when to power up the machinery.

Tisa had sought him out and sent him here so he could see for himself what her group was capable of, and what presumably she was trying to stop. Mercer tried to put his mind around what exactly that was. He couldn't. She'd made the tower, which must have cost tens of millions of dollars, sound like a small part of what her people could accomplish. This was a mere demonstration. He felt adrift. If this was a sideshow, how much bigger could their main goal be?

"Are you okay?" Jim asked. "You went pale there for a minute."

"I'm fine," Mercer said slowly, unable to convince himself or McKenzie that he was okay.

"Something big's happening, isn't it? Like maybe what Spirit was talking about. A government conspiracy?"

Mercer tried to shake off the feeling of being overwhelmed. "This is one time I think Uncle Sam's innocent, but we are in the middle of something big."

"What are you going to do about it?"

"Get pissed." Jim gave him an uncomprehending look. "You don't need to know any of the details, but since this whole thing started I've been a step behind, reacting rather than taking the initiative. It's like I'm being led around like a bull with a ring through its nose. I get shown clues that only lead to more questions. I've got to find a way of taking charge."

McKenzie still didn't understand what Mercer was saying, not that it mattered. Mercer knew his feelings. Ira had withheld truths from him and so had Tisa, both using him for their own purposes. He'd forced Lasko to finally come clean, and when he reached Greece, he'd have to do the same with Miss Nguyen.

A light drizzle fell across the tarmac as Mercer stepped from the air force cargo jet with two dozen rowdy marines ready for their first night on American soil in six months. They'd been part of a counterterrorism team assigned to the Philippine Islands. Mercer had gotten a lift on their flight to Hawaii with a little help from Ira Lasko.

Standing at the bottom of the ramp, Mercer paused as the men filed past, a few he'd spoken with on the plane wishing him well, the rest eager to use up everything in their wallets. A flight-line technician wearing a shiny rain slicker and commercial-quality ear protectors approached.

"Dr. Mercer?"

"Yes."

"Could you come with me, please? Admiral Lasko is waiting for you."

Mercer was led to an open-topped utility tractor. The technician hopped behind the wheel, leaving Mercer a tiny perch on the back of the vehicle. He held his bag on his lap as the tractor lurched across the parking apron. Hangars and a control tower lined one side of the vast expanse, while the rest was lost in the darkness.

Twisting so he could see where they were headed, he spotted a Gulfstream jet like the one Ira had procured to fetch him to Area 51. Sheets of rain poured

from the aircraft's swept wing, but the boarding hatch
was open and inviting light spilled onto the asphalt.
The tractor shuddered to a stop next to the jet. Over
the whine of the idling engines, Mercer heard the line
worker tell him this was his plane. Mercer jumped
from the tractor, gave the man a wave and hauled
himself up the boarding steps. Ira was waiting for him
just inside the luxury cabin.

Mercer had expected to meet with the admiral for
a debrief in Washington. He was grateful for the private plane after eleven hours cooped up with a bunch
of rambunctious marines, but he would have preferred
to sleep through the flight. He'd spent an additional
three days on the *Sea Surveyor* while Jim McKenzie
and his team tried to repair the submersible. Mercer
had gotten some instruction on the Advanced Diving
Suit from C.W., but in the end they decided that it
wasn't the optimal platform to study the mysterious
tower and abandoned the idea of a tandem dive. It
would be a week or more before *Bob* was functional
again and a team could continue their investigation.

"Almost a week at sea and no tan?" the admiral
teased.

Mercer was pale, drawn and exhausted. "Damn ship
was dry. I've lost my alcohol flush."

"I made sure this bird's stocked. First round's on
me." They shook hands and Ira became serious.
"How'd it go? Really?"

Mercer tossed his bag into an overhead and
dropped into a plush leather captain's chair. Ira had
the ingredients for a vodka gimlet waiting on the table
between them. Mercer mixed them each a drink, took
a quick appreciative sip, then downed it. "The more
I think about this situation, the worse it gets. I can't
figure out exactly who we're up against. In Vegas they
were a handful of armed goons and a woman with a
strange story to tell. Now I see them as a damned

army with some serious funding. There was a naval architect on board the *Surveyor*. He and I went over the video we'd managed to shoot. He estimates that tower cost at least a hundred million dollars."

"Any ideas about what it's designed to do?"

The aircraft commander came over the intercom to tell his two passengers to strap in, they had clearance to take off. The jet engines' pitch became a shriek as they rolled across the taxiways. Mercer waited until the sleek aircraft had lifted from the ground before answering Ira's question.

"Obviously it was sited over a previously undiscovered methane hydrate deposit."

"You were rather circumspect when you called me from the ship," Lasko interrupted. "What is this stuff? I've never heard of it."

"First, the reason I couldn't give you any details is that I think that someone was monitoring the *Sea Surveyor*'s communications. That's how they knew when to turn the tower on."

"I can check with the navy. They might have had that area under surveillance by then. If there was a ship close enough to eavesdrop, maybe they have a few pictures of it."

"Good. Now methane hydrate is nothing less than the future of fossil fuel energy on the planet. It's basically ice that has trapped methane gas within its crystal lattice. I'm not an expert, but I've read there's more than enough energy locked in these benthic hydrocarbon deposits to fuel our power needs for centuries. In fact, hydrate reserves are larger than coal, oil, and natural gas combined. The best part is the lion's share is found right off our own coastlines. The major oil companies are scrambling to develop the technology to tap these reserves, but it's still years away.

"The problem is that these deposits can be unstable. An undersea landslide or an earthquake can cause bil-

lions of tons of methane hydrate to vaporize and
erupt. That's what makes exploiting it so difficult. A
drill rig could upset the hydrates' equilibrium and
cause an eruption that destroys the rig and releases
tons of greenhouse gas. Environmentalists are currently doing everything in their power to prevent further exploration."

"Figures," Ira muttered.

"The danger's real. About eight thousand years ago,
a massive deposit off the coast of Norway was released
by an undersea avalanche. The three hundred fifty billion tons of hydrates that reached the atmosphere
raised temperatures about twelve degrees all over the
world and helped bring a swift end to the last ice age.

"I don't know how this group found a deposit of
hydrates so far out in the ocean. As far as I know no
one's ever looked there before. As for the tower itself? It's either designed to keep the hydrates chilled
by pumping cold brine solution into the seafloor or it
was built to heat the hydrates and cause a catastrophic eruption."

"But why? Why would someone do either?"

"No clue. If they wanted to sink ships, it would be
cheaper just to blow them out of the water, so I don't
think that's it. My money's on it being built to keep
the hydrates stable. When she got the distress call
from the *Smithback*, the *Sea Surveyor* was performing
research on deep-ocean currents. I interviewed a few
of the scientists. It appears they were tracking a jet of
warm water that hugged the ocean bottom. It runs
from the Philippine Sea toward the Aleutian Islands.
This stream wasn't there a decade ago according to
data from a previous NOAA expedition. They hypoth-
esize that global warming is what's caused this current
to develop. I believe that Tisa Nguyen's group discovered it years ago, knew about the hydrate deposit and
realized that if they didn't do something to prevent the

heat from melting the deposit we'd have a potential environmental catastrophe."

"Could this have been as bad as the one in Norway?"

"Don't know yet. When I left, they were hanging a magnetometer off the stern of *Sea Surveyor* to determine the extent of pipework buried under the mud. So far they've found that three square miles of the bottom are rigged with cooling pipes. The ROVs on the *Sea Surveyor* can't accurately measure the depth of the hydrate layer, but it's pretty clear the field is extensive and only a fraction of the gas was released when they hit the *Smithback* and the *Surveyor*. Jim McKenzie, who heads the submersible team on the ship, plans to stay in the area until they can get their sub running again.

"I hope you take care of the people on that ship. They're performing above and beyond the call for us."

"The navy can't get their own research submersible to the site for at least three more weeks so the folks out there now are getting whatever they want in return. Don't worry." Ira paused. "You said a minute ago that you thought someone was monitoring communications on the *Surveyor*. Is that your theory for why the gas erupted when you were down at the tower?"

Mercer told him about the acoustical signal Jim McKenzie detected. "I think Tisa's group has been using the tower to keep the hydrate deposit stable for years. Then there was some kind of schism within the organization. She wasn't too specific, but I bet the splinter group co-opted the tower for themselves and decided to reverse the machinery. Please don't ask why. I have no idea. All I know is that after Vegas, I don't think their agenda matches ours."

"Speaking of Vegas." Ira retrieved a briefcase from a nearby seat and snapped open the lid. The manila report he handed to Mercer was stamped TOP SECRET. "A lot of the science is beyond me. I don't think Briana Marie knows the meaning of layman's terms, but she explained the gist."

"What is this?" Mercer opened the folder and thumbed through pages of text and graphs.

"Evidence that Tisa Nguyen lied to you."

That startled Mercer. For the past few days he'd focused on her as his only source of credible information. "Come again?"

"She lied to you about how her group discovered we ran a secret test at Area 51."

She'd lied? Mercer downed his second drink and fixed another. Had he fallen for the oldest trick in the intelligence game, believing her because she was exotic and beautiful?

Anger flared behind his eyes. How could he have been so stupid? True, he'd just come a breath away from being killed, and it was understandable that his guard was down, but he'd done nothing in the days since to verify her story. Thank God Ira wasn't thinking with his glands.

The anger he felt toward her intensified the anger he directed at himself. Now more than ever he was anxious to get to Greece. He took a sip. "Okay, tell me what you found."

Ira recognized the recrimination written on Mercer's face. He'd expected no less from his friend. "According to what you said, they knew about the test because of a seismic disturbance inside Area 51, right?"

"That's what she told me, an anomalous earthquake."

"Dr. Marie pulled USGS records for the day the submarine materialized under the mountain. There were dozens of earthquakes in the west, but none of them close to Area 51. The biggest was a four-point-two near Barstow, California, which they said was an aftershock of the quake that hit Bakersfield a few months back. There were two three-point-fours in Washington State and a three-oh near Reno. The sub didn't cause any detectable disturbances when it came back."

Mercer sat quietly for a second, searching for and finding the flaw in Lasko's statement. "How did they know you were doing something out there? She knew the date, time, everything."

"Randall," Lasko answered. "They must have gotten to him, or maybe he was already part of their group. Either way, he must have told them something was up even if he didn't know what it was."

Again, Mercer pondered the logic, wondering if he wanted to exonerate Tisa because she was right or because he *wanted* her to be right. He hated the doubt. "Obviously no one at the excavation site knew the nature of the experiment you'd run, but did any of them even know the date it happened?"

"They weren't supposed to," Ira replied. "That doesn't mean it didn't slip somehow. I know what you're trying to do, Mercer, but you have to look at this reasonably. The only way she could know the timing of our test is through a security breach at the mine site. Someone talked and Donny Randall passed on the information. Later, he must have received orders to sabotage the job—the cave-in that brought you on board and later the explosion."

"And when he failed they tried to gun me down in Vegas."

Could it be that easy? Mercer asked himself. It made sense. At least more sense than Tisa's group detecting the emergence of the submarine through some other, unknown way. Yet a doubt lingered at the back of his mind. What was it? What were they missing?

Tisa's group had found a hydrate deposit where no one had ever thought to look and secretly built an enormous machine to protect it. Either feat was incredible and showed a tremendous level of sophistication. Why couldn't they have the capability to discover Ira's secret project through some extraordinary means?

"So where does that leave us?" he finally asked.

"That's up to what you learn in Greece."

"Tisa told me about some unusual phenomena in the Pacific to get my attention. Well, she got it. Now I hate thinking what's going to happen in Santorini."

"By the way, do you want backup?"

Mercer shook his head. "That'll spook her. Don't ask me how or why, but I know she's on our side and that's why we're meeting in such an out-of-the-way place. She probably could have told me whatever she needs to back in Vegas or anywhere else. She must feel comfortable on Santorini, like it's out of reach of the splinter faction she's trying to protect me from. If I show up with a bunch of men with earphones shadowing me, she may bolt."

Ira nodded. "I can buy that. A driver will be waiting for you at the airport. He'll be holding a sign saying Harry White."

"Nice touch." Mercer smiled.

"You'll have to take the ferry to Santorini because the package he'll have for you won't pass an airport security scan, if you know what I mean."

"Gun?"

"Beretta 92, as you seem to favor."

"Now that's backup I do appreciate."

Mercer stood at the rail of a three-hundred-foot inter-island ferry, glazing across the waves. The view from this ship was little different from what he'd seen from the *Surveyor* on the opposite side of the planet. His eyes felt gritty and his body was starting to ache from so much travel and so little sleep. Ira's revelations about the possibility that Tisa had been lying to him only deepened his exhaustion. He'd spent the flight from Washington mulling the consequences and his next moves. He had a real fear that her group had installed towers like the one he'd seen near Guam over other hydrate deposits. The ecological devastation of a massive coordinated release of gas was incalculable.

The ferry was heavily loaded and it seemed hundreds of people were on deck waiting for the first sight of the island of Thira, better known as Santorini. A young German couple apparently on their honeymoon stepped close to Mercer, almost brushing into him. He turned so the blond husband wouldn't feel the heavy automatic pistol slung under Mercer's arm.

There was a commotion of pointing near the distant bow and soon everyone pressed to the rail. The smudge just forming in the distance was Santorini, a paradise of dazzling whitewashed buildings and domed roofs painted a distinctive blue seen on travel posters worldwide. Formed by volcanic eruptions, the crescent-shaped island had once been substantially larger until a cataclysmic blast thirty-six hundred years ago had destroyed half of the caldera and jettisoned a cloud of ash that many archaeologists believe caused the destruction of the Minoan civilization on Crete several hundred miles south. Home to black sand beaches and some of the most spectacular views in the world, Santorini was heavily developed as a European tourist destination.

As the weather-beaten ferry motored nearer to the island, more and more passengers found their way to the railing. With the height of the tourist season still months away, Mercer was still pressed by throngs of half-drunk backpackers pointing excitedly at their first glimpse of Fira, the island's largest city. Situated inside the flooded caldera, the town clung precariously to the cliffs as if it had grown out from the living rock. Even from a distance it gleamed in the sun.

The ship passed inside the protective arms of the caldera and the steady waves that had rocked them since leaving Piraeus ceased abruptly. The more inebriated vacationers lurched on their feet. The bluffs towering over the ferry were barren stone and the small island in the center of the caldera was nothing more than a pile of rubble. If not for the town, Santorini looked primeval.

The big ferryboats usually docked at Athenios, about a mile beyond Fira, but none of the passengers disembarking were taking an automobile onto the island, so the lumbering craft edged toward the open-air port at the foot of the mountain directly below Fira. Nearly a hundred passengers hastily broke themselves from their reverent gawking and headed below to the pedestrain disembarkment ramp.

Mercer waited at the rail while they made their mass exodus. The small dock was soon a sea of milling humanity. There were three ways up to the town.

There was a winding footpath of switchback stairs that people could climb. They could ride one of the dozens of sturdy donkeys that shared the path. Or there was a modern cable car that shot straight into Fira. Admitting he was too tired to hike the ascent and dismissing a donkey ride as too touristy, he decided on the cable car, but only after it made several runs to ease the congestion.

He hefted his light bag and meandered down two decks to where the ramp had been lowered. Once on the cement quay, the heat hit Mercer full force. There was no wind in the volcanic bowl and flies rose in clouds from the manure piles left in the donkeys' wake. People climbing the trail looked as bowed as Sherpas under their packs. A few had already given up and were headed down again to take the cable car.

Mercer had to wait ten minutes for his turn to pay for the ride and climb onto the glass-enclosed car. Around him people chatted animatedly in a Babel of differing languages. To his ear, most sounded German or Scandinavian, though there were a trio of twangy Australian girls and a young American couple who looked like they just stepped out of a hippie commune. Through it all he could feel their excitement and wished a little would rub off on him. They were here for the trip of a lifetime. He didn't know what to expect and in his present frame of mind he began to regard the unknown with suspicion.

The Beretta felt comfortably cool under his left arm.

The cable car lurched as it started up the steep mountain, swinging free for a moment like a pendulum. As they rose, the view grew more expansive and breathtaking. Far out in the caldera a snowy-sailed yacht searched for a breeze to send her on her way. In the distance the sun was beginning to blush, shooting lances of ruddy light skipping atop the waves. More of the town was revealed as well—narrow twisting alleys, barrel-vaulted churches, fabulous houses with balconies hanging hundreds of feet over the water.

If this was a favorite spot for Tisa, Mercer could understand why she felt safe here. It was an enchanting place, full of charm and dramatic beauty. He wished he were here for a vacation with Tisa rather than whatever she had planned.

The cable car shuddered as it reached the upper station. To the right, hundreds of mostly young tourists had gathered along the stairs and promenades of Nomikos Street, the most popular spot in the town to wait for Santorini's notoriously beautiful sunsets. Their faces were pointed at the sun like flowers.

Mercer instinctively scanned the crowd, looking for anything out of the ordinary, like pairs of men wearing jackets that could conceal guns or someone watching people rather than the view. He spotted a few of those, but they were young men on the hunt for women or women on the prowl for men. On the ship he'd overheard enough people to know that Fira was famous across Europe for its nightlife.

The cable car doors slid open and Mercer followed the passengers outside, thankful because the miasma of patchouli oil from the bohemians was burning his sinuses. People often wore the pungent essence to mask the reek of marijuana in their clothes. Mercer would have preferred the dope.

He allowed the tide of people to push him toward Nomikos Street as he looked for Tisa. He was careful to keep one hand on his bag and the other casually draped across the shoulder holster so no one accidentally bumping into him would feel it. The crowd was too dense to pick out a single person and Mercer was drawing attention to himself by not watching the sunset as everyone else.

The faces around him were bright with anticipation, eagerly awaiting the simple delight of a setting sun.

They were here to make a ritual out of the usual. Mercer had never felt more detached in his life. From the moment the gunmen had attacked him at the Luxor he'd felt a building sense of dread, like he'd glimpsed only the tip of an iceberg. Even if more of it hadn't been revealed yet, he sensed it lurking just below the surface.

In the jostle of people still spilling onto the promontory overlooking the caldera he didn't feel the figure sidle up to him until it was too late.

He reeled back and found himself staring into the laughing eyes of Tisa Nguyen. She'd just kissed him. He hadn't realized she was almost as tall as he was. "I just knew you'd come," she said with a mixture of excitement and embarrassment at her unbidden display.

Mercer didn't speak. It was the crimson sun or the romance of the moment or maybe it was something deeper. No matter what the cause, he knew that he'd never seen anyone look more beautiful than Tisa standing there like an ancient high priestess holding rites at dusk. She wore sandals and a tight sleeveless dress that poured seamlessly down her body, rising at her breasts and flaring in at her waist. Her skin shone with a fresh tan that made the dress appear even whiter than white. She almost glowed.

"Er, hi," Mercer managed to stammer.

"What a smooth rejoinder," she teased. "Sorry I startled you, but you looked so serious. You were ruining the sunset by being so gloomy. What were you thinking?"

Mercer was about to tell her how hollow he felt. The words were already formed. Instead he smiled and said, "I was thinking how much better the view would be if you showed up."

Tisa smiled at the compliment. "Wishing makes it true."

He studied her in the dying light. It wasn't just the

outfit or the tan, he saw. Something else made her appear so buoyant. He remembered the suffering he'd seen in her eyes when she'd saved his life and looked for it again. Her sloe eyes were bright and clear. There was no trace of the agony that had made her vulnerable. Then, even as he watched, it flooded in, darkening her expression, crowding in on her simple happiness. Tisa turned away. It was as if just seeing him reminded her of her suffering.

"I suspected you'd actually come a day early," she said. "I've met every ferry entering Santorini since I got here."

Mercer hated that he'd already poisoned her happiness. "I would have if I could," he said awkwardly. "You left some compelling evidence that I should take you seriously."

She looked stricken for a moment. "You have to believe I didn't know about that ship that sank. I heard it on the news. I was sick." Her words came as a rush. "When I told you something unusual was going to happen in the Pacific, I expected that a research ship called the *Sea Surveyor* was going to discover the elevated levels of methane and eventually discover the tower."

"I just came from the *Surveyor*."

"Then you know they were doing studies on deep-ocean currents. Part of my job within the Order is to monitor some of our more prominent sites around the world, to ensure that nothing happens to them. I learned months ago about the *Surveyor*'s mission and was sure that they would find the hydrate deposit. Please, I didn't know about the navy ship that went by there earlier."

Her tone was plaintive. Mercer glanced around. A few tourists were watching them. From their sour expressions, it looked as though they thought Mercer and Tisa were having a lovers' quarrel and fouling the romantic atmosphere. "We should get out of here," he said.

Tisa immediately understood. "Where are you staying?"

Ira's office had handled the travel arrangements. From inside his jacket pocket Mercer withdrew his itinerary. "Let's see, the Hotel Kavalari."

"Okay. I don't think it's far."

"You don't know?"

"Hey," she protested playfully, "I've never been here before and I've spent most of my time at the ferry dock waiting for you."

Since the moment she asked him to meet her on Santorini, Mercer had believed she knew the island well and felt safe here. It was yet another assumption that had been proven wrong.

The sun was well down on the horizon and the crowd was beginning to disperse. Tisa led Mercer toward the center of town, climbing a winding set of stairs to Ipapantis Street. The narrow lane was hemmed in by bars that were just getting going and glittering jewelry shops that were just closing. The air was scented with cooking smells, lamb and beef and the light aroma of the world's premier olive oils. Packs of rowdy teens roamed in search of the opposite sex, their mood carefree and alive.

Like so much of the town, the rambling hotel was built into the cliff face and the rooms were accessible only by walking down rickety stairs. The maître d'hôtel checked Mercer in and led him and Tisa down three flights along the serpentine steps to a private balcony and the room. The room itself had been carved into the stone, and once inside they saw the bathroom had been left as undressed rock.

Mercer tossed his bag on the bed and excused himself to use the bathroom while Tisa stared at the darkening sea lapping a hundred feet below. He shaved as quickly as he could using the tepid water, dragged a stick of deodorant under his arms, and changed his shirt.

He paused coming out of the room. A breeze had kicked up, snapping and tangling Tisa's hair around her head. She'd removed her glasses and faced the salt-tinted wind with her eyes closed. Her mouth was slightly parted, as if tasting the air. He was struck again by her beauty and how innocent she looked when he could not see her eyes. He committed the moment to memory.

Tisa felt his presence and quickly put on her glasses. She turned to face him. She looked guilty. "Do you want to talk here?"

Mercer grinned. "Nope. I want a drink. I spotted the hotel bar two floors above us."

Five minutes later they were seated at an intimate table overlooking the caldera. The night had turned chilly and tall gas heaters threw coronas of warmth over them both. Not trusting an unfamiliar bartender with his usual, though not usually popular, vodka gimlet, Mercer had a double vodka and soda with a standing order for at least two more. Tisa drank water.

"Okay, now we can talk," he said, feeling the knots of muscle at his shoulders losing a fraction of their rigidity. "Tell me about the tower."

"In order for you to understand, I have to give you a little background. Do you know anything about acupuncture?"

Mercer hadn't expected such an odd question and was taken aback. For a fleeting moment he was back in an underground cell in Panama with a psychotic Chinese torturer named Mr. Sun, his skin pierced with hundreds of tiny needles that Sun used to induce unimaginable pain from all parts of his body. The memory was fresh and while Mercer hadn't been physically harmed, the mental scars still felt raw. The old terror welled up, forcing him to swallow heavily at his drink to cleanse his throat. "I know a bit."

Tisa hadn't seen his discomfort. "Then you know that the body is connected by force lines that transfer a person's chi, or essence, and that these pathways can be manipulated to relieve stress or pain."

"Or to cause it," Mercer said mildly.

"There is a dark side to the art," she acknowledged. "But used properly, acupuncture is a proven healing technique that works on animals as well as people. Do you believe that?"

"How's this? I don't not believe it."

"Good enough. Now, what if I told you the earth was like the human body and that it too has pathways for a chi force."

"Are you talking about magnetic lines?"

"No, not a tangible force. Something more"—she sought the right word and failed—"intangible." She paused again. "I will give you the proof in a while, but for the sake of this discussion, accept that the earth has a life force, like a person.

Mercer nodded. "I'll give you the benefit of the doubt. For now."

She shot him a secretive smile, as if she would make him pay for his skepticism. "This force is very real, you'll see. Now if someone can detect the force and understand how it concentrates in certain places on the earth's surface, they can also manipulate it."

Mercer raised an eyebrow. "Acupuncture for a whole planet?"

"Exactly!" Tisa was delighted he understood.

"Please don't tell me you built the tower as a giant acupuncture needle to ease earth's aches and pains."

She frowned at his mocking tone. "In a sense, that's exactly what it is. What I'm about to tell you can be verified by checking oceanographic data. Over the past fifteen years a new ocean current has developed in the Pacific that is raising mean bottom temperatures."

"Yes, I know. I spoke with scientists aboard the *Sea Surveyor*. My theory is that your group knew about it, and also knew that a large hydrate deposit was right in the current's path. You built the tower to keep it stable."

"You do understand. Methane hydrate can exist in only a very narrow range of temperatures and pressures and the new, warmer current would eventually cause a tremendous release. We had to do something. The tower uses the current itself to power machinery to chill a special liquid that keeps the deposit from erupting. Some methane manages to escape, however. That's what I thought the *Sea Surveyor* would find and follow back to the site."

"You said that you monitor other sites for your organization."

"The Order."

"Yes, the Order. Are there other towers like the one I was just at?"

"That's the only one, but I think I know what you're really asking. Are there other installations that can be used to harm people? The answer, I'm afraid, is yes. But I don't know if my—if the splinter faction I mentioned has tried to gain control of them. I doubt it because many sites have full-time employees. The tower was easy for them to commandeer because it ran autonomously."

"If you knew about the current and the methane hydrates, why not tell the world? The UN or someone? Why do it yourselves."

"Because that is what we do, or at least that's what we've been doing for almost twenty years."

That shook Mercer and he asked incredulously, "Your group is a hundred years old?"

"Oh, gosh no. Its roots date back almost five hundred years. It's only been the past two decades that we've done anything other than monitor the earth's chi."

"Five hundred?" Mercer rocked back in his seat.

He had assumed the Order had only formed recently, another New Age fringe group speaking of chi and force lines. Five hundred years made it feel more like a religion.

"Yes, since the time of Admiral Zheng He and China's treasure fleets."

"I'm not familiar with—"

"Not too many people are," Tisa said. "Zheng He was a eunuch slave who became one of China's greatest military commanders. From 1405 to 1433 he was in command of seven epic journeys that ranged as far as the Persian Gulf, Madagascar and the mainland of Africa. Some say he went to South America too, and there's archaeological evidence to back that claim. His ships were the most magnificent ever built and the largest too. The treasure ships were four hundred feet long at a time before Christopher Columbus used a puny ninety-footer to discover America. If I'm not mistaken, Admiral He's ships were the biggest until the Industrial Revolution."

"I had no idea."

"You're the victim of a Western-biased education," she said to tease. "This period during the Ming Dynasty was the only time in China's history that they looked beyond the Middle Kingdom and sought trade with other nations rather than wait for traders to come to them. The Ottoman and Persian empires were in full flower and the trade of goods and knowledge were unprecedented. The Ming navy was the most powerful in the world and stood poised to dominate the sea-lanes had they chosen. No nation could have stopped them. And then the emperor decreed an end to ocean commerce and China once again closed her borders to all but a few struggling along the Silk Road. The fleet of ships was destroyed, crews and captains who'd seen the distant lands were put to death. Much of what had been brought to China was burned."

Mercer was enthralled with her story, imagining the vast wealth the Chinese must have accumulated. "Why?"

"No reason need be given. No one dared question the orders of the emperor. But one man did. He was a Confucian scholar named Zhu Zhanji, a master scribe in the emperor's court who decried the destruction and risked his life to spirit away the best of what the traders had brought back. The cache included scrolls and texts gathered from the four corners of the globe, works of advanced mathematics being developed in the Arab world, as well as priceless pieces of art, ivory carvings, gems and tons of gold. It was a storehouse of knowledge and human ingenuity, perhaps the greatest ever amassed."

"You're describing something along the lines of the Library of Alexandria."

"Perhaps some of that collection was part of what Zhu gathered. Who knows? Legend has it that an observer standing on a tall mountain couldn't see the entire length of the caravan. Zhu Zhanji took the treasure trove deep into western China, into an isolated valley called Rinpoche-La, and bade the local people to guard it well. Zhu died on his return to the imperial court and the archive appeared lost for all time. But Zhu hadn't chosen this valley by accident.

"Rinpoche-La was an enigmatic place, fabled because even though it was high in the foothills of the Himalayas, it remains warm year-round. The village was built near geothermal springs deep inside the mountains, allowing for a standard of living not found anywhere else in that barren part of the country."

"Sounds like James Hilton's book, *Lost Horizon*."

"His story of Shangri-La is very likely based on the legend of Rinpoche-La," she concurred, "similar to how Bram Stoker was inspired to write *Dracula* after hearing of the Transylvanian king Vlad the Impaler. For a hundred years the archive was left in vast underground storehouses beneath the monastery. Then some of the monks began to decipher what Zhu had left them. One particular part of the treasure caught their attention."

"I assume the gold."

"More Western bias," she teased. "No, it was a set of blueprints and some texts, a gift to the emperor from the Sultan of Muscat, perhaps the richest man in the world at the time the treasure fleets roamed the Persian Gulf. No one knows how he came about the documents. It is believed they were created by one of his great mathematicians. When I heard these stories as a child, I imagined him to be like an Arab Leonardo da Vinci. It took generations for the monks at Rinpoche-La to understand the full potential of what they were studying, and many more years, centuries, in fact, for them to attempt to build the oracle described in the sultan's plans."

"An oracle?"

"They called it the Navel of the World, a machine that could accurately measure the earth's chi. They completed the work in the 1850s and set about to see if the machine was right. And soon found it was. Uncannily so. For years they sent people to chronicle the effects of the chi and report back to the Lama what they'd seen. And that's the way it remained until the summer of 1908 when a cataclysmic event upset the planet's delicate balance of forces."

The year triggered another memory for Mercer. "Can I venture a guess as to the exact date? June thirtieth, 1908."

This time it was Tisa's turn for a moment of stunned silence. "How did you . . . ?"

"That's when a meteorite slammed into Siberia near the village of Tunguska and leveled several thousand square miles of forest. The blast was heard in Scandinavia and darkened the sky as far as London. Can't be too many other cataclysmic events that year."

Her eyes were still wide. "Few people have even heard of the event and yet you know the exact date."

"I'll tell you the story why sometime," he said evasively, then steered the conversation back to her tale. "You believe the impact changed the earth's balance in some way."

"Not the planet's, obviously, but the chi forces. Up until then, the earth behaved as the oracle at Rinpoche-La predicted. After the event, the predictions were no longer accurate. The Lama and his acolytes became concerned. The times and locations between predicted events diverged further as the years passed. Twenty years ago it was decided that the Order had to do something to correct it. We would heal the earth and restore its proper balance of chi."

"And the tower is one way you do this?"

"Oh, no," Tisa dismissed. "That is just one small project. A short-term, ah, Band-Aid." She smiled at her turn of phrase. "Our main efforts are a little more subtle. You see, to rebalance the world we must focus on points where the earth's chi lines intersect. This is becoming more difficult because humanity is also beginning to affect chi with such things as atomic bomb tests and hydroelectric dams that shift rivers. These all change the force lines."

Mercer was having a hard time keeping the skepticism from his expression. There could be some truth in the history Tisa had told him, but he didn't believe a word about the interpretation. He was taunting when he said, "So you guys must hate what China is doing at the Three Gorges Dam, the biggest hydro project in history."

"On the contrary," she replied quickly. "Members of our group were on the committee to see it built. Three Gorges is an important nexus point for chi. The weight of the water is helping to bring the earth balance."

Mercer scoffed. "Come on, Tisa. This is ridiculous."

"Eight years ago you were approached by a company called Jaeger Metals to help them in the development of a copper mine in Brazil. Do you remember that?"

"Vaguely," Mercer said uneasily. "I turned them down. How do you know about that?"

"Because the Order controls Jaeger Metals. Do you recall why you refused the job?"

"They wanted to shift billions of tons of overburden for a copper deposit that didn't justify the expense. I tried to tell them they were pouring money into a hole with no bottom but no one on the board of directors cared."

"Do you know what happened to Jaeger?"

"Yeah, they went ahead with the project, dug a three-mile-wide, eight-hundred-foot-deep pit in the middle of the jungle and went bankrupt."

"What you didn't know, what no one knew, is that spot in the jungle was a chi point and by removing all that dirt we managed to regain five minutes of accuracy."

"I—" Mercer checked his sarcasm. Could that possibly be true? At the time, he'd suspected that the whole debacle was a financial swindle of some sort. He'd followed the story in trade magazines after bowing out and recalled that Jaeger had blown about seventy million dollars before giving up, but when the mining company folded no one came forward with a complaint. An SEC investigation after the collapse found all the money had come from a private source that was satisfied with Jaeger's "good faith" efforts. Could Tisa's group be that private source? Could all they have wanted was a giant hole and not the copper?

They did build an undersea tower just to keep a hy-

drate deposit stable, a little voice reminded him. This appeared to be an organization where you couldn't question their methods or their motivation.

Tisa watched the play of conflicting thoughts in Mercer's eyes. She looked pleased. "Jaeger's just another example of how we work. You should see the oil field we paid a company to develop in the middle of Australia, about a thousand miles from the nearest oil deposit. They thought we were nuts but took our money and drilled eleven hundred wells for us, every one of them dry." She frowned. "I hate to admit all that work only corrected another six minutes. Don't worry, you'll understand better tomorrow."

"What happens tomorrow?"

"You just have to wait and see. I ask for one night of patience. If you don't think I'm right then, well, nothing matters much after that."

She spoke earnestly, and Mercer recalled what she'd said the night they met. "The end of the world?"

"As we know it, yes." In the moonlight, her eyes began to glisten.

Mercer knew it didn't matter if he believed what she was saying. It was abundantly clear that Tisa was certain. The deep melancholy that so wracked her features was back, worse than ever.

"What time is it?" she asked, just to say something.

"Eight o'clock. That reminds me. I have something for you." Mercer hastily reached into his jacket pocket. He opened and then handed across a slim black case. Inside on a bed of satin was a woman's gold Raymond Weil watch. "I remembered you don't have one and always seem to ask for the time. I bought it for you at Dulles on the way to Greece."

Mercer had expected her to be delighted. Instead Tisa regarded the watch as though it were a poisonous snake. He was at a loss.

She quickly regained her composure. "I'm sorry. It's

beautiful. It's just that I, well, I've never gotten in the habit of wearing one, but for you I will." She snapped it around her slender wrist and studied it for a moment. "Thank you."

He hadn't known what to expect when he saw her again. But certainly it wasn't the disaster this night was turning out to be. He reached across the table and took her hand. "I'm sorry about the watch. Obviously I hit a nerve. How's this? For the rest of the night we'll just be two people on a date in the most romantic place I've ever seen. We will eat too much for dinner, have too much ouzo and forget the rest of the world even exists. What do you say?"

Tisa wiped at her eyes and smiled. "A date? I guess that wouldn't be too bad."

He stood and set a handful of bills on the table, eager to get away from the dark mood he'd seemed to create at the bar. "Then let's get at it."

They climbed back to Ipapantis Street, flowing with the tide of revelers until they came upon a tiny restaurant that had an even more spectacular view than the hotel bar. There were only six tables. The elderly owner was in the kitchen. His spry wife served as waitress. She brought a bottle of wine without waiting to take their order and a moment later brought bread and garlic-scented olive oil. She never asked what they wanted to eat. Apparently the restaurant didn't have menus. Their dinner was going to be whatever the chef decided. And by the second course they knew to trust his decisions. The meal was excellent.

For a while, Mercer and Tisa were uncomfortable together. The conversation started and stopped a dozen times. After her second glass of wine she admitted that this was the first date she'd been on in a long time.

"I find that hard to believe. You're beautiful. You must have to beat men off with a stick."

She looked into his eyes. "You think I'm beautiful?"

"Good God, don't you own a mirror? You're stunning."

Her smile spread and her cheeks turned flush with embarrassment and delight. "Thank you."

"If I knew you could smile like that, I'd have told you hours ago." Mercer was pleased with himself. "And truth be told I haven't been on a real date in a while either."

"Oh, please. You must have had dozens of women."

"I—well, yes, sort of." The comment had caught him off guard. "What I mean was I don't date that much. I'm traveling seven or eight months out of the year, and I don't think much of the idea of a one-night stand."

"Though you have had them."

"Uh, a few," he admitted, not wanting to tell her the truth but unwilling to hide it from her. "I guess I just haven't taken the time to get involved with any-one seriously."

"Maybe you haven't found the right person."

Mercer laughed. "You don't happen to know a guy named Harry White, do you?"

"I don't think so. Why?"

"You two sound a lot alike."

"Is that good or bad?"

"He's my best friend. It's good."

"Now that's someone I'd like to hear about. Philip Mercer's best friend. Tell me about this Harry White."

After that, things went better. With Harry as a sub-ject, Mercer didn't even have to try to get Tisa laugh-ing. When they left the restaurant two hours later neither was surprised at how natural it felt to hold hands as they strolled. Mercer had removed his shoul-der holster in the men's room and tucked the gun into the back of his slacks so he could drape his blazer over Tisa's shoulders.

There was no need for any artless wile on Mercer's part or false coquettishness from Tisa. Both knew where the evening was headed as they walked and talked, and yet that certainty made neither impatient. Everything unfolded at such a natural pace that when they finally arrived back at Mercer's hotel they simply continued down the stairs to his room without pause.

There wasn't one moment of awkwardness. They felt only the joy of discovery as their lips met for the first time and as clothes began to pile on the floor. Together on the soft bed, their acts became more intimate until Mercer found himself doing things he hadn't done since his days of college experimentation. But this wasn't about pushing boundaries, it was about Tisa giving more and more of herself and he being willing to receive. There wasn't any fear of going too far, for when he looked in her eyes he saw he'd just scratched the surface.

They did not separate, but clung tightly to each other as they both drifted toward sleep. It was only as the last spark of consciousness faded that Mercer recognized the words Tisa had panted as she reached her climax. He could have sworn she'd been repeating, "I love you. I love you."

In the moments between sleep and consciousness, in the blending of the dream world and the real, there was a moment of clarity where Mercer often found inspiration. He was not yet aware of his surroundings—that was a minute away—but his mind felt unimpeded and open to new ideas. Without realizing why, he played back his conversation with Tisa about chi forces and locus points. Then that scene became overdubbed with his own words to Ira Lasko a scant twenty-four hours earlier. They were talking about global warming and Mercer told his boss that the planet had rhythms and cycles we had yet to detect.

It seemed that he and Tisa had been discussing the same concepts, only she had a name for it. He'd dismissed her philosophy as Eastern legends and New Age bunk, but what if it wasn't? What if it was the very same thing he believed, that we know more about outer space than our own planet and momentous discoveries await us if only we took the time to look.

And then the thoughts diverged once again, leaving him with two separate ideas that couldn't be reconciled. That was his last thought before coming fully awake.

The light pouring into the room was pearly and wan. With the room's door open, the air tasted fresh with the scent of the sea. As his eyes adjusted he saw Tisa on the balcony. Because the deck was screened on three sides and open only to the ancient volcanic caldera, she stood completely nude as she made the slow, balanced moves of the Tai Chi ritual, her supple body twisting in lissome poses. As he watched, his mind flashed back to their exploits during the night. He felt a familiar stirring.

Tisa's moves became more complex, and intense. Soon she deviated from Tai Chi to commence her morning contortion exercises. She'd taken the quilt from the bed so she could practice more freely. As she moved, Mercer became entranced. She exercised without guile, but he found the poses increasingly erotic. At one point only the crown of her head and the tips of her toes remained on the ground as she formed a backward arch. Her skin was stretched across her torso and her breasts rode high and proud. He could not hold back a moan.

Tisa flipped around as agile as a cat, peering over her shoulder at him, her eyes wide and mischievous. "I was wondering when you'd notice me out here." She swung up to her feet and sauntered to the bed. She dropped next to him and her hand disappeared under the covers. "So it is true. Men do have a thing for limber women."

"Limber, hell. Some of what you were doing would shame Gumby."

She bent and kissed him deeply, her lips soft against his. Mercer reached for her and dragged her into the bed. Her body had cooled from her exercises but quickly warmed against his and soon became almost hot to the touch.

It was another hour before they got out of bed. Tisa left Mercer in the shower so she could go to her own hotel and gather her things. They would meet at ten for brunch. When she returned, Mercer lounged on the terrace, a Bloody Mary at hand to ease the lingering effects of too much ouzo. She'd left her luggage with the concierge and carried only a beach bag.

She took a proprietary sip of Mercer's drink. "Fur of the cat?"

He smiled. "Hair of the dog."

"Ah, that's right. English is an easy language to speak but has too many idioms."

"What is your native language? If you don't mind my asking, what is your ethnic background?"

"I grew up speaking Vietnamese at home. My father was half Vietnamese and half French. My mother was from Paris. In the village where I was born, the native language was a blend of Tibetan and Chinese."

"You were born in China?"

"At Rinpoche-La," she answered as if he should have known. "How do you think I know so much about Zhu and the archive and the oracle? I was raised to be a watcher until my mother fled the village with my half brother and me. I returned when I was eighteen."

"Why?"

Tisa paused. "You must understand the size of the Order. Literally millions of people support us in one form or another. We control yoga studies, temples, and special schools. We also run organic farms on four continents. Go into any specialty food store in the United States and I can show you dozens of products that are produced by Order-owned companies. Most people who work for us have no idea. A yoga instructor in Miami pays a franchise fee to a company in California, who then pays a fee to another corporation in a country with loose banking laws. Eventually the money ends up in our coffers and no one knows we even exist."

"That's where the money for the tower came from?"

"Partially. Any group that lasts for as long as we have is usually wealthy beyond measure. If someone invests a dollar when they're a child, it's worth thousands when they retire, right? Now expand that scenario to span generations."

"We're talking millions."

"Billions, actually."

"You returned to be part of all that?" Mercer prompted after Tisa lapsed into silence.

"I returned because I was stupid and spiteful. I was never really happy in Paris. Rinpoche-La was a village of a thousand people and I was the daughter of an important man. In Paris I was another half-breed left over from France's colonial past. I was isolated and lonely. There were a few people in the city who knew my identity. They were some high-ranking members of the Order. Because of my father they treated me as an object of veneration, not a person.

"Naturally, like any headstrong teenager I blamed my mother for all misery. When I was old enough, I sent word to my father that I wanted to join him. He arranged everything."

"That must have been painful for your mother."

"Doubly. My half brother had already returned to Rinpoche-La a couple of years earlier. She died a short time later in a train accident never knowing how sorry I was." Behind her glasses Tisa's eyes were wet. "I think we should talk about something happier than my childhood."

"From the sound of it that should be easy. How about the violence in the Middle East? Or maybe world famine?"

She understood Mercer's sense of humor. A smile touched her trembling lips. "What about the AIDS crisis? Much happier."

"I do have one more question for you," Mercer said seriously. "When we met, you told me how you knew about me and the work I've done."

"Yes," she answered cautiously.

"Why? I mean why me in particular? There are hundreds of prospecting geologists."

Tisa paused. "When I rejoined my father at Rinpoche-La, my first job for the Order was to collect information about large-scale mining operations. It was part of our efforts to determine how much human development was affecting the earth's chi. Over the course of a few years I saw your name come up again and again. I was a bit intrigued about how you were at the epicenter of so much work. While I've followed the careers of many mining engineers, I think I paid special attention to yours. More than anyone else I came across I saw you balance humanity's need for raw materials with a sense of environmental awareness."

"There are a few dozen conservation groups who'd disagree with you," demurred Mercer.

She made a face. "Most of whom are so misguided they don't think we even need raw materials. Like I said there's a balance and I believe that on this issue your views parallel mine. I know you've refused jobs that others greedily took because you felt the damage far outweighed the benefit."

"Or maybe they weren't offering enough money," Mercer countered, just to hear her reaction.

"You're being disingenuous."

He grinned. "Okay, you found my dirty little secret. I'm not a corporate money grubber after all."

Tisa's eyes sparkled with mischief. "I wouldn't go that far. How about a money grubber with a heart?"

The rest of the day passed in a sweet blur of meandering strolls and aimless conversations. They blocked out everything but themselves and the perfection of the island. For Mercer only one thing marred the day. It seemed that ten times an hour Tisa would ask him the time. She did not wear the watch he'd given her, which he didn't mind, but her obsession with time was something he couldn't understand.

They were sitting on a quiet beach on the eastern coast of Santorini when she asked yet again and he told her it was quarter of five. She bit her lip, her gaze fixed on the horizon. Mercer knew that their idyllic escape was at an end.

"We have to go," she said sadly. "It's almost time for you to see your proof." She placed her hands on each side of Mercer's face. "I want you to know that today was the most enjoyable I've had in a long time. I can forget so much when I'm with you."

"Tell me what's so horrible that you have to forget, Tisa."

She released him and got to her feet, brushing sand from her backside. "You'll know in a little while."

They found a taxi in the village of Monolithos and negotiated a fare back to Fira to pick up their luggage and take them to the city's main dock south of town. The road hugged the cliff and descended to sea level in a dizzying string of switchbacks. The narrow tract was clogged with trucks climbing up from the dock. The vehicles were laden with produce and supplies that kept the island habitable. Teens on rented motorcycles darted between the trucks and tore up the road, their whining exhaust echoing off the mountains. The driver cursed one particular biker who came around a blind curve in his lane as he overtook a lumbering ten-wheeled truck. The silver bike juked back into his own lane with inches to spare.

Tisa turned to Mercer. "I read that at the height of the tourist season there's a motorcycle accident every day on Santorini and a death at least once a week."

"To a kid only old people are mortal."

They rounded another curve and could see the open dock far below. Beyond ranks of shipping containers a ferry even larger and older than the one that had brought Mercer here disgorged a stream of cars and trucks while an equally long line of vehicles waited their turn to board. The double-ended ferry had the battered appearance of a veteran New York taxicab. Her paintwork had been faded by years in the fierce sun and she had fared poorly in her fight against the tough Aegean storms. Her lines were boxy and blunt and her flanks were deeply scarred by careless captains who used her bulk in port to push aside other craft.

Because her forward loading ramp gaped open, she reminded Mercer of a bloated fish trapped on a beach and gasping for air.

"Looks like they're running late," he said.

"What time is it?"

"What does it matter? It'll take a half hour to load all those cars."

"Please."

"It's six fifteen."

Tisa ticked off on her fingers as she made a mental calculation. She let out a relieved breath. "We'll be okay as long as we're not too late shoving off."

"What are you talking about?"

"Proof, dear doctor. Your proof."

Tisa had to pay the cabbie because last night Mercer had given the hundred dollars' worth of drachmas to the couple that ran the restaurant as appreciation for the sumptuous meal.

"So where are we going?" he asked as they joined the line of people at the amidships passenger ramp loading.

"I think the ferry's next port of call is Crete, but I'm not sure."

The vague answer made little sense to Mercer. "You don't know where this proof of yours is?"

"Oh, it's right here on Santorini, but the best way to see it is from a distance."

On board, Mercer and Tisa stashed their meager luggage in one of the coin-operated storage bins outside a shabby middeck cafeteria. Tisa kept a single bag and Mercer asked to stash his pistol in it so he didn't have to wear his sports coat. The day had been a hot one and inside the ship the press of humanity already made sweat ooze from his pores.

Tisa bought several bottled waters in the cafeteria and said enigmatically, "We might need them later."

They climbed to the top deck and found a space at the ship's rail shaded by one of the smoke-darkened funnels. Twenty minutes later the ferry's horn gave a great mournful blast as the vehicle door was secured and lines cast off. She eased from her slip with ponderous dignity, and as soon as she felt waves broadside she started to roll like an overweight woman on uneven pavement. Just a few dozen yards from the black cliffs that reflected the last of the day's heat like mirrors, the air was much cooler, freshened by the trade winds blowing past the island.

Tisa set her bag at her feet and rummaged through it until she found what she wanted. She handed the bundle to Mercer. It was a book wrapped in stiff waterproofed canvas. The volume was leather bound and ancient; the binding crackled as he opened it.

"You are the first person outside the Order to ever see one of our chronicles." She gazed at the book with reverence.

"What is this?" Mercer scanned a brittle parchment page but couldn't read the words, or even recognize the language.

"For almost two hundred years the monks and villagers from Rinpoche-La and later others who became part of us have left the mountain redoubt in order to verify the predictions made about the earth's chi forces. Each person carried a journal like this to write observations about the event."

The words "event" and "predictions" sent a chill down Mercer's spine as he finally understood what Tisa had been saying all along. "You're talking about earthquakes?"

"Yes," she said somberly, "and volcanic eruptions too."

"No one can predict earthquakes." Mercer shook his head. "It's impossible."

"Which is why I didn't tell you the truth that night in Las Vegas. You would have thought me more insane than I probably seemed. Admit it. Had I said we could predict earthquakes you never would have agreed to meet me. I had to get you here so I could show you proof."

"This book isn't proof, Tisa."

"What time is it?"

"Quarter of seven." And then he got it, what Tisa meant by proof. He felt breathless. "My God, we're here to watch an earthquake."

"According to the original journal entry it should have hit the island two days ago at noon. I said last night that ever since the Tunguska blast the oracle's predictions have been off. The new calculations say it should hit in about twenty minutes." She took the book back from him and opened to one of the latter pages. She handed it back. Mercer couldn't read the faded script so he concentrated on the numbers written along the side of the page. One he saw was the date two days past and others he recognized as longitude and latitude coordinates. Tisa then gave him a modern tourist map. Santorini was circled and he saw that the coordinates matched exactly.

"When was this written?" Mercer whispered, still unable to fully grasp the implications.

"In 1850," she answered. "This particular chronicle is of seismic activity around the Mediterranean. There are others for the other parts of the planet. If you'd like I can show you where it mentions the Izmit, Turkey, quake that hit in 1999 and killed so many, or the cycles of Mount Etna's eruptions."

"You knew about these events before they happened?"

She nodded. "The journals are kept by a council of archivists and were only given to watchers a short time before an eruption or earthquake, just long enough

for them to get there so they could report their find-
ings. Over the past twenty years, as the media has
become globalized and the Internet has grown, the
council has stopped sending watchers because news
reaches Rinpoche-La on its own.

"We do have groups around the world, members
who don't know the full scope of our prognostication.
They provide details if we need them to help us correct the time differences that cropped up in the prophecy since 1908."

"Jesus, Tisa, if an earthquake is about to strike the
island we have to warn people, we can't let them die."

Mercer launched himself from the railing. Tisa had
to race to grab his arm before he descended down to
the lower deck to find someone to take him to the
captain. "Relax. The oracle says the quake is a small
one. I would never put you in danger."

"How small?" he asked dubiously.

"Just enough to rattle some windows and panic a
few cats." She smiled.

"But the others, like the one that struck Turkey?
Why didn't you send out a warning? My God, you
could have saved thousands of lives."

She shook her head. "It is forbidden. I told you,
only the archivists have access to the chronicles and
only they understand how the oracle works. Because
watchers aren't really needed anymore, we never learn
what the oracle had said until after it happens. We
then verify the prophecy in order to determine if our
efforts to correct the chi imbalance have had an effect.
I'm not supposed to have this book," she admitted in
a soft, remorseful voice. "I stole it from the archive
so I could convince you."

She suddenly became angry. "This is what has
caused the schism within the Order. Some of us feel
that it is our duty to humanity to tell the world what
we know. Others, like those that tried to kill you at

the Luxor, take a harder line and want to remain in the shadows. They don't even believe we should actively try to correct the growing chi disparity."

"That's how you knew about the experiment," Mercer said, more to himself than her. "Those quakes that hit in Washington and near Reno hadn't been predicted, had they? They were triggered somehow by Dr. Marie's experiment."

"After they happened, it sent the archivists into a panic because the chronicle said there wouldn't be any activity in those areas for many months. This was something far beyond the previous imbalances we'd detected before. Something severe had occurred. Something we had never seen before. They dispatched several teams to the United States to discover the cause. Some felt certain that the oracle was no longer reliable."

"What is the oracle?"

"I've only seen it once, when I was a child, but—"

The rumble came from all around them, a vibration that built in their bodies before it became a sound that reached their ears. It was low on the register, a bass that struck in a continuous wave. Several passengers lining the rail to watch the island in the twilight looked at each other in confusion. The moment stretched. A woman screamed as the sea puckered under the seismic onslaught of a mild earthquake. A few rocks dislodged from the massif ringing the caldera and tumbled to the water. The splashes looked like torpedo strikes against the base of the bluffs. Flocks of birds took wing all over Santorini and seemed to further darken the sky.

And then the quake subsided, the sound fading even faster than it had grown. An uneasy buzz flew through the passengers, a few looked sickly pale, a few dismissed the moment with nervous laughter.

Mercer remained rooted in place, his knuckles white

on the steel railing, the line of his mouth grim. Even before it had struck, Mercer knew Tisa hadn't made up her story. She hadn't lied about a single thing and the implications were beyond belief. The best minds in science, experts in geo-mechanics and fluid dynamics and other branches of geology, had been working for years to give citizens a few hours' notice of an impending quake. Their efforts had failed miserably. They couldn't give even a moment's warning. And now here he stood with a centuries-old book that gave the exact time and place of an earthquake, a feat of prediction he couldn't possibly explain. He was overcome by superstitious awe but also the thrill of the potential. He had to understand. He had to learn everything Tisa knew about the oracle.

As he turned to face her a figure striding across the crowded deck caught his eye. It took him a fraction of a second to understand who he was seeing, place him in context and react to the threat. He dropped the journal and tore at Tisa's hand at the same instant the person closing in on them realized he'd been spotted.

Donny "the Handle" Randall shot Mercer a wolfish grin and reached under the left arm of his windbreaker.

Tisa glanced over her shoulder as Mercer pulled her from the rail. She didn't recognize the big man who accelerated after them, but behind him was someone she did know, her brother, Luc. Her heart tripped like she'd just been shocked. In the stark illumination of the deck lights she saw the glow of a knife held flat against his leg.

At the top of the stairs leading into the ship, Mercer shouldered aside a pack of German students coming up from the cafeteria. Pitchers of beer went flying. One of the drunker ones cursed him and took an awkward swing at Mercer's head. The blow missed and the kid punched one of his own friends, sending him down the metal stairway. Someone shouted and a panic began to radiate from the epicenter of the altercation. The surge of passengers slowed Randall's rush across the deck.

"Give me my gun," Mercer called as he dragged Tisa down the clogged stairs.

"It's in my bag on deck!"

He gave her hand a squeeze as if to say that it wasn't important while furiously thinking how to get out of this trap. No doubt Donny had backup. The slender guy behind him looked like he was part of Randall's team. There would be others, too. They'd come after him with a half dozen men in Vegas, believing he would be trapped in his room. On board the ferry where he really was trapped they'd probably double the size of their team to be certain they got him.

At the bottom of the stairs was an open mezzanine stretching the width of the ship. Sickly potted palms lined the walls. To the left and right were corridors leading to cabins and passenger lounges. The whole area was jammed with people, some leaning against the walls or sitting on their luggage, others just milling around. A steady stream of passengers passed through the cafeteria doors. While no one paid him and Tisa any special interest, he knew Randall's backup was coming. A second set of stairs across the mezzanine ascended to the top deck. Donny would expect Mercer to hide amid the twisting interior corridors, not double back, so he led Tisa up the stairs before Donny and the man with him could see where they were heading.

Back in the cooling breeze Mercer realized his body was bathed in sweat, although his breathing remained steady and his heart had slowed after the initial shock of seeing Randall on board. He cut through the crowd and scooped up Tisa's bag from where she'd left it.

Once the familiar heft of the Beretta was in his hand, he felt the odds had evened slightly.

The lights of Santorini were mere pricks against the darkening horizon. Between the ferry and the island, a white motor yacht seemed to be keeping pace with them, hanging a mere thirty yards or so from the side of the ship. Mercer doubted its presence was a coincidence. He looked beyond the cabin cruiser at the receding island. Estimating distance at night was notoriously difficult but he judged the island was too far away to swim to. They had to get off the ferry, and if they were to survive they needed a boat. The ship's life rafts were inflatable and capable of carrying forty people. Each was encased in bulbous fiberglass capsules. Mercer briefly examined the complex tangle of wires and pulleys that launched them and knew he'd never get one overboard in the minutes he had before Randall found him on deck.

"What are we going to do?" Tisa's eyes were wide with fright, but not for herself. Her half brother would never hurt her. She feared for Mercer.

With Tisa in tow he took off toward the ferry's bow. "When we came aboard, I noticed a big chest near the gangway. The label said it contained a six-man inflatable. If we can get to it we can get off this tub."

They cut past a circle of students ringing a young woman playing guitar and were a dozen paces from another stairway when a pair of men in matching nylon windbreakers came around a ventilator stack. Mercer paused for an instant, judging angles and distances, mindful of the passengers farther forward.

The gunmen gave no such thought. Automatic pistols appeared from under their jackets and the first shots exploded across the open deck. Amid the screams of panic from the teens behind Mercer came the higher keen of an injured woman. He dropped to the deck, shoving Tisa to the side, and fired intentionally above the gunmen to avoid hitting anyone on the far side. The assassins ducked out of view, giving him precious seconds to roll out of their line of fire.

The crowds still lingering at the rails had started a headlong stampede off the top deck. One person ended up going over the rail and into the black water below. Mercer and Tisa became caught in the tide of fleeing bodies, fighting to stay on their feet as the mass of people half ran, half fell down a staircase.

Once through the bottleneck of the stairs, the crowd spread. Mercer and Tisa lost the cover they provided. Just a few feet away, another pair of men wearing the same windbreakers were studying faces, searching for their quarry. This time Mercer didn't hesitate. He hammered the first with the butt of his pistol, a savage blow to the back of his head that dropped the gunman instantly. The second was angled away from the crowd enough for Mercer to ram the Beretta into his gut and pull the trigger without worrying about the bullet's follow-through.

The shot was muffled by the man's body, but not enough to prevent another stampede. An alert crewman hit the fire alarm and its piercing shriek added to the din. Mercer fought against the flow of the crowd, shoving and punching a path until breaking clear into a corridor.

"They're trying to kill us," Tisa gasped as they ran from the melee behind them.

"You just noticed?"

"But one of those men, up on deck. It was my brother, Luc." She still couldn't believe it. "He'd never hurt me. He, he, he loves me."

Mercer didn't know what to say, although he understood the bitterness in her voice when she talked about the schism within the Order. Her brother was on the other side and now felt that his beliefs meant more than his sister's life. Who the hell were these people? he wondered. Obviously fanatics, but about what? Nothing Tisa had told him the night before made him consider this level of zealotry.

The only answer was that there were parts that she hadn't explained yet, something that had triggered violence in a group that had remained passive for centuries. Fear or power, those were the only two motivations he could think of. They feared some upcoming event or sought power through their oracle. And considering what the oracle did, he could imagine what they feared.

"You have got to tell me what's going on," he said sharply, checking that a cross corridor was deserted before continuing his flight. "In Vegas they were after me. Now I think they want you."

Tisa opened her mouth to reply when a shot passed between them an instant before the concussive roar of the pistol filled the corridor. Mercer fired a snap counter shot and pushed Tisa ahead of him as they ran down the hall. At a sharp bend in the corridor, Mercer paused to see who was behind them. The hallway was clear, but as he watched, Donny Randall ducked his head from around a set of double doors. Mercer fired two quick shots. As he turned to flee farther into the ship, he caught sight of another man behind Donny. It was the guy with the knife he'd seen on deck. Two things he knew right away. The first was that this was the same guy who'd indifferently tossed the woman over the balcony at the Luxor, and the second was that he looked like Tisa's twin, not just a brother.

Tisa waited at an open hatchway, an access to the utilitarian parts of the ship prohibited to passengers. The lighting was flat and metallic, bare bulbs in wire cages. The walls were gray steel. A staircase as steep as a ladder descended into the gloom below. The air was hot and heavy with the stench of burned engine oil. Mercer stepped over the coaming and followed Tisa down.

Their lead would only last a few seconds before the confines of the stairwell became a slaughterhouse. Tisa nimbly danced down the steep steps, Mercer hot on her heels. When they reached the next landing, the level where the gangway was located, she tried the hatch only to find it jammed. She stepped aside. Not only couldn't Mercer move the handle, he saw that long ago the door itself had been welded to the frame.

"Remind me to take this up with the captain," he remarked offhandedly as he moved Tisa back to the ladder.

A shot split the air, a sharp noise that beat on their eardrums. The bullet sparked a half dozen times as it ricocheted off railings and walls. Barely in control of their descent, Tisa and Mercer plunged down one more level. Though his ears were ringing, Mercer heard the sounds of pursuit. He was too low on ammo to fire a delaying shot.

The next landing was the main car deck and also the bottom of the access shaft. If this door was welded too, Tisa and Mercer were as good as dead. The mechanism to unlock the heavy hatch was stiff and creaked like nails on a chalkboard. Mercer heaved the lever upward at the same time he pounded his shoulder into the steel. A thick crust of corrosion around the jamb held the door in place. He stepped back and launched himself again. The door crashed open and his momentum carried him onto the ferry deck. He fell and rolled into a parked Volvo hard enough to dent the driver's door. Tisa already had the door closed behind them by the time he regained his feet. He helped her resecure the lock. A red fire ax hung from a rack nearby. Mercer wedged the handle into the mechanism to prevent it from opening again. Both he and Tisa fell against the wall, feeling safe for the first time since seeing Donny on deck. They'd run just a short distance yet panted like they'd completed a marathon.

As he struggled to calm his breathing, Mercer surveyed their surroundings. The ferry's car deck stretched from stem to stern, a forty-foot-wide steel tunnel with a twenty-foot ceiling of support girders. The paint had been yellowed by years of exhaust and neglect. The air reeked of diesel fumes. The steel decking was covered in a nonskid material that had long ago become smooth.

The hold was divided into three rows, automobiles flanking the inner lane, which was reserved for heavy trucks in order to maintain the ferry's stability in rough seas. With massive cables holding them closed against the rush of the sea, the tall loading doors at bow and stern resembled the drawbridges of a castle.

The cavernous space vibrated with the power of the engines, which had to be nearby. Thick exhaust stacks rose along the wall from floor to ceiling. Waste heat made the hold uncomfortably hot.

This close to the waterline, the steady whoosh of water rushing along the hull had a lulling resonance that drowned out nearly all other sounds. Mercer tightened his grip on the Beretta to remind himself they weren't out of danger yet. More than likely Donny had enough men to cover all the exits from the hold. He could then take his time hunting down him and Tisa.

The clank of steel on steel was muffled by the heavy door. Mercer whirled, bringing up the Beretta, ready to meet Randall's charge if he somehow broke through the hatch. A second passed and then a few more. Nothing happened.

"Hey, Mercer, can you hear me?" Donny shouted from inside the access shaft.

Mercer scanned the ranks of vehicles looking for movement. He suspected Randall would try to keep him talking while his men gained entry to the hold from another direction. Nothing seemed out of the ordinary.

"Come on, buddy. I know you're there," Donny called. When Mercer remained silent, Randall continued. "No matter, bud, I'll do the talking. See, here's the deal. In about ten minutes a lot of folks are going to die because you had to survive the flood in the mine back in Nevada. Ironic, huh? You got more lives than a cat and the people on this boat have to suffer for it. I can't blame Luc for underestimating you at your hotel. Hell, we both done that.

"Not this time. Luc figured you and his sister would be here tonight to watch that earthquake. Hey, hell of a thing, being able to predict quakes, huh? Anyway, we been on this boat since it left the mainland. Had us plenty of time to make certain, ah, preparations. Soon as we took off from Santorini, my men secured all entrances to the car deck except this one. If we couldn't get you topside, the plan was to force you down here, and we gotcha good.

"Now you tell that girl with you that Luc didn't want her hurt, but hey, shit happens."

"Cut the crap, Donny, and tell me what the hell you want."

"I knew you were there," Randall crowed.

"Yeah, yeah, you're a master strategist, Donny," Mercer spat. "Congratulations. What do you want?"

"I want to watch you die, but that ain't gonna happen. Instead I'm going to get off this tub and about five minutes later explosives are going to blow the bottom out of her. I bet you'll be the first to drown."

Mercer and Tisa exchanged a stricken look. "You sick bastard, why are you doing this?"

" 'Cause you missed your chance to die in the mine, buddy."

Swamped by feelings of responsibility, Mercer didn't

hesitate. "If you only want me then open the god-damned door and get me. Leave Tisa and the other passengers out of it."

"No can do. I already busted the lock on this side and my finger's real itchy to trigger the fifty pounds of 'splosives we stuck down in the engine room. When the water finally closes over your head and you're about to suck it into your lungs, I want you to think about how this was all your fault."

"I'm going to kill you," Mercer raged. The blood pounding in his ears blocked out any other thoughts. "I swear to God I am going to reach down your throat and pull out your heart."

Randall laughed. "Two little problems there, Mercer. One, you ain't gonna get out off this ship alive, and two, you should know by now I don't have a heart."

"Randall!" Mercer shouted, pounding •his fists against the hatch. "Hey!"

Randall was gone.

"Mercer?" Tisa called, touching his arm, trying to calm him. "Stop, please. There must be another way out of here, a ventilator shaft or something."

He slapped the door a final time, certain he heard Randall's laughter as he climbed up the stairs. "Okay, you're right." He took several deep breaths, purging his anger, turning it into action. "You take this side. I'll check along the port side." He looked into her eyes. "We'll get out of this, I promise you."

Her smile was genuine. "I know we will."

Mercer crossed the deck at a sprint, zigzagging around cars and trucks until he reached the bow. This side of the ferry was identical to the opposite, steel walls ribbed by structural girders. He found two door-ways, but as Donny had promised, the locks wouldn't budge, even when he used another fire ax as a lever. He swept farther aft. There were a couple of vent grilles, but they were too small for even Tisa and her contortion skills to slip through. The hold's main vents were on the ceiling, hopelessly out of reach and also too narrow to allow them to escape.

He met up with Tisa at the stern loading ramp. "Anything?"

She shook her head. "What time is it?"

"Jesus, Tisa, not that again."

She wasn't stung by his tone and said gently, "No, I mean how much time before he detonates the explosives?"

Mercer didn't bother looking at his watch. "It could come at any time." He hopped onto the hood of the nearest car, an old Audi, then climbed onto the roof. He scanned the hold, looking for the safest place to wait out the explosion. To plant charges that would blow out the bottom of the ferry, Donny must have gained access to the machinery spaces below the car deck, like he'd boasted. Logically there would be areas at the very bow and stern he couldn't reach, nor would he need to. Enough plastique near an amidships fuel bunker would turn the ferry into an inferno. Surviving that was their first priority.

He jumped off the car and looked into other vehicles. A nearby Fiat was unlocked. He opened the rear door. "Inside, quick." Mercer shoved the front seats forward and motioned Tisa to fold herself onto the floor. He got in after her and covered her body with his own. "Keep your eyes shut and your mouth open—it will keep the pressure wave from blowing out your eardrums."

Mercer knew the wait would be intolerable. The minutes would drag by like molasses as the inevitable approached, not knowing if the initial blast would erupt right below them.

But it wasn't. They waited only seconds before the ship lurched under them, a jarring rattle that shoved the Fiat into an adjacent ten-wheeled tanker truck. Then a second explosion rocked the ship, a brutal onslaught much worse than the initial blast. A fuel tank? Mercer wondered, even as a third charge detonated near the ferry's bow.

After the roaring echo died away, he chanced opening his eyes. The lights high in the ceiling had gone out, leaving the hold in the muted glow of emergency lamps. There was no fire he could see, no telltale flickering. For that he was thankful, yet over the chorus of car alarms he heard something just as deadly when he levered open the Fiat's door—the unmistakable rush of water pouring into the ferry. Fire alarms had gone off and several red strobe lights pulsed urgent warnings in time with the Klaxon.

He stepped from the sedan and knew the ferry was doomed. Mercer had to give Randall credit for placing his explosives at the bow. Traveling at fifteen knots, the vessel's forward motion would act like a pump to force seawater into her bilges and engineering spaces. Against such a torrent, there was no way to swim out through the torn hull plating. If they waited for the ship to equalize enough to make their escape, the ferryboat would likely be resting on the bottom of the Aegean.

"What are we going to do?" Tisa asked as she stood at his side.

"I'm working on it," Mercer said absently as the merest outline of a plan formed in his mind. He slapped the polished steel tank of the fuel truck parked next to the Fiat. It returned a dull ring. Full. Plenty of mass.

The stern door was twenty-five feet wide and nearly as tall, covered with horizontal ripples to improve traction for vehicles struggling into or out of the boat. The large hatch was held closed by tension maintained on cables connected to large drum-shaped motors mounted high on the wall. Although the ship had lost power, the cables remained rigid. In theory, it would be possible to force open the door if Mercer could cut the cables. The doors had reminded him of castle gates and he thought the fuel tanker would make the perfect battering ram.

The driver had left the cab door unlocked and Mercer swung himself onto the seat. Already he could feel the ship tilting toward the bow. The truck reeked of stale cigars, sweat, and garlic. A porn magazine lay open on the passenger seat. The key wasn't in the ignition or atop the sun visor. Mercer reached under him to feel along the floor, then checked the glove compartment and the small trays built into the plastic dashboard. Nothing. There was a map pocket built into the door panel. He reached in and came out with a hand covered in dark, sticky goo.

Cursing, he smeared the gunk on the seat and leapt back to the deck. The ship's list was even more pronounced, maybe ten degrees.

"So much for driving us out of here," he said to Tisa, who watched him silently, "but I'm not through with the truck yet."

He'd earlier tucked the Beretta into the waistband of his pants and now drew it as he approached the cables securing the loading ramp. He'd counted his shots and knew there were four left. "Go get the ax I wedged into the door we came through," he ordered and placed the automatic's muzzle an inch from the thick cable.

Mercer fired one deliberate shot, angling the barrel so the ricochet wouldn't come back at him. The nine-millimeter slug cut through half of the inch-thick wire braid. He aimed again and fired a second time, cutting through half of the half that remained. Tisa returned and stayed at Mercer's side as he crossed athwartships to repeat the procedure with the second cable, nearly severing it with his last two bullets.

She handed him the ax. Mercer had to brace his feet. The ship was down by the head and the angle continued to grow. In a few minutes, any cars not firmly held by the nonskid deck would begin to fall toward the bow. He hefted the ax and chopped at the cable. The metal vibrated with each hit, sending painful shivers up his arm even as he cut a dozen strands with each blow. He chopped again and again using a smooth rhythm learned long ago in the forests of Vermont, where he and his grandfather had cut trees for firewood to heat their home for the winter.

The seventh strike did it. The cable parted with a writhing snap as the sudden release of tension yanked the stay through several pulleys. Without wasting a moment he returned to the first cable and managed to shave off three strokes to part the wire. With the ship sinking by the bow, the stern door remained firmly in place, held fast by gravity.

Toward the front of the ship, a compact car with bald tires lost its fight with the ever-increasing deck pitch and the vehicle skidded into the automobile in front of it. The momentum caused this car to begin to slide forward. In seconds, half the port-side row of cars were in motion, careening down the inclined deck in a chain reaction. Their slide ended with cars crashing into the bow doors. Mercer distinctly heard the slosh of water amid the crunch of metal. The hold was beginning to flood quicker than he'd hoped.

Perfect.

They returned to the tanker truck. "Tisa, I want you to go around and find as many blankets as you can, plastic sheeting too, tarps, things like that."

"Okay." She was off without questioning his odd request.

Mercer turned his attention to the valves that controlled the fuel in the giant tanker. The valves required a special tool, which he found in a storage bin mounted to the chassis in front of the back wheels.

He opened one of the valves and a jet of gasoline arced from the tank in a noxious golden stream. The stream was powerful enough to climb as high as the stern doors before falling to the deck and running back under the tanker. It sluiced down the deck in sheets, mixing with the water bubbling up at the distant bow. The stench made Mercer's head spin.

A car on the starboard side lost its battle with gravity and smashed into the ferry's prow.

"Are you all right?" he shouted, fearing for Tisa.

"I'm fine. What's that smell?"

"Gasoline. I'm emptying the tank."

"Oh."

Mercer opened a second valve, doubling the flow. He had no idea how long it would take so he moved down the line of trucks. The next rig was an eighteen-wheeler, and the cab was unlocked. The ferry hadn't settled enough to overcome the truck's massive weight, but as Mercer climbed in he saw the parking brake had been set and the transmission left in gear. Once he had everything in place he planned on launching the truck down the sloping deck then easing the tanker after it. For his scheme to work he needed plenty of open deck if the tanker's momentum was going to be able to smash open the stern door.

Tisa returned a few minutes later with her arms full of sleeping bags and a roll of plastic. She had to brace her hip against the tanker's front fender to stay upright. "I got what you wanted," she called to Mercer, who had remained up at the valve controls. "Will you tell me why now?"

"Get near the cab," he ordered. More than two-thirds of the gasoline in the truck had drained down into the growing pool of water filling the forward section of the sinking ferry. Mercer noticed that the air had cooled dramatically and realized the engines had long since been silenced. He cranked the valves closed and joined Tisa near the driver's door.

"Water weighs eight pounds per gallon, seawater a little less. I estimate this tanker holds five thousand gallons and I've drained about three thousand."

"Leaving two," Tisa said.

"Leaving air," Mercer corrected. "Three thousand gallons worth of air, or buoyancy equal to twenty-four thousand pounds. Factoring in that the remaining gas is also lighter than water, I estimate that this tank is more than buoyant enough to make the entire truck float like a piece of Styrofoam."

Tisa's eyes lit up. "When the hold fills with water, the truck will float up and smash open the door. We'll rise to the surface."

Mercer nodded. "Provided the cab doesn't flood first."

Tisa held up her bundle. "That's what this is for."

"You got it."

They worked side by side, tearing sleeping bags into strips to stuff into the air vents, and using a roll of duct tape they found in the glove compartment to tape over the gaps around the windows and along the passenger door, sealing off where the brake, clutch, and gas pedals came through the floorboards, and anyplace else they thought water could enter the cab. Through it all, they ignored the sounds of the ship sinking deeper into the water and the growing surge of water creeping up the deck. The remaining automobiles on the port side slid down into the pile of smashed vehicles at the bow.

By the time they finished most of the car alarms had gone silent because their electronics had been shorted by the advancing seawater.

"I think we're set," Mercer pronounced. "I need to clear the deck behind us so I can control our slide down. We can't allow the truck to get tangled in that pileup down there. I'll be right back. I'll be coming back fast so stay on the passenger side but keep your foot on the brake."

Stepping out of the cab and looking down the three-hundred-foot length of the ferry was like standing atop a ski jump. And at the bottom lay a pile of mangled automobiles pressed against the bow in a cauldron of water that swirled ever higher. The creeping surface spurted in foaming geysers as air pockets trapped within the tangle of cars erupted. The view was disorienting. So far none of the trucks, with their numerous tires and better traction, had started their inexorable slide.

Mercer had to grip the tanker's bodywork with one hand and lean far back on his heels to keep his footing as he made his way down the inclined deck. Once at the truck's front bumper, he dropped to his backside and crawled like a crab until reaching the rear of the eighteen-wheeler. On his feet once again, he clung to the trailer's side and slowly eased his way along its length. He finally reached the tractor and clambered along it until he could open the driver's door. He reached up for the handle, and as soon as he released the catch the door flew open with a violent jerk. Keeping his body partially outside the truck, he reached across the seat and jimmied the gearshift into neutral.

The truck shuddered as the strain of keeping it in place fell solely on the parking brake. The tires gave a single chirp as the eighteen-wheeler slid a fraction of an inch. Mercer wiggled farther out of the cab, took a shallow breath, and popped the brake release.

The truck dropped away like an avalanche of metal, smashing into the school bus in front of it, sending it into a moving van until the whole string of oversized vehicles raced for the bow. Mercer had just barely dropped clear as the semi hit the bus and he watched as the wall of trucks vanished into the gloom. He lay on the sloping deck like a fly stuck on sticky paper, his arms and legs spread flat.

With precise movements he turned onto his stom-

ach, peered once more over his shoulder to see that
the deck had become a steep featureless wall and
began to climb up to the tanker, still holding tight,
although it wouldn't be for long. If its tires slipped
now, the truck would roll right over him.

He climbed upward, his fingertips exploiting every
irregularity in the deck to give him purchase. Once he
reached the truck, he could feel the bodywork judder-
ing as it wanted to succumb to gravity. Mercer climbed
into the cab, placing his foot on the brake before Tisa
took hers away. Without waiting, he cranked the
transmission into neutral and took away just a fraction
of the pressure he kept on the brake pedal. The truck
moved an inch or two before he jammed in the
pedal again.

Keeping the rig straight and his motions smooth, he
eased the truck down the deck. It seemed to take
forever and they were almost at the top of the pile of
wrecked vehicles when the ferry lurched suddenly and
a gout of water erupted from the pool at the bow.
The truck slammed into the rear of the semitrailer
and immediately water began to surge around the
front wheels.

It was strange to consider that the water level wasn't
rising. The apparent upward advance came because
the ferry was sinking. In minutes, roiling water lapped
at the side windows and continued to climb even
higher. Mercer recalled the feeling of diving in *Bob*,
although this was a far cry from the high-tech submersible. Tisa reached for his hand.

The oily water passed over the hood, rising above
the roof. The cab was completely submerged.

"The moment of truth." For some reason he
couldn't explain, Mercer was whispering.

Tisa replied in kind. "For what?"

"To see if this old girl has some fight left in her."

The cylindrical tank felt the first hint of buoyancy

and the truck shuddered as it shifted against the wreckage. The shriek of metal seemed amplified by the water, a tearing sound worse than any Mercer had ever heard. But no matter how buoyant, the truck couldn't break free of the other vehicles.

"Come on, come on," Mercer urged under his breath, noting the cloth stuffed into an air vent was glistening with moisture. "Float, you pig, float."

Without warning the truck did a sudden pirouette and fell onto its side. The tanker pulled its bumper free, allowing the vehicle to scrape against the canted deck as it remained level with the steadily rising tide of water.

An explosion outside the hold shook the entire ferry. The volume of water flooding the ship doubled. Held at sea level by the air trapped in its tank, the truck remained in one place as the ship sank into the abyss at an ever-increasing speed. She was near vertical now and Mercer could imagine her blunt stern raised high, her propellers gleaming in the moonlight.

Mercer wondered grimly how many hapless victims remained near enough to the doomed ship to be sucked under when she vanished beneath the waves.

Tisa cried out and lunged at a toggle switch on the dash that had broken away, allowing water to dribble in around the cracked plastic. She held her hand over the weeping gash. The blankets at Mercer's feet were sodden. As the truck floated up from the bow, there was just enough light penetrating the dark waters for Mercer to count the support girders lining the wall. He estimated the stern door was at least seventy feet above them. Water found more openings into the cab.

"Are we going to—"

"It'll be close," he answered, not needing her to finish the question.

The ship continued to fill with water. The auto deck wasn't the only space flooding. Her bilges and upper

decks too were drowning, a few passengers too slow
or too disoriented to escape after the initial explosion
dying silently in the black water. The ferry was actually lower in the water than Mercer thought, and sinking faster than he believed possible. The truck was
fifty feet from hitting the stern door when her stern
rail vanished under the waves, leaving the sea littered
with hastily launched lifeboats and hundreds of wailing passengers.

The water in the inverted cab was up to Mercer's
knees. Tisa braced her feet against the dash to keep
them dry. The truck sloshed across the hold because
the ferry corkscrewed as she sank. Mercer couldn't
tell how far they were from hitting the door.

"Tighten your lap belt," he said unnecessarily. He
and Tisa were buckled as tight at they could be. "Get
into the crash position they teach you on airplanes.
It'll protect you from whiplash."

They ducked down, holding their chests to their
knees. The position was uncomfortable for Mercer,
but he lacked a tenth of Tisa's flexibility.

Outside the ferry, water pressure exploited the
smallest entrances into the ship, forcing air from any
voids with increasing fury. The last and greatest empty
chamber on the ship was the car deck. Air trapped at
the still-sealed stern had formed a taut bubble that
needed just a tiny more impetus to blow open the
eight-ton ramp. The gasoline tank was made of heavy-
gauge noncorrosive steel and hit the door at nearly
seventeen miles per hour. The truck's upward rush
ended in a savage impact that whipped Mercer and
Tisa brutally, though none of the windows cracked.

"What happened? Are we free?"

Mercer didn't say anything for a moment, his opti-
mism fading with each passing second. The ramp
hadn't been blown open. "No, damn it. We're not
light enough to force open the door. We're trapped."

Water continued to pour into the cab. It was up to Mercer's waist and climbing. He could feel pressure building in his ears. They were probably forty feet below the surface by now and falling by the second. He knew there were two choices: wait for the water to slowly fill the cab or simply break a window and end it quick.

There was no light for him to see Tisa, but he could feel her hand in his. She gave him a squeeze. She also understood their options.

"Just do it," she whispered with eerie calm, as if she'd known it would come to this all along.

"I'm sorry, Tisa."

"It's not your fault. You did everything you could."

"No, I mean I can't do it." His voice was fierce, unbending. "I'm not giving in, not until I can't hold my breath for one second longer."

Like a piece of flotsam, the tank truck rolled along the door, edging away from the stout hinges at the base.

Water continued to pour into the cab, covering Mercer and Tisa, forcing them to unsnap their belts and struggle to find the diminishing air pocket. Tisa came up sputtering, her hair plastered against her head. Her arms went around Mercer.

"I don't want to die, Mercer. Oh my God, I really don't want to die." She sounded surprised to realize she had a survival instinct.

The truck rolled once again, tumbling the pair as though they were caught in a washing machine. They had to fight to find air.

The tanker came to rest at the very top of the door, pushed there by the streams of bubbles still rising from deeper in the hold. The added force of buoyancy was just enough to crack the door open a fraction of an inch. Air gushed through the opening, forced through by the tremendous pressure. The heavy door was pushed farther back on its hinges. The truck rolled again in the surge of air and suddenly it was scraping across the threshold. It hung suspended, half in and half out of the plummeting ferry, gripped tight by the heavy door.

Mercer held his face pressed tight to the top of the cab, taking shallow sips of air, allowing Tisa the lion's share of the few remaining breaths. They'd been in the water ten minutes, not nearly enough for the cold to affect them, but still both trembled as if suffering hypothermia.

"Mercer. I—" A wave forced water down Tisa's throat. She spat and gagged to clear her lungs. "I want you to know—"

Like a cork from a shaken bottle of champagne, the pressure of air in the big tank wouldn't be held any longer. Shoving aside the door the ten-ton truck popped free and rocketed toward the surface amid a fountain of bubbles.

The motion was so violent that Mercer's last breath left his mouth half filled with foul water. His lungs burned and he felt the muscles of his diaphragm convulsing to draw air. Tisa couldn't be faring any better, he thought, as the truck spiraled upward.

From a depth of sixty feet, the trip to the surface took just seconds. The tanker exploded from under the waves like a breaching whale, slamming back to the sea with a splash that nearly capsized a nearby lifeboat. Several survivors struggling in the water were almost crushed when the heavy vehicle spun to find its equilibrium.

Mercer was thrown into the windshield when the tanker broached, shattering the glass and what felt like his skull. He kicked free from the cab, reached back for Tisa and dragged her through the opening. Holding her limp body in one arm, he stroked for the surface, his lungs screaming.

He surfaced next to the bobbing truck and sucked in great drafts of air. Crisscrossing searchlights mounted on a dozen lifeboats cut the dark night. The only sounds were boat motors and pleas for help. The sea was littered with the dead and dying.

The front half of the tanker was underwater, allowing Mercer to wedge himself into the rear wheel well. Tisa wasn't breathing. He held her to his chest and was able to pinch off her nostrils and begin to breathe air into her lungs.

Tears mingled with the salt water stinging his eyes. "Come on, come on," he called softly, his mouth inches from hers, his senses alert for the slightest sign of life. He continued CPR, trying to massage her chest to keep her heart going. His precarious position on the tanker made his efforts extremely awkward. He gently blew more air into her body, feeling her lungs expand with each cycle. Tisa remained inert.

And then she coughed up a mouthful of bile and water. Mercer didn't care that he took most of it in his face. Tisa coughed again, a deep retching that seemed to rip the delicate tissues in her chest. Mercer turned her in his arms so it was easier for her to clear her lungs, all the while rubbing her back and murmuring reassurances.

It took her several minutes to regain her breath enough to speak, and even then Mercer urged her to stay quiet. In that time a dozen stranded passengers had floundered their way to the tottering truck, clinging to precarious handholds wherever they could find them. One man tried to climb the tank, but Mercer reached out a hand to prevent him from upsetting the vehicle's delicate balance.

He wasn't paying attention to the boat that approached the tanker. From his position it was just a murky outline behind a dazzling searchlight. As it neared, a few people struck off from the tanker to climb aboard the rescue craft.

Mercer watched absently as the strongest swimmer reached what he thought was a lifeboat and made a grab for the gunwale. A shadowy figure in the craft lofted something high over his head and brought it down with a sickening crunch that carried all the way to the tanker truck.

What the . . . ?

Another man looped an arm over the boat's low transom. He too was struck over the head. He screamed shrilly but his shout was cut off with another savage blow. A searchlight beam swept the lifeboat and Mercer saw that it wasn't one of the boats from the ferry. This was a sleek white powerboat, about thirty feet long. Its European styling reminded Mercer of the large motor yacht he'd seen tracking the ferry. That's how Donny had made his escape, a launch from the big yacht. And now he had returned. Why?

The answer was obvious—to make sure that he and Tisa were dead.

"Tisa, we have to get away," he whispered urgently. "Your brother's back."

She peered into the darkness. The area around the speedboat was becoming chaotic; the crew aboard were whacking at those struggling in the water as though they were marauding pirates bent on plunder. Though the light was bad, and Tisa near-drowned, she recognized the lithe form of her brother standing in the speedboat's bow. Behind him, Donny Randall smacked at people like an Arctic hunter cracking the skulls of baby seals.

She turned back to Mercer, barely able to see his features in the darkness. "I'm sorry," she said, and touched his cheek. "This is the only way. He won't hurt me."

"What are you—?"

"Luc," Tisa shouted. "I'm here. Please. I love you." She pushed away from the tanker and began swimming before Mercer could stop her. "I'm here, Luc. It's Tisa." She paused in the water, looking back at him. Her face was a pale oval hovering just above the black water. "Oh my God! Leper Alma, Mercer. Watch for Leper Alma."

The speedboat knifed across to where she struggled, deliberately running over two survivors clinging to a single life jacket. The craft circled around, and when it reached Tisa, Donny Randall lifted her from the water as easily as a kitten. From where he clutched the tanker truck, Mercer watched horrified as she fell into the waiting arms of her brother.

In the few moments the speedboat had idled, it had attracted dozens of swimmers brave enough, or desperate enough, to chance getting aboard. Donny and another crewman armed themselves with oars once again, but despite their best efforts they were becoming overwhelmed by the press of struggling humanity. Tisa spoke a few words to her brother. Luc ordered the boat's driver to get them back to the yacht before they were swamped.

Mercer watched it all, unable to believe what he was seeing. Tisa had willingly sacrificed herself to save him. She'd gone to convince her brother that she alone had survived and he was dead in the hold of the ferry. He had no idea what Luc would do to her. She hadn't told him much about her brother—he felt deliberately—but the impression he had was that their problems went far, far beyond the ideological split within their Order.

He didn't know what to think, what to do. He was at a complete loss. Even maintaining his grip on the tanker truck didn't seem worth the effort. He'd barely found her and now she was gone.

Someone knocked into him, bringing him back to his situation. It was a boy of about eight, wide-eyed and frightened, his skinny shoulders nearly slipping through his life jacket. Mercer grabbed the boy and held him close. The child hugged him fiercely, crying in Greek, calling out for his mother in such a clear voice that Mercer felt his heart's ache deepen further.

In moments two dozen other swimmers were clustered around the tanker and it fell on Mercer to distribute them around the truck to keep the rig from upending. Soon overloaded lifeboats had rafted alongside and the truck became the center of the survivors' universe. Men gave up their spaces in the boats for women and children while ship's officers gave their spots to tourists.

Two hours later a ferry from Santorini reached the floating atoll of boats to take on those left alive and commence the grim task of collecting the corpses. Many people would later recall how terrorists in a speedboat had clubbed survivors in the water and kidnapped a young woman, though no one could give an accurate description of the men or their vessel or how they'd escaped. Nor could anyone describe the American who'd miraculously popped up from the depths in the tanker truck to organize the rescue effort and save countless lives.

The dream diverged from reality at the same place for the last three nights. Holding tightly to each other against the truck, Tisa and Mercer waited in the dark for Donny and Luc Nguyen to give up their search. In the dream, Tisa didn't call out to her brother and swim away. In the dream, she stayed by Mercer's side. In the dream Mercer was happy.

Reality came with the discreet chime of a Tiffany alarm clock. Mercer woke with an emptiness the past few days of activity had been unable to fill. The light filtering through the skylight above his bed was sodden and gray. The third straight day of rain matched his mood perfectly.

He turned to disable the alarm and came face-to-face with a long muzzle and red droopy eyes. Drag had been awaiting his chance. Now that Mercer was awake, the basset hound began to lick at his face, his tail thumping against the blankets like a sluggish metronome. Since Mercer's return from Greece, the mangy dog had forgone his master, asleep on the barroom couch, and settled on the king-sized bed. Each morning he'd waited for the alarm before adding his own wet affection to prod Mercer out of bed.

"Those aren't the kisses I wanted," Mercer said as he scratched the hound's floppy ears, "but I appreciate the gesture." Drag wormed his way partially under the covers and presented his substantial belly for a little attention.

The dream always left Mercer bathed in sweat, so while Drag burrowed deeper into the warm spot on the bed and snored blissfully, Mercer took a quick shower and dressed, putting on jeans, T-shirt and sneakers. Down at the bar getting coffee from the automatic machine he looked fondly at Harry White asleep on the couch, his prosthetic leg on the floor next to him, his mouth slack. Harry had slept over ever since Mercer had returned. Although they hadn't talked much beyond the bare facts of the past few weeks, Harry recognized that Mercer was hurting and refused to leave him alone. He'd wait until hell froze over for Mercer to be ready to discuss what he was feeling.

Drag sauntered down the spiral stairs, passed the bar and continued to the foyer, his nails clicking against the tile until he reached the front door. He woofed softly, demanding to go out.

By the time Mercer returned from the walk around the block, Harry was sitting on his customary stool with a cigarette between his lips. He'd poured himself a cup of Mercer's tarry coffee rather than make his own pot and had a pen ready to do the *Washington Post* crossword puzzle. Mercer slid the paper to his friend and stepped behind the bar to turn on the room's industrial air filter.

"You know," Harry rasped, then cleared his throat. His voice didn't improve. "Drag got used to sleeping in your bed when you were gone. If you let me have it back, he wouldn't bother you in the morning."

"It's not the bed, Harry—it's the fact you get up to take a leak a dozen times a night."

"What can I say? I've always had a small bladder."

"Small bladder, enlarged prostate, tomato, tomahto."

"Potato, potahto, let's call the whole thing off." Harry sipped at his coffee and made a face. "You got any Bloody Mary mix back there?"

"Yeah. It's that crap Tiny pawned off on me. You won't like it."

Harry dismissed Mercer's warning with a wave. "You think I'm drinking it for the mix? Just use good vodka."

Mercer snorted, thinking that Harry White should be added to death and taxes as life's inevitabilities. He fixed the drink and placed it next to Harry's ashtray.

"So are you spending your day on the computer again?" Harry asked, wrapping his long fingers around the glass.

Mercer had spent the first twelve hours after his arrival at Dulles Airport three days ago being debriefed by Ira Lasko and a joint team of CIA and FBI agents. He told them everything he knew about Tisa, her organization, the attack on the ferry, and her cryptic final words, which he still didn't understand. He'd been through such meetings before and was able to keep his temper in check as they went over the same information again and again, trying to coax more out of him. At the end of the debrief, the agents had packed up their recorders, cameras, and notebooks and left the conference room near Ira's office without comment.

Mercer and Ira were alone. "Now what?" Mercer had asked.

"Now nothing," Ira said. "They'll write up their report and fill in any gaps they can. I'll go over it and forward it to my boss, who might or might not pass it to the president."

"Ira, Tisa Nguyen laid her life on the line to convince me that her group can predict earthquakes. I'm sure she didn't do it just to impress me. I think something big is coming, something she wanted, no, *needed* me to know. She's giving us a warning, or at least part of one."

"This Leper Alma she mentioned?"

"Yes. She told me the where, but didn't have time to give me the when. Now I admit I have no idea what Leper Alma means, if it's a place or the name of a nuclear power plant or what. But I think that whatever it is it's about to be destroyed by an earthquake or a volcano."

"We'll look into it, of course."

"Look into it?" Mercer snorted. "I'm the one who brought you this information and you're cutting me out of the loop."

"I'm not cutting you out," Ira shot back, "but Christ, look at yourself. You're a mess. You've pushed yourself for the past month without a break. Let the analysts do their job while you get some rest. In a day or two I'll call and let you know what they've come up with."

"Meanwhile Tisa is God knows where and no one's going to lift a finger to help her." Mercer was disgusted.

"For the time being that's out of my hands. You've given us a lot and it's going to take a while to substantiate your claims."

"Claims? How many people died when Donny Randall blew up that ferry? Forty? Fifty?"

"Forty-seven."

"Wouldn't you call that substantiation that these bastards need to be stopped?"

"And they will be, but I'm not going off half-cocked."

"The way you're acting I doubt you even have half a one," Mercer said angrily, twisting Ira's cliché. "Are we through here?"

Ira held Mercer's gaze but said nothing. As soon as Mercer closed the door behind him, Lasko shook his head and reached for the phone book in a bottom desk drawer. He found the number he wanted.

"Tiny's."

Ira recognized Paul Gordon's high-pitched voice. "Paul, this is Ira Lasko. I'm a friend of Mercer's. I've been at your bar a few times with him."

"Yeah, I remember. What can I do you for?"

"Have you seen Harry White?"

"Morning, noon, and night."

"Any idea where he is right now?"

"In the can. Hold on, he's coming out now. Want to talk to him?"

"Yes, thanks."

"Admiral," Harry boomed. "What's going on? Where's Mercer?"

"He's back. Just left my office." Ira paused, thinking how he wanted to phrase his next statement. "I'm worried about him. Something happened to him in Greece. I've never seen him like this before."

"What happened?"

Ira told Harry about how the ferry was sunk.

"That ain't it," Harry said. "Mercer's been in worse jams than that. What else?"

"Well, there was this woman."

"Ah, now we're getting someplace. What happened to her?"

"Mercer went to meet her. She had some information. After they escaped the ferry she was kidnapped by the group she belonged to."

"Terrorist group?"

"We're not sure yet."

"Doesn't matter anyway," Harry said. "You've known Mercer a couple of years, but not the way I do. What you gotta understand is he's basically an overgrown Boy Scout and he takes responsibility for everything and everyone around him. It's what drives him. Right now he's blaming himself for that woman getting nabbed and he's not going to stop until he gets her back."

"I know all that. This seems more somehow. He's taking this personal."

"He takes everything personally."

"No, Harry, you're not listening. Personal, as in to heart."

Harry needed a moment to get what Ira was driving at. The idea was shocking. "You don't think he's . . . I mean he can't be in . . ."

"I don't know," Lasko answered. "All the signs are there."

"Holy shit! Who would have thought it? Our boy in love. I admit this is new territory for me. As long as I've known him, he's never fallen for anyone. He came close once with an oil heiress, good-looking girl with more money than sense, but even that was just a temporary thing."

Harry paused. He was torn. Part of him wanted Mercer to find that kind of happiness while an equal part feared for what that would do to their friendship. Nothing, he decided quickly. Mercer wouldn't fall for a woman who didn't appreciate the company of a crippled rummy and his stinky dog. And when he accepted that, he knew he'd do everything in his power to help Mercer get her back.

"I wanted you to know," Ira said. "Can you keep an eye on him? Try to get him to talk. He's bottled up pretty tight and I don't want to see him blow."

"You don't have to worry. No matter how tight he gets wrapped, Mercer knows his limits. He needs a little time, is all. But thanks for the heads-up. I'll watch him for the both of us."

"You're a good friend, Harry White."

"Yeah, well, truth be told, so are you, Ira. I'll talk to you later."

Harry had hung around Mercer's place in the days since, watching and waiting for his friend to open up. Meanwhile, Mercer spent his time on his computer searching for everything he could about the legend of Rinpoche-La. What he found confirmed much of what Tisa had told him about the Chinese treasure fleet and the extraordinary voyages of Admiral Zheng He. There was little about Zhu Zhanji and the fabled treasure he'd spirited away and absolutely nothing about her organization. He did learn that the Chinese were the first to attempt developing accurate earthquake sensors. These were delicately balanced porcelain pots that when filled with water became unstable. The slightest tremor would cause water to spill from one of the multiple dragon mouth spouts. The direction and amount of water spilled would tell those watching it where and how strong the quake had been. The earliest one found was almost two thousand years old.

As for the mythical village, the Internet provided a great deal of conjecture but little in the way of fact. Most of what he found was on Web sites dedicated to mysticism and New Age mumbo jumbo. They said Rinpoche-La was the last truly unspoiled place on earth, a sort of terrestrial Nirvana where the inhabitants were free from the daily burden of human existence. They put the village's location high in the Himalayas, deep in the Gobi Desert and a thousand locations in between.

The writers sounded so flaky, Mercer determined that no one had ever tried a scientific approach to finding the hamlet. He contacted a commecial satellite imaging company in La Jolla, California, and requested every high-resolution photo they had of the north flank of the Himalaya Mountains for the past five years. That's where Tisa indicated she'd been born, and at five hundred dollars per picture, the cost of expanding the search beyond that area would be staggering.

As it stood, the weeks he'd spent consulting in Canada for De Beers would cover just a portion of the price of the two thousand prints that had been delivered late yesterday afternoon.

Until he studied the pictures, he would put the

search for Rinpoche-La out of his mind and concentrate on the second puzzle Tisa had given him. Leper Alma.

"Yup," Mercer finally answered Harry's question about his day's plans. "Another wasted effort on the computer. I can't do much else until I hear from Ira."

"Sure you can." Harry held up his empty drink. "Pour yourself one of these and relax for a while. I'll call Tiny and see if he'll open early or maybe we can take a ride up to Pimlico to watch the ponies."

As tempting as it sounded, Mercer shook his head. "I can't."

"Killing yourself won't get her back," Harry said softly.

Mercer froze. He wasn't surprised Harry had figured out what was driving him so hard; he probably understood Mercer's motivations even better than Mercer did. He was just startled that Harry had brought it up. In their unwritten code, neither man discussed their emotions much. Each carried several lifetimes' worth of scars and saw little need to irritate them further.

"Do you love her?" Harry prodded.

"I don't know." Mercer's reply was slow, deliberate. "Maybe. We only spent one day together, not enough time to know for sure."

"When it comes to love, no one's ever really sure."

"That sounds like something you heard on Oprah."

Harry smirked. "Jerry Springer. Overweight teen cross-dressers in love with their teachers was the show's topic." He turned thoughtful. "The amount of time you spend with someone doesn't matter. A day, a week or a year. It's all the same. Christ, there are couples who spend a lifetime together only to finally admit they've hated each other since day one."

"Too true. More than anything, Harry, I'm pissed that some asshole has denied us the opportunity to find out."

"And what if it isn't love?"

"I'd still go after her for no other reason than the chance to kill Donny Randall."

Harry smiled and slapped the bar. "Now that sounds like the Mercer I know."

"So what the hell do I do?"

"Pour us that drink for one thing and I guess keep doing what you're doing. Only don't think about why you want to find her. It'll cloud your judgment. Concentrate on the how."

Not bad advice, Mercer admitted, considering the source. "What's the longest you've ever spent with a woman?"

Harry gave him a lecherous look. "An hour and ten minutes, but that was at midnight when the clocks roll forward."

"Seriously."

"Seriously? About six months. This was years ago when I first moved to Washington and thought it was time to settle down."

"What happened?"

"I realized that when I was with her I wasn't being true to myself. I was already settled by then and was using her just to legitimize my life. For a while I hid my feelings in a misguided attempt to protect her. Big mistake. The night I broke up with her, she was expecting me to propose. She had no idea how I really felt. It was one hell of an ugly scene. I know it was for the best. I could have faked it for a while longer, years maybe, but in the end it wouldn't have worked. I'm sure someday she realized it too. I guess in your situation, you have to ask yourself if you are still who you're supposed to be when you were with Tisa. And that's a trickier question than it sounds."

"I know it is," Mercer agreed. "And the truth is I don't know yet."

"But when you *were* with her?"

Mercer didn't hesitate. "Yes."

Harry sat back in his stool, a smug expression on his weathered face. "There you go then. Go back to work, but at three o'clock we're going to Tiny's and I'm going to buy rounds until one of us is blind drunk. That's not an offer. It's a threat."

With a fresh pot of coffee in hand, Mercer left Harry to his crossword puzzle and went down to his office. The room was decorated like the bar, with green carpet and plenty of oak and brass. In one corner was one of Mercer's prize possessions, a blackened piece of lightweight metal that had once been a girder of the airship *Hindenburg*. Passing the credenza by the door, Mercer's hand brushed a slab of a bluish mineral called kimberlite. He considered this particular rock, which was the lodestone for diamond mining, his personal good-luck charm. It had been presented to him by a grateful mine manager whose life Mercer had saved.

He sat at the antique desk and ramped on to the Internet. He typed "Leper Alma" into a search engine and groaned when he saw there were a quarter million matches. He had no idea what the name meant yet the computer readily matched it to two hundred and fifty thousand Web sites.

After an hour's worth of education about leprosy, he knew he was on the wrong track. There were only a handful of leper colonies, or leprosariums, left in the world and none of them was affiliated with the name Alma. Nor were there any famous lepers or physicians who treated them named Alma either.

"Wrong track?" he muttered. "I'm not even in the right station."

He'd obviously misheard what Tisa had told him. The trick now was to recall her exact words. Mercer got up from his desk and went to the closet in the corner of the office. Amid the junk, files, and miscellaneous paperwork that was easier to shelve than sort, Mercer found a large shoebox. He returned with it to his desk. He pulled out a soft towel from the box and spread it across his desktop, then set a foot-long piece of railroad track in the center. Cans of metal polish, rags, and scraps of steel wool came next.

For thirty minutes he worked on the rusted section of rail, working the metal with the concentration of a diamond cutter facing a priceless stone. The repetitive act of polishing the track was the way Mercer helped focus his mind. It was a habit he'd formed in school as a way to alleviate the pressure of studying without turning his brain to mush, much the way Winston Churchill built brick walls in the yard behind Number 10 Downing Street even during the bleakest days of the Blitz.

A half hour after starting, he'd purged his mind of everything but those fleeting seconds as Tisa swam toward her brother. He could again feel how his movements had been slowed by the weight of water and the throb from where he'd hit his head against the tanker's windshield.

"I'm here, Luc. It's Tisa." Her voice echoed across the dark sea, a cry that rang clear over the background of misery. Her head was barely above water as she swam awkwardly for her brother's boat. Halfway there she stopped, turned back to Mercer, her body shuddering as she treaded water. "Oh my God! Leper Alma, Mercer. Watch for Leper Alma."

He heard it the same way again and again. Leper Alma. Leper Alma.

Forcing himself to watch her vanish time and again was worse than the emptiness he'd woken to for the past three days. His heart beat furiously, and yet his hands maintained their unhurried rhythm as he scoured rust from the length of railroad track.

It had been too dark to see her mouth. Even from

a few yards away her face had been a pale oval struggling just above the surface. Leper Alma. She'd bobbed in the water as she'd said those words, he recalled now. A wave had passed close by, raising her head slightly, but also covering the lower part of her face as she spoke.

It hadn't been leper. The second syllable had been her clearing seawater from her mouth. Lep Alma. He was close and his hands began to work faster, the dull metal between his fingers growing bright under the chemical and physical assault.

The solution came and he dropped the polish-soaked rag on his desk and rolled back in his chair. She'd either said Le Palma or La Palma. He turned to the computer, unconcerned that his fingers left smudges on the keyboard as he typed the names into the search engine.

The computer turned up tens of thousands of matches, but just fifteen minutes after starting in on the first entry he was on the phone to a geologist in Cambridge, England, named Robert Wright. Mercer didn't know Wright, but the Ph.D. was mentioned prominently on several Web pages about La Palma. After an hour-long conversation, he made a frantic call to Admiral Lasko.

"Ira, it's Mercer. We've been searching in the wrong place. I misheard what Tisa said. It wasn't Leper Alma. She said La Palma."

"We know," Lasko said.

"Huh? How?"

"I put the NSA's cryptoanalysis computers on it. Their report was sitting on my desk yesterday morning. They tore apart the words phonetically and came up with a couple thousand matches. The most obvious was La Palma, one of the Canary Islands, volcanic but dormant."

"Not according to the scientist who's spent his entire career studying the place. I just got off the phone with him."

"You're talking about Dr. Wright? I've already had people go over his research and frankly we're not that impressed. On more than one occasion he's been accused of falsifying data to fit his model."

"Are you willing to take the chance he's wrong?"

"We're taking a wait-and-see attitude right now."

"Ira, listen to me. This whole thing has been Tisa's way of warning me about a La Palma eruption. I'm certain of it. Obviously she did it far enough in advance so we could do something about it. But I don't think we have time for your wait-and-see attitude. If you've read some of what Dr. Wright predicted, you understand the consequences."

"Give me a little credit, will you? A team's already been sent to the island to monitor the situation. They arrive today. Another group with equipment more sophisticated than anything Wright has seen should get there tomorrow. We're on it, Mercer, but right now there's no need to panic."

"Have you told the president?"

"I passed it up to Security Advisor Kleinschmidt. I don't know if he took it any further."

"We have to find her, Ira."

"Who? Tisa?"

"That mountain's going to blow no matter what your teams tell you. She's the only person who knows when. We need her, damn it." Mercer slowed, taking a breath to calm himself. "I agree that monitoring the island is the best course right now, but we have to talk with Tisa before it's too late."

"Even if we wanted her, we don't have a clue where she is."

"I'm working on that," Mercer countered quickly. "If I pinpoint where I think she is, will you authorize a rescue?"

"I . . . I'll think about it. That's the best I can do."

"Then that's all I'll ask." Mercer cut the connection and felt better than he had in days. He was able to put the appalling consequences of a La Palma eruption out of his mind only because he was thinking about Tisa. She had the answers he needed, and Ira was beginning to box himself into a corner to allow Mercer to find her.

With most of his luggage spread from Canada to Vegas to the bottom of the Aegean Sea, Mercer went to the second-floor guest room where he kept an old set. From the bar, Harry saw him lugging the bags upstairs. "What are you doing?"

"Packing."

"For where?"

"Africa, at the least. China if I get lucky."

"You gotta talk to your travel agent. Your itineraries are all screwed up."

Once he had both bags packed, he returned to the bar with the box full of sixteen-by-sixteen-inch satellite pictures from the imaging company in California. He'd requested they be stacked chronologically so that the first ten pictures showed the same spot on the earth over the past five years. The next set was an adjacent segment of ground over the same period of time. Dividing the file box in half, Mercer handed Harry one of the two magnifying glasses he'd brought up from his office. He turned up the bar lights and explained how the pictures were organized.

"What am I supposed to do?"

"Look for clouds that don't move."

"Huh?"

"Tisa told me the valley of Rinpoche-La is fed by a geothermal hot spring. There should be waste heat from the spring that will show up as steam. If each picture of the same spot shows a cloud, we've got a possible hit."

"Not a bad idea. How many pictures?"

"Two thousand. And if we don't find her in this batch, I'll order more."

Harry bent to the first picture, muttering. "And they say chivalry is dead. You do remember that Romeo only killed himself over Juliet. He didn't force his best friend to go blind."

Mercer couldn't suppress a smile. "Less discussion, more dissection."

They gave up late that afternoon. Neither was trained in the arcane art of photo interpretation and the pictures didn't have anywhere near the resolution Mercer expected. In the images shot from a hundred miles above the earth, glaciers looked like the dense, stationary clouds they were searching for. In five hours they'd located thirty-five potential locations for Rinpoche-La and had covered barely a quarter of the pictures Mercer had bought.

They did end up going to Tiny's after having some Chinese food delivered for dinner. As for Harry's threat to get Mercer blind drunk, they had only two drinks apiece. Both had headaches from squinting at pictures all day and weren't in the mood to add to the pain.

Mercer took Drag out for the last time just before midnight and climbed the spiral stairs to bed. By the time he finished brushing his teeth and using the urinal tucked in a corner of the master bathroom, the basset was spread across both pillows. Mercer didn't have the heart to disturb the old dog so he resigned himself to the corner of one pillow he'd been left and settled in for another round of nightmares.

The phone rang at two fifteen. Mercer was wide awake before the end of the first shrill chime. He knew who was calling and what he'd hear. He squeezed his eyes shut, trying for a moment to retain the simplicity he was about to lose. True, the call might bring him closer to Tisa, but it would also introduce him to a world on the brink of Armageddon. She hadn't been exaggerating when she'd said life as he knew it was about to end.

On the second ring he answered by saying, "It's already happening, isn't it?"

"Yes." Ira sounded like he hadn't been to sleep yet. "A deep strata seismograph indicates La Palma's becoming alive."

"How long until a car gets here?"

"Ten minutes, maybe less."

"Where am I headed?"

"The White House."

"See you there." Mercer cut the connection.

The rain that had been falling for days finally abated, leaving the streets clean and fresh. Halos of mist draped the streetlamps. At this hour there was no traffic or pedestrians. Even the city's homeless were hibernating.

The Cadillac carrying Mercer swung into the back entrance of the Executive Mansion and braked at a guardhouse. After vetting the driver and passing a mirror under the chassis to search for bombs, the guard asked Mercer for identification and checked his name against an electronic clipboard. The car was waved through.

Ira was waiting for Mercer at the West Wing entrance wearing a suit but no tie. They shook hands silently and the admiral led him into the building. They moved along dim corridors and passed several quiet offices before coming to a closed door.

"The president doesn't know the nature of this briefing," Ira informed him. "Kleinschmidt called him thirty minutes ago and just said there's a crisis."

"Who else is in there?" Mercer asked.

"Admiral Morrison." C. Thomas Morrison was the charismatic chairman of the Joint Chiefs of Staff, the uniformed leader of the United States military, and possibly the next occupant of the Oval Office. "Paul Barnes of the CIA and Dick Henna from the FBI."

"I haven't seen Dick in a long time," Mercer remarked. They'd been friends for several years but their busy schedules had taken a toll on the relationship.

"This isn't a social call," Ira reminded.

Mercer nodded grimly.

Ira knocked and waited for an aide to open the heavy door. This was the Cabinet Room, a long space dominated by a massive conference table. The president sat at his traditional seat at the center of the table sporting a polo shirt and twenty hours of beard. John Kleinschmidt, the national security advisor and Ira's direct supervisor, was just settling in at the president's right. Paul Barnes was seated to his left. Unlike the others, he'd taken the time to don a fresh suit and tie. Even Admiral Morrison was out of uniform. Mercer and Barnes had butted heads on several occasions and their mutual dislike was evident in the single glance they afforded each other.

Ira took the chair opposite the president and indicated Mercer was to sit next to him. Dick Henna, the bulky director of the FBI, gave Mercer a friendly nod. Someone handed Mercer a mug of coffee and stepped aside when he declined the offer of cream.

"I'm sure the esteemed members of the Fourth Estate are wondering about this late-night meeting, and quite frankly so am I." The president had the rare ability of making a mild rebuke sound friendly. He spread his large hands on the polished table. "Ira, you want to tell me what we're doing here at this godawful hour?"

"Mr. President, I believe you've met Dr. Philip Mercer, a member of my staff."

"On several occasions," the president said with an easy smile. "I recall telling him after Hawaii nearly seceded from the union that one day he'd be working for me. How's that Jaguar of yours?"

"Fine, sir." Mercer was astounded the president

knew what kind of car he drove and waited only a
second for an explanation.

"You probably didn't know that I paid to replace
the one that got destroyed during the Hawaii crisis. It
was easier for me to cut the check than to bury the
expense where some forensic accountant from the
GAO could find it."

"I'm flattered."

"It was a small price to pay for what you did for
this country." The chief executive turned serious.
"And since you're here again, I suspect you're about
to do my administration another favor."

"If it's not too late."

The president turned his startling blue eyes to Ira.
"Okay, tell me what's going on."

Ira didn't clear his throat or shuffle papers or any
of the normal delaying tactics people used when
they're about to dole out bad news. He shot straight
ahead. "Through an intelligence source Mercer has
been cultivating we learned of a potential volcanic
eruption on an island in the Canaries called La Palma.
On my order, a team from the U.S. Geologic Survey
has been sent there, and about two hours ago they
confirmed that the island may be in the first stages of
an eruption."

"Pardon me for a second," the president interjected.
"But why do we care?"

Ira tapped Mercer. "You're the geologist. Want to
explain it?"

Though Mercer hadn't heard of La Palma until a
few hours earlier, he spoke with the confidence of an
expert. "For those that don't know them, the Canaries
are a group of islands in the Atlantic about a hundred
miles off Morocco's west coast. They're Spanish
owned and are considered a vacation getaway for
snowbound Europeans. La Palma is the westernmost
of the islands and, in terms of geology, the youngest

and the most volcanically active. The latest eruption was in 1971, but the one that concerns us occurred in 1949.

"That year, the Cumbre Vieja volcano, which dominates the southern third of the island, erupted over the course of several days. This in itself isn't unusual. She generally pops every two hundred years or so. What made the 'forty-nine eruption unusual is the four-meter-wide crack that appeared along the center of the island. The western flank of the island, a chunk of rock about a hundred twenty cubic kilometers in size, slipped a few feet toward the sea and stopped."

"Why did it stop?" the president asked.

"Because Mother Nature wanted us to dodge a bullet, sir. There are two geologic features that make La Palma particularly dangerous. The first is that the composition of the island's soils allows for it to build up in very steep slopes. In fact La Palma is one of the steepest islands in the world. By rights, the slab of rock should have kept sliding down into the water. We got incredibly lucky. But maybe not for long.

"About ten years ago, a British scientist named Robert Wright floated the idea that a significant eruption could further loosen that slab of rock, allowing it to crack through completely and crash into the ocean. Such an event would produce a catastrophic wave, a phenomenon called a mega-tsunami. The supposition garnered a few doomsday headlines when he published his research, but no government took the idea seriously and certainly no large-scale analyses have taken place."

"What is a mega-tsunami?" asked the Joint Chiefs chairman.

"Though commonly called tidal waves, a tsunami has nothing to do with tides. Generally they're caused by undersea earthquakes and their size is limited by the amount of crustal displacement, which is fortunate because rock can only take so much strain before it snaps. That's why we'll never experience an earthquake much above eight-point-six. Most geologic faults slip long before they contain enough energy to cause a quake of even magnitude seven. Therefore an undersea earthquake will cause a tsunami of corresponding size. If a fault drops twenty feet, the wave will top out around twenty feet."

"That doesn't sound so bad." This came from the caustic director of the CIA, Paul Barnes.

Mercer rounded on him, not bothering to keep the anger from his voice. "Tell that to the three thousand residents of Papua, New Guinea, who were killed by such a wave in 1998." He turned his attention back to Morrison but kept an eye on the president. "In contrast, a mega-tsunami is caused by a rockslide, and the only limit to the size of the wave is the amount of debris that hits the water. Petroleum geologists working in Alaska in the 1950s found evidence of such a wave in Letuya Bay. Ringing the bay was a line where the old-growth forests inexplicably ended. It was as if some force had ripped out every tree up to about five hundred fifty feet above sea level."

"Five hundred fifty feet?"

"That's the height of the wave created when a huge chunk of granite sheered away from a cliff and hit the bay."

"That's impossible," Barnes opined.

Mercer shifted his gaze to the president. "Three years later a group of fishermen were caught in a tsunami more than a hundred feet tall in the same area. Only a handful survived."

The president looked grave. "And you're saying that another eruption in the Canaries will cause such a mega-tsunami?"

Mercer shook his head. "The chunk of granite that created the wave in Alaska weighed a couple thousand tons. If La Palma lets go we're talking half a trillion tons of rock. That's an energy pulse equal to the total U.S. power consumption over six months." That fact had come from a research team in Switzerland with verification from several computer modelers.

The men around the table paused, reflected on the enormity of what Mercer described.

Dick Henna cut the silence by clearing his throat and asking, "You said that two things make La Palma particularly dangerous. One was how steep the island is. What's the other?"

Mercer wasn't surprised it was Henna who'd picked up on that. Unlike the president, Paul Barnes or Ira's boss, John Kleinschmidt, Dick had worked his way through the ranks to his current job. He was an investigator at heart, not a politician.

"Dikes," Mercer said.

"Excuse me?" the president and Henna said simultaneously, shooting each other quizzical glances.

"La Palma is comprised of volcanic rock that is very permeable to water. The island absorbs rain like a sponge. However, there are formations, called dikes, of very dense basalt that cut along the spine of the island like a picket fence. These dikes act like dams that trap the rainwater, forming tall columns of supersaturated soil. It's believed that the dikes are solid enough that they wouldn't be affected by the seismic shocks associated with an eruption."

"So where's the danger?"

"An eruption begins with magma filling chambers deep under the island. The heat from an influx of molten rock will begin to boil the water trapped in these columns. As we all know from high school physics, water expands as it heats, but it cannot be compressed. This would put incredible pressure on the dikes. The failure of one or many of them is inevitable."

The president leaned forward. "And this would trigger the landslide and cause the mega-tsunami?" Mercer nodded and the president asked the obvious follow-up. "What kind of damage are we talking about and what can we do to minimize it?"

"According to the computer modeling done a few years back, the wave will be one thousand feet tall and would have already traveled outward at least sixty miles in the first ten minutes after the landslide. It would cross the ocean at about five hundred miles per hour, radiating in all directions. North Africa would be hit first. The wave will have abated to three hundred fifty feet by then and fortunately that part of the continent is sparsely populated. Loss of life would be minimal. Next would be Spain, Portugal and then southern England. The wave crest at this time will top out at over a hundred feet, still carrying enough energy to ricochet and radiate through the English Channel and completely drown all of the Netherlands."

The faces around the table paled with sickly fascination.

"Nine hours after the landslide," Mercer continued, "the wave is still traveling at jetliner speeds. It will scour everything off the Bahamas and Bermuda and the archipelago islands stretching from Puerto Rico to Venezuela. Nothing would remain behind. No plants, no people, no evidence anything had ever called those places home."

Jaws were beginning to slacken, but the men around the table were tasked with protecting the United States and someone, Mercer wasn't sure who, asked, "What about us? What happens when it hits us?"

"The wave will hit Miami first. It'll be eighty feet tall and be about forty feet thick at the base, a surge unlike anything ever seen. At five hundred miles per hour the kinetic energy is almost incalculable. Every structure, road, bridge, and building within fifteen miles of the coast will be destroyed. At twenty miles, there's a chance a few of the more solid buildings will remain, though they will be completely gutted, first by the initial wave pulse and then again when the water drains back to the sea.

"This scenario will play out all along the East Coast from Florida to Maine. Jacksonville, Savannah, Norfolk, Washington, Philly, New York, Boston. All of them are wiped from the face of the earth. That's roughly forty million dead. And these are just the figures for the United States. Add an equal amount of dead in the Caribbean, Africa and Europe."

"And the number of injured?" Ira asked.

"It'll be like the World Trade Center."

The men understood. Like many around the nation, they'd donated blood to help the injured survivors only to discover that in such a tragedy there were none.

"If this is really going to happen, what about evacuating the eastern seaboard?"

Admiral Morrison took that question. After a lifetime in the military, he had the background in logistics. "You're asking about relocating fully one-fifth of our population, Mr. President. It would take months just to coordinate where to put them all."

"Do we have months?" the chief executive asked Mercer.

"The truth is, we don't know, sir." Mercer gathered his thoughts for a moment. He was standing on top of a precipice. The wrong word could send him over the edge. Or more accurately send Tisa over the edge.

"Over the past fifty years," he started, "scientists have made strides in predicting cataclysmic events like earthquakes and volcanic eruptions. There are certain signs we can look for to tell us what's happening deep underground long before anything is visible on the surface. The presence of microshocks, tiny swarms of earthquakes, is one. New seismographs are hundreds of times more precise than ever before. From soil taken from core samples we can detect elevations in diffused gasses like CO_2, a precursor event to an eruption.

"All of this gives us an idea that a volcano's coming to life. This is the type of evidence the team Admiral Lasko sent to La Palma has found. But this isn't a guarantee that a mountain's about to erupt. Volcanoes give off signs all the time only to fall dormant once again."

"You don't believe the recent activity on La Palma will end soon, do you? You believe the island is going to erupt."

"Yes, Mr. President, I do. And we all should."

"Why?" Paul Barnes's voice dripped acid.

"Ira mentioned I was cultivating a contact. That's not entirely true. She approached me first." With a quick glance around the table, Mercer realized that he had the lowest security clearance and needn't keep anything back. He began his tale from the moment the two agents first arrived at his house and told it straight through. When he finished, it appeared that everyone had questions and was eager to parse his story.

The president staved off the onslaught with a wave. "Do you believe her?"

"I've never doubted the presence of her organization. I saw it in Vegas, the Pacific, and aboard the ferry. Her claim about predicting earthquakes I would have dismissed as fantasy except I saw the book and felt the Santorini quake myself. She knew when and where it was going to hit. That's not a coincidence and judging by the size of the journal she carried, I believe her group's had this ability for a long, long time."

The president was about to ask another question,

but Mercer forestalled him. "Please don't ask me to explain it. I can't. What she showed me flies in the face of everything I've ever learned as a geologist and yet I can't refute the evidence."

Several seconds passed. They were waiting for the president.

Mercer glanced at Ira, who gave him a small shrug. His bald head was covered in sweat. Mercer had always assumed that Ira had become comfortable in the corridors of power. He'd retired from the navy with two stars, so dealing with the nation's elite shouldn't have been anything new. And yet this meeting made him sweat. He was on the line here, Mercer realized. By bringing him in, Ira was tacitly backing him. If the president dismissed the claims, Ira would be out of a job by morning.

Mercer shot him a wink filled with more bravado than he really felt.

The president laced his fingers and set them carefully on the table. "There's been an interesting change to what is expected of this office over the past few years. The American people now count on their president to be omniscient. They expect us to know the motivation of every ally and enemy and divine the consequences of every action. Mistakes are no longer an option.

"I think this started during the Gulf War when people saw the precision of force projection. They began to believe that if we could slam a bomb through a designated window, we can damn well do anything. People now presume that this kind of precision should extend to the economy and foreign affairs. Put simply, people think that I have a crystal ball sitting on my desk in the Oval Office.

"Obviously I don't. I have the authority to order the evacuation of fifty million people, but what if thousands are killed in a panic and nothing happens. Or I can order the evacuation and those that are saved will blame the government for not preventing the catastrophe in the first place. Another option is to do nothing, believing that this crisis has been concocted by a gullible scientist influenced by a fringe group and no one will be the wiser."

Paul Barnes folded the leather-bound binder in front of him as if the meeting was over. "I think that's the best course."

The president didn't appear like he was going to stop the CIA director.

It was now or never. "There's one more option, sir," Mercer said quickly.

The chief executive almost smiled. "I was hoping there was."

"I believe Tisa Nguyen gave me enough time to do something to prevent this from becoming a disaster. We're seeing the first signs of an eruption. That doesn't mean the eruption is imminent. It might take six months. It might be six years." Mercer paused. He wasn't being dramatic; he was thinking about the aftermath if his next words were true. "Or it might be six weeks. She is the only person who knows for sure. We need to find her. With the information she can provide, we're in a better position to understand what we're up against."

"Do you know where she is?"

"Possibly, but I need help. I spent the day going over commercial satellite photographs looking for a telltale sign of where Rinpoche-La could be located. I have to admit the person helping me and I aren't photo interpreters and I kind of think it was a colossal waste of time."

"*Harry* helped you?" Dick Henna asked incredulously.

Even Mercer had to admit asking a pair of eighty-year-old eyes to scan thousands of pictures was a long shot. However it was the only shot he had and he was desperate. He gave a little rueful smile. "Well, he was there and didn't hinder me. That's about all the help he could give."

The president turned to his national security advisor. "John, what's that group over in Maryland that does our photo work?"

"We've got the National Reconnaissance Office, but I think you're talking about the National Imaging and Mapping Agency in Bethesda."

"NIMA, that's the one. Dr. Mercer, where exactly were you looking?"

"The northern slopes of the Himalayas."

Paul Barnes rounded on Mercer, his eyes bulging. *"China?"*

Mercer maintained his composure. "I believe so, yes."

The president turned to the CIA chief. "Can you get her out?"

"Mr. President, please," Barnes entreated. "Even if we can find her town, which isn't likely, it would take weeks to mount a rescue op. We have precious few assets in China. Most of them are in the cities and wouldn't last five minutes in a rural area without authorization."

"What about sending in some of our own people?"

"If this was the Cold War and the target was in Eastern Europe or Russia I'd say there's a shot. In China, forget it. A Special Operations force would have to come in overland from Nepal or Pakistan, crossing one of the most heavily fortified borders in the world. They wouldn't make it five miles before being picked up."

"What if the team is made up of Chinese-Americans?"

"I don't have that kind of manpower. All our Chinese-American agents are analysts or translators. None of them is trained for fieldwork."

"A budget of three billion a year and you don't have one Asian James Bond?" Dick said archly.

"Gentlemen," the president cut in smoothly, "we're going to concentrate on locating Rinpoche-La first and hammer out how to get her afterward." Henna and Barnes mumbled an assent in unison. "Mercer, I would like you to draft a memo for the people at NIMA to tell them exactly what they're looking for. Finding needles in haystacks is their specialty, but I'm sure they'd appreciate anything you can give them."

"Yes, sir."

"And then I'd like you to pack for La Palma."

"No, sir."

The chief executive wasn't used to being defied. He looked more startled than upset. "Excuse me?"

"I said no, Mr. President. I trust the people Ira sent to the island are more than qualified to study the volcano. They're specialists in that field. I am not. I'd be in the way. I think you'd be better served if I accompanied whoever is sent in to rescue Tisa."

"Out of the question!" Barnes thundered. "I will not allow a civilian to join one of my teams. If you think you'd be in the way around volcano specialists on La Palma, just what do you think you can add to a contingent of CIA operatives?"

Mercer could have gloated. Lord knew, Barnes deserved it, but the director was just trying to protect his fiefdom. The CIA should have known about this case long before Mercer handed it to them on a platter. Barnes was humiliated, and needed to do some damage control to reestablish his authority. It wasn't in his personality to work with Mercer so he was lashing out instead. "Mr. Barnes, you're forgetting a very basic fact. None of your people have the slightest idea what Tisa looks like. In this situation, a composite sketch based on my impressions won't do a rescue team much good."

Making ready to reply, Barnes let his mouth close. There was nothing he would say. Although Barnes couldn't see Dick Henna directly, the FBI director put his hand over his mouth so no one could see his smile.

"You have a point there, Doctor," the president said. "I assume you know what you might be getting into?"

"Yes, I do. I wouldn't consider it if I didn't know it was so important."

"Then if we do go in to get her, consider yourself on board." The president stood and swept the assembled group with a stern look. "For now I don't want this getting too far beyond this room. Make the inquiries you need but keep it quiet. If this eruption is as serious as we believe we have a small window of opportunity before the media get wind of it. We all know what'll happen then. Dr. Mercer, on top of everything else, you are my special science advisor. I want options."

"Options, sir?"

"To save our country. We may only have a couple of weeks or months. I think we all agree that evacuation is pretty much out of the question. Even if we could pull it off, the United States would cease to exist as the country it is now. The same goes for the sections of Europe that get hit too. There must be a way to prevent the eruption or stabilize the side of the volcano. Those are the options I want."

"I understand," Mercer replied, thinking that the president didn't have a clue what he was asking.

The western portion of Tibet had never had a substantial settled population. There was little pasturage for nomadic shepherds and few areas low enough in elevation to support farming. For this reason, the Chinese military, following their invasion in 1950, maintained a tight cordon and used the land for their own purposes. There were a few political prisons, but mostly the region was given to observation and radar installations securing the borders with Nepal and India. Tibet had been annexed as a buffer state and the Chinese kept their cushion rigid. Except in closely monitored tour groups, foreign travelers aren't allowed much outside of the Tibetan capital of Lhasa, and the western reaches of the country are particularly restricted. Military patrols sweep the few roads on a regular basis and no one is ever granted overflight rights. The handful of drug smugglers who tested the air defenses soon found themselves painted by ground-based radar and in the sights of MiGs or Sukhoi fighter jets a short time later.

The country at the roof of the world has always been steeped in legend and mystery and no place was more unknown than the western borderlands.

To keep their valley's secret, the Order had a strict protocol for reaching Rinpoche-La. The trek from the Nepalese frontier never followed the same route twice and never took less than two weeks, and even this pushed the threat of detection. That time frame didn't include the days spent in Katmandu evading the Chinese informants that infested Nepal's capital city, each eager to make a few yuan by reporting suspicious parties.

Moving hard and ignoring the safety protocols, Luc Nguyen forced the group carrying his sister from Nepal to Rinpoche-La in a mere eight days. They risked using trucks on open roads and took minimum shelter when specially modified helicopters that could fly in the rarified atmosphere of the Himalayas thundered through mountain passes. The choppers often patrolled the area searching for people trying to flee the worker's paradise that the Chinese had imposed on the people of Tibet.

At twelve thousand feet, the wind was a constant presence. Whether a soft summer zephyr or the shrieking gales of winter, the wind never stopped moving through the valley, funneled by peaks that rose a further eight thousand feet above the valley floor. The mountains were jagged and barren, scoured clean of snow and soil except in protected pockets and veins. While much of Tibet is renowned for its rugged beauty, the land around Rinpoche-La was particularly harsh and ugly. Isolated in an isolated country, the nearest town was sixty miles east and there were no connecting roads, just a barely marked footpath that only the heartiest could attempt.

Construction on the monastery at Rinpoche-La began in 1052 under the guidance of the Indian scholar Atisha and was added on to in fits and starts until its abandonment in 1254 to protest how Godan Khan, Ghenghis's grandson, had made the Lama of the Sakya Buddhists regent of all Tibet. Because Rinpoche-La was at the outskirts of the Tibetan kingdom, it remained completely forgotten save for the handful of self-sufficient villagers who eked out a liv-

ing in the shadow of the huge building. That was until
Zhu Zhanji, the Confucian who defied the emperor,
cached the knowledge of Admiral Zheng He's historic
sea voyages. There were no records in the Order's
archive describing how Zhu Zhanji knew of the valley's existence. It remained one more of the legends
that surround Rinpoche-La.

The nearly six hundred years since saw countless
invasions of Tibet from the south and the east and the
north, culminating in the totalitarian occupation by
the Chinese. Even as they slaughtered an estimated
one million Tibetans and doubled the country's population by the forced migration of ethnic Han Chinese,
Rinpoche-La remained nestled in its valley, unknown
beyond rumors and the whispered tales of nomads
who rarely ventured close to the intimidating mountains. Beyond its geography, the valley was further
isolated by a river that was barely negotiable in winter
and seemingly impossible to cross in summer.

The monastery dominated the end of the valley, a
five-story central structure surrounded by various out-
buildings and a thirty-foot-tall, ten-foot-thick wall of
mortared stone. Behind the hermitage, the valley
dropped away in a sheer hundred-foot cliff, hemmed
on each side by towering stone ramparts. The village
lay at the monastery's feet, clutches of stone buildings
that seemed to grow out of the living rock. Because
the valley was little more than an ax stroke cut into
the mountains, little light filtered to the floor and this
was diffused by the steam escaping through countless
geothermal fissures.

It was the steam that provided the village shelter
and also its means of survival. The microbes that
flourished in the scalding waters of the hot springs
were the basis of a bizarre food chain similar to that
found in the deep-sea thermal vents called black
smokers. In the absence of sunlight, creatures de-

pended on chemosynthesis, the transformation of chemical, rather than light, energy into life. Around the black smokers, microbes fed off the exotic plumes of chemicals belched from the earth's interior and in turn fed a myriad of odd creatures: tube worms that grew to six feet or more, mussels and crab species found nowhere else and fish able to withstand the tremendous heat. The difference at Rinpoche-La was at the top of this food chain were goats and yaks that ate nutrient-rich aquatic weeds and provided meat and wool and milk for the villagers. A further advantage to those living amid the geothermal vents was that heat was provided for them. There was no need to gather wood to warm their homes or cook their meals, a time-consuming necessity that handicapped the rest of Tibet's rural population. Over the generations, the valley had become its own self-contained, self-sustaining ecosystem.

On an upper story of the monastery a window sash rattled as a fresh gust of wind blew by. The candle on the table flickered and shadows jumped along the stone walls of the cell. Tisa barely looked up from where she sat, a cup of pungent butter tea cooling at her elbow. She was physically and spiritually drained, but she knew the bed in the corner would provide no succor. In sleep lay the nightmares that had plagued her for so long.

Added to them were her fears for Philip Mercer.

She was sure he had survived. When she'd left him on the floating tanker truck and struck out for Luc's boat, she'd tried to convince her half brother that she alone had escaped from the sinking ferry. He hadn't believed her, but the crush of survivors trying to board the speedboat nearly capsized the vessel and forced him to motor away before mounting a search. Mercer would have surely been rescued when word reached Santorini that the ferry had gone down.

No, her fears were based on what she knew was coming. She wondered if she should have bothered giving him the warning about La Palma now that she couldn't be with him. Mercer would doubtlessly figure out that the volcano was going to erupt and she was just as certain he would try to minimize the devastation. He'd go to La Palma and be one of the first to die. Her interference had sealed his fate. She'd only just discovered that in their short time together he'd evoked emotions she'd thought she was incapable of. She'd fallen in love with him. Now he was gone forever.

She knew now that whoever said it was better to have loved and lost than to never have loved at all had no idea what they were talking about. She looked at her wrist where for a few hours she'd worn the watch he'd given her. It was the sweetest gesture she'd ever seen. He couldn't possibly understand why she wouldn't wear one, couldn't know the fear she had of time itself, how finite it was and how she couldn't stand the constant reminder.

She wished now she'd kept it.

The monastery was so solidly built that it seemed to absorb all sound. Tisa didn't hear the footsteps outside her door, didn't know anyone was coming for her until the heavy iron lock slid back against its stop.

She remained bowed, not needing to look up to see that it was her brother who had come for her. "Leave me, Luc."

"You know I would never do that," he whispered. When they were together at Rinpoche-La, they spoke Tibetan. For some unknown reason, when they were on the outside they conversed in either French or English.

She raised her head. She'd lost her glasses during her escape from the ferry. Her spare pair weren't the correct prescription, forcing her to squint slightly to focus her vision. Like her, Luc was dressed in voluminous wool pants, a fine cotton shirt and a heavy cloak. She noted he'd taken to carrying a pistol belted around his lean hips. "What did you hope to accomplish by bringing me here?"

He crossed the murky room to stand behind her. She could feel his hands near her shoulders but he refrained from touching her. "I just want to keep you safe."

"From what?" she snapped. "Inevitability?"

"Tisa, it doesn't have to be like this. I forgive you for trying to warn the world. At times, even I thought that we should. In the end, we both know it's for the best that we don't."

She turned in her seat to look him in the eye. "Best for who? Who are you to decide?"

"I can ask you the same question. For centuries the Order has done nothing but watch as cataclysms destroyed nations, laid waste to entire regions, and killed millions. No one ever questioned our need to remain silent. Just because the scope is so much greater now doesn't mean we should part with our traditions."

"Luc, if we don't do anything a hundred million people will die outright and many more later as civilization unravels."

"This is where you and I disagree, dear sister. I don't see that as a bad thing. Civilization as it is today is fundamentally flawed and can't be sustained. Its demise is certain. Rampant consumption in the west and exploding populations in the developing world are either going to bleed the planet dry or collide in a monumental war that will destroy both. The eruption on La Palma is a pressure relief valve, a way to turn back the clock a century or two and give humanity a chance to learn from its mistakes rather than continue to build on them.

"This is the very nature of evolution—the adaptation to changing circumstances. Those that can do it will survive, those that can't will perish. The planet doesn't care which species resides at the top of the evolutionary ladder so long as it can endure the tests thrown at it. We've done well for so long that we forget we're here only by the earth's grace."

Tisa couldn't form a response. Far from growing blank, her mind was a swirl of images and thoughts, a torrent that crashed like a hurricane. In the months since she'd learned about the La Palma eruption, she'd strived to find a way to avert it, or at least reduce the impact. She'd remained confident that she could make a difference. That knowledge had given her the determination and courage to continue. Hearing her brother now, she understood how useless it had all been. For the first time she knew she was going to fail.

There was no escaping Rinpoche-La. Upon her return she'd seen that Luc had mobilized dozens of followers into a loose army. Like her brother, they all seemed to be carrying guns. Even if she could slip past the guards and make it out of the valley, she'd never survive the trek to Nepal. Darchen, the closest Tibetan town, was out of the question too. It was a backwater village with a heavy military presence. She'd be arrested the first time she tried to hitch a ride to Llasa.

Luc began to massage her shoulders. Tisa didn't have the strength to shrug him off. "We'll be safe here. When the time comes we will rejoin the world and take our rightful place. The oracle will guarantee our primacy."

"I want to see the Lama," she said, trying to keep from sobbing.

"Of course." Luc stepped back to allow Tisa to stand. He smiled at her, a patronizing look that said he could see past her anger and not care about her pain. "Whatever you want is yours for the asking."

He led her from the cell. In this wing of the lamasery, the hallways were wide and lined with rooms once used by some of the hundreds of monks who'd lived here. Precious prayer scrolls called *thangkas* adorned the paneled walls. The floors were made of tropical woods, burnished to a mirror gloss, then mostly covered by intricate carpets. He took her to one of the central mezzanines where a staircase seemed to float in space yet was large enough to accommodate a dozen people walking abreast. Oil lanterns lit the way. The ground floor was an open space several acres square, cut by marble columns that supported the floors above. There were so many supports that the grand entrance was called the stone forest. The ceiling gleamed with gilt.

It took several minutes to cross to another set of stairs that descended below ground level. This passage was part of a dormant geothermal vent, and once at the bottom of the steps the passage took random twists and turns that had once been an ancient lava tube. After a hundred yards they came to a towering door. Luc unlocked it with a key kept on a long leather thong around his neck. He gave Tisa an appraising look.

She remained expressionless. Three months had passed since she'd last been here and taken the chronicle from the archive that lay beyond this door. Only the archivists, the most venerated members of the Order, had the key. Luc had not been among them then. Her brother must have been busy consolidating power within the Order. She feared what else had changed.

The archive chamber was dark until Luc turned on lights powered by a geothermal generator buried deeper under the monastery. The walls were draped with heavy, moisture-absorbing carpets to protect the priceless volumes. The rugs were replaced on a regular basis and the ones here appeared fresh and vibrant.

The air was chilled, not damp exactly but clammy and claustrophobic. The chronicles were arranged along two walls in shelves that stretched from the floor to the ten-foot ceiling. There were several antique desks for the archivists and drawers filled with maps and manuscripts. This wasn't where Admiral Zheng He's cache was stored, although a few pieces were generally kept here for reference. The bulk of that horde was in another chamber Tisa had never seen.

When she'd taken the book she'd shown Mercer, she had tried to disguise the theft by spacing out the nearby journals. Luc, or one of his underlings, had reformed the tight ranks and the gap where the chronicle once stood was as obvious as a missing tooth. From the blank spot to the end of the last shelf were six more journals awaiting the time when the predictions in them could be verified.

Luc crossed the room and opened another locked door. Tisa's unease increased. She hadn't seen the Lama in almost a year. Even back then his health was failing and his mind had lost much of its keen edge. She dreaded that he'd died in her absence and her brother was leading her to his ossuary. That would explain how Luc had taken such complete control over the monastery and the Order.

They continued down the volcanic tube, their way lit by bulbs strung along the ceiling. Tisa suspected this was an alternate route to the oracle chamber, the subterranean cavern where centuries earlier devotees of Zhu Zhanji had constructed the oracle based on designs that dated from long before the scholar took possession of Admiral He's historical treasures. The air in the tunnel turned warmer the farther they descended, fueled by the earth's fiery heart.

At last they came to an open area that had been finished off with elegantly paneled walls and a carpet-strewn wood floor. The room was furnished with ornate sofas and chairs covered in watered silk. Glittering chandeliers hung from the coffered ceiling like crystal stalactites. The architectural details of the handcarved moldings were lost under heavy layers of gilt. Through an open doorway Tisa could see a bedroom dominated by a massive four-poster bed. It was only the lack of windows that betrayed the space as something other than a room fit for royalty. She'd never seen this part of the monastery and didn't understand what it was. Luc indicated she should go into the bedroom.

The chamber was much dimmer, shadowed and ominous. There was a gamey odor in the air, like meat on the verge of rotting. Sensing a presence, she stilled her breathing. Someone was on the bed, hidden by darkness. Her heart began to hammer and her palms turned slick. As Tisa approached the bed, she couldn't still her quivering lips. She knew whom she was about to see. The rasping breathing that first caught her attention stopped suddenly and the figure on the bed let loose with a crowlike caw.

Tisa's hand flew to her mouth to stifle a scream. She slowly made her way closer, angling across the room so light could reach the figure leaning against the headboard. Behind her Luc adjusted a light switch and the level of illumination grew. Tisa gasped.

The Lama no longer wore his ceremonial blue robe. He was naked, his thin chest rising feebly as he struggled to breathe. His body was hairless save the coarse gray nest at the juncture of his legs. The hair atop his head was as fine as silk thread. His face was more deeply wrinkled than any she had ever seen. The creases seemed to vanish into his skull. His mouth was a blackened, toothless hole, his limbs little more than desiccated sticks. He wasn't yet seventy but appeared ninety. She discerned all this ruin in a glance, but what held her were his eyes. They were those of someone with severe retardation. They remained bright, but there was no curiosity behind them, nothing to indicate the creature peering through them even knew who or where he was.

Soft cords bound his left hand and ankle. The right side of his body was held rigid by some paralysis.

Tears burned Tisa's eyes. She turned to her brother, unable to hide her pain and confusion.

"Two months ago," Luc explained as if discussing the weather. "The doctors say it was a massive stroke. It would have been better had the old bugger died. I've actually thought about putting him out of his misery, but the others believe his condition is a portent and that the date of his death will have special meaning."

Tisa reached out and brushed a wisp of hair back across the Lama's forehead. He looked at her trustingly, but without recognition. Unable to keep her composure, a wracking sob tore into Tisa's chest. The pain was like a lance.

"Ah, dinner's here," Luc said from the doorway, unmoved by his sister's personal agony.

Tisa glanced over her shoulder. A local woman Tisa didn't recognize hesitated at Luc's side, torn by duty and the unexpected presence of a stranger in the Lama's bedroom. She was pretty, not far out of her teens, with a round face and freshly washed hair. She was dressed simply in a long skirt and a loose blouse of cotton. She carried nothing, no tray or bowl from which to feed the Lama.

"I'm not sure that you want to stay for this," Luc said as the girl made her decision and drew closer to the bed.

The high Lama cawed again, becoming animated at the sight of the young woman. The girl paused, her dark eyes darting from Luc to Tisa. Luc made a "go ahead" gesture with his hand. Tisa remained uncomprehending. The Lama tried to reach for the woman with his bound hand, his motions directed at her chest.

It was then that Tisa saw the wet patches at the swell of the woman's bust. She was a nursing mother, her breasts heavy with milk.

Tisa whirled away, unable to hide her revulsion as the woman began to undo her buttons.

Luc laughed. "It's the only way he'll eat," he explained cavalierly. "Though we did have his teeth pulled. He kept biting the wet nurses."

The Lama's agitated noises were suddenly replaced with a contented mewling. Tisa refused to look, although her brother watched for a moment. She stormed past him.

"How could you?" she hissed so hard it hurt her throat.

He grabbed her by the shoulder and spun her into his arms so their mouths were inches apart. "I told you it would have been better if the stroke had killed him. The pillar of our community has been reduced to an infant. Maybe it is punishment for continuing the program to counter the time drift that developed in the oracle's predictions. The Order should never have started moving rivers, constructing towers, and digging holes in an effort to change earth's chi."

Tisa twisted so she wouldn't have to look at her brother's face, a visage so much like her own. "I hate you."

"One of these days you'll see things my way. Not now, I understand, but soon, very soon." He kissed the top of her head and released his grip. "In the meantime I'll make sure no harm comes to you, as we wait together for the world to be transformed." He looked past her shoulder. Donny Randall stood at another entrance to the living quarters. "Take my sister back to her cell, Donny, then meet me in my office."

Tisa couldn't stop crying as the big man lumbered

at her heels through the sprawling building. She'd been away a few months, but it had been even longer since she'd seen the Lama. She should have stayed. She could have prevented Luc from usurping power as he had. Her duty was here, at Rinpoche-La, not on the outside. Had she not wasted so much effort contacting Mercer, maybe she could have saved a portion of the Lama's dignity and with it the purity of the Order.

Half a millennium of planning and surviving was about to unravel in a way even the oracle couldn't have predicted. For centuries the Order had been free of the pettiness that had destroyed so much that was rational in the world, the squabbles that blossomed into wars, bankrupting nations and killing millions. The innocence they had enjoyed for so long was lost, as lost as the Lama's mind.

Maybe Luc was right, she thought, capitulating to her own inner darkness. Maybe nothing humanity had created was worth saving. After all, she'd seen there was an ugly reflection to all things beautiful. The first joyous cry of a newborn was the same sound as the dying wail of a starving child. The same techniques that created great cathedrals helped the construction of concentration camps. The same laboratories that produced chemicals that cured also made those that killed. Art and music and free expression had all been perverted by hate by those bent on sending their own unholy message. Religion, politics, family, it was all so easily distorted that little of the good behind these ideals remained.

She trudged up the steps to her cell, barely able to shoulder the burden of her feelings. Her strength was gone. Since she'd first learned the mysteries of the Order, she'd always held hope that she'd been selected for a special task, that she would be the one to break the cycle that had kept the Order together but doomed it to the role of Cassandra, the figure from Greek mythology endowed with the gift of prophecy but unable to convince others of the future. She realized now that it didn't matter that she had convinced Mercer. Events were inalterable. Her true purpose, she saw bitterly, was to witness the end of everything, to be the last watcher stuck on the fringes of calamity.

Tisa had dammed up so much in her life, watched as devastation overran the world, stood by knowing she could have helped, all the while fighting for a time when she could make a change. Time had been her enemy, the most hated element she'd ever known. She'd fought it for as long as she could, hoping she could steal a moment and slay the beast. But there was no stopping time and only now was she willing to concede defeat.

They reached the upper floor. Donny fumbled with a key ring as Tisa stepped into her cell.

"What time is it, Mr. Randall?"

"Huh?" Donny looked up from his work, lost count of the keys and had to start from the beginning to find the right one.

"I asked for the time."

"How the hell should I know? It's nighttime. Don't worry about it."

"I guess maybe I won't." She eased herself onto the bed.

Once Randall had the proper key, he could turn his mind to his next concern. "Your brother's going away in a couple of days. My orders are to keep an eye on you. I just wanted you to know my eye isn't the only thing of mine that's gonna be on you, if you know what I mean. You ain't got much tit, but I figure if you were good enough for Mercer, you're good enough for me too."

Tisa had expected this was coming. Randall had done little to hide his leering interest since shortly after he'd pulled her from the Aegean. "Fine. By all means, rape me all you want. I just hope you understand that molesting me isn't going to get you any closer to the person you really want."

"Yeah, and who's that?"

"It's obvious you're using me as a surrogate for Mercer. He's the one you want to rape. He's the one you want power over. You're only with me so you can pretend I'm Mercer."

Donny bristled. "Are you calling me some kind of fag?"

"No. I'm calling you a deeply sick person. And if you touch me even once, I am going to hurt you in ways you've never imagined."

Randall pulled himself to his full height, the top of his head scant inches from the underside of the doorframe. "Brave words now. Let's hear them again when your brother's gone and I've got a knife to your heart."

"Then I'll do us both a favor and walk into it."

Not understanding what she meant, Randall the Handle shot her a scowl and slammed the door, jamming the key in the lock as though it were an act of violation.

At another time, Tisa would have been scared, but she truly didn't care any longer. Being raped by Donny Randall was nothing, a small taste of the shame she was just beginning to sense from her own failures.

The next day Luc knelt before an altar on the monastery's second floor. The smell of incense was thick and the low dirge of chanting monks reverberated around the spartan temple. To the disciples behind him it appeared that Luc was deep in prayer. He was in fact thinking about his next course of action but he understood the symbolic role he had to play. While the Lama lived, he couldn't don the sacred blue robe. However, by acting out the Order's mysteries and rites he was laying the foundation for his eventual consecration.

In the months since the Lama's stroke, Luc had steadily brought the Order's younger brothers to his cause. Like him, they were drawn to the promise of power in the wake of the cataclysmic destruction of civilization. It was the old guard who resisted the changes he wanted to implement. Luc would soon leave Rinpoche-La again. Tisa had always been a poor liar and he knew Mercer was still alive. While there was nothing Mercer could do about the eruption, Luc wanted him dead. But before he could fulfill that mission, he had to solidify his position here in the monstery.

The prayers went on for six straight hours. As the voices of some monks faltered, others took up the chant. Even Luc added his voice, one more small deception. As the sixth hour ended, Luc came to his feet. Despite the forced inactivity, his muscles hadn't cramped and he moved easily.

"My brothers," he called softly. While the fifty younger monks stopped chanting immediately, it took several minutes for the dozen older monks that Luc had invited to this special prayer to return from their trances.

"My brothers," Luc repeated. "Your voices have helped guide my thoughts at this troubled point in our history. I have been too long away from Rinpoche-La yet even just a moment home restores my spirit and clears my mind."

"Time has no meaning when one has peace," Yoh Dzu remarked. He was the Lama's secretary and the voice of the more conservative arm of the Order. His words were part of a familiar litany, a not-so-subtle rebuke to the discord Luc's actions had created.

"And yet time stalks us even if we have peace. Because peace isn't a possession, but a state. That is precisely what I want to discuss with all of you. The state of the world and the state of the Order, for the two are more entwined now than ever."

"That was not always the way," an ancient monk muttered. "For many generations the world and the Order were separate."

Luc seized on that comment. "Since our present Lama was given the right to wear the blue robe, he has changed the nature of the Order from passive watchers to active participants. He embarked us on a path of interference, of trying to correct the discrepancies between the oracle and physical reality. I stand before you and say that it was a mistake."

Several heads nodded. A young monk Luc had coached said, "His mistakes have cost us and they have cost him."

"Laying blame at the feet of a dying man is not taking a stand," Dzu scolded.

"It is not blame, brother. It is fact. The world and the Order are no longer separate." By invoking the Lama's controversial decision to try to realign the earth's chi, Luc had carefully sidestepped his own responsibility in drawing attention to the Order. "Even if we stopped now, our presence has already been detected."

"This was debated many years ago," Dzu pointed out. "We understood the risk then and accepted it. We all agreed that we had to do something to heal the earth and return the oracle's accuracy. It is an unfortuante circumstance that we are without the Lama's guidance when the time came to face the consequences."

"Perhaps not unfortunate, but auspicious. Unlike our Lama, I have spent a great deal of my life in the outside world. I understand how it works. The La Palma eruption is going to spark unprecedented fear, and what people fear they hate. What they hate, they kill. Word will soon spread about us and how we knew about the volcano. The world leaders cannot lash out at a mountain, but they can come after us."

"Why would they do that?" an older monk asked innocently. The man had never set foot outside the valley and had been sheltered from the corruptive nature of the world.

"Because that is their way. Startle a snake and it will strike. It doesn't matter to it that you meant it no harm."

"But I would not blame the snake," the elder brother said.

"Nor I," Luc agreed. "But the outside world does not think like us."

The old man grasped the analogy. "I think I understand. When I was a young man I once burned my hand picking up a stone that was too close to a fire pit. In anger I kicked out the fire. Afterward I could not understand why I did it, for it was not the fire's fault."

Luc smiled. "You were given a taste of human nature's darker side, one that is amplified outside the valley to the point where nations wage wars over rumors."

"What can be done?" Dzu asked.

"I do not know, but I fear that we can no longer rely on the monastery's isolation to protect us."

"Is that why you and some of the others are carrying weapons?"

"Yes, brother. I fear for our safety."

"Would you take a life to protect your own?" Dzu asked.

"No," Luc lied. "But I still debate whether I would do it to defend the oracle."

The statement sent a shocked murmur through the older monks. The taking of life, either a human's or that of the lowliest insect, was anathema to everything the Buddhist Order believed.

Luc cut through the chatter. "That is the question that faces us all, the one we must answer before I take my leave of Rinpoche-La."

"Is our situation truly that dire?" Dzu, who had been Luc's sharpest critic in the months since the Lama's stroke, was falling under Luc's spell.

"It is. We must all recognize that our way of life will soon come to an end. It is how we go forward from this moment that will determine the Order's ultimate fate."

"I for one can never kill, no matter the circumstances." Dzu crossed his arms over his chest as if that settled the discussion.

"And many agree with you," Luc said. "I would never ask anyone to act against his vows. But I need to know if you would prevent others from acting in ways that you would not? What if they believed that killing to protect the oracle was the right choice? Would you stop them?"

"That question should be easy to answer. Life must take precedence over all other considerations." Dzu paused. "Even if the oracle was threatened, killing to preserve it is wrong."

"As wrong as those who may kill to destroy it?"

"Are there degrees to that kind of sin? I don't know, perhaps. This is a matter I have never contemplated."

Luc took on a sincere look of sympathy. "It is something I have not stopped thinking about for some time now." It was a struggle to keep from smirking. He had so twisted logic that he now had the monks thinking about committing murder. "Here is something else for your consideration, something that has occurred to me over time. For one hundred fifty years the Order has had within its power the ability to save countless lives by warning those about to die and yet we did not. By rights those deaths should be on our collective consciences. Is not a lie of omission still a lie? Why then would the deaths of those who come to harm us be more wrong?"

His question was met by silence.

Finally Dzu spoke. "In some ways I hear the voice of our Lama in you, Luc. He stood in this very room when he proposed that the Order heal earth's chi. He was very convincing and after a short debate we agreed to his plan, although some secretly believed it was a mistake. How do we know that your intentions aren't also a mistake?"

"You must all agree that passivity is not an option. No matter what we do, the Order is forever changed."

"I see that, yes."

"If we do not defend ourselves when they come for us, we will cease to exist. The oracle will be destroyed."

"So you say."

"All I am asking is for you to consider that we are worth saving, that we should survive and emerge whole after the eruption." He turned his attention to the elder monk. "Brother, would you not prevent a man from beating the snake that bit him."

"Yes, I would."

"That is all that I ask. I do not blame those of you who wouldn't protect the snake, but I ask you not to stop those that would."

The door at the back of the temple room creaked open on its iron hinges. A gust of fresh air swirled in, diluting the cloying smell of the joss sticks. Donny Randall wouldn't enter the chamber but just his presence at the threshold interrupted the meeting.

"I believe Mr. Randall is here to tell me everything is ready for my trip back to Nepal." Luc smiled at the assemblage. "Were it that I could stay and pray with you for our Lama's recovery and for guidance in these troubled times."

"We shall pray for your speedy return to us, Luc." Dzu got to his feet and embraced him. "You do the Order proud and while I don't agree with some of what you said, I know your heart is good and your thoughts pure."

"Bless you," Luc replied and hugged the older man more fiercely.

He crossed the carpeted floor and joined Donny. Together they strode down the hallway away from the temple and the reek of incense that burned Luc's eyes.

"How did it go?" Donny asked.

"Better than I expected." Luc snickered. "The old men are so confused they don't know what to do. Even Dzu is looking for someone to lead them."

"They'll make you Lama when old toothless kicks the bucket?"

"Without a doubt."

"And then?"

"And then things get run my way. With the United States and Western Europe in disarray, the world's balance of power will immediately shift to China, Japan and the nations of the Pacific. It will take a year, maybe two, before the world economy has adjusted to the fact that most of its biggest consumers are dead. By then people will have realized that the great cities that were destroyed were little more than black holes that absorbed everything and produced only more mouths to feed.

"The planet's natural resources like coal, grain, timber and oil will not be affected, only their means of distribution, and those can be rerouted. Take away New York as a financial capital and a new one will emerge in Australia. Scour away the beaches of Miami and people will vacation someplace else. Adaptation is perhaps mankind's greatest skill. The eruption will force humanity to realize the suicidal path they were on and buy enough time to correct it."

"Where does that leave us? The Order, I mean."

"Interestingly, it is the nations of the Pacific basin that will be least affected by the eruption, yet they remain the most vulnerable to earthquakes and volcanoes. We will be in position to warn them about impending catastrophes."

"For a price?" Donny asked.

"For a price," Luc agreed.

Where Randall saw storehouses of gold, Luc saw power, raw unadulterated power of a kind not held since the Roman Caesars. Nations would give him anything to protect themselves and perhaps even more to not warn their enemies. How much was it worth to the Saudi government to know that a major earthquake was going to strike Iran on a certain date and disrupt their oil shipments for weeks or months? How much would the Japanese pay to have enough warning to evacuate Yokohama when an undersea slide sends a tsunami washing over the port? That kind of knowledge was worth something beyond mere money.

After just one or two demonstrations Luc was certain he'd be given virtual control of the world.

Paul "Tiny" Gordon backed out of the ladies' room brandishing a plunger and cursing the antique plumbing. He flipped the sign on the door so it read OUT OF ORDER. Not that it mattered. Sundays were notoriously slow and even on a busy night his bar catered to an almost exclusively male clientele. The few women who did venture in weren't the type to be deterred by using the men's lavatory.

Nursing a vodka gimlet at the bar, Mercer smiled good-naturedly. "The laundry joint again?"

Tiny's was part of a run-down strip mall anchored by an industrial laundry facility. On a regular basis, the toilets belched thick curds of detergent foam.

Tiny tossed the plunger into the back room and stepped onto the platform behind the bar that allowed him to look his seated customers in the eye. "Damn landlord won't do anything about it and the last time I talked to the owner of the laundry he told me that the detergent's keeping the lines clear and I shouldn't complain."

"The joys of running a business." Mercer checked his watch. It was past four in the afternoon. Lasko was running late.

The front door opened. In the reflection of the mirror behind the bar, Mercer saw Harry unclip Drag's leash. The pooch and his master ambled into the bar, the basset making for a pile of blankets Tiny kept for him in a corner and Harry for the bar stool Tiny kept for *him* to Mercer's right. Tiny had mixed a Jack Daniel's and ginger ale by the time Harry eased into his seat.

"Where were you last night?" For the first time in a week, Harry hadn't slept at Mercer's. "You didn't come by."

Harry shot him a lecherous smirk. "I came someplace else."

Mercer and Tiny groaned.

"What brings you here so early?" Harry asked.

"Ira wanted to meet and I needed to get out."

"Think they found Tisa?"

"That's my hope."

"And you're going to go get her."

Mercer sipped at his drink. "That's my plan."

Harry looked to Tiny. "The charming prince storming the castle to rescue the fair damsel? Is his life a cliché or what?"

"You gotta wonder what that makes us."

Mercer indicated his glass. "Obviously you're the alchemist who concocts the healing potions that keep me going."

"And Harry?"

Harry straightened. "I see myself as the sage providing insightful advice."

"Sorry, Harry. Drag's the insightful one. You're more like the court jester."

The door opened again. Ira paused to let his eyes adjust to the bar's gloom and his nose adjust to the smell of old beer and stale cigarettes. He wore khakis and a golf shirt with boat shoes on his feet. The clothes appeared fresh. Mercer suspected he'd been in his office all weekend and had changed for the meeting, which coincided with his commute home.

"Whatchya drinking, Admiral?" Tiny asked.

"Dewar's rocks." Ira slapped Harry on the back. "How you doing, Harry?"

"Fair to partly cloudy. How about you?"

"About the same, maybe a chance of precipitation."

The admiral turned to Mercer. "Let's grab a table."

They collected their drinks and moved to a booth. Ira set a briefcase on the floor after withdrawing a file folder.

"Is that what I think it is?" Mercer asked.

Ira opened the folder and slid it across. "The valley of Rinpoche-La."

The folder contained dozens of satellite photographs. The top picture was a wide-angle shot encompassing hundreds of square miles of rugged snowcapped mountains. Smears of clouds obscured many of the peaks.

"You're looking at the Himalayas from one of our polar orbiting birds," Lasko explained, his voice raspy with exhaustion. "This is the satellite's minimum resolution but about the same as you got from that commercial platform."

"Looks about right," Mercer admitted.

"Using the report you prepared about geothermal activity in the valley, the photo interpreters tasked an infrared bird to shoot the region."

Mercer turned to the next picture in the stack. The photograph was of a black field shot through with white specks.

"Each white dot represents an appreciable heat source. Everything from factory smokestacks to cooking fires. They filtered out known sites, like towns and villages, and anything along established roads." The next picture was the same image but more than three-quarters of the white flecks were gone. "These are the spots we focused on. To be on the safe side, we did this across the entire Himalayan range. In total there were eight hundred seventy-seven targeted sites."

"And they checked them all?"

Ira simply nodded. "If something looked promising, they cranked the resolution and fed the image to the computers for further enhancement. We found a lot of military camps that the Pentagon hadn't known about and"—he flipped to the second-to-last picture—"one lost valley."

Mercer studied the image. The satellite camera was looking straight down at two barren mountain ridges. They were so close together, the valley between them was little more than a jagged line. To the north, where the mountains ended in a high plateau, a dense layer of clouds obscured what little of the valley could be discerned. A river cut across the mouth of the valley as it wended around the twin mountain ranges.

"Are you sure?" Mercer did little to hide his disappointment. He'd expected to see the monastery Tisa had described and the village where she'd grown up.

With a dramatic flourish Ira flipped the picture over to reveal the last in the series. "This what you're looking for?"

Mercer couldn't believe the clarity. It was as though the picture had been taken from a couple hundred feet, not hundreds of miles in space. He could see individual tiles in the monastery's multitiered roof and make out sheep being herded along a nearby path. He could even see there was a rip on the left sleeve of the shepherd's cloak. The compound was enormous, a square parcel fenced by a stone wall with the lamasery at its center. The building itself was easily the size of four city blocks.

Ira retrieved another stack of pictures from his case. "These are everything we got. I guarantee these are the only shots ever taken of that place."

"Why do you say that?"

"Because we didn't have them in our archive and no one else in the world has the technology to produce them. Besides, if the Chinese knew the valley existed, don't you think they would have razed it by now?"

"How far into China is it?" Mercer was too rapt to look up from the photos as he asked. It was almost as if he was searching for Tisa's upturned face, knowing that at that precise moment her picture was being taken, one that Mercer would shortly see.

"A hundred sixteen miles as the crow flies," Ira answered. "But we're talking about an area where you can't get a crow to fly. The average elevation between there and Nepal is over ten thousand feet and the mountains themselves are impassable. A team sent in on foot would take weeks to reach Rinpoche-La."

That got Mercer's attention. "We don't have weeks, Ira."

"I know. I saw the latest from La Palma. The team there reports that the tremors are increasing in severity and duration. They also tell me that the westward side of the volcano is beginning to show displacement. I think that means the mountain's starting to bulge."

"That's what it means, all right. The pressure in the magma chamber has reached a point where it can distort the outside of the volcano. If it keeps up, La Palma could explode like Mount St. Helens."

"Those are the same words they used. What they won't do is make predictions about when it'll blow."

"Like I explained to the president, they can't do that. In a normal circumstance, they couldn't even say that it will erupt. When most volcanoes rumble to life they stay active for a few months or even years and go dormant again without any kind of eruption. We're only certain about La Palma because of Tisa and only she knows exactly when. Have you thought about how to get her out?"

"We can't get her out, at least not in time."

"What do you mean can't?" Mercer stabbed a finger at one of the pictures. "She's right here."

The admiral held up a hand. "I said we can't get her out. I didn't say we can't get you in."

Mercer stared blankly. Ira climbed from his seat and peered out the bar's plate-glass window. He gave it a rap with his knuckle and returned to the booth. A moment later a black man with a shaved head and massive shoulders pushed through the door. He was dressed all in black and sported dark glasses. One cheek bulged with a wad of tobacco.

He scanned the room from behind his shades, projecting menace that would have withered a normal bar crowd. Harry and Tiny merely gave him a passing glance and returned to their conversation. His gaze settled on Mercer.

"I hear you want to join the Monkey Bombers," he said in a rich baritone.

Mercer blanched. He'd recognized Captain Booker Sykes the moment he made his entrance but hadn't put the Delta Force commando together with Ira's boast about getting him to Rinpoche-La. Once Mercer understood the nature of the weapons Sykes worked with, he'd agreed that the nickname, monkey bombs, was much more apt than the military designation, MMU-22. Manned Munition Utility 22.

Sykes grinned at Mercer's pallor and slid into the booth next to Ira.

"I've had the best minds in the Pentagon on this operation and there's no other way," Lasko explained. "Obviously just asking the Chinese for permission is out. We can't slip a team over the border because of the timing involved and the probability of them being picked up. We can forget an insertion via a regular parachute jump. The Chinese have unbroken radar coverage throughout the region. Even flying nap of the earth, a transport plane wouldn't make it twenty miles into China before they scramble MiGs for an intercept. It's the MMUs or nothing."

Mercer kept his eyes on Sykes. "Do they really work?"

"For the past twenty drops the sensors in the pods indicate the passenger would have survived."

"Sensors? You mean you haven't made a manned jump yet?"

Sykes looked hesitant. "Well, the first forty or so

drops weren't survivable. Hell, the first couple were so bad we had to dig what was left of the pods out of the desert floor. The techs needed some time to work out the kinks. They think they have it now."

"Jesus." Mercer shook his head. "Well, I was the damned fool to insist on coming along. What about extraction after we reach Rinpoche-La?"

"That's the other wrinkle," Ira informed him. "As soon as you establish contact with Miss Nguyen you'll have a secure satellite phone to relay any information she has about La Palma. Once we have that, the urgency is gone and you can take all the time you need to hike out to the Nepalese border."

"A hundred sixteen miles?"

"More like two fifty," Sykes corrected. "There's a whole lot of mountains we have to walk around."

"Better and better." The thought of being reunited with Tisa kept the misery from Mercer's voice, but not the sarcasm. "How does it play now?"

"Tomorrow morning an air force transport will take you to Area 51 for two days of orientation with Sykes and his team. From there you'll be flown to a staging point on the island of Diego Garcia in the Indian Ocean. That's where you load up the MMUs for the flight into Tibet."

"How long's the flight?"

"We're estimating six hours but it could be longer," Sykes replied. "It all depends on how far we have to detour around the heaviest of the Chinese radar coverage."

"And no in-flight movie, I suppose."

The commando laughed. "At least the MMUs have been modified to include a relief tube."

There wasn't any need for Mercer to think about the dangers. He would go no matter what scheme the Pentagon savants had concocted to get him to Tisa. "Hey, Harry," he called across the quiet bar. "You have to modify your rescue story. I'm not charging the damsel's castle on a horse. I'm dropping on it from out of a dragon's stomach."

Harry didn't miss a beat. "Just as long as you make the moat of the situation."

A thousand miles south of the Indian subcontinent, the islands of the Chagos Archipelago were like a handful of emeralds tossed on the blue waves. Dense tropical jungle, sugar sand beaches and azure reefs gave the islands their beauty. The extraction of copra oil from coconuts once gave them a thriving economy. All that changed in the 1970s when the British established a military base on one of the islands, a seventeen-square-mile atoll called Diego Garcia. At the time, it was a Cold War outpost for monitoring Soviet ships plying the Indian Ocean.

Over the next twenty years the island was gradually expanded. At the same time, it was handed over to the United States. Today, only a handful of the three thousand military and civilian support staff on the atoll are British citizens.

Diego Garcia gained a measure of fame as a staging area during Operation Desert Storm for B-52 bombers pounding Iraqi positions in Kuwait. Upgrades to the facility allowed it to base B-1s and B-2s during the Afghanistan campaign and again in 2003 for the ouster of Saddam Hussein.

Strapped in the observer's seat behind the pilot of the C-17 Globemaster cargo jet, Mercer had a clear view as the giant aircraft descended from out of the clouds after twenty hours of flight. The atoll was shaped like a squashed circle, an open ring of coral and sand that bulged on one side. It was there that an air base had been hacked from the jungle. As the plane dropped farther, he could see the long runway paralleling the beach and acres upon acres of parking ramps. He counted two dozen aircraft before giving up. Behind the landing strip was a village of prefabricated buildings constructed for those posted at this isolated location. Farther on was Camp Justice, a facility built in the wake of the September 11 attacks that housed military personnel involved in the global war on terror. Beyond the island nothing but ocean stretched to the horizon.

"We call it the dirt aircraft carrier," the pilot called over the intercom, her voice filled with a Texas drawl. "Folks based here call it Gilligan's Isle with guns."

"Ever been here before?" Mercer asked Sykes, seated next to him in the second observer's seat.

"Couple of times. Damn! That was a secret. Remind me I have to kill you later."

The pilot eased back on the quad throttle controls and activated the thrust vectoring system that allowed the two-hundred-eighty-ton aircraft to land in less than three thousand feet no matter how large the load she carried. The air was thick and humid and the four engines labored.

Thundering over the runway threshold, the Globemaster floated on ground effects for a few hundred feet before settling on its multiple landing trucks. Without concern for passenger safety beyond getting them to their destination alive, the air force major slammed home the thrust reversers and Mercer pitched against his harness.

Almost immediately the plane slowed to taxi speed and swung off the 11,800-foot runway.

Now that they were on the ground, Mercer saw that the planes he'd noticed during their descent were B-52s, the venerable strategic bomber whose crews were generally younger than the aircraft they flew. At the end of the parking ramp were four futuristic buildings that looked like flattened domes. These round structures measured two hundred fifty feet wide and were almost six stories tall. The C-17 taxied to a spot in front of the last building and the pilot cut the engines. After being assailed by the whine of the turbojets for so long, the silence was disconcerting.

Mercer peered through the windscreen. The building was a hangar with open clamshell doors. Tropical light flooded the interior and yet the aircraft in the center of the cavernous space seemed to absorb it all. Although he'd seen the same plane the day before at Area 51, seeing it deployed and knowing what they would be attempting soon sent the first pangs of fear into his gut. Mercer's fists clenched and he had to consciously work to get them to relax. Sykes noticed but said nothing.

Officially designated Spirit, the bat-winged B-2 had been dubbed the stealth bomber by the media. The aircraft in the hangar was part of the 509th Bomb Wing out of Whiteman AFB, Missouri. She was number 82-1065, a last-generation block 30 with every conceivable upgrade the builders at Northrop and the air force could devise. With an unlimited range due to her in-flight refueling capability, the stealth was the ultimate weapon of the U.S. doctrine of force projection. It could carry a variety of payloads in her rotary launchers, everything from thirty-six cluster bombs with their hundreds of individual bomblets to eight five-thousand-pound GBU-37 "bunker busters" to sixteen B83 multimegaton thermonuclear bombs capable of leveling entire cities.

For the past several months this particular B-2 had been stationed at Area 51, the linchpin to the development of the MMU-22—what Sykes's troops affectionately called the monkey bomb.

The concept for this secret weapon came from the military's perceived need to covertly insert a commando team inside an area protected by heavy air defenses. Up until the development of the MMU-22 the only options were for troops to land beyond the radar umbrella and slog in on foot or risk a HALO (High Altitude Low Opening) parachute jump off the back ramp of a C-130. However, the Hercules cargo plane was as stealthy as a zeppelin and not much faster. Something better was needed, a covert way to get Special Operations soldiers to where they needed to be.

In the late 1990s, a British defense contractor was working on the development of pods that could be mounted under the wings of the Harrier jump jet. These man-sized capsules were designed for the rapid evacuation of wounded soldiers from deep behind enemy lines. Someone at the Pentagon expanded on the idea and wondered if it was possible to infiltrate troops the same way, but using a stealth platform such as the B-2 or F-117 Nighthawk fighter/bomber. From that abstraction grew the MMU-22.

The pods were slightly larger than telephone booths, doped in radar-absorbing composite material and formed in angular shapes to deflect incoming radar. Using the same global positioning satellite system that gave American bombs such precision, an onboard computer steered the MMU-22 as it fell. At a predetermined height, usually the minimum safe distance above the ground, the parachute would be deployed. Booker Sykes claimed accuracy of within twenty feet even in a crosswind of up to thirty knots.

Inside the pod, a Special Forces soldier was provided with enough room to stretch out, storage for combat harnesses, packs, equipment and the weapons necessary for their mission. While confining, the monkey bombs were lined with high-tech memory foam that made them relatively comfortable, provided the person inside didn't suffer from claustrophobia. As Sykes had mentioned, there was a relief tube for a soldier to empty his bladder as well as a closed-circuit television attached to a camera at the bottom of the pod to give a view of the landing site during the descent.

Sykes loosened his safety straps and leaned over to Mercer. "Little more intimidating now that we're here, huh?"

The B-2 resembled a black manta ray, its partially buried engine nacelles being the gills to feed the four General Electric F-118 turbofans, the bulbous cockpit the creature's eyes. Even resting at its hard stand, the aircraft radiated menace. "I was thinking the same thing."

Ten minutes later they were sweating on the tarmac. A steady breeze carried the iodine taste of the sea but provided no relief from the humidity. The ramp at the back of the C-17 was down and the aircraft's loadmaster was coordinating a fleet of forklifts to remove the MMUs from the plane's hold. Despite the tight security at Area 51 and here at Diego Garcia, the pods were crated in containers labeled MACHINE PARTS and wouldn't be unpacked until they were in the hangar and the doors closed. There were eight MMUs in total, seven for Sykes and his Delta Force team and one for Mercer.

The six men, hand selected by Sykes, were perhaps the best-trained soldiers the United States had ever produced. They all came from the army and had excelled from their first days of basic training and in their extensive training since. Specialists in all forms of combat, they'd also learned to operate with initiative and flexibility. They were tighter knit than brothers, hard men who had trained through the human instinct of self-preservation to put their lives in the hands of the others. In Kosovo and Afghanistan and Iraq and a dozen other hot spots around the globe their bonds had been tempered by combat.

Because the occupant of the monkey bomb was virtually powerless once the weapon was loaded into the B-2, Mercer's two days of orientation in Nevada was more for the Delta operators to assess him for themselves. New members seconded to the team, soldiers who'd already proved they belonged through years in the military, still needed months of initiation and indoctrination before they were accepted.

It wasn't enough for the men that Sykes had said Mercer was all right. He had to prove it himself. In the thirty hours he'd spent with just the men, not Sykes, he was forced on two five-mile runs, endured numerous timed sprints through an impromptu obstacle course, expended about a thousand rounds of ammunition on a firing range and went on three static line parachute jumps (the jump master had explained why he wanted to see three jumps by telling Mercer anyone can fall from an airplane once, only a few will try it a second time and only damned fools go back for thirds and those were the kind he wanted).

In the end, the team's senior noncom, Angel Lopez, a streetwise Honduran immigrant who went by the nickname Grumpy, had pronounced Mercer just marginally more fit than a week-old corpse. In keeping with the sequence of names the men chose for each other—Sykes being Doc, the son of a preacher who struck out consistently with women getting called Bashful, the team's jokester going by Dopey, and so on—Mercer was given the ignominious name of Snow White.

Mercer and Sykes strolled past the hangar. In the background they could hear Grumpy snarling at the men. "H'okay people, we got twenty hours until we launch and twenty-four hours of work. I want a full weapons check, equipment breakdown and ammo load distribution in twenty mikes."

At the edge of the aircraft ramp, beach sand blew across the asphalt in airy streaks. The wind had kicked up, a steady beat that flattened their clothes. Sykes hunkered down to a squatting position and took up a stick to draw random shapes in the dirt.

"What's on your mind?" Mercer asked after a moment.

Sykes kept his eyes on his drawings as he spoke, his voice solemn. "We haven't had a chance to talk since Dreamland. I just want you to know that Grumpy says you did okay back there. That's a hell of a compliment coming from him."

"So I gathered." Mercer sensed this wasn't what Sykes wanted to say.

"The boys are calling you Snow White."

Mercer grinned wryly. "I've been called worse."

"Yeah, I bet. Anyway, I've been with Delta for eight years now. I've lost a few men during that time. A good guy named Tom Hazen in Colombia, a heck of a sharpshooter in Pakistan, a gunny who got killed when his chute didn't open at Bragg. A couple of others.

"These guys died doing their job. It's part of the risk we take. But the thing is we *take* that risk. It isn't given to us. Some ugly pops an ambush we're too stupid to see, we deserve to get killed. That gunny packed his parachute wrong, he deserved not to have it open. You following me?"

Mercer knew where Booker was headed, but remained silent, knowing it needed to be said.

"Admiral Lasko tells me you've been in some real hairballs over the past few years and with some pretty good operators too. SEALs in Alaska, Force Recon in Africa. Some army spec dogs down in Panama last year. Don't take this the wrong way, hell, there ain't no right way, I guess, but I don't want you thinking all that earned you a place here."

"I never thought it did," Mercer replied softly.

"I like you. I think you'll do okay up there, but you

have to understand my mission is about getting certain information back to the admiral. It's not about protecting Miss Nguyen and it's not about protecting you. If at some point you become a liability to that mission, or if you put one of my men at risk, don't think I won't drop you myself."

"I'm taking this in the spirit it's given. It's not personal, I know."

"It's not, but this whole thing has my hackles up. We've never had a Snow White tagging along with the team before and that has me spooked."

"You love them, don't you?"

In the distance Grumpy was chewing out Sleepy, the marginally laziest man on the team. "Not them as individuals," Sykes answered, "but the ideal of what they are. Faces come and go, but the team is still the same. Am I making any sense?"

"It's the old saying about hating the president but loving the presidency. Only you're talking about respect and honor, much truer feelings, ones that are harder to develop and sustain. You've felt this way for years now. It's as much a part of you as the color of your skin. I'm not a member of your team, never could be, and you're afraid that my going in with you will affect the balance somehow."

Sykes nodded. "Something like that, I guess. I don't mind being dropped out of a bomber in nothing more than a high-tech coffin or facing overwhelming enemy forces. I just like to know everyone who's at my back."

"There's nothing I can say that'll put you at ease so I'll keep my mouth shut."

They looked each other in the eye, a silent current of understanding flashing between them.

For the twelve hours the Delta team was slated for sleep, inside the hangar was a flurry of activity to prepare the B-2 and the eight MMUs. As Sykes had said, he and his men were only responsible for getting information out of Rinpoche-La. Mercer had been given the additional job of finding a way of turning that information into a practical plan. In an office off the barracks where the team snored away, he sat hunched over a laptop staring at the latest geologic reports coming out of La Palma.

The news wasn't good. The numerous fumaroles, gas-emitting vents that dotted the volcano, were pumping out deadly aerosols with the force of jet engines. The discharge rate of noxious elements such as carbon dioxide and sulfur was rising exponentially. Rain as caustic as sulfuric acid was falling on parts of the island.

While the eastern side of the mountain was showing signs of displacement, the western, and more dangerous, flank hadn't begun to slip. Yet each passing minute raised the temperature of the water trapped inside the volcano. It was only a matter of time before the increased pressure cracked the rock and the half-trillion-ton slab went crashing into the sea.

The president had hoped to keep the news of the potential eruption to a minimum, and it appeared for the time being his wishes were coming true. There weren't any dramatic pictures for the media to focus on and the few so-called experts being interviewed downplayed the potential of a massive eruption because La Palma's last jolt in 1971 hadn't affected the fault. Instead, the press was focused on a Hollywood corruption scandal that was ruining the careers of several top-ranked actors. Mercer blessed the American fascination with fame and the misguided belief that the oceans still afforded isolation from the rest of the world.

Ever since he'd been asked to find a way to minimize the effects of a La Palma eruption, Mercer had spent countless hours examining the problem. He came at it from every direction, dissecting and discarding each scenario that occurred to him. Feasibility and practicality didn't factor in his thinking. All he wanted were options. And as he'd known since the president first asked him to try to deflect a volcanic blast, there wasn't a whole lot to be done except hope the other scientists working on the project were more inspired than he was.

Dawn found him asleep on the cradle of his arms.

The morning was spent in a locked room, where Sykes went over operational details. From the satellite photographs, a detailed model of the monastery and its environs had been constructed. The model maker had gone so far as to include a flock of sheep from a children's toy farm.

The plan was simplicity itself. The back of the monastery hung precariously over a hundred-foot-tall wall of dressed stone that divided the valley into an upper and lower section. The wall, as substantial as that protecting any castle, spanned the width of the valley, and had doubtlessly deterred generations of soldiers from attempting an assault from the rear. The surety of the wall's impenetrability made it less likely to be guarded and thus the logical choice for Sykes's team. Under the cover of a moonless night, the MMUs would be directed to land in the lower valley at the base of the wall. There weren't any discernible trails from the meadow to the upper valley so Bashful and Happy would free-climb the wall, anchoring ropes for the rest of the team as they ascended. From there it would be up to improvisation and luck to infiltrate the building and find Tisa. As a precaution, each man carried his own satellite phone to broadcast the eruption date once they'd gotten it from her.

Two hours before the afternoon takeoff, the team members began to don their gear. Maybe it was because Harry's jokes about Prince Charming storming a castle had remained fresh in his mind, but to Mercer it seemed the process was like knights suiting up in their armor. Meticulous care was given to every detail. The weapons had all been cleaned and test fired the day before. Ammunition magazines were checked for the stiffness of their springs. Batteries for their comm gear and the sat phones were fully charged. If there was even minor wear on any piece of equipment it was discarded for another.

As the men were doing this, technicians swarmed the bomber and monkey bombs doing their last-minute checks. The two pilots performed their walk-around and were ready to board through the bottom hatch.

A blacked-out van took the commandos from their barracks to the hangar. Once inside with the door closed, the men piled out of the vehicle and assembled under the enormous flying wing. The large bomb bay doors were open. Although the air force had given this plane the name *Spirit of Wyoming*, the crew had added a nickname. Painted on one of the barnlike bomb doors was a fluffy cloud. Extending from it was a downward-pointing hand with its index finger extended. The drawing was vague as it emerged from the cloud but grew more detailed closer to the fingertip, as though its presence was becoming more real. The bomber's name was written underneath. Invisible Touch.

As was tradition during the preflight for this flight crew, a portable cassette deck pounded out the Phil Collins song by the same name.

Mercer eyed the MMUs. Sykes was right. They did look like coffins, especially with their lids open. The foam lining was covered in a microfiber that had the sheen of casket satin. Great.

The team stowed their gear in compartments built into the bombs, making sure straps were cinched tight and nothing rattled. Once they were set, the pilots shook hands with each commando and climbed into the B-2's belly.

At the side of one of the monkey bombs, Sykes called his group for one last pep talk. "For the next six hours we're nothing more than passengers who"—he glanced into the open capsule—"have about the same amount of room as folks who get stuck in coach."

There were a few nervous chuckles.

"We've been working with this system for a couple of months now. We've all taken a tethered drop from the twenty-foot tower and know how to handle a landing. The only thing we have to worry about is the chute opening. And that's something we face every time we go so that means there's no difference in this op from any other we've ever done. We don't have to sweat it. Once we're on the ground we know what to do."

"Rules of engagement?" Bashful asked.

"Take down anyone with a gun or anyone threatening you. The only person we care about is Tisa Nguyen. Snow White's given us a pretty good idea what she looks like, but don't take chances. Any woman under the age of say, forty, is off limits."

Bashful raised his hand. "Even if they're coming after us, Doc?"

"Ain't no *chica* coming after you, man," Grumpy retorted and the men laughed.

"Anything to add, Snow?"

Mercer looked around at the confident faces. "Just that these guys blew a hole in a ferryboat in Greece two weeks ago to stop Tisa from talking to me. They killed almost fifty people. Take Doc Sykes's advice. They won't give quarter so don't offer it. And if one of you tags a big bastard who dyes his hair like Elvis, you earned yourself two weeks on the Caribbean island of your choice with the woman of your choice."

"Hoo-yah!"

"Except for Bashful," Mercer added. "You monkeys will have to get him the girl."

With that the meeting was over. It was time.

Two air force technicians helped Mercer into his MMU. Harnesses went around his legs and waist and over his shoulders. He was asked to unbutton the fly of his black fatigues and was given an appropriately sized sleeve for the relief tube. From down the length of the hangar he heard Dopey complaining that even their biggest one was too tight.

"You don't put it over your mouth," Sneezy joked back.

Mercer's helmet was jacked into a communications console and the closed-circuit television was tested. The camera was placed on the bottom of the pod and on the four-inch flat screen he saw workers bent over the other capsules like something out of a sci-fi movie. He was shown the climate controls and ventilators and the mouthpiece for a specially concocted fruit beverage full of electrolytes and minerals. Two hours from the launch, he would draw from another tube. This brew contained stimulants and natural painkillers plus something to counter the effects of altitude sickness. Sykes warned Mercer that after drinking the potion it would be best if he didn't submit to a drug test for a month or two.

"How do you feel, sir," the tech asked, his hand on the lid ready to close Mercer in.

"Like I'm about to be interred."

"Then you're good to go."

The lid came down and a vacuum system engaged to seal the MMU. Mercer cracked his jaw to adjust to the slight change in air pressure. The television screen was four inches over his face. The lighting inside the MMU was subtle and warm, a concession to the men who had to endure them for long flights.

A minute later Mercer's pod rattled as the special

cargo lift that had come with the team on the C-17
hoisted the MMU from its cradle and trundled over
to the B-2. Clamps on the bomber's rotary launcher
clasped the capsule and drew it up into the bomb bay.
No sooner had Mercer gotten comfortable again than
another MMU was attached and the launcher spun. It
was like being a bullet as it was loaded into a revolver.
The launcher was designed to carry eight nuclear
bombs and had been modified to carry four MMUs.
The first four went into Mercer's side of the aircraft,
and the remaining were fed into the stealth bomber's
second bay.

External power cables were attached, as were the
supplemental communications lines so the men could
converse during the flight. After making each man call
out his status, Sykes notified the pilots on the flight
deck that the men were ready.

"Status board in the green, Doc. Taxi truck's coming now. ATC gives us priority and there isn't a recon
satellite pass for another seventeen minutes. We'll be
cruising at a classified speed and at a classified altitude. Our flight time to target is also classified. So lay
back and relax. We here at Cloak and Dagger Airways
wish you a pleasant journey."

The jagged winged aircraft was drawn from its re-
vetment and pulled to a parking slot adjacent to the
main runway. A ground crewman unhitched the tow
tractor, snapped the pilot a crisp salute and motored
away.

Deep in the B-2's hull the first engine spun to life,
followed seconds later by the other three. Although
the powerful turbofans straddled the bomb bay, the
noise level inside the soundproofed MMU was only
slightly louder than what passengers experienced on
an airliner.

The pilot performed one final test of the aircraft's
complicated control surfaces. Satisfied, he ran up the

engines and the menacing plane began to roll under its own power.

In front of the aircraft, the end of the runway vanished in the wavering curtains of a heat mirage. Behind the plane, hot exhaust created the same effect so the bomber looked like a wraith enveloped in a chimera. Even on the ground the B-2 was otherworldly, like no aircraft ever built.

The engines' roar turned into a scream as the Spirit picked up speed. Using less than a third of the runway, the B-2's nose lifted and she took to the sky. The landing gear snapped closed as the bomber began climbing for the safety of the upper troposphere, high above commercial traffic.

From inside the bomb bay, the ascent felt smooth. The men made a few bad jokes and bantered for a while, but soon grew quiet as they settled in for the six hours of being locked in the MMUs with their thoughts and fears. After a while Mercer was able to forget where he was and what they were about to attempt. His mind drifted through countless random thoughts, and while he knew he should be thinking about the impending eruption on La Palma, he found himself focusing on Tisa.

Just one day and night with her had created a deeper impression on him than any woman he'd ever been with. He sought justifications and rationales for his thoughts and admitted that this wasn't something he had conscious control over. He'd strayed from the path of what was logical and crossed into an emotional realm he seldom approached. The answer to the fundamental question of if he loved her wasn't clear yet, but he did face the truth that he wanted to.

Mercer had earned the reputation as one of the best mining engineers and prospecting geologists in the world by making deliberate calculations and expertly assessing risk versus reward. Like so many other driven men he'd used those same analytical skills on his personal life as well. The result was a string of short but intense relationships that he ultimately cut short. The reasons were varied but underlying all the breakups was his belief that the affair would ultimately fail anyway and it was better for the women to have it end quickly. For the first time he got a sense that it was his own fear of getting hurt that made him end those other relationships. He wasn't doing it to protect the women. He was doing it to protect himself. By breaking up quickly, he shielded himself from the risk of possible rejection and the associated doubts that came with it.

"Goddamned strange place for an epiphany," he muttered as the plane streaked across the Indian Ocean.

And also for the first time, he believed in risking that kind of pain for the opportunity to be with Tisa. He had always been comfortable gambling with his life. That was part of any miner's job. Now he was growing comfortable with risking his lifestyle too. He drifted to sleep with that thought foremost in his mind.

Hours later, the internal intercom squawked to life. "Gentlemen, this is the flight deck. We're about an hour from the border with Tibet. Not that we expected they would, but Indian civilian and military radars have failed to pick us up. However we're approaching the Chinese air defense net. Once we get closer to the border we'll be dropping to the deck and may be forced to find a route where their radar coverage is thinnest. There's nothing to worry about, but you guys may get tossed around down there." He clicked off, returned a second later, and quipped, "Oh, and depending on conditions we might have to dodge a mountain or two."

The strategic bomber's flight path had kept it over the ocean for as long as possible, allowing her to top her tanks with an aerial refueling from a KC-10 tanker over the Arabian Sea. The plane made landfall north of Bombay and headed in a northwesterly diagonal across India toward Nepal. Cruising at forty-five thousand feet, too high for anyone on the ground to see or hear, the B-2 still skirted all the major population centers as extra insurance.

Now that they were nearing the Himalayan foothills it was time to drop closer to the ground and employ the aircraft's sophisticated terrain following/terrain avoidance (TA/FA) system. One of the one hundred sixty-two onboard computers would take control of the plane, mapping out and following a route through the mountains while at the same time keeping clear of Chinese radar installations. Even though the stealth's shape and skin gave it the radar cross section of a bird, the classified radar-detection system made certain that even that small of a picture wouldn't appear on an enemy's scopes.

The final piece of stealth gear to be employed was perhaps the most classified on the aircraft. Because of its unusual shape and mission needs, the B-2 flew below the speed of sound. Had it been able to travel faster than the thunder of its own engines, like the B-1b Lancer, acoustical detection wouldn't have been a concern. Even with the engines shielded within the hull to deaden some sound, the Spirit flew within an envelope of noise generated by its four turbofans and could be heard coming miles off at low level. To counter this, the design team created an antinoise generator, a device that matched the frequency of the sound waves and produced waves of its own at the exact opposite amplitude. While consuming an enormous amount of fuel, the top secret apparatus effectively canceled out the jet's bellowing roar. With the device in operation and at five hundred knots, the B-2 sounded barely louder than a well-tuned Harley-Davidson.

The Himalayan massif quickly came into range. The barometric altimeter showed fifteen thousand feet, but the plane was only a thousand above the ground. Trained for this kind of flying, the pilots were relaxed in their seats as the sophisticated controls moved of their own accord. The Spirit followed the path mapped by its GPS and radar, rocketing through steep valleys, slewing around ramparts that towered ten thousand feet above the bat-winged plane. It was a ride on the ultimate roller coaster, one in which the car determined where to put the tracks it was to follow.

The plane ate the distance across Nepal in twenty minutes and was a dozen miles from the Chinese border when the computer detected the first antiaircraft radar. In minutes a CRT screen in the cockpit lit up with dozens of radar contacts. The coverage appeared solid, a veritable minefield stretching the length of the frontier and projecting fifty miles into the country. Added to this was the presence of microwave towers built intentionally to detect a stealth bomber penetration. The towers emitted an invisible barrier of energy that the plane would have to fly through.

The idea behind the barrage of microwaves wasn't to find the plane directly but rather to detect the hole it created when it cut across the net, much the same as sonar operators focus on quiet spots in the otherwise noisy seas to find modern noiseless submarines. Detractors of the B-2 had called this low-tech solution reason enough to scrap the $2 billion planes.

The veteran pilot watched the terrain map unfolding on the screen in front of him, trying to guess their route before the computer found it. There were several radars in the H and E bands to their west and a powerful microwave tower directly ahead. The tower appeared to be on a mountaintop. The computer banked the bomber so it steered close to the tower but a thousand feet below it in a valley only five hundred feet wider than the plane's 172-foot wingspan.

The pilot would have made the same maneuvers, although his solution came seconds after the computer's.

Jagged crags of granite seemed to reach for the plane as it plunged into the steep valley seconds before breaking the microwave beam. She hugged the canyon floor, flying low enough to blow snow off the ground. Once the threat board showed clear, the heavy bomber shot out of the gorge, passing directly over a sleepy little village.

"There'll be a story or two down there come morning."

"If they knew comic books they could tell the local commissar that they were buzzed by Batman."

"They were."

With their clear view out the cockpit and ample time to prepare, the violent maneuvers seemed routine for the flight team. In the bomb bay, it was quite different.

Mercer was certain his shoulders would be black and blue. The sudden jukes and jinks slammed him around inside the MMU, straining his safety harnesses with each furious bounce. And if it weren't for an iron stomach, he would long ago have lost his lunch.

The wild ride went on for twenty minutes, with changes of direction, attitude and speed coming with dizzying regularity. The fact that the men were horizontal in the pods and couldn't gain equilibrium made it all that much worse.

"This is the flight deck," the pilot called after a moment of relatively level flight. "We just penetrated the heaviest concentration of SAM sites and radar installations anywhere on earth and as far as the Chinese know this bird's sitting in a hangar in Missouri. We'll be over the drop zone in ten minutes. This ship's at her most vulnerable when the bomb bay doors open. To minimize the risk the rotary launcher's gonna spit you out like watermelon seeds. If you think the past few minutes were rough, you ain't seen nothing yet."

For Mercer the waiting had become easier. He'd spent so much time worried about finding a way to save a planet full of people that it was almost a relief to only worry about saving one, Tisa. With that goal so close, his blood felt charged. The others were feeling it too. The bad jokes were beginning again.

"Five minutes to drop," the pilot announced what seemed just seconds later.

"Okay, people," Doc Sykes called out. "Tighten those straps, stow your relief and water tubes and button those flies. Once we're on the ground, I want Dopey to rig the MMUs' demolition charges with a four-hour delay. Sneezy's his cover. The rest gather on me ASAP and we'll make the assault on the wall. The two of you can catch up when you're done. By then, Happy and Bashful will have finished their ascent and we'll be ready for the climb. Turn on your external cameras and everyone give me a status report."

By the time the Delta operators and Mercer told Doc they were ready, the pilot informed them the drop was in one minute.

Mercer's sense of well-being evaporated. Facing a thirty-thousand-foot plunge in what amounted to a futuristic life-sized tin can, he knew that once the rotary launcher released the MMU his fate was out of his hands until the pod touched down. Sykes had said the first forty or so drops hadn't been survivable. He'd later confided that a few of those that were survivable would have resulted in broken limbs, internal injuries, or worse. Mercer tried to recall his frame of mind when he'd blackmailed his way onto this mission and cursed the person he'd been then.

"Okay, boys, doors open in five, four, three, two, one."

The hydraulic whine was drowned instantly by the screaming torrent of air that whipped into the large bomb bay. Mercer had only a second to sense the buffeting when the rotary launcher engaged. He couldn't feel the other MMUs being jettisoned, but every two seconds the launcher advanced one slot and another was gone. After three quarter-rotations of the launcher it was his turn.

The mechanism spun to the lock position and the clamps holding Mercer's MMU released.

The instant the monkey bomb was free of the Spirit it began a four-g deceleration that shoved Mercer's internal organs toward his feet. Somewhere high above he felt his stomach calling for him to come back. Winglets deployed from the sides of the MMU to prevent the pod from tumbling as it transited into free fall. The drop was like a runaway elevator, only there seemed to be no bottom. Reaching its terminal velocity of one hundred twenty miles per hour, the stealthy MMU plummeted from the sky, unseen, unheard and completely undetectable. Clutched so tightly, one of the plastic handgrips on the side of Mercer's body snapped off. He could barely force air into his lungs. At some point he became aware that he was screaming and probably had been since the MMU fell clear.

He remembered the television screen, but it showed nothing but blackness. He could only hope the GPS system was keeping the MMU on track, otherwise he'd have no chance of hitting the target and would likely crash into the side of a mountain.

"Come on," he silently prayed. The chute should have deployed by now.

The designers had mistakenly not installed altitude displays for the soldiers inside the monkey bombs. He was sure he'd already passed the minimum safe distance above the ground and nothing was happening.

Jesus, the thing had malfunctioned.

What he didn't know was that the MMU was working flawlessly, the stabilizing fins making constant adjustments to keep the weapon on target while the laser
range finder knew to the inch how close it was to
the ground.

At a thousand feet the onboard computer released
the drogue chute to ease the shock of the main parachute deploying a moment later. As the MMU drifted
downward, the range finder switched to secondary
mode and began searching for the flattest place to land
within a three-hundred-foot target area.

The strain of the chute billowing open came as
sweet pain. Mercer took his first deep breath since the
initial release and felt the adrenaline spike subside.
He let go of the handgrip and heard it clatter down
toward his feet. The closed-circuit screen flushed green
as night-vision enhancers activated. Details on the
ground were hard to make out, but even the murky
glimpse was a welcome relief.

As his view resolved, Mercer could feel the MMU
make adjustments to his flight path by controlling the
ram-air parachute. In a moment he saw a flat plain
immediately below his feet. It drifted out of view as
a crosswind caught the pod, then came back as the
computer made automatic corrections.

Sykes had trained him not to watch the landing to
prevent himself from tensing. He closed his eyes at
what he thought was the last second and had to wait
almost fifteen more before shock absorbers at the bottom of the MMU touched down. As designed, the pod
fell onto its back and the chute rigging was sheered
away so the yards of black nylon couldn't act as a sail
and drag him across the landscape.

Mercer flipped a protective cover off the button that
opened the pod and mashed it with his fist. The seal
maintaining pressure in the pod hissed and the door

opened slightly. A cold wind exploited the tiny opening and whipped the hatch all the way open. The first breath of the icy mountain air seared his lungs. Mercer coughed.

He unsnapped his harnesses and rose unsteadily. Around him he saw a monochromatic world of grays and the outline of steep mountain cliffs. If not for the tough grasses growing along the rocky valley floor, the scene could have doubled for a crater on the moon. The air temperature was in the low thirties, yet he would occasionally feel the warm caress of steam from a geothermal vent.

A figure loomed out of the darkness. "You okay, Snow?" It was Grumpy. He had already donned his equipment and cradled his M-4, the stripped-down assault version of the M-16. Night-vision goggles covered half his face.

"Yes, just a little shaken."

"Don't sweat it. That was one hell of a ride. Get into your gear, we're moving out." He turned away quickly.

Mercer grabbed his arm. "Hold it, did everyone make it down safely?"

Grumpy didn't look at Mercer when he said, "Sneezy's chute tangled. He's dead." The noncom shook off Mercer's hand. "This op better be worth his life, man."

"It's worth all of ours," Mercer said to Grumpy's back as he vanished into the darkness.

Sykes took the news of Sneezy's death by ordering Sleepy to cover Dopey as he worked on each MMU to activate their self-destruct mechanisms. Now that they were on the ground, the mission took precedence. Grieving for the fallen man would come later. He led the team northward toward the monastery's back wall, about a quarter mile from where the MMUs had dropped in a cluster.

Mercer expected to have trouble breathing at twelve thousand feet and knew his lack of altitude sickness symptoms like headaches, dizziness and pulmonary distress was due to the drug cocktail he'd consumed on the flight. The black fatigues he'd been given also protected him from the near-freezing temperatures and the wind that was beginning to shriek down the valley, corralled by the mountains and vectored like a jet into his face. Because of the constant streamers of steam that blew from the geothermal vents ringing the valley, his night-vision goggles could not gather enough ambient light. He left them dangling around his neck as he ran, exposing the area around his eyes to the biting cold. Soon his skin was numb.

The wall at the rear of the monastery was made of smooth river rocks mortared together with primitive cement. Through the streaming haze of steam high above them, they could see a portion of the building's

pagoda-style roof. With curt hand gestures, Sykes
fanned out his men to cover the climbers as they unlimbered their rope and equipment. Mercer took a
position on the far left flank, tight against where the
stone wall met the cliff. He donned his night-vision
goggles and scanned the top of the wall and the surrounding rocks, which had hundreds of crags that
could easily hide observers. The barrel of his M-4 followed the smooth motion of his eyes.

In the center of the towering wall Bashful and
Happy, whose real names were Bobby Johnson and
Bruce Morrelli, were ready to start their ascent.
They'd studied it for ten minutes, mapping their route
with the practiced eye of professional climbers. They
would scale the wall independently, carrying coils of
rope and the necessary gear to secure the lines once
they reached the top. Each also carried a silenced Beretta in case a sentry wandered by. Every member of
the team was competitive to a fault, driven to surpass
their comrades at all costs. But when it came to a
mission, they knew this wasn't a game and the two
men began the climb with caution and little thought
to the progress of the other.

As if gravity didn't apply, Bashful and Happy
seemed to float up the wall, their arms and legs in
constant motion as they exploited the tiniest flaws in
the mortar for finger- and toeholds. Mercer, who had
done some climbing out of necessity rather than recreation, had never seen anything like it. In minutes they
had traversed half the distance to the top and he had
to force himself not to be distracted by the display.
He turned away and checked his surroundings again.
His weapon's safety was off, though he kept his finger
clear of the trigger guard.

"Doc, this is Dopey." Mercer heard the voice over
the hearing-aid-sized speaker in his ear. "MMUs are
rigged. Three hours and fifty minutes to bingo. Sleep
and I are on our way in."

"Roger, Dope," Sykes replied.

Bashful reached the top of the foundation wall a moment ahead of Happy. There was a squawking flurry as he rolled over the cornice. The men on the ground tensed as several owls exploded into the night. Bashful remained out of view and Happy froze a foot below the ledge. The seconds dragged.

"All clear," Bashful finally called over the tactical radio.

Happy finished his climb. They scouted the area immediately around them for five minutes to satisfy themselves that the birds hadn't alerted anyone before using a muffled nail gun to drive spikes into the stone. They secured pairs of carabiners for the ropes and a moment later the thick lines tumbled to where Sykes waited.

"Grumpy on line one, Snow on two," Sykes ordered. "Dope, what's your ETA?"

"I'm fifty yards behind you, Doc."

"You're on rope one when Grumpy hits the top. Sleep, you take two when Snow's secure." As he spoke, Sykes clipped Bashful's and Happy's combat equipment to the ropes so they could be hauled up.

Mercer had been issued special clamps that would allow him to climb the rope as easily as ascending a ladder. He clipped them to the line, took a moment to stare up the rock face and marvel at the skill of the two commandos. To him the wall was as smooth as glass and angled near ninety degrees.

"Move it, Snow," Grumpy prodded.

Mercer looped the clamp's strap under his foot, lifted his leg and applied slight downward pressure for the clamp to bite. He stepped up, repeated with his other foot and was instantly two feet off the ground. He slid the clamps strapped to his wrists upward, took another step with his right foot and quickly found his rhythm. The thirty pounds on his back would have become an issue had the climb been higher, but he could take the added strain for a hundred-foot climb.

To his left, Sergeant Lopez, a.k.a. Grumpy, was twenty feet higher on the rope and climbing like a machine, his legs pistoning in perfect synchronization. Mercer didn't even try to keep up.

At the top of the rope Bashful took a handful of Mercer's uniform to haul him over the cornice. They were in a wide unsheltered terrace covered in square flagstones. Twenty yards away the monastery loomed above them, supported by a colonnade stretching the length of the building. The structure itself rose in tiers that vanished into the clouds. A soft glow filtered from the single arched doorway. Several upper rooms were also illuminated. To the left and right were small round structures he guessed were chapels. Other than the prayer flags ripping and snapping from atop dozens of poles, nothing moved on the courtyard.

In the minutes it took for the rest of the team to make the climb and haul up the equipment, Mercer kept his back pressed to the low wall surrounding the terrace and watched for movement. Once assembled, the team moved to the lee of one of the small chapel buildings for Sykes's final orders.

"All right, my little dwarfs, from here on we run out of plan. We'll go through that door over there and search floor by floor in teams of two. Snow, you're with me. Grump's the lone gun on the ground floor. The longer we avoid detection the more we can cover, but by the looks of this place there are probably two hundred rooms in there and Snow thinks there's a lot of underground stuff too. At some point we're gonna be spotted. Be ready."

"Hoo-yah," the men whispered in unison.

Sweeping around the chapel, the men jogged to the rear of the monastery, rifles at their shoulders, eyes peering into the shadows around the ranks of columns. The double doors stood fifteen feet tall, made of some exotic wood bound with ornate iron straps. There were no locks. With six guns covering him, Grumpy pulled on one of the five-foot-long handles. No matter how well balanced, the door was massive and he had to change his grip to ease it open. The tongue of light that seeped under the door grew. Mercer saw he wasn't the only soldier sweating despite the chill.

When the door was open wide enough, Sykes tapped Dopey on the head. The commando dropped to his belly and ducked his head for a second-long peek into the building. He looked again, more slowly this time, his head swiveling as he searched the interior.

"Clear," he said as he crawled forward.

The men followed him in, with Grumpy taking the drag slot. The room was twenty feet square, lit by oil lamps, and had no discernible purpose. The walls were paneled in dark wood while the floor was dressed stone. Other than the lamps, the space was empty. A door on the far side was the only way out.

This time Sykes made the first visual reconnaissance. "This is it," he whispered. "The next area is open, lots of doors and hallways and a big staircase."

He shouldered his assault rifle and pulled a silenced pistol. "Mercer, keep on the M-4. You're my cover. Let's go."

Pouring out of the antechamber, the men rushed into the monastery's central mezzanine, the sound of their advance deadened by the rich carpets on the floor. Grumpy peeled off to the right to begin searching independently while the rest moved to the stairs, climbing hard because of their exposure. Sykes motioned Bashful and Happy to check the second floor as he raced past the landing and continued upward. They skipped the third floor and Dopey and Sleepy were ordered to investigate the fourth. Mercer and Sykes reached the top landing. Halls ran off in three directions. Sykes arbitrarily went left with Mercer at his heels. The hallway was lined with small empty rooms and twisted crazily. Narrow staircases ran down to the floor below, creating a dark three-dimensional maze.

"This is going to take forever," Sykes said after five minutes of opening doors on empty rooms. He opened yet another. The room was bare but inexplicably had its own set of steps leading down to the fourth floor. "And with all these staircases, someone can easily outflank us once we make contact."

"Let's hope there aren't that many of them."

Sykes looked at him hard. "Do you believe that?"

"Not for a second."

Backing out of the room, Mercer bumped into someone. He whirled, bringing the rifle around in a blur. The stock caught the figure on the side of the jaw and dropped him to the floor. Sykes pushed past, his pistol held an inch from the unconscious man's head as he patted him down with his free hand. His search turned up nothing.

The man was in his sixties, painfully thin and deeply wrinkled. He wore the robes of a monk. His breathing was even, though blood dribbled from a gash on his cheek.

"Jesus!" Sykes hissed. "You didn't say anything about noncombatants here."

"I didn't know." Mercer's heart still hammered from the shock of the unexpected confrontation.

Sykes keyed his throat mike. "Dwarfs, this is Doc. We just ran into an unarmed monk. This place may be crawling with civilians. Be on the lookout." He gestured to Mercer. "Let's go."

He hadn't taken more than three steps when another monk rounded a corner. Sykes raised his Beretta. The monk, who was younger than the first, froze, his dark eyes widening at the sight of two black-clad soldiers inside the monastery, one of them holding a pistol on him, the other an automatic rifle. He dropped to his knees and cried out in Tibetan.

Sykes put his finger over his lips to silence the frightened man, but the gesture did no good. His cries grew louder and sharper. Sykes glanced back to mutter a disgusted oath at Mercer. The monk dropped his hands toward his waist. Mercer saw the movement. He held his fire for an instant, hoping Sykes would turn to see what was happening. There was no time for a warning.

As soon as he saw the gun coming from under the monk's robe, Mercer fired a single shot. The rifle's crack echoed down the hall as the man was blown back, scarlet drops spraying from the bullet hole in his forehead.

Sykes turned to see the gunman fall flat. His pistol lay on the floor next to him. "Contact," he said coolly into the radio on the off chance his men hadn't heard the M-4's sharp bark in the otherwise silent monastery. "Shot fired. If they didn't know we're here before, they sure know now." He unscrewed the long silencer from his pistol and tossed it aside before holstering the weapon and reaching for his M-4. "Nice shot," he said to Mercer. "Thanks. I screwed up."

He looked down the long corridor, trying to hear if anyone was coming for them. "This is going to get real ugly, real fast. There are seven of us on unfamiliar ground facing an unknown number of enemies. Situations don't get much worse."

"Look on the bright side," Mercer said softly.

"What bright side?"

"I was hoping you'd think of one."

Sykes took point again as they continued their search for Tisa. Every minute or so one of the other teams would report their progress. So far Grumpy was the only other person to make contact. He'd left an elderly woman bound and gagged in a temple room.

They'd covered no more than a quarter of the top floor in fifteen minutes. Sykes was becoming agitated. Someone must have heard the shot and yet no one was coming to investigate. It meant either no one else was here or they were laying an ambush.

A long burst of automatic fire from downstairs tore the silence. It was countered by the familiar crackle from a pair of M-4s.

"Sit rep?" Sykes shouted into the radio.

There was no immediate reply, and with his concentration split between his men and his own surroundings, he didn't hear the whispers from around a corner. Mercer did and dove flat, knocking Sykes to the floor as three men charged around the hallway firing Chinese knockoffs of AK-47s. The jagged fire spitting from the barrels gave the dim corridor a hellish cast.

The barrage flew over their heads as Mercer and Sykes lay prone. Mercer fired off a quick burst that raked one attacker across the torso and punched through the shoulder of another. Sykes added his own shots, dropping the uninjured man with a head shot and finishing off the wounded one with a double tap to the chest. The hall vanished behind a swirling veil of smoke as an oil lamp's contents dribbled like a flaming waterfall onto the carpet. Sykes stayed low as he moved ahead to check around the corner. "Clear."

Mercer followed, taking the opportunity to change out his magazine for a fresh one even though he'd only fired a half dozen rounds. Before the next bend in the corridor they came across an open door. The room beyond was simply furnished, a bed, a small table and a bureau. A smoky lamp gave the spartan room a funereal cast. A window shutter rattled in its frame. Below the stench of cordite and the growing smell of burning wood from the hallway, Mercer detected a familiar scent. Not a perfume, but something more subtle. He moved to the bed. The blankets were still warm. He drew them to his nose and inhaled. The familiar scent drove a current through his heart.

"Tisa was just here," he said. "Those men must have been a rear guard to delay us." He realized bitterly that had he not fired that first unsilenced shot, they might have taken her guards unaware.

"Dwarfs, this is Doc. We just missed the target. We're still on the fifth floor, west side. Grumpy, cover the main staircase on one—everyone else move west and keep sharp."

The fire from the spilled lamp was growing as the ancient carpets on the floors began to burn. Flame licked at the walls, burning through the dried timber as if they'd been doused with gasoline. The pitch that had been used to caulk the joints in the wooden ceiling ignited like fuses when the flame touched it. In a few minutes the fire would eat its way into the roof, and once it opened a hole to feed its growing appetite for oxygen, it would burst into a raging inferno. The air was already becoming unbreathable.

Sykes and Mercer slipped on the gas masks they carried. Mercer had to use the flashlight attached to his rifle to cut through the thickening smoke.

More gunfire erupted downstairs.

"Doc, this is Sleep. We just tagged three of them on the fourth, but I think the target has already slipped down to three."

"Roger that. Bashful, you copy?"

"Affirmative. Hap and I are on our way."

"Keep them from reaching the ground floor," Mercer said. "If they escape underground there could be a thousand ways out of the tunnels and we'll lose them."

Behind them the fire finished off the ceiling and began attacking the roof supports. The tiles above were extremely heavy and it didn't take much for the section of roof to start sagging. More wood splintered and a twenty-foot chunk of timber and ceramic tiles crashed to the floor, sending up a shower of sparks and dancing flames. The sudden rush of frigid air tore down the hallways like a hurricane, pushing a wall of fire ahead of it.

Mercer sensed the danger as soon as he heard the roof collapse. He pushed Sykes hard and began to run. The hallway grew painfully bright as the flames raced after them. The heat became unbearable.

Each twist and turn in the corridor slowed the men but not the fire. The walls and carpet were hundreds of years old, tinder dry, and seemed to explode at the slightest brush of flame. They'd be engulfed in seconds.

The stairwell was hidden in a small alcove and Mercer almost missed it as he ran. The sound of the raging fire made it impossible to speak so he tapped Sykes and stopped. He pointed back to the alcove. Sykes didn't understand, and rather than try to gesture an explanation, Mercer dodged into the fire, ducking low and keeping his weapon ready. He felt along the wall and located the alcove. Sykes bumped into his back. Mercer found the stairs and was about to drop flat to see under the curtain of smoke when the floor lurched. Farther down the corridor a section let go, dropping down to the fourth floor and spreading the fire. Like tipping dominos, more of the floor collapsed, cascading into a growing chasm of flaming debris.

Without knowing what was below the violent swirl of smoke, Mercer threw himself down the stairs, twisting so he used his heavy pack to cushion the blow. The wood steps disintegrated when he impacted and a burst of machine-gun fire raked the spot he'd hit. He fell through the staircase, landing hard but managing to turn onto his belly. A pair of men wearing Western clothes stood a dozen paces away, momentarily confused by what had happened.

Sykes sent a barrage from above, missing completely but drawing their attention. Mercer cleared his weapon of splintered wood and fired. The first gunman dropped, the second remaining on his feet as Mercer pumped more rounds into him. He finally fell.

"Clear," he shouted and slowly got to his feet.

Sykes had to jump from what little remained of the fifth-floor landing. He hit the ground and rolled. The air here was clearer and both men stripped off the restrictive gas masks.

"Which way?" Sykes asked.

"Looks like they were protecting the hall to the right."

"Let's go."

"Dopey, it's Doc. We're on four now. Watch yourself. The fifth is burning and looks like the fire's spreading."

"Roger, Doc. It's already eaten through a few spots."

"Grumpy, what's happening on one?"

"Quiet, sir. A couple of old monks came down the main stairs five minutes ago. They didn't see me and I let them leave the monastery through a side door."

"Stay there. We're working our way down. Bash, you seen anything on the second floor?"

"Negative, Doc, but that don't mean much. There must be fifty staircases here. The target group could have gone through when Hap and I were checking another area."

"I know," Doc acknowledged. "Do your best."

He and Mercer exchanged a worried look and took off at a dead sprint, smoke pouring off their uniforms like vaporous cloaks. Above them the fire raged unchecked.

This floor was much more ornate than the one above. The carpets were thicker, the gilt more plentiful, the rooms better furnished. In one Mercer spied a collection of delicate vases near an open window. They were so thin that he could see the weak orange glow from the upstairs fire through them. He could only guess at their value. Another room was papered in incredible examples of calligraphy and ink and brush paintings.

Tisa's Order sat on a priceless horde of Chinese art, perhaps the greatest outside government control. The entire structure was a living museum and in an hour or two the centuries-old building, filled with untold treasures, would be nothing but a smoking ruin.

"Doc?" It was Grumpy, whispering so softly that Mercer had to press the speaker deeper into his ear.

"Go, Grump."

"I've got the target. They're about fifty yards away, crossing the main foyer."

"How many with her?"

"Twelve to fifteen. Tell Snow his Elvis look-alike has her in a hammerlock."

Mercer picked up his pace, shedding his heavy pack as he ran. He had enough ammo in the pouches attached to his harness to see this through. Sykes struggled to keep up. He ran blindly down the first staircase he came across. At the landing, a group of monks clustered fearfully near a full-sized statue of Buddha. The reclining figure was covered in gold, and the Enlightened One's half-closed eyes were fathomless blue cabochon sapphires. It appeared the monks were trying to find a way to save the statue. Mercer was sure they'd debate the rescue until the fire killed them where they stood. He fired a burst from his M-4 into the ceiling above the men and they scattered like pigeons.

Unbelievably, the third floor was more opulent than the fourth. What Mercer didn't know was that the monastery was laid out so novitiates lived in splendor when they joined the Order, and only as they learned the mysteries and mastered their own desires would they move up the building, shedding luxuries and amenities as they progressed. Only after decades of service would they be allowed to occupy the stark topmost floor. It was the reverse of how the rest of the world worked, where those gaining success could accumulate and enjoy tangible fruits of their labor.

A door just off the landing opened and someone tossed an object into the hallway. Mercer threw himself back, dropping and rolling behind the golden statue an instant before the grenade detonated. The concussion was a hammer slap to his ears. Part of the statue's gold veneer melted, and drops were blown across the foyer to splattered against the wall like gilded Rorschach blotches. The statue itself, made from the aromatic wood of myrrh trees, had been shredded by the blast. One of Buddha's jewel eyes was missing; the other had been turned to powder.

The door opened again and a figure ducked his head out before retreating an instant later. Mercer searched for his rifle and saw it lying three yards beyond his reach. A young monk stepped through the door to check his work, a pistol in one hand, a second grenade in the other. He searched the area with his eyes, seemingly unconcerned with the destruction of the priceless statue. He spotted Mercer cowering behind the figure's pedestal. His gun came up and he fired a snap shot that blew off the remainder of Buddha's head.

Before he could take better aim, Sykes dropped the monk with a shot from up the stairs. He joined Mercer on the third floor. "Are you okay?"

Mercer barely heard Sykes's voice over the ringing in his ears. He nodded anyway. With Tisa only two floors below, nothing else mattered. He gathered up his fallen rifle as two more robed men fired at them from down the hall. They were well protected behind a massive cabinet covered in ornate scrollwork. Mercer unclipped one of the concussion grenades he'd been issued. He pulled the pin and held it for a moment before lobbing it down the hall. He and Sykes covered their ears and screwed their eyes closed. In the confined space, the flash/bang had nearly the same effect as a fragmentation grenade.

One of the men staggered from around the tall bureau and collapsed. Mercer charged forward, firing three-round bursts to keep the other pinned. He stopped just short of the cabinet, held his gun around the corner and fired blind. When he looked, the second monk lay in a pool of blood, his woolen robe holed a dozen times.

"Clear," he shouted back at Sykes and continued on, looking for a stairwell to get him to the ground floor.

Two stories above them, the fire had weakened a secondary support column for the building's pagoda roof. The massive timber failed under the load of the baked tiles. The result was as if that part of the monastery had been dynamited. Tons of wood and barrel tiles fell inward in an implosion that pulled more material into the crater. The sloping roof lost the counterweight of its own construction and the entire eastern side of the temple sagged. A flood of loosened barrel tiles went crashing into the courtyard in an avalanche that quickly formed twenty-foot mounds of rubble.

The other three sides of the roof swayed, shedding tiles like a fish being scaled as wind tore through the burning structure. Lances of flame climbed seventy feet into the air, fueled by the ancient wood and bellowslike gusts funneling down the valley. As the building shifted, windows exploded from their frames in staccato pulses, first north, then south, until the glass from two thousand panes littered the ground.

Inside, Mercer was thrown against a wall as the floors above began to pancake. One wing of the monastery collapsed entirely, dragging more sections with it. Dust billowed from the heap of wreckage in waves of ash and debris that engulfed the length of the valley. It was so heavy that even the ferocious Alpine winds couldn't clear it. Mercer ran blindly, feeling the building tearing itself apart.

"Sit rep," he heard Sykes shouting over the radio.

"Doc, it's Grumpy. The target's past me. I couldn't risk a shot. They went through a door about fifty feet off the main foyer. It's not an exterior door so I think they went underground."

"Shit," Mercer cursed as the others reported their position and progress. Tracking her in the enormous monastery was hard enough. Trying to find her in the warren of tunnels he was sure was under the building would be next to impossible.

As more of the building came down, he expected the defenders to give up the fight and try to save themselves, but as he came to a staircase, someone down on the second floor fired up at him.

Mercer pulled the pins from a pair of flash/bangs and let them roll down the steps. The explosion blew apart the bottom of the stairs and the whole structure nearly collapsed. He loosed a short burst from the M-4, tentatively stepped on the top stair and leapt back as the staircase caved in.

He and Sykes abandoned the ruined stairs in search of another.

"This is Bash, me and Happy are on the first floor. Grump, give me your position."

Mercer tuned out the radio chatter. The third floor was burning freely now. The air was full of smoke and sparks that singed his skin and burned away tufts of hair. After what seemed like an endless search, the confining hallways opened up to a long balcony overlooking a mezzanine. This wasn't the main foyer where the team was assembling, but a secondary space that was still larger than the lobby of most hotels. A set of stairs spiraled down along three walls, descending past the second floor and ending at the first. Standing at the railing, Mercer and Sykes swept the area through their rifle sights. It appeared deserted. They were about to descend when the wall behind them disintegrated and a torrent of flame exploded across the landing. They were both lifted from their feet and launched down the stairs.

Mercer tucked himself into a ball as the scalding pressure wave blew him over the steps. Rolling as he fell, he was hit repeatedly by Sykes tumbling right behind him. He caught a boot to the mouth that split his lip and another to the lower back that felt like it had gouged out a kidney. He smashed into a wall hard enough to arrest his headlong plunge and managed to get a hand on Sykes to stop him too. They climbed to their feet.

Mercer cleared his mouth of blood. "You all right?"

Sykes grabbed his trigger finger and winced as he straightened the misshapen digit. It had broken when it got caught in the trigger guard of his assault rifle. "Fine."

A startled shout from below gave them a second's warning to fall flat before auto-fire raked the staircase. Tufts of carpet and wood splinters filled the air as rounds tore through the steps. They were pinned. Above them the balcony was an inferno; the newel posts burned like roman candles, and banks of smoke poured over the landing. Below, the unseen gunmen were getting more accurate. Bullet holes appeared in the wall a foot from where Mercer lay.

"Bash—Snow and I are pinned," Sykes radioed. "I don't know where the hell we are, but we need help." He fired over the railing, drawing redoubled counterfire.

"I hear you," Happy replied. "Hold one."

"We don't have one, Hap."

Down below, one of the fanatical Order members

cocked an RPG-7 under his arm and fired the rocket-propelled grenade at the stairs. The explosive-tipped shell impacted well above Mercer and Sykes, but the charge blew the cantilevered stairs from the wall. The entire structure began to tilt, wood pulling from the wall with a sound like an agonized moan. The staircase had been pegged to the wall with two-inch-thick dowels that remained in place as the steps collapsed. Mercer reached across the widening gap between the stairs and the wall and took hold of one of these pegs just as the section he was lying on fell free.

Sykes just managed to grab his own dowel.

The staircase crashed to the first floor, leaving both men hanging on the wall twenty feet above the ground, exposed and unable to defend themselves. The killing shots were a moment away.

But the gunfire came from outside the foyer. Bashful and Happy had engaged.

Mercer didn't waste a second. If not for the debris of the collapsed staircase he could have let go, but the pile of shattered wood was unstable and even a drop from a few feet invited a broken leg. The dowel projecting from the wall was easily two feet long. He shifted his grip and began to pendulum his body, arcing across the void to reach the next peg in line, about three feet in front of him and two feet farther down the curved wall. He snagged it with his left hand and let momentum swing him down to the third. Like a child on the monkey bars, he looped his way down the wall as bullets sliced crisscrossing tracks through the smoke.

At the bottom he found cover amid the demolished staircase, but he did not shoot at the robed gunmen across the foyer. Sykes was barely halfway down and Mercer couldn't risk drawing fire until the commando was safe. The instant Sykes dropped next to him, Mercer sighted in on one of the gunmen and put a bullet into his chest. His partner fumbled with another RPG-7. Mercer fired again, catching him in the hip as he pulled the rocket launcher's trigger. The missile went errant, climbing straight up on a column of flame until it impacted on the burning ceiling three floors above. The explosion seemed to shake the monastery to its foundation. More of the roof came down. One chunk landed on the gunman, crushing him flat.

The shooting suddenly ceased as Bashful and Happy dispatched the last of the killer monks. "I think we're clear, Doc."

"Roger." Sykes stood.

Mercer and he teamed up with the other two and together they ran to the main mezzanine, where Grumpy, Sleepy and Dopey waited to continue the search. The first floor was ablaze now. The floor was littered with smashed tiles and soot lay thick on every surface. If not for the wind howling through the building, the monastery's interior would have been hotter than a furnace.

"Where'd they go?" Sykes panted. He wiped grime from his face.

Grumpy nodded down a hallway. "There's a door down there. I saw them as they went through. On the other side it looks like a cave or something."

Mercer nodded. "This place was built on top of a geologic hot spot, like Yellowstone Park. That must be one of the old lava tubes they went down. I was afraid of this."

"Why?"

"A typical building only has four sides and so many exits. You can't get too lost. But down there you take one wrong turn and we could end up miles from where they've got Tisa."

A tremendous crash on the far side of the monastery ended the rest of the discussion. The building was coming down. Either they had to get out now or follow Tisa's captors into the subterranean labyrinth.

Sykes gestured Grumpy to take point. They ran to the doorway, fanning out as Dopey, their demolitions expert, checked it for booby traps. Finding nothing around the jamb, he stood aside to use the butt of his M-4 to ease the door slightly. It creaked on its hinges, swung open a foot and exploded in a blinding flash.

Dopey remained silhouetted against the blast for a fraction of a second before his body was blown ten feet down the hallway. He tumbled against a column. Much of his uniform had been stripped from his body, as well as most of his skin.

The blast wave rolled over the rest of the men, covering them in powdered stone and wood shavings. Behind them a stone column collapsed and a section of the second floor smashed into the foyer. Flames rose from the debris.

"Goddamn it," someone screamed as they raced from their cover positions. Sykes was the first one at Dopey's side. Grumpy and Mercer stayed back, covering the tunnel entrance with the M-4s in case the explosion brought an ambush. The rest of the men clustered around their fallen comrade. Their movements were purely reflex. There was nothing any of them could do. Dopey had been killed instantly.

"That's two the fuckers got," Sykes hissed. "I want them. So help me God I want them."

They approached the still-smoking cave entrance. The men carried their rifles high, shoulders hunched, fingers curled around triggers. The barrels were in constant motion, sweeping corners and shadows.

Beyond the ruined doorway, the tunnel was a circular fissure that ran down into the earth. A few lamps bolted to the ceiling provided dingy light. It was deserted. The men stayed in a tight group as they inched into the shaft. In the tight confines, staying together reduced the risk of friendly fire and allowed them a denser barrage of counterfire if they were attacked.

The passage corkscrewed and twisted as they went, providing blind corners that needed to be scouted and slowed their progress. Mercer could feel Tisa slipping further and further away. How long ago had she come this way? How far ahead was she?

Sykes was leading the party and dropped down on his haunches, holding up a gloved fist. The men stopped and lowered themselves. From around the next bend a bright glow crept up the tunnel. Sykes moved forward cautiously, his boots making a bare whisper on the stone floor.

He paused at the corner. "Jesus. Come on."

The men ran up. The chamber had once been richly appointed with antiques, desks, lamps, and tall bureaus. Two walls were dominated by bookshelves. Mercer recognized the texts from the single journal Tisa had stolen from Rinpoche-La. These were the watchers' archives, the books on which scribes had written the oracle's predictions that people had gone out to verify.

Everything was burning. The shelves, the furniture, and the books. There wasn't enough air in the room for the flames to grow high, but enough remained for the priceless artifacts to smolder and blacken before their eyes. Mercer was certain that Donny Randall had set the fire to delay them.

As Sykes and his team searched through the growing smoke for an exit, Mercer tried to approach one of the shelves. The heat was intense, as if the room was an oven. He made a grab for one of the books, only to have it disintegrate in a burst of flame and ash. He tried for two more with the same results. At his fingertips was the knowledge to save millions of people and yet it was out of reach.

He unbuckled his combat harness and let it drop to the floor, then stripped off his battle jacket.

"Mercer, what are you doing? We gotta go!" Sykes had found the door out of the chamber.

"I have to save them!" Mercer shouted over the crackle of burning wood and parchment. He scanned the rows, hoping to find how the chronicles were arranged, but couldn't make out the titles through the smoke. He made a guess that the last books were the most recent. Using his jacket, he swept the last three books from the shelf and bundled them as quickly as he could.

They were as hot as bricks from a kiln and his hands blistered. He ignored the pain, clamping the jacket tightly around the books, trying to smother the embers. He was too slow. Curls of smoke grew from the fabric and it began to blacken. He tried to beat at those spots with his hands, but it did no good. The entire bundle caught fire. Mercer jumped back, momentarily blinded by the flash. The precious collection burned like a torch—lost for all time.

"Mercer, let's go!"

He turned reluctantly from the chronicles. The remainder of the shelves were sheeted in flames. Centuries of painstaking work was gone. He snatched up his harness and rifle and followed Sykes deeper into the ground.

For ten minutes the men wended their way along the tunnel until they came to another open chamber. This one was much larger than the archive, with towering ceilings adorned with chandeliers and ornately carved furniture. It resembled something out of the palace at Versailles.

Grumpy and Sykes entered first, staying tight to the wall as they made a circuit of the room. The rest of the men covered them from the tunnel's mouth. A dozen paces in, Bashful barked a warning. Sykes and Grumpy dropped behind a massive urn. Bashful fired to his left, his rounds chewing the frame off a doorway. From across the room a monk stepped from behind a screen and fired back. Grumpy opened up from a prone position, stitching the monk from groin to shoulder.

In seconds other armed monks appeared all over the room. The level of fire grew to a roar that rattled the chandeliers. One of the monks tried to fire a rocket-propelled grenade but was cut down a moment before he got it to bear. Mercer loosed a long fusillade and ran for cover behind a desk. Another monk dashed out to recover the fallen weapon and managed a snap shot that cratered the rock face above the tunnel.

The men tumbled from the opening as stones and rubble began to fall around them. Sykes and Grumpy poured out rounds to cover them and as soon as Mercer changed out his magazine, he fired over the top of the desk, taking two monks and forcing several others to retreat.

No one needed to order an advance. The men knew they had only seconds before the enemy regrouped. In leapfrog dashes they charged across the room, holding their fire as they ran but opening up again when they had cover.

Mercer was halfway across when a grenade was tossed in his path. He jumped through a doorway to his right and backed himself against the wall. The detonation blew the door from its hinge but left him unhurt. He took a moment to look around as the commandos flushed the defenders from the outer chamber.

The room he'd landed in was dominated by a large bed. Tapestries covered the walls. He thought the room was unoccupied until he spied a naked skeletal man propped against the bed headboard. Through mindless eyes he watched Mercer watching him. The pitiable creature began to giggle.

"What the—?"

The giggle turned into a shriek and the madman started to claw at his skin. His long fingernails tore bloody trenches from his arms and legs. He threw the ribbons of flesh at the heavy cerulean drapes hanging across the far wall of the bedroom. The clots of skin and tissue clung to the hangings while droplets of blood trickled down the rich blue fabric. Horrified by what he was seeing, Mercer couldn't help but notice that the curtain seemed to billow slightly at the spot where the man was throwing bits of his body.

He stayed low and circled around the bed. As soon as the crazed figure saw Mercer was moving to the drapes, he stopped tearing at himself and made a cooing noise. Mercer reached the spot and used his rifle barrel to probe the cloth. There was an opening behind the drape.

"Is that what you were trying to tell me?" he asked the old man.

The man's expression remained vacant. His toothless mouth hung slack.

Mercer lifted the drape. Behind it was a door that had been left ajar. A warm breeze blew from deeper inside the complex of tunnels. It had a sharp scent, like machine oil.

"Sykes!" Mercer called on his throat mike. "Sykes, can you hear me?" He heard nothing but static. The team had fought their way out of the first room and was doubtlessly chasing the monks farther into the mountain. The intervening rock was blocking the radio signals. "Bashful? Happy? Anyone read?"

He turned to check the bedroom entrance, hoping that at least one of the Delta operators had stayed behind to find him. He'd barely taken a step toward the exit when the old man screamed again and ripped a strip of skin off his hip.

Mercer froze. "Easy, now. I just need to check something."

He took another step. The lunatic heaved the piece of meat at the secret door and reached across himself to tear another chunk from his shoulder.

"Okay, okay. I get the point. I'll go through the door." As soon as he turned back to the portal, the old man settled on his bed, his thin chest rising and falling as fast as a hummingbird's.

The tunnel beyond the bedroom was much smaller than the lava tube the men had used to get this far, forcing Mercer to crouch. There were no lights, and the lamp attached to his M-4 had been damaged during the fighting. Its beam was an anemic glow that barely cut the gloom.

Every twenty paces or so, Mercer paused, cocking his head to listen for any movement. He sensed more than heard the rhythm of heavy machinery farther down the shaft. The impression coincided with the oil smell that was growing stronger. The warm air felt charged with electricity.

He silently prayed that the old man hadn't led him down a dead end.

Three hundred yards into the tunnel, the path branched. Mercer paused at the fork, holding his breath, trying to determine where the oily breeze was coming from. He shut off his flashlight.

There! To the left was the faintest trace of light. He stealthily padded down the tunnel. The light grew stronger and the machinery noises seemed to be growing louder too. He could see the shaft was ending in what could be another chamber. He dropped low, crawling on the smooth rock floor, making his movements as slow and silent as he could. His M-4 was at the ready.

Rounding a slight bend, Mercer froze.

Indeed it was a chamber, a cavern that towered more than a hundred feet. The space was longer than a football field, wider too. It was like being at the entrance to an enclosed sports arena. But it was what sat in the center of the cave that stilled his heart and choked his breath in this throat.

He'd never seen anything like it—couldn't imagine something like it could even be built.

Mercer had found the oracle.

The attack came from Mercer's right, a slashing blow moving so fast it seemed to crack the air. He brought up his rifle in a purely reflexive block. The head of the twelve-pound sledgehammer hit the weapon's receiver, crushing the mechanism, and the force of the impact knocked Mercer off his feet. He landed on his back five feet down the tunnel. He used the momentum to shoulder roll to his feet, disoriented but charged with adrenaline.

Donny Randall stood in front of him at the tunnel's mouth, the long-handled hammer held at port arms. Mercer didn't bother to aim. With the M-4 held at his hip, he pulled the trigger.

The weapon remained silent.

Randall charged.

Mercer raised the gun to ward off the next powerful swing of the hammer. The strike sent shivers up his arms and drove him back several paces. He retreated farther, dropping the M-4 and reaching for the Beretta hanging from his belt. Behind Randall the oracle glowed.

The pistol had just cleared the holster when Donny reacted. Mercer was out of range for another swipe with the hammer so he threw the tool like a javelin. The steel head smashed Mercer's right hand, deadening his fingers and pitching the pistol into the dark recesses of the access tunnel.

Randall retreated back into the oracle chamber. Mercer searched for the fallen pistol but couldn't find it. The hammer had landed nearby and he snatched that up at least to have a weapon. Facing Randall the Handle unarmed wasn't an option. He dropped onto all fours, sweeping his hands blindly along the stone at the same time he watched for Randall's return.

He caught a glimpse of something metallic just as Donny's shadow loomed over him. He spun flat as Randall swung down at him with another sledgehammer. He twisted just enough for the head to miss him, but the side of his face was peppered with stone chips gouged from the tunnel floor by the blow. Mercer used the butt end of his own sledge to crack Donny on the shin, unbalancing him and allowing Mercer to scramble to his feet.

No one knew the origin of hammer dancing. It was almost as if it had cropped up spontaneously wherever men, hardened by labor and charged with savage competitiveness, gathered. It was a way of settling feuds in the slag heaps of Pennsylvania mill towns, and among black workers in the tail piles of Johannesburg's gold mines. Mercer had seen it once on an oil platform in the swamps of the Niger River delta. The workers wagering on the outcome claimed they had invented the sport, but Mercer suspected men were betting on hammer fights in the pharaoh's quarries when they were building the pyramids.

There were no rules to hammer dancing. And the outcome could not be questioned. One man was standing and one man was dead. The victor was usually crippled for life.

"I've wanted to dance with you since Vegas," Donny sneered as he backed out of the tunnel to give himself room. "And I'm gonna lead."

Mercer tightened his grip on his hammer, testing the tool's balance and trying not to show the fear coursing through his veins. He knew he'd never find his pistol so he followed Donny into the oracle chamber. Stepping into the cavern, Mercer felt like a gladiator entering the Colosseum.

The oracle sat in the middle of the cavern, an enormous sphere reaching for the chamber's rocky ceiling. Mercer estimated it was at least four stories tall. Below the sphere was a partitioned area furnished with antique desks and divans. The floor under the furniture was layered in carpets.

Randall's dyed hair gleamed under the lights atop the wood scaffold ringing the top of the oracle. His grin remained fixed, his feral eyes on Mercer, watchful and expectant. He was eager for the fight, confident that his superior size and strength gave him the advantage. He'd probably done this a few times before.

He wore a pair of loose workman's coveralls and steel-toed boots. With his sleeves rolled up, Mercer could see his forearms were as thick as footballs. The four-foot length of the sledgehammer looked puny in his huge hands. He was back far enough from Mercer to hold the hammer out straight in one hand, and he slowly brought it to the vertical using nothing but the power of his wrist. It was a staggering demonstration of his strength, leaving Mercer to hope that his eyes hadn't bulged.

"Mercer!"

The cry came from near the towering sphere. The way the light played against the oracle's glittering surface, Mercer could barely see the diminutive figure at its base, but he knew the voice. Tisa. She appeared unhurt but was tied to a chair. That must be where the archivists interpreted the oracle's predictions, he thought, although he had no idea how the device worked.

The instant his eyes shifted to see her, Donny lunged forward, swinging his hammer in a wide, powerful arc. Mercer stepped back a pace but was unprepared for how effortlessly Randall could reverse the stroke and move in on him. The hammerhead came an inch from his chest and would have shattered his ribs had he not fallen back another step. He had his hammer up when Donny cut the strike at him again, carving a wicked S in the air. The handles met with a dull knock. Donny shoved and Mercer went sprawling.

The big man stood firm, not pressing the advantage. He wanted to draw this out and toy with Mercer before beating him to death. His grin widened, showing a gap where two of his side teeth had been.

"All that money you make in an office someplace made you soft. You ain't as tough as people say."

Mercer remained on the ground for a moment longer, taking his time getting to his feet so that when he launched himself at Randall, Donny wouldn't expect it to come. He swung in an uppercut, judging the distance so all Donny had to do was sway back on his heels to avoid the blow.

Donny remained rooted, tipping back so the hammer swung past his head. Mercer let the momentum carry him forward and around so as he pivoted he could chop down at Randall's hip. Donny parried and the steel hammerheads crashed together with a ring like a cracked bell.

Mercer dodged away, unable to meet Randall's brute strength when fighting on the inside. Randall came at him, swinging wildly. Some swipes Mercer ducked, others he parried. Each time Donny's hammer struck Mercer's, Mercer was forced to give ground. Even these deflected blows were taking a toll. His arms ached and his palms were losing feeling. His grip on the hammer was becoming lax. Donny Randall didn't seem the least affected. He swung and chopped as though his hammer were a toy sword. While Mercer panted, Donny's breathing was even and steady.

They had moved to within fifty yards of the oracle.

Mercer saw for the first time that its surface wasn't smooth as he'd assumed. It was rippled and made of either the most lustrous brass he'd ever seen or pure gold. It was also far larger than he'd estimated. He added another twenty feet to its height and diameter.

The two circled each other, making halfhearted feints. Donny lifted his sledge over his head, coming down on Mercer like a pile driver. Mercer caught the strike on the haft of his hammer and was nearly driven to his knees. The two hammerheads locked.

Donny heaved on his sledge, trying to pull Mercer's hammer from his hands. Mercer managed to hold on but was bodily thrown ten feet when the heads separated. This time Randall gave no quarter. He stalked across the chamber, slashing back and forth with his maul. Mercer scrambled back, unable to parry the swipes, only just managing to avoid being hit.

He came up fast against a large antique desk. The oracle loomed overhead. Mercer barely had time to note that the ridges covering the outside of the golden orb were mountain ranges and plateaus. The oracle was an intricately detailed globe on an unheard-of scale! Donny swung again. Mercer rolled to his right, around the desk's leg. The hammer split the wood, upending the heavy piece of furniture. The scrolls and leaves of parchment that had littered the desktop flew like scattered birds.

Randall fought through the mess, swinging his hammer again and again, as tireless as a machine. His face remained an expressionless mask. From the floor, Mercer drove his hammer at Donny's ankle, a weak effort that forced the bigger man to move aside only to feel if the blow had been worse than it felt. Mercer scrambled up on the far side of the ruined desk.

Tisa was shackled to a nearby chair. She'd screamed when the table had shattered. Now she watched wide-eyed as Donny shifted away from Mercer and took three long strides across the work area toward her. He stopped when he stood above her, the head of his hammer resting on her bent knee.

"Hey, Mercer, wanna see something cool?" He raised his weapon.

Mercer got to his feet. The oracle chamber felt as hot as the burning monastery above him. He was bathed in sweat. His muscles felt drained, rubbery.

"I thought you were here to dance with me." His voice came as a rough croak. "Can't change partners now."

"This will only take a second." Donny had enough animal cunning to know if he injured Tisa, Mercer would come at him, blinded by rage. An easy victim.

He watched Mercer as he raised the hammer a bit higher. He could let gravity drop the heavy mallet and the bones around Tisa's knee would turn to pebble-sized chips.

Something within the oracle lurched, a mechanism of some sort that gave a steadily rising ticking sound directly above the trio. Donny looked up, Tisa looked at Mercer and Mercer rushed Randall.

He caught the movement a moment too late. Mercer's swing lacked power because it came from his off foot. Still, the steel head caught Randall in the stomach, driving deep into his flesh. Donny doubled over, curling tight in a spasm that ripped the hammer from Mercer's hands. When he wheeled away, Mercer's hammer was still lodged in place. Donny dropped his own.

Mercer bent to scoop it from the stone floor and went to finish the fight. He took his eyes off Donny for only the split second necessary to grab the fallen sledgehammer. Donny moved fast, faster than Mercer could have believed. His strike hadn't been anywhere near as damaging as he'd thought. Donny had gained a firm grip on Mercer's hammer. His face showed pain, but also a fierce hatred and a deadly determination. Mercer just got his hand on Donny's hammer when Randall waded in. He swung once at Mercer's shoulder, a glancing blow that spun Mercer in place, presenting his vulnerable back to his opponent. Donny couldn't get the hammer to swing around quick enough so he rammed the butt end into Mercer's spine.

The agony was a spike driven so deep Mercer felt the hammer was going to explode from his abdomen. He roared as pain flooded his nervous system, nearly short-circuiting his brain. Donny kept up the pressure, screwing the wooden handle into Mercer's flesh, tearing the ballistic material of his fatigues and ripping into his skin. Perversely, his own blood lubricated the handle, allowing Donny to jam it deeper into the wound.

He was slowly being skewered.

Mercer let his legs collapse from under him. The handle tore from his back with a wet sucking sound. He rolled away from Donny as fast as he could. The wound left a trail of blood dappled on the stone. He got back to his feet in time to meet Randall's charge, barely able to parry the hammer swing. He continued to backpedal, exchanging ground for the moments he needed for the worst of the pain to abate.

"Bet that felt good," Donny taunted. "It'll feel even better when I shove this thing up your ass."

Mercer smiled around the agony. "You should buy me flowers or candy first."

"In a minute I'm going to hammer that grin from your face and make you swallow your teeth. After that you're gonna beg me, Mercer. You're gonna beg me to let you die." Donny wiped at his brow, smearing his hair dye across his forehead. "You still think you're better than me?"

Mercer glanced around and saw something that

gave him the start of a plan. "I have a better barber, that's for sure."

"You ain't nothing. All that money, all them people talking about how good you are. It don't mean shit down here. Here it's just you and me. You think that Ph.D. of yours is gonna save your life?"

"No. The fact that you're a goddamned moron is going to save my life. I came here with fifty Special Forces soldiers. While you're bragging about how tough you are, they're sweeping the tunnels. They should find this room in about two minutes."

It was clear Randall hadn't considered Mercer's backup. His eyes narrowed. "Then I'll kill you in one."

Behind Mercer was a set of black iron stairs that spiraled to the scaffolding surrounding the top section of the oracle. Even as Donny was making his last threat, Mercer was in motion. The stairs were tight, a narrow corkscrew that made it impossible to mount more than two steps at a time. The confining structure shook as Donny raced after him.

Around they went, climbing ever higher. Halfway to the top, the oracle was close enough to the stairs for Mercer to reach out a hand and touch. He almost stopped running when he looked closer at the mysterious machine. The oracle was an enormous clockwork mechanism. Tiny brass gears and ratchets covered the oracle's surface. Openings allowed him to see inside the device. Within the oracle was a complex collection of pistons, springs and cogwheels that drove plates on the surface. Some of the gears inside the machine appeared to be twenty feet in diameter, like something out of a factory.

That's how they did it. The oracle was a model of the earth's tectonic plates, the huge slabs of solid rock that glided on the planet's liquid mantel. Somehow the builders had known about plate tectonics and crustal

displacement long before it was discovered by Western science. Tisa had said that the plans for this machine were centuries old even before they were
brought to China five hundred years ago. Meaning the
designers had had generations to observe the earth's
movement, extrapolate how that motion would affect
other regions and create a machine that could accurately predict future geological events.

As he moved past the globe's equator he noted the
Hawaiian Islands were sharp cones jutting from the
near featureless plain of the Pacific basin. A cylinder
half filled with mercury projected from the central island. It had to be Kilauea, Mercer realized, the volcano that had been erupting on Mauna Loa for years.
The mercury must represent the volume of lava that
belched from the volcano over a certain amount of
time. Near it was another, smaller mercury vial. It was
Loihi, the newest island in the Hawaiian chain. Mercer
knew that the top of this volcano was still deep underwater. Craftsmen must be able to add to the oracle,
he thought, when new discoveries about the earth
were made.

He quickened his pace, climbing up the Pacific side
of the oracle. There were the Aleutian Islands and the
Bering Strait. He could see the rift valleys that crossed
Alaska. Small brass armatures kept the miniature
plates together but could allow them to shift suddenly
if there was a significantly sized earthquake.

Mercer reached the top of the stairs at least one
story ahead of Donny Randall. The platform ringing
the oracle wasn't nearly as wide as he'd hoped, and
the wood scaffold was old and water seeping from the
cavern roof had rotted it in places. He'd planned on
waiting at the head of the stairs to ambush Donny,
but there was hardly enough space on the landing to
stand and nowhere to swing the sledgehammer. The
scaffold was hemmed by rock on one side and a tall

but rickety railing overlooking the globe on the other. The lights blazing off the oracle's facade were blinding.

Donny reached the last twist in the spiral stairs. He paused, watching the landing, and once he was satisfied that Mercer couldn't attack, he came all the way up.

"Two minutes for your rescue, huh?" He was slightly out of breath from the six-story climb.

"Among other things I'm an eternal optimist," Mercer panted. He stayed well back from Donny on the circular catwalk, needing the space to think how he was going to get out of this.

Below them, at the top of the oracle globe, the gold sheets that covered the Arctic Ocean had been removed for maintenance. Looking down was like looking into the guts of a mechanical monster. Massive wheels turned slowly inside the oracle, driving ever-smaller cogs and gears, transferring the tremendous geothermal energy of the mountain redoubt into the finite movements of the delicate surface mechanisms, each capable of infinitesimal shifts along fault lines and tectonic plate boundaries. The interior of the oracle was as complex as an antique pocket watch but a thousand times its size.

Donny skulked forward, his hammer dangling by his waist. Mercer wasn't fooled. Randall could have the sledge in position for a strike much faster than he could. Mercer continued to back away, keeping one eye on his opponent and one on the model world below them.

Randall suddenly lurched, halving the distance between them, his hammer arcing back and forth. When it struck the cavern's stone wall sparks shot from the steel head; when it hit the wooden railing, splinters flew. Mercer timed his counterattack when Donny was at his full extension and his shoulder was exposed. He darted forward, ramming with the hammer rather than swinging it. While his strike lacked Donny's power, it did connect. Donny grunted and he had to lower his hammer. Mercer tried for another hit, but Donny had already recovered. He swept aside Mercer's thrust and twisted his upper body so he could drive his elbow into Mercer's ribs.

Mercer went down. Randall tried to stomp on his head. Mercer rolled and the blow missed. Donny's foot exploded through the wood floor and vanished up to his ankle. Mercer was just able to slide out of the way as Donny swept his hammer at him again. He couldn't prevent Randall from yanking his foot from the shattered floorboard.

They fought their way around the ring of scaffold. Their hammers flew in furious strikes and the sound of their battle resonated across the cave. But neither could gain an advantage. Mercer was quicker than Randall, but the few glancing blows he'd inflicted only seemed to make the big man more determined. Donny seemed indefatigable. And as Mercer tired, he knew it would only take one mistake to lose the hammer dance.

Half the railing had been destroyed as they fought. Lights had been shattered and power cords ripped from their mounts so electrical cables arced and snapped, shooting sparks across the wooden deck.

Mercer was weakening. His back felt like a hot coal had been placed in the wound. He would have to end this soon or Donny would tear him apart. Donny fired a wild swing with his hammer. Mercer ducked under the blow and launched himself into Randall's chest. They smashed into the cavern wall with enough force to burst the air from Donny's lungs. Mercer choked up on his hammer and used the head as an extension of his fist, pumping punch after punch into Donny's stomach, trying to stop him from reinflating his lungs.

Randall was dazed enough to stand still for five blows before he roared and shoved Mercer away,

nearly sending him over the railing. Donny came at
him, swinging the hammer over his head. The sledge
smashed through the railing next to Mercer and the
whole section began to collapse. Mercer spun away,
managing to stay on the platform as Donny's momentum started to take him over.

Randall grabbed the banister with his right hand
and Mercer slammed his hammer into the exposed
appendage. The bones were crushed flat yet Randall
the Handle managed to swing his own hammer using
only his left. The shot caught Mercer under the arm.
Donny didn't have the angle to crack ribs, but the
impact knocked Mercer aside and left him gasping.
With his right hand dangling uselessly at his side and
the big hammer clutched firmly in his left, Randall
charged Mercer, any rationality driven from his mind
by the pain of his near-severed limb. Spittle flew from
his lips with each gusting breath.

It was almost as if the past fifteen minutes had been
a game to Donny Randall, a prelude for the moment
he was maddened enough to finish the fight. He swung
savagely, slashing and chopping with his hammer.
More of the railing exploded when he hit it. Fragments
of stone flew from the divots his counterswing gouged
from the cavern wall. Black-dyed sweat rained from
his head.

Mercer could barely back away fast enough. He
didn't dare try to parry Randall's immense swings. The
impact would have torn the hammer from his hands.
The stairs were halfway around the scaffold. If he
turned to make a run for them, Randall would be on
him in a second. There was only one option and he
took it without hesitation.

The railing was four feet tall, but right behind Mercer was a section of rotted wood that had been damaged earlier in the fight. The instant he'd backed next
to the opening he tossed himself from the platform.

The drop was ten feet, a relatively easy leap had he

not been so seriously injured. He landed hard, sprawled against the top of the mechanical globe, nearly losing his hammer in one of the open access panels. He managed to turn onto his back in time to see Donny jump after him.

Randall landed a few feet away and tried to steady his fall with his ruined right hand. He shrieked as the sharp end of the broken bones shot through his skin in a dozen spots, saturating his hand in blood. Mercer got to his feet, bracing himself on the slick surface by wedging his foot against the six-inch-high ridge that was Alaska's northernmost mountain range. Randall had his hand up and Mercer took aim. His swing didn't need power, only accuracy.

The hammer's steel head caught Donny on the up-raised wrist. The remainder of the bones in his lower arm disintegrated. The force was enough to shred the tendons and skin that had been keeping the hand attached to his wrist. The member flew free. Blood fountained from the stump.

"That's for . . ." Mercer paused, unable to remember the name of the miner Randall had killed when he flooded the DS-Two mine. "Damn it, that's for being a fucking prick."

Randall couldn't defend himself so Mercer's next swing carried every ounce of strength left in him. He hit Randall in the chest hard enough to detach his sternum. Donny staggered but didn't fall.

He lurched around in a circle holding his arm aloft while turning blue because he couldn't draw breath. He finally slipped on the blood drooling across the surface of the oracle. He landed on his side and began to slide down the sphere. That's when he became aware of what was happening and tried to save himself from falling off the golden globe. He twisted and kicked out with one leg, arresting his plummet by catching the lip of an access panel.

When he tried to stand, his foot slid into the mechanism.

Mercer was five feet above Donny's position so he couldn't see what was happening inside the machine. But suddenly Randall's blank stare turned into fear and then panic. Donny tried to jerk his leg free of the hole and fell backward, sliding farther down the globe until Mercer felt as much as heard his knee joint pop. Inside the clockwork oracle, Randall's foot had caught between a large pinion gear and a saw-motion rack of metal teeth. Each quick ratchet of the gear drew his foot deeper into the machine.

Somehow Randall struggled upright again. His screams drowned out all other sounds, echoing off the cavern, rebounding again and again in a chorus of unbearable agony. Mercer didn't enjoy watching what was unfolding, but he wouldn't look away. He kept his eyes locked on Donny Randall's as the oracle's remorseless mechanisms chewed his leg and pulled him deeper inside.

When his leg was half gone, Randall could no longer remain upright. He toppled into the hole and became tangled in more of the machinery. His cries lasted a few seconds more as he was literally eaten alive, his limbs plucked from his body before his torso was consumed. Somewhere deep inside the bowels of the oracle, his severed head dropped free, only to get stuck between a pair of gears and crushed.

"Bet you didn't predict that," Mercer said as he clambered along the oracle to find a way off its crown.

The huge machine shuddered just as he found a ladder that could be pulled down from the overhead scaffold. A steady vibration built from inside the oracle, as though a flywheel had become unbalanced and was fighting against its bearings. Something tore loose with a metallic squeal. A jet of mercury shot from a nameless volcano on Russia's Kamchatka Peninsula.

"Mercer?" Tisa shouted from far below, her voice nearly lost in the din of the damaged machine. "What's happening?"

Unbalanced by Randall's body falling through its gears, the machine tore itself apart. A piston exploded from the side of the oracle, poking a huge hole in its skin and scattering hundreds of intricate parts. Mercer pulled the ladder down and stepped off the oracle just as a huge gear rammed through the top of the machine, spitting a shower of brass and gold shrapnel.

Forced onward by geothermal pressure, the mechanism continued to grind upon itself, the intricacy of its design causing its downfall. Each component of the oracle was directly connected to every other, so when one was wrecked the damage spread geometrically. The plate containing the entire continent of Africa sheered from its mounts and dropped to the cavern floor.

Swaying on the scaffold, Mercer realized that Tisa was directly below the oracle. The structure was threatening to collapse. He raced around the platform, dodging sparking power cables and charging through a fire that had caught along one section. He reached the spiral stairs and threw himself down, unconcerned how the tower wobbled. He was doused by liquid mercury gushing from the Hawaiian Islands. Doubtlessly some of the carcinogenic fluid seeped into his bloody wounds.

Fifteen feet from the ground he heard voices over the noise and vibration. He hadn't considered that other members of the Order would be around. He had no weapon other than surprise, and once that wore off he was no more capable of defending himself than Harry's toothless basset hound.

"Snow, you here?" The voice was in Mercer's head, a fantasy that Sykes had found him. "Snow, come in."

Not in his head. In his ear. The tactical radio. "Doc, is that you? It's Snow. Where are you?"

"I'm in a cave with a big gold globe that looks like it's about to fall apart."

Mercer sagged. The people he'd heard below weren't more fanatic monks. Sykes and his Delta commandos had found him. He reached the ground floor. Above him, the surfaces of the oracle were a blur as the mechanisms inside destroyed themselves. Sykes stood a short distance off, covering Grumpy and Happy as they untied Tisa.

Mercer rushed past the two men and was nearly bowled over when Tisa threw herself into him. Their tears mingled as their lips sought each other out. Tisa was drawn and exhausted, her eyes washed out by her captivity. She hadn't been allowed to bathe in days and her hair felt as brittle as straw. Mercer simply didn't care. She was alive, and that was all that mattered.

"I knew you'd come for me," she said. "I don't know how, but I knew you'd come."

"You never gave me your phone number. How else was I going to get in touch with you to ask for a second date?"

"Mercer," Sykes interrupted. "We've gotta go."

He couldn't let go of Tisa completely, so as he pulled away he held one of her hands. "What's the situation?"

"Serious unless Miss Nguyen knows a way out of here. We chased the last of the defenders into a bunch of dead-end tunnels. We got them, but there ain't no way out except the way we came in."

"And that's blocked by the burning monastery."

"How about it, ma'am?"

"There is a way. I used it once when I snuck into the oracle chamber when Luc and I were children. But first I have to go back for the Lama."

"Was that the old man in the room with the secret entrance here?" Mercer asked.

"Yes." Her tears changed from joy to sorrow. "I must save him."

Mercer looked to Sykes and nodded. The commando leader wasn't going to argue.

The three surviving Delta soldiers led them back to the bedroom. Mercer wanted to stay at Tisa's side but something he'd noticed forced him to pull Sykes back from the party as they moved up the tunnel.

"None of you are wearing your packs. What happened?"

"Noticed that, did you?" Sykes jammed a plug of tobacco into his cheek.

"You lost all the satellite phones." It wasn't a question.

"Yep. Grump's was shot to pieces and Hap's was smashed when he took a fall and mine's upstairs with yours. I'm guessing both are nothing but melted plastic by now."

"What about the others?"

"Blown to shit along with my men. Sons a bitches claymored us."

"I'm sorry," was all Mercer could reply. Without those phones there was no way to get Tisa's information to Admiral Lasko.

They reached the curtain covering the secret bedroom entrance. Tisa was the first one through. She rushed immediately to the bed. The Lama didn't move. He remained flat on the bed, his lower body covered with a sheet, gaining him a measure of dignity in death he'd been denied in life.

Tisa knelt at his side, holding one of his birdlike hands in hers. Her face was hidden by her hair, but by the way her body convulsed, her sobs were apparent. Mercer knelt next to her, waiting for her to say what she needed.

"He was so good." Her voice cracked. "He didn't believe in violence and had he known the magnitude of what's going to happen I know he would have wanted us to tell the world. People die every day. It is what makes us human. He didn't think it was our place to warn others about what we know. But he would have changed his mind about La Palma. He would have warned you."

"He was the Order's spiritual leader?"

"And more." Tears streaked down her cheeks. "He was my father." Her tone turned bitter. "It was Luc who ruined everything. He wanted the Order to be an authority in the world, a nation with automatic superpower because of what we knew."

She looked at Mercer. "I am so sorry I involved you."

"Why?"

"Because you can't make a difference. You can't stop what's going to happen. Luc has won because the earth can't be changed."

"That's not true. The future isn't set by the oracle, Tisa. It's created by people like you and me, people who believe they can change things for the better. Tell me—how much time do we have? When is La Palma going to erupt?"

Mercer needed a year. With a year he had an idea how to stabilize the western flank of the Cumbre Veija volcano and prevent the catastrophic slide. In the moments Tisa took to answer him he cut the estimate in half.

Give him just six months and he could do it. It would be close, some material would crash into the sea, but not enough to devastate the Atlantic basin. With six months to work he could save the millions who lived along shorelines of America and Europe, although the property damage would likely run into the billions of dollars.

Grant me six months, please, he thought as Tisa proudly gave her answer. "Five weeks."

Mercer went numb. Five weeks? It wasn't possible. Tisa couldn't have cut it so close. She'd said all along that she wanted to warn him with plenty of time. Five weeks was as useless as five minutes. The volcano could erupt in five seconds for all the good he could do with the time she'd given him.

Still on his knees next to the bed, he deflated and fell into Tisa. The greatest calamity in human history was about to unfold and he no longer had the strength to care. His blank stare turned Tisa's self-satisfaction into dismay, then fear. She grabbed for his hand. "That's enough time, isn't it? You can evacuate the islands and warn people living along the coasts."

Mercer raked his fingers through his hair. His skin prickled and he felt like he was going to vomit. He swallowed a mouthful of watery saliva. He looked into Tisa's eyes. Below her alarm he could see vestiges of her pride that she'd defied the Order to give the world a warning. She'd never thought beyond the warning, what was involved once people knew La Palma was about to erupt. The Order had cast a dismal shadow over her entire life and she'd thought she'd escaped it by divulging her secrets to him. She'd freed herself and now he had to put her in a prison of guilt from which there would be no liberation.

Even before he spoke, she could sense it. Her entire body began to tremble. Mercer would have given anything, his own life even, to spare her from learning her warning did no good.

"When the volcano erupts, one side of it is going to crash into the ocean. The waves it creates are going to wash across the Atlantic, destroying most of southern Europe and America's east coast. Those areas are home to a hundred million people. They can't be evacuated because there's no place to put them. And even if they did move away from the shores in time, there would be nothing left for them to return to. They would be permanent refugees. There's no way to feed and house them. Rather than all of them being killed in one catastrophe, they'd die over time, slowly succumbing to disease, starvation, and the breakdown of social order.

Tisa had begun to hyperventilate. He stroked her head. "You only learned about the eruption a few months ago, right?" She nodded and tried to speak but gave only a low keen. "Even that isn't enough time. It would take at least a year for any workable plan to take shape. A couple of extra weeks wouldn't have made the slightest difference. You can't blame yourself for something you weren't aware of. Although I know you will. You're a lot like me."

Sykes had given Mercer and Tisa a few minutes alone at the side of the bed. He cleared his throat to get their attention. "I'm sorry to do this, Miss Nguyen, but we have to get out of here. We still have to find a way to pass your information to the admiral."

"It doesn't matter anymore," she said flatly.

"Excuse me?"

Mercer got to his feet and crossed to where Sykes and his men waited by the secret exit. "We only have five weeks before La Palma blows."

"What? Jesus! It's going to take two just to trek out of the valley."

"I know."

Sykes thought about that for a minute. "My orders were to get that information to Lasko. It makes me no never mind if the answer's five weeks or ten minutes." He yanked the Velcro flap off his watch to check the time. "It's oh four hundred. Once we get to the surface, we can rest up until noon and then start for Nepal. I've got a feeling the secret's out about this place and pretty soon the Chinese army will come swarming."

Mercer nodded. "No matter how bad a mass evacuation is going to be, it's the best we can do. We need to give Ira every extra second we can. We might want to consider splitting up. I'm in no shape for a trek over the Himalayas. The wound in my back isn't as bad as it feels but it is going to slow me down."

"That's not a good idea."

"Booker, every extra minute you give Admiral Lasko means an additional thousand lives saved. I'm going to hold you up."

Sykes said nothing but it was clear he knew Mercer was right. His men, though exhausted by the firefight, were in peak physical condition. They could do the trek out of China in half the time if they didn't need to worry about Mercer. "What about you two?"

"I think Tisa should go with you. Maybe I can convince her. I'd follow you as soon as I was ready."

"And if the Chinese show up before then?"

"It's a risk I have to take."

Sykes laughed. "I still haven't figured out if you're brave or an idiot."

"Sometimes there isn't much of a difference."

"Hoo-yah."

Mercer returned to Tisa's side, dropping to his knees next to her. His back had stiffened and the movement opened the scab. Warm blood trickled into the waistband of his fatigues. "Captain Sykes and his men are going to run for the border. They can make it a lot quicker without me. I want you to go with them. You know these mountains. They need you as a guide."

She sniffed. "I'm not leaving you. I can talk to some of the villagers. A couple of them can get Sykes to

Nepal. You and I will go together when you're strong enough."

"Tisa, I—"

"This is an argument you aren't going to win, so don't bother fighting it. I'm staying with you."

"There's a good chance the Chinese are going to find Rinpoche-La. The fire could have been spotted by a helicopter patrol."

"Mercer, you forget I grew up here. I know where all the hiding places are. I can keep you safe if they come."

Just like Sykes knew Mercer was right about leaving him behind, Mercer knew Tisa was correct now. "You're pretty remarkable, you know that?"

She touched his face. "So are you. Would you ask Captain Sykes if one of his men could carry my father. I want to see he gets a proper burial."

Mercer was about to volunteer for the duty himself, but he was in no condition even if her father weighed no more than ninety pounds. "They'd be honored, I'm sure."

Sykes kept point as they returned to the oracle chamber in case they encountered pockets of resistance. The oracle had demolished itself. The outer sheath was split in dozens of places, and much of it had fallen off the machine so now it resembled a shattered eggshell. The mechanisms inside were twisted into unrecognizable shapes. Pipes carrying superheated steam that powered the oracle spewed jets of vapor that were quickly filling the lofty chamber. The walls of the cavern ran with condensation and the temperature had climbed past one twenty. The huge space was becoming a scalding sauna.

Tisa paused at the base of the ruined machine. "Good," she said after a moment. "I'm glad it's gone."

"I can understand how you feel," Mercer agreed.

"The temptation to abuse its power is just too great. It's a testament to your Order that it wasn't subverted long before now."

The hidden entrance that Tisa had found as a child lay on the far side of the cavern. It took forty minutes just to locate it and a further two hours to negotiate the twisting tunnels. She didn't remember the exact route to the surface and led them down countless dead-end branches.

They came out in a cave high atop a craggy bluff midway between the village and the monastery. The sun was just rising, a pale wash that barely penetrated the valley. The air was cold and laced with the heavy smell of burned wood. Nothing remained of the monastery except a few upright support timbers and a smoking fifty-foot mound of debris.

There were maybe two hundred huts in the village clustered around a central square. From their vantage it appeared the people were packing up to leave. They too understood that the fire would eventually attract attention. Their simple life of supporting the monks who tended the oracle was over. Several of the wood buildings were aflame. The villagers would leave nothing for the army when they came.

"Are they loyal to your father or your brother?" Mercer asked.

Tisa was helping position her father's body for when they came back to get him. "The Lama. I doubt any of them know Luc tried to take over the Order."

"So they'll help us?"

"I believe so."

Sykes shot Grumpy and Happy a look to tell them to stay alert as they descended the trail to the valley floor.

They were halfway to the village when the eerie morning silence was shattered. The narrow confines of the valley masked the approach of the helicopters until they burst over the rim. There were three of them, two huge Russian-made Hind-D gunships and a French-built Aerospeciale Gazelle in civilian colors. Laboring at the high altitude, the three helos were still as nimble as dragonflies.

Mercer and his party were caught in the open. The nearest cover was a hundred yards away and one of the Hinds was thundering straight for them. The other swooped low over the village, its multiple missile racks and chin-mounted machine cannon at the ready.

The Delta commandos had dropped flat at the first sign of the choppers and watched their approach through their gunsights—a purely reflexive action since the 5.56-millimeter rounds from the M-4s were useless against the heavily armored Hind. Mercer and Tisa remained on their feet. After a moment, Sykes and his men realized the futility of their position and also got up, holding their weapons low against their bodies in a nonthreatening pose. There was no place to run and no way to fight their way out.

"How did they get here so fast?" Grumpy shouted over the helo's deafening roar, his clothes and hair rippling under the onslaught of the blades' downdraft.

"No idea," Mercer said, keeping his eyes fixed on the pilot hovering twenty feet above him.

The other Hind wheeled away from the village. With the first gunship providing cover, the second chopper flew within thirty yards of the team and settled on its landing wheels. A side door crashed open and eight Chinese soldiers outfitted for cold-weather combat jumped to the ground. Each carried China's type-87 assault rifles, a 5.8-millimeter bull-pup design that was so new that only the country's special forces had been issued them.

Sykes, Grumpy and Happy slowly unslung their M-4s and let them drop to the ground, keeping their hands in the air. The leader of the Chinese commandos made a gesture with the barrel of his rifle for the team to step away from their weapons.

"What's going to happen?" Tisa asked.

Sykes spoke out of the side of his mouth. "Four armed Americans and a Chinese national caught in a secret valley that housed an ancient monastery the government had not known about? I suspect they'll congratulate us on our discovery. Then shoot us."

The Chinese made no further threatening moves, not that they needed to. There was nothing Mercer or his people could do. The words "dead to rights" ran through Mercer's head.

With the Americans covered by soldiers on the ground, the first Hind reared away to make room for the Gazelle. The elegant copter was more befitting an executive helipad atop a skyscraper than these rough surroundings, but like the Hinds it had been modified for high-altitude duty. As soon as the skids took the craft's weight, a soldier in the copilot's seat leapt out and opened the rear door.

Two men stepped to the ground. One was Chinese, a middle-aged man wearing a greatcoat and general's stars on his cap. The other was a Westerner wearing a blue suit and polished loafers, as if he hadn't been prepared for the flight. His only concession to the frigid temperature was a garish ski jacket festooned with colorful lift tickets.

The Gazelle's turbine spooled down and relative quiet returned to the valley.

The general stepped ahead of the civilian until he was standing in front of the team. He looked each up and down as though they were soldiers on parade. He paid particular attention to Tisa, though his appraisal was more respectful than sexual. He finally got to Mercer.

"I suspect you are Dr. Philip Mercer?" The general's English was passable. His voice grated from a lifetime of harsh unfiltered cigarettes, one of which he lit with a brass windproof lighter. The smoke blew back into his face, forcing him to squint.

Mercer kept his expression neutral. "That's correct."

"I am General Fan Ji. By order of the chairman of the politburo, I am placing you and your people under arrest for espionage. You have already been found guilty and your punishment has been determined. Immediate execution."

Overhead, a hawk screamed.

"If the guy in the suit's my lawyer, tell him I won't take the plea bargain."

The general's smile revealed yellow uneven teeth. "A joke, yes? One of your American sarcasms?"

"It's called gallows humor."

"Ah, like from your western movies. The man is not your lawyer, Dr. Mercer. He is Hans Bremmer, the German chargé d'affaires from Katmandu, the highest-ranking diplomat we could find on short notice."

"Is he here to make sure our blindfolds meet the specifications laid out in the Geneva Convention?"

"More sarcasm?"

"Impertinence."

"No matter. He is here because the politburo has also decided that your sentence is to be commuted. You are to be flown to the border and released. However if you or any of the others return to the People's Republic, your death sentence will be reinstated and you will be executed."

"I don't—"

Bremmer came forward. He was in his mid-thirties, with sandy blond hair and the healthy glow of someone who enjoyed the outdoors. He held his hand out to Mercer. "I apologize for this but to secure China's cooperation, they insisted on your arrest before I was allowed to get you out. I'm sure you understand that diplomatic protocols must be maintained."

"What the hell is going on?"

"The situation on the island of La Palma has changed. Your government has been in contact with the Chinese since shortly after you took off from Diego Garcia. I guess you were under radio blackout. I wasn't cleared for those types of operational details."

"What's happening on La Palma?"

"I'm sorry, Doctor. I don't know." Behind the diplomat, the Chinese soldiers were transferring fuel from drums carried in the hold of the Hind gunship to the Gazelle. "My ambassador ordered me to meet General Ji at the border and accompany him to this location. I am to fly you and your team to Katmandu. An American aircraft will be waiting to take you from there to the Canary Islands. I understand there's a plan being discussed that requires your expertise."

Mercer, Tisa and Sykes exchanged an identical look of disbelief. A few minutes earlier they were facing a death sentence, before that a weeks-long hike to civilization, and before that the understanding that nothing could prevent the impending cataclysm. Mercer shook off his surprise and pumped Bremmer's hand again, this time with much more feeling. "What the hell are we waiting for?"

They were airborne ten minutes later, leaving behind the smoldering remains of the monastery and a thousand hapless villagers who were being rounded up by the Chinese.

"What will happen to them?" Mercer asked Tisa as she stared out the Gazelle's window long after they lifted out of the valley.

"They will kill some. Others will be jailed. The rest will be relocated, doubtlessly far from each other." She looked at him with the same bottomless sorrow she'd shown him so many times before. "The people of Rinpoche-La avoided the Chinese occupation for more than half a century. I guess that's something to be grateful for."

"I'm sorry," he said lamely.

"It's not your fault." She took his hand, then added so he couldn't hear, "It is mine."

The aircraft waiting for Mercer in Katmandu was a Citation executive jet on loan to the government from India's defense ministry. The plane's interior was as opulent as a rajah's palace. The stains Mercer's uniform left on the picked silk cushions were likely permanent. Unfortunately, the aircraft's regular passengers were Sikhs and did not drink alcohol. The galley produced a hearty breakfast and aromatic coffee but not the shot of booze he was dying to lace it with.

Because the Citation was crammed with every conceivable communications device, he had very little time to enjoy his meal before he was on a video conference call with Ira Lasko and a team of scientists stationed in Washington and others already on La Palma. The Delta commandos were stretched in the plane's rear bunks and Tisa was curled in the seat next to Mercer, asleep.

"I think we're ready to get started," Ira said as the last participants acknowledged they had video and audio feeds. "For those of you who don't know him, I want to introduce Dr. Philip Mercer, the president's special science advisor and the man who first alerted us to the potential eruption along the Cumbre Vieja."

Mercer recognized a couple of the scientists, mostly geologists he'd met over the years, as well as Dr. Briana Marie. He greeted them by name, heard the names of the others and promptly forgot them.

"Mercer, first of all, bring me up to speed. Then I'll fill you in on what's been happening on our end."

"The only pertinent fact we need to deal with is that the eruption will occur in five weeks, on the eighteenth to be exact."

The eight faces on the split computer screen reacted to the news with a gamut of expressions, from disbelief to fear to anger. Then as one they began to talk and debate.

"Admiral Lasko," one of them, a stentorian volcanologist from the Smithsonian, clamored over the swelling tide of objections. "You indicated we had months of buildup before the event. Five weeks is not enough time."

"It's going to take five weeks just to determine where to bore the blast holes," another protested.

"We might as well issue the evacuation order now," a third, wearing a paisley bow tie, sniveled.

"Ladies, gentlemen, please," Lasko repeated until the scientists quieted. "Mercer, are you sure about the date?"

"As sure as I can be, Admiral." Mercer maintained a professional distance from Ira until they could speak privately. "It came from the same source as the Santorini prediction."

"Very well." He drew a breath. "We had an idea how to counter the effects of a mega-tsunami, but we required at least four months, probably longer."

"I assume your plan was to detonate a nuke on the eastern side of the mountain so the western flank would implode into the volcano rather than slip into the sea."

Ira wasn't the least surprised that Mercer had independently developed the same strategy as a team of the world's top scientists. "That was the general idea, yes. The computer models we ran say the bomb needed to be buried at least eight hundred feet into the eastern slope to get the desired results."

"And let me guess, the models can't pinpoint the exact location until we drill some test holes."

Ira nodded. "Which will take weeks we don't have. Add in the time to bore eight hundred feet for the bomb and we're way past the deadline."

The bow-tied pessimist chimed in. "That's why the evacuation should be ordered now. Nothing can be accomplished on La Palma in five weeks. It's a waste of time to even try."

Mercer ignored the comment and kept his focus on Ira Lasko. "You've modeled for a surface detonation?"

"We did," Briana Marie answered. "Such a blast wouldn't change the Cumbre detachment fault. It would still slip in its entirety, possibly as a result of the explosion. We ran dozens of locations and various yields up to one megaton."

"No offense, Doctor, but take off the kid gloves and pump up your yields. Model a blast with fifty megatons and see what that does."

"Besides irradiate southern Europe and western Africa?"

"Most of the people living there are going to die anyway," he snapped back. "Shielding them from radiation then cleaning the fallout is the better, and cheaper, alternative to displacing them for the next two or three generations."

Mercer wasn't angry at her, but at himself. Since deciphering Tisa's warning about La Palma, he thought he hadn't limited his thinking when in fact he had. Even a minute ago he never would have considered setting off such a nuclear explosion. Now he knew that no option was too outlandish. Exposing two hundred thousand people to a hefty dose of radioactive contamination in order to save a hundred million was the kind of sacrifices they had to consider if they were to succeed.

"There has to be a better way," a young volcanologist currently on La Palma said.

"I hope there is, but we have to explore every avenue. What did your models say about an underwater blast on either the western or eastern side of the island?"

Dr. Marie glanced away and admitted, "We didn't run those scenarios."

Although he'd been out of the loop with these scientists, Mercer took it for granted that as the president's special science advisor he'd spearhead any effort to minimize the damage from the eruption. However, he would be relying on them for everything they could give over the next weeks. With that in mind he kept the recrimination from his voice. "Why don't you look into that before we consider higher-yield nukes. We might get lucky."

"I'll get on it as soon as we're done here." It was clear she appreciated his conciliatory tone.

"To those of you on La Palma right now," Mercer continued, "I'd like to see an underwater survey of the coastlines on either side of the Cumbre fault zone."

"What are we looking for?"

"Vents. I'm just thinking out loud, bear with me. You were all in agreement earlier that you needed to drill eight hundred feet for the bomb to collapse the volcano." On Mercer's computer eight heads nodded in unison. "What if we can find an old vent that allows us to get even deeper into the mountain?"

Dr. Marie's eyes lit up. "If we go deep enough, we don't need to be so precise with the weapon's placement. A kilometer or two in either direction might not matter. Rather than cutting open the volcano with a chisel, we can smash it with a sledgehammer."

Her metaphor made Mercer wince. The handful of over-the-counter painkillers he'd found in the aft washroom did little to ease the fire in his back or the countless other aches and pains.

The young volcanologist on the island, Les Donnelley, typed notes onto a laptop computer mounted below his video camera. "I can hire a fishing boat, if there are any left here."

The comment triggered Mercer's next questions. "What is the situation on the island? What's happened in the past twenty-four hours?"

"For one, the media picked up on the story," Ira said with a mixture of irritation and relief. He would have liked more time to work without public scrutiny, but also appreciated that people could make their decisions about evacuating early. "It broke just as you took off from—" He stopped before divulging Mercer's mission. "It broke early yesterday in New York. The networks have been preempting ever since. The panic hasn't been as widespread as we first feared, but most people are still in shock. The president is going to address the—"

"No," Mercer interrupted. As much as he cared about how the world was taking the news that a hundred million people might perish, he couldn't let it distract him. "Tell me what's happening on the island. From now on that is our focus. Let the politicians and disaster-relief people debate evacuation strategies and refugee issues. We stick with the science."

"All right. Les, you want to fill him in? You're in charge on La Palma."

"You're aware that the island is comprised of dozens of volcanoes, each one corresponding to La Palma's history of tectonic activity. The one that concerns us is the San Juan volcano. It was the actual volcano on the Cumbre ridge that erupted in 1949 and caused the fault to slip." Donnelley was covering familiar ground to the video-conference participants and moved on quickly. "Up until yesterday morning our time, the monitors placed around its summit and near some of its secondary vents and fumeroles were quiet considering the activity on the island's extreme southern tip."

"And that's changed?"

"Yes, Dr. Mercer. Unlike previous eruptions here that were localized to one finite area, this one seems to be affecting others as well. San Juan shows every sign that it's about to blow. We have some equipment lowered down a bore hole. We're detecting a hundred microquakes an hour, and temperature and pressure are both up, leading us to believe that the magma chamber is beginning to fill."

Mercer's expression was grim. "This dovetails into the five-week prediction."

"I have to agree, though I don't understand how you can say that with any degree of confidence. It could take much longer."

"Trust him on that," Ira said. "It'll be in five weeks."

"What else is happening?" asked Mercer.

"The Spanish government has ordered a full evacuation of the island. The people here are taking it very seriously. Gas and ash levels are rising. Several elderly have already died and a previously unknown vent near the Teneguia volcano suddenly burst open under a school. Forty-three students and three teachers were asphyxiated. With Teneguia erupting at the southern tip of the island and San Juan showing signs in the middle of the island, people here recognize how the two are joined by the fragile Cumbre ridge. They don't want to be anywhere near here if it goes."

"There's something we have all overlooked," the twerp in the bow tie interjected. "No one has gone to the United Nations about this. I mean they know about the potential of a mega-tsunami, but don't we need permission to detonate a nuclear device on another nation's sovereign soil. Don't forget they're still smarting because we lost several bombs off of Spain's south coast in the late 1960s. They won't take too kindly to us intentionally blowing up one of their islands."

"Who are you again?" Mercer spat.

"Professor Adam Littell of MIT."

"And your specialty, Professor?"

"Fluid dynamics with an emphasis on wave propagation," he replied archly.

"We all know about the waves if we can't stop the slide so we don't need your services. Kindly turn off your camera."

"Excuse me?"

"Admiral Lasko, can you cut him off?" No sooner had Mercer made the request than the portion of his computer monitor showing the professor went dark.

"He does raise a good point," Lasko said.

"That's for the politicians, Admiral. Let them worry about it. I suspect when the UN's secretary-general realizes a fifty-foot wall of water is going to wash away his shiny skyscraper he'll see that the right thing gets done."

"Provided it's the right thing," Briana said.

"That's why we're talking." Mercer drained his coffee and poured more from a sterling carafe. "Okay, other ideas to minimize a slip. Has anyone thought about trying to blast the western side of the Cumbre ridge into strips? Or what about pinning the top layer of material to the underlying rock to hold it in place?"

His questions were met with blank stares.

"Someone start an equipment list." Ira nodded to an assistant off camera. "We need as many rotary drill trucks as we can get to the island, machines capable of boring at least a thousand feet."

"Once you drill the holes, what do you use to pin the rock together?" Les Donnelley asked.

"The drill pipe itself. We'll leave everything down hole and move to the next site with new bits and new drill string. That means we need drill mud, pipe, as many diamond bits as we can lay our hands on and enough support personnel to keep crews working around the clock."

"And your idea about cutting the slope into strips?" Ira prompted.

"Expert explosives people, liquid explosives, blast mats, detonators. The works. I'll call Bill Janson at Blastech in Houston. I've worked with him a few times at the open pit mines out west. He's the best surface blaster in the business. Admiral Lasko, you'll have to organize transport. What's the airport at La Palma?"

"Not big enough" Donnelley said. "The Canaries' international airport is on the nearby island of Tenerife."

Once Mercer got started the orders came crisp and concise. "We'll fly equipment to Tenerife, then either take it to La Palma by boat or get the airport there extended. Probably be a good idea to plan on both. Gas masks, a field hospital, thermal suits capable of taking at least five hundred degrees, fifty thousand gallons of diesel fuel to start. Fresh water because the natural springs on La Palma are either going to dry up, boil over, or turn to sulfuric acid. We need boats, security personnel—"

"What about food?" a consultant from the U.S. Geologic Survey asked.

"There should be enough left behind by the residents for us to scavenge," Mercer said without pause. "We'll need it in a week or so. Right now I'm giving the top priorities. Admiral Lasko, where is the *Sea Surveyor*?"

"She was just relieved by the navy's submersible

tender *Endeavor* and her two minisubs. I think she's in Guam."

"Contact the ship. I want Charlie Williams and another diver on a plane with their NewtSuits." Mercer thought for a moment and added, "We might need a larger submersible too. Get one from one of the oil companies operating in the North Sea or maybe the French. They have a couple that might be closer to the Canaries."

"What else?"

"Portable industrial refrigeration systems, burn specialists, firefighting helicopters, cylinders of liquid oxygen, scuba gear, bulldozers—Caterpillar D-7s or larger—a case of Grey Goose vodka and a couple of bottles of Jamaica Gold lime juice, and of course the nukes."

"What type and how many?"

His ascension to the head of the project came so smoothly and so naturally that it suddenly hit Mercer that he was being given control over nuclear bombs and had every intention of setting off one or more. The thought held his attention for only a moment. "I don't know yet, but put the wheels in motion to get them."

He went on uninterrupted for five minutes, naming anything he thought they had the remotest chance of needing. When he was done, the others added items they thought would be useful until it became clear they were talking about a mobilization on the scale of going to war. And that's exactly how Mercer saw it. This was a war against Mother Nature herself. Win or lose, he was putting everything he had into the fight.

The conversation came to a close as the sleek jet was on final approach to Al-Udeid air base in Qatar. Mercer closed the laptop and glanced at Tisa. She was awake.

"I've been listening to you." Her eyes and voice

were soft from sleep. "You really think we have a chance?"

"A slim one," Mercer conceded. "It comes down to logistics and our ability to find an underwater vent that goes deep enough into the volcano for us to collapse the eastern face."

"What happens if you succeed?"

"What do you mean?"

She sat up and sipped from his cup of cold coffee. The bitter taste did more to wake her than the caffeine. "Won't there be a tidal wave if the eastern part of the mountain crashes into the sea?"

"Yes and no," Mercer said. "There will be a wave, but nowhere near the size of the mega-tsunami if the western slope collapses. The danger there is one huge slab of rock, about five hundred cubic kilometers, hitting the water at one time. That energy is what creates the big wave. If we blow out the eastern side of the San Juan volcano, we can reduce the internal pressure trying to loosen that slab. I'm sure someone's modeling for it as we speak, but the waves from the nuclear blast will dissipate rather than maintain a solid front. I bet the worst won't be more than a dozen feet when it hits Africa. Given that area is sparsely populated we have more than enough time to evacuate the coastline."

He stopped talking.

The way Tisa looked at him, hearing but not listening, entranced by his voice rather than interested in the details, made Mercer believe even more that they could pull it off. Her steady, trusting gaze filled him in a way he'd never experienced. The obstacles, or at least his fear of them, retreated as her eyes wove their spell around him. Mercer felt—no, he corrected himself, she made him feel—capable of doing anything.

He moved closer so their mouths met. Their eyes

remained open, searching and finding what they both longed for. Even as the plane made contact with the runway and the engines shrieked to slow it, the spell endured.

While several of the other islands of the Canary chain had paid the price for succumbing to tourist dollars, La Palma had remained virtually untouched. Partially it was because the people didn't particularly relish the idea of their home being overrun, but mostly it was the relatively young age of the island in terms of geology. The Atlantic swells that battered La Palma hadn't yet carved the towering cliffs into the pristine beaches so coveted by European vacationers.

Lashed by constant winds and chilled by ocean currents, La Palma had remained rugged and sparsely populated with a little more than eighty thousand inhabitants. The Cumbre ridge and the twelve-mile-wide Caldera de Taburiente cut the island into distinct segments. The northern part was covered in forests of Canary pines and tree heather, while in the south only hearty grasses and cultivated grapes grew from the volcanic soil.

At its highest point, the seventy-eight-hundred-foot Roque de los Muchachos, stands a cluster of observatories, silvered domes housing some of the most powerful telescopes in Europe. Far from smog and light pollution, La Palma made an ideal place to observe the heavens.

That was until the earth began to stir. And even the

massive concrete foundations under the observatories couldn't dampen the earthquakes that made the entire island shiver.

In the two weeks since his arrival, Mercer had logged some eighty hours crisscrossing the island in various helicopters. The chopper he was currently riding, a navy Seahawk off the amphibious assault ship *Belleau Wood*, thundered over the harbor of the island's capital, Santa Cruz de La Palma, or S/C, as the locals called it. Half a dozen cargo ships waited at anchor for their chance to unload equipment for the effort to prevent the slide, and then carry islanders to Tenerife, where charted jetliners were ready to take them to Madrid and settlement camps being built in the center of Spain.

Farther out to sea, American and Spanish warships maintained a tight quarantine to prevent the flotilla of hired yachts from approaching. Despite the dangers, the eruptions had become the latest "must see" event for the wealthy elite. For now, the military was allowing them to approach to within twenty-five miles of the island. In a few days, the cordon would be pushed out to fifty and the airport at Tenerife would be closed to private aircraft, ending the stream of journalist-laden planes that buzzed the island.

From his vantage, Mercer could see the security personnel manning checkpoints on the roads leading out of the city. Each guard had a high-speed Palm Pilot that continuously updated destinations for the trucks, heavy equipment and fuel tankers that poured off the cargo ships. This was to ensure that no work crews were idled because they ran out of diesel or parts or any of the hundreds of items necessary for the project. Already the army of drill trucks working along the western slope of the Cumbre ridge had gone through six miles' worth of twenty-foot lengths of drill pipe and enough lubricating mud to fill a small lake.

"There it is," the navy pilot said over the intercom, pointing to a lone ship several miles south of town.

The ship was the one-hundred-foot *Petromax Angel*, a sturdy service boat belonging to Petromax Oil. With her blunt bows and extreme width in the beam, she wasn't an attractive vessel, but she'd been designed to maintain the oil rigs and production platforms in the near-Arctic conditions of the North Sea. She personified function over form and came equipped with twelve-thousand-shaft horsepower, dynamic positioning systems, a submersible, saturation diving chambers, and two ROVs. The *Angel* also came with the compliments of the company's president, Aggie Johnston, a woman out of Mercer's past who had donated the boat despite, or maybe because of, his involvement. He didn't know which.

It took Mercer several moments to spot the ship. Her hull was painted vivid red, her deck was clear green and her superstructure was covered in safety yellow. Even these garish colors were obscured by the ash and smoke that filled the air and wreaked havoc with all the machines in operation around the island. Each morning everyone on La Palma woke to the daily ritual of shaking out their clothes no matter how tightly sealed their bedrooms.

The sky was a constant overcast of putrid greens and grays. The satellite pictures Mercer had seen showed the sickly plume spreading eastward from the prehistoric ax-shaped island. No matter how often he brushed his teeth or how much water he drank, Mercer's mouth always felt gritty. The only place safe from the ash was upwind in a helicopter, and even there the air was heavy with the stench of sulfur.

The pilot brought the Seahawk over the *Petromax Angel*'s fantail, flaring the helo over a clear spot on the deck. The navy chopper was too large to land on the workboat's pad so he hovered just above the deck. Mercer opened the copilot's door, tossed his duffel to the metal deck and leapt the four feet. He paused as a crewman slid open the rear door and helped Tisa make the jump. Mercer caught her and the two remained crouched until the Seahawk peeled away.

Charlie Williams and Jim McKenzie were the first to greet him. They'd boarded the *Angel* at Cherbourg, France, along with their gear, which had been flown in from Guam on an air force C-5 Galaxy. It was the first he'd seen of the two since the dive on the USS *Smithback*.

"I don't know whether to thank you or curse you for calling us in," Jim greeted, shaking hands.

"It all depends if we succeed."

"He's only speaking for himself," C.W. said. "I wouldn't want to be anywhere else in the world right now. Talk about your opportunity of a lifetime."

"I bet even your wife approves of this one."

"Only after she conned Jim into letting her come."

That surprised Mercer, but he let it pass. Her presence here didn't matter. He introduced Tisa to the two marine scientists and asked, "You guys have everything you need?"

"What we didn't bring," McKenzie said, trying to light his cigar against the wind, "the folks here on the *Angel* have. But with an entire cargo jet to fill, we stripped about everything but the plumbing out of the *Surveyor*."

"And the second diver? Alan Jervis?"

C.W.'s typical jovial expression faded. "He won't be diving again. Kind of delayed shock or something. The night after you left he woke up screaming. The docs had to dope him up just so he could sleep. He's still in a hospital in Guam."

Mercer was shaken. Jervis had seemed fine the few extra days Mercer had spent on the *Sea Surveyor*. "I had no idea."

"Neither did we," Jim agreed, puffing on his Cuban. "But it does happen."

"You're okay, aren't you?" Mercer asked C.W.

The lanky Californian grinned. "Taking risks is why they pay us. Seriously, I'm fine. Spirit and I talked a lot about it. I think what happened down there scared her more than it scared me. That's why she insisted on coming. We have a backup diver. Scott Glass. He's damned good."

"And your team is settled here on the *Angel*? No problems with the regular crew?"

Charlie dismissed the notion. "Are you kidding? Underwater technology is one of the few areas where academia leads industry in having the latest and greatest. Their guys would love to get their hands on my suits. As we sailed down from France we already decided to use *Conseil*, the ROV we brought, rather than the two owned by Petromax. We finished the software download this morning."

Jim cut in, "Besides, we all know what's at stake here. No one is going to fight a turf battle with so much on the line."

Mercer nodded. "All right. Les Donnelley spent last week talking with every local diver still left on the island and has taken temperature readings all the way around La Palma. He's pinpointed three volcanic vents along the eastern coast below the Cumbre ridge that may suit our needs. Two of them show a steady rise in temperature so we think they are active. The third has remained dormant. It's down a hundred eighty feet so few have dived into the tunnel. We don't know what to expect."

"How hot is the water around the other vents right now?"

"At their mouths, about eighty-four degrees. That's twenty above the ambient water for their depths."

"My ADS can take temperatures up to two hundred," C.W. stated.

"We may need that capability if this last vent pans out. For now we'll check the dormant tunnel with the ROV before committing anyone to the water." Mercer handed Jim McKenzie a notebook opened about halfway. "Here are the coordinates. Get these to the captain and let's get to it."

C.W. and Jim left Mercer and Tisa alone at the rail of the stubby workboat. A half mile from shore the island didn't look dangerous. They could almost pretend the pall was just smoke from a forest fire and not the sulfurous discharge from deep within the earth.

"I find it interesting," Tisa noted, looking up at him. Even in the ruddy glow of the near-eclipsed sun, her dark hair shimmered. "People take orders from you as though they've worked for you for years."

Mercer demurred. "The three of us shared a pretty wild experience."

"Not just Jim and C.W. Others too, even your boss, Admiral Lasko."

Mercer looked out across the waters to the island. "I never really thought about it. I see something that needs to be done and if I can't do it I find people who can. I think the trick is finding the right people. Any idiot can manage a group who knows what they're doing." He smiled. "All I have to do is make sure I surround myself with experts and I get to look good."

She slapped him playfully on the arm. "Fool."

Six hours later, the *Petromax Angel* was in position near where Les Donnelley, the chief volcanologist on La Palma, had thought there was a suitable vent. The boat's bow and stern thrusters were slaved to the dynamic positioning computer that was receiving updates every half second from global positioning satellites. She was as stable as if she'd been anchored to the seafloor.

Jim McKenzie sat in the glow of several video monitors, his hands on the joysticks that controlled *Conseil*, their ROV, which they'd named after the assistant to Professor Aronnax in Jules Vernes's *Twenty Thousand Leagues Under the Sea*. Behind him in the control were Mercer, Tisa, Charlie and Spirit Williams, and a mix of people from Petromax and the crew Jim had brought from the *Sea Surveyor*. The control van bolted to the *Angel*'s deck hummed with computers and the hiss of air purifiers. The doors had to remain closed because of the dust and the air-conditioning labored to dispel all the body heat.

Outside of the steel box, workers were monitoring *Conseil*'s umbilical as it unreeled from the huge stern-mounted spool. The bug-eyed ROV sank deeper into the waters.

Jim had a well-chewed cigar clamped between his teeth and a fresh pitcher of ice water at hand. His fingers were light on the controls, and the cameras on the unmanned submersible had become his eyes.

The ROV was the size of, and roughly the same shape as, a queen-sized bed but was made of high-strength steel, carbon fiber and composite ceramics. It carried four sets of extreme-low-light stereoscopic cameras, as well as a manipulator arm, pressure and temperature gauges, and a chemistry suite that allowed it to analyze water on a continuous basis.

"Okay, boys and girls," Jim said without looking at his audience. "We're dropping through one fifty. *Connie*'s board shows green."

On the monitor they could see virtually nothing other than the glare from lights mounted directly above the cameras. The ROV was still falling, and Jim kept it well away from the island's underwater basalt foundation.

"What's the temp?" asked a Petromax technician.

"A bracing sixty-two degrees," Jim answered. "No sign of volcanic heating."

Mercer was relieved. The San Juan volcano loomed
directly above their location. While lava had begun to
jet from vents on the southern part of the island, San
Juan, in the island's middle, merely rumbled and occasionally belched ash.

Designed to probe the deepest parts of the world's
oceans, *Conseil* had no problems as Jim brought the
ROV to a hover at one hundred eighty feet, a depth
that even a scuba diver could work.

"The vent should be a hundred yards ahead of us
and a bit to the left," Jim intoned as he spooled up
the nimble craft's propulsors.

He eased the ROV forward, keeping one eye on
the video feed and another on the sonar screen that
was mapping the irregularities of the undersea cliff.
An accidental brush with the rock, even this shallow,
could damage the remotely operated vehicle.

"All right, I see the cliff."

On the screen a murky shadow resolved itself into
a jagged promontory of solidified lava. As he nosed
the craft forward for a better look, the team could see
the lava had formed in long ropes that had once shot
from the vent like toothpaste. This pillow lava, as it
was called, was what they all expected. To Mercer it
looked like the ruins of a Greek temple, with the
longer, straighter pieces of lava resembling fallen
columns.

"Judging by the size of that lava," he said, "I'd say
our vent is big enough." The shafts of rock were easily
fifteen feet in diameter.

"We're below the vent." Jim brought *Conseil* up
ten feet, then another thirty.

They lost sight of the pillow lava but didn't spot the
vent opening. He swiveled the ROV, searching along
the dark cliff for the blacker spot of the volcanic
vent. Nothing. He dropped *Conseil* back to their original starting point, moved ten feet to the left and

allowed the robot to ascend. The dozen pairs of eyes watching the screen all thought they saw the vent, but it was their desire, not reality. Once the ROV had risen above the layer of pillow lava, Jim sank her again and started a new search lane another ten feet to the left.

They ran fifty vertical lanes before the area of lava ended entirely. Four painstaking hours had been wasted.

"No one said this was going to be easy," Jim opined, undaunted by the job. He maneuvered *Conseil* to where they first encountered the lava and methodically started the next stripe ten feet to the right.

"I thought I put us right on the spot," Les Donnelley said miserably.

"Don't sweat it, man," Charlie offered. "We learned a long time ago that you can't find anything underwater until it wants to be found." He turned to his wife. "Any dowsing tricks you can use to help?"

Spirit squeezed his hand. "Sorry, lover, that only works when you're looking for water. How about you, Dr. Mercer? You always seem to have a bag of tricks up your sleeve." Her voice dripped sarcasm.

Mercer didn't notice. "Not this time."

"Oh, that's right. You only perform miracles when your own ass is on the line."

He shot her a look, but let it pass.

After another hour and ten more search lanes, the lava field petered out once again.

"Damn." The mild expletive was the most emotion Jim McKenzie had shown since starting the search while the others were showing signs of their anger and frustration. "The vent that spewed this stuff must have been sealed sometime in the past. So now what?"

They'd covered a mere thirty-five hundred square feet, a tiny fraction of the cliff face. Without a more precise idea of the vent's location, they could spend the next week scouring the undersea wall without finding it.

"I am so sorry, guys," Les kept repeating. "The divers I talked to were certain there was a vent here."

"Go back to our original starting point," Mercer ordered, "and let *Connie* descend."

"Why down and not up?" Spirit Williams challenged. "The vent could be above where we've searched just as easily as below."

"It's a guess," Mercer admitted. "But an educated one. Charlie can back me on this. He's a more experienced diver than I am. I think the answer is nitrogen narcosis, also called rapture of the deep. It's a feeling that can overwhelm a diver working at depth not unlike drunkenness. You get impaired judgment, lack of motor coordination and feelings of euphoria. Now suppose the divers Les talked to had been affected by nitrogen narcosis when they discovered the vent. Chances are they would have been deeper than they thought, not shallower."

C.W. nodded. "Makes sense to me."

"And what if they were a mile south of here, or a mile north when they dove?" Spirit countered.

"They were on the surface when they fixed their position," Charlie answered her challenge. "I'm sure they could read a handheld GPS."

Spirit didn't like that her husband defended Mercer and shook off the hand he had around her waist. She crossed her arms over her chest and stormed out of the control van.

Jim ignored her outburst. "I think Mercer's on to something. I'll let *Connie* sink down to three hundred and see what we see."

"That's way below how deep a diver can go on scuba gear."

"Better safe than sorry."

Jim backed *Conseil* away from the cliff and let the ROV slowly drift deeper into the abyss. He kept the cameras pointed straight down so he could avoid any rock outcrops as the little robot sank.

At two hundred seventy feet they found another platform covered in ropes of pillow lava. "Bingo!"

The cell phone in the pocket of Mercer's khakis vibrated. Rather than disturb the others, he stepped out of the control van. The air was crisp but heavily laden with fine ash particles. It had a metallic taste and Mercer couldn't take deep breaths without the urge to cough.

The sun was setting beyond the Cumbre ridge. It silhouetted the volcanic formation, creating an undulating line of darkness and light. Because of the ash in the atmosphere, the color was more melon than yellow. To the south, where molten rock fountained from the Teneguia volcano, the sky's glow was unworldly and hellish.

He fished the phone from his pocket and flipped it open. The caller-ID feature showed Ira Lasko's number. They spoke at least ten times a day. "What's the latest?" Mercer answered.

"I've got something for your file of the most ridiculous things you've ever heard. The North Korean delegation to the United Nations is willing to drop their objections to us using a nuke on La Palma if we give them permission to test one of their own. Get this—they say that a detonation on the island is a peaceful use of nuclear weapons and that their test would also have a beneficial purpose."

"Yeah, beneficial in scaring the crap out of Japan and South Korea. What's the UN's reaction?"

"Publicly they don't have much choice but to allow it. The way the resolution was drafted every nation has to agree for us to get permission. Privately, as soon as they run their test, the germane countries are going to sanction them even further into the Stone Age."

Mercer snorted. "What else is going on?"

"The team at Lawrence Livermore have come up with the weapon you need. It's an old W-54 SADM."

"Saddam?"

"Small Atomic Demolition Munition. It was developed in the fifties to be fired from the Davy Crockett recoilless rifle. The engineers have modified its plutonium implosion core to push up the yield. Originally it was a one-kiloton warhead. They've brought it up to four and a half, which Dr. Marie says should be sufficient."

"Provided we can find the vent," Mercer said.

"No luck yet?"

"We're closing in," was all Mercer would give. "How big is the bomb?"

"Ah, hold on. About two feet square."

"Sounds like the legendary suitcase bomb."

"It is, or was. When they increased the yield they had to add shielding. It weighs in at two hundred sixty pounds."

By attaching lifting bags to the warhead, Mercer was confident that the ROV could position it in the vent.

"Can I call you back in a minute?" Ira asked suddenly. "My boss is on the other line. I think it's important."

"Sure." The call had already been cut.

Mercer stayed at the rail, leaning far over to watch the occasional boil of water when the thrusters kicked on to keep the *Petromax Angel* in position. The control van door opened. Tisa stood poised until she spotted him. As project director Mercer rarely slept in the same place on two consecutive nights so they'd had very little time together since their arrival in the Canaries.

Yet even these absences, and the shadow of the impending cataclysm, couldn't spoil their budding relationship. She made every second magical, like the candlelight bath in his hotel room, or the midnight stroll she'd taken him on through gnarled olive trees. In the very heart of the grove, she'd erected a tent for them.

She smiled as she sidled up to him, slipping her arms over his shoulders and drawing his mouth to hers. "I think I should be jealous," she said.

"Jealous, why?"

"That woman, Spirit. I think she's in love with you."

Mercer was even more confused. *"What?"*

"You have to admit she is beautiful." He could tell she was teasing him.

"I suppose so," he said, as if giving the question serious consideration, "if you're one of those guys who goes for women with long legs, a big chest and dark smoldering eyes," inviting a quick slap to the hip.

She massaged the spot in widening circles until she had a firm grip on his backside. "I'm not kidding about her. She's attracted to alpha males. I bet back home she and C.W. are the center of their social group. Out here her husband looks to you for leadership. She doesn't like it, while at the same time she's also attracted to you. That's why she's always nasty."

"You got all this from the tone of her voice?"

"Oh, she's not that subtle. When you're not looking she can't take her eyes off you. And since I don't think she owns a bra, her arousal can be obvious."

Mercer burst out laughing and it took several moments for him to catch his breath.

"What's so funny?"

"My life is starting to sound like a cheesy potboiler. Pretty soon you and Spirit will get into a catfight and then Charlie and I will have to defend the honor of our women or something."

"Won't happen that way. If she tried to fight me, C.W. would be busy planning her funeral. You know, it's funny how people can adapt to anything. Here we all are, standing at the edge of disaster and we all continue to act on our basest emotions."

"That's part of being human. We can adapt to any misery, our capacity for it sometimes seems bottomless. I read someplace about romances between inmates in the Nazi concentration camps. If people can retain their humanity there, it can endure anywhere."

"You think we will recover if we can't prevent the avalanche?"

"As a species, absolutely. As a civilization, who knows?" Mercer's phone jiggled.

"I'm back," Ira said, his tone ominous.

Mercer caught it instantly. "What happened?"

"That was Kleinschmidt. He just came back from a meeting with the president's national security council. As you can imagine, the president is under tremendous pressure to order an evacuation of the East Coast. Some say the order should have been given weeks ago. The idea of impeachment's been floated. Meanwhile every senator and representative from Maine to Florida is clamoring for federal aid."

"I told you I don't care about the squabbles in Washington."

"This one affects you. Originally you were given four weeks to stabilize the western side of that volcano and detonate the nuke, leaving one week for an evacuation if it doesn't work. The president has decided to bump that up by a week in order to give people fourteen days to hightail it out of the danger zones."

Mercer couldn't respond.

"I'm sorry to hit you with this. It came right from the Oval Office. There was nothing I could do to stop it."

"They call this a compromise, right? Jesus. Ira, if what we're doing here fails, even those towering intellects on Capitol Hill have to understand an evacuation won't mean shit. Taking away that week kills my chances while gaining almost nothing on the other end."

"I argued that point, John Kleinschmidt argued that point and so did the vice president. On the other side were about fifty politicians representing forty million frightened Americans. We didn't stand a chance. If it's any consolation, the situation is much worse in Spain and Portugal. Both countries' prime ministers have stepped down. And some of the Caribbean islands are in full-out revolt. Cuba, Haiti and the Dominican Republic are about the only places where people have a chance to survive and even there it's chaos."

"Are we doing anything to help?" Mercer asked, disregarding his own edict about not paying attention to world reaction.

"People who have their own boats have been arriving in Florida and a few in Texas. The Immigration Department's not even bothering to count them. As for the rest, Christ, even if we wanted to we couldn't save a fraction of the millions of people living down there. If we had every cruise ship and freighter in the world ready to take them off, we could *maybe* evacuate one of the smaller islands."

"I shouldn't have asked," Mercer said, feeling the anguish in Ira's voice. "I knew the answer already." He put his arm around Tisa's slim body, needing her warmth to soak into him. She snuggled close.

"Mercer?" Les Donnelley called from the control van. "We found the vent! You were right."

"Ira, we found the vent," Mercer said into the phone. "I'll talk to you tomorrow."

Mercer folded the cell back into his pocket and strode to the van. "Great news." He gave Les a congratulatory high-five.

"It was right below where we first looked, like ten feet to the left."

Back in the control room, Mercer looked over Jim's shoulder. The lava tube was almost perfectly round and about eight feet in diameter. The high-intensity lamps attached to *Conseil* could penetrate only twenty feet into the aperture before their glow was absorbed.

"Looks pretty clear," Mercer said. "Our first lucky break of the day."

"We found it in a day," Jim replied. "I call that lucky too."

Mercer put his hand on McKenzie's shoulder. "I'll tell you the rest after we explore the tube. Any change to the temperature?"

"Nope. Nice and cool. The vent's still dormant."

"All right, send in the ROV."

Jim pulled a microphone to his mouth to talk to the men on deck manning the spool. "We're about to enter the vent. Spool out three hundred extra feet of cable so it doesn't snag." He looked over his shoulder at Mercer. "The cable's armored, but . . ."

With gentle touches on the joysticks, he eased *Conseil* into the tube, keeping the robot exactly centered. The rock had been polished glassy smooth by the tremendous heat and pressure of the lava it once discharged, and it ran as straight as a sewer pipe, but he was careful not to scrape the tunnel lining and damage the ROV.

After the first three hundred feet, the team was starting to feel they had found what they needed. More cable was stripped from the reel and Jim sent *Connie* deeper under the volcano.

At five hundred feet the tunnel had shrunk so there was only a few inches' clearance on each side of the ROV. The temperature was also on the rise, up to eighty-four degrees. This in itself wasn't an issue, but it meant that magma was heating the water. Somewhere deep in the volcano, lava was boiling near the tube.

"I still think we're okay," Jim said. "We can strip *Conseil* when we make the run with the bomb. There are a few struts and sensors we don't need that'll reduce her width. I'm just worried about the heat."

Without warning the lights on the ROV went dark.

"What the . . . ?" Jim checked his console. "We've got a problem."

"The lights?" Tisa asked.

"Across the board. *Connie* just went dead. I've got zero telemetry." He continued to scan his computer readouts, searching for the problem. "Goddamn it!" he roared. He grabbed for the microphone. "Bridge, this is McKenzie. What the hell are you doing up there? We're drifting." He pointed to the screen where it showed their coordinates. They were more than five hundred feet from where they were supposed to be.

"Hold on, Mr. McKenzie," the officer on watch called back. "I'm checking right now. Yes, I see we have drifted. I don't know what happened. It must be a computer glitch."

"Glitch my butt. Were you even watching the screens?"

"Of course. Everything was fine but now we're off course. I can't explain it."

"I can. You weren't doing your job." Jim switched channels on the PA system, uninterested with the man's excuses. "Deck, this is the van. The ROV is down, reel her back in. Nice and slow. No more than twenty feet a minute. She's in the tube and I don't want her banged up."

It took an agonizing hour to retrieve the cable. While the others went to dinner, Mercer and Jim stood shoulder to shoulder at the rail to watch the operation. And when the last of the cable appeared their worst fears were realized.

They'd recovered a thousand feet of armored data line but no ROV. When the *Petromax Angel* drifted from her assigned position *Conseil*'s tether had snapped.

"We have to send in C.W. to attach a towline," Jim said in a defeated monotone. "*Connie*'s blocking the pipe and we need to get her out of there."

"We can still use it to insert the bomb, right?"

McKenzie shook his head and spat into the sea. "When that cable snapped, it opened a conduit to the sea. Right now water's wicking through the tether and slowly filling the interior of the *Conseil*'s interior. It's cooked."

"Okay, we'll use one of Petromax's ROVs."

"They're camera platforms only, half of *Connie*'s size. What does the bomb weigh?"

"Two hundred sixty pounds."

"With that kind of payload, they'd sink like a stone."

"What about attaching air bags?"

"I won't take the chance of a bag hooking on something and deflating. We have to insert the bomb with the NewtSuits. Besides, those ROVs can't function at temperatures above a hundred and twenty."

"The water's eighty-four."

"Right now. Tomorrow it'll be a hundred. The day after, who knows?"

"So we do it with the Advanced Diving Suit," Mercer stated. "It's not our first option, but we knew there was a chance."

"I know. I just don't like it. If something goes wrong, *Conseil* can be replaced. Divers can't."

Later that night, Mercer lay in his bunk beside Tisa. He was going over in his head how the ship could have drifted from its position and caused them to lose the ROV. He and Jim had confronted the watch officer and the helmsman on duty. They insisted neither had left their posts in the minutes leading to disaster. Two off-duty crewmen had vouched for them as well. They'd been on the bridge wing photographing the lava glow to the south. That left a computer glitch, an unlikely explanation since the GPS worked fine now and the chances of it failing when the ROV was most vulnerable stretched credibility.

Staring at the ceiling, Mercer knew the only explanation was sabotage. Someone on board wanted them to fail. His suspicion turned first to Spirit Williams. Only she didn't have a motive. As he sought one, it dawned on him that the signal Jim McKenzie had intercepted in the moments before the hydrate cooling tower had activated could have been sent from the *Surveyor* and not some mystery ship that no one had been able to locate. Someone on the research ship would have known exactly when to turn on the massive impellers in order to kill the divers.

That realization took Spirit off his suspect list. He could accuse her of a lot of things but she was obviously devoted to her husband. He couldn't picture her sending the signal, knowing that C.W. was right in the path of the boiling methane hydrate.

He folded his arms under his pillow as Tisa tucked herself tighter against him, her mouth near his neck.

If not Spirit, then who? Scott Glass, the alternate diver, hadn't been on the *Surveyor*. He'd joined Jim and C.W. in California. And those two hadn't done it, he was sure. That left the five technicians who had made the trip from Guam with McKenzie.

Mercer didn't even know their names, which he supposed made it easier for him to have them confined to their quarters until after the bomb went off. For good measure, he'd lock up Spirit too, just so he wouldn't have to listen to her mouth. Maybe he'd ask Tisa to be her jailer.

Now that he'd satisfied himself as to the who—and the why didn't really concern him; who knew why fanatics did anything?—he still found himself wondering about the how. How had they made the ship drift off course?

Tisa shifted. Mercer knew he'd remain awake until he solved the mystery, so he moved her a little farther and swung off the bed. She gave a soft moue of annoyance and settled back to sleep.

He dressed in the dark, not bothering with his boxers or socks, and slipped out of the cramped cabin. The corridor was deserted, but he felt the presence of the ship, the thrum of her generators and the whoosh of air through the ventilators. He passed the cabin Jim was sharing with Scott Glass. He could hear Jim's snores through the closed door and pitied the diver. The next cabin in line was Spirit and C.W.'s. He heard voices.

He paused. It was three o'clock in the morning.

He couldn't make out what they were saying, but it sounded like an argument. Charlie must have told her that the ROV had been lost and he and Scott were going to have to place the nuclear weapon themselves. Mercer could imagine her reaction.

He moved on, found a flight of stairs and climbed to the bridge. He didn't know the watch officer, but the red-haired Irishman knew him and greeted him by name. "Kind of late for a stroll, Dr. Mercer. I'm Seamus Rourke." Most of the *Petromax Angel*'s officers and crew were from the British Isles.

"No rest for the wicked." They shook hands.

"I thought it was the weary."

"Both." He helped himself to coffee from the urn on a counter at the back of the spartan bridge. "Can you show me the GPS receivers."

"You too, huh? I've been sitting here thinking about that since I heard what happened and I kind of thought sabotage. But the receivers are on the antenna mast outside. You can't get to them without accessing a service ladder that's kept locked. Only the captain and chief engineer have keys and I already checked the padlock. No one messed with it."

"That blows my theory."

"There is another way," Rourke suggested.

"I'm all ears."

"There is such a thing as a GPS scrambler. It's only

available to the military so they can prevent enemies from accessing the positioning satellites or at least messing with their reception."

"That's right! I think Saddam Hussein tried to use them during Iraqi Freedom. As I recall they didn't work."

"Not against the equipment used by the U.S. Air Force and Navy, but it might confuse our gear long enough for us to drift off station. The *Angel*'s a good boat but she was state-o'-the-art when Maggie Thatcher was hanging her girdle at Number Ten."

Rourke's idea had merit. "What would one of these scramblers look like?"

"Probably just a little black box. Something that could be tossed overboard. I doubt we'd ever find it even if the saboteur kept it with him. And there's also the chance that our receivers were scrambled by somebody onshore. We're close enough."

Mercer hadn't thought of that. Had there really been a ship over the horizon from the *Sea Surveyor*? That opened the possibility that someone on the island had the jammer. Eleven thousand workers were currently on La Palma along with about a thousand die-hard locals who had yet to evacuate. Not one had been screened by security. There hadn't been time.

The tall officer looked Mercer in the eye. "I want to know why. Why would they do it? We're trying to save the world. Why would someone want to stop us. No one gains."

"It's not about gain." Mercer set his cup next to the coffeemaker and turned to the door. "I think it's about maximizing loss." He hadn't forgotten that Tisa's brother, Luc, hadn't been at Rinpoche-La and was still at large.

Mercer found his way to the deck. The air felt heavier than before and charged with static. Lightning licked along the distant Cumbre ridge, caused by the

ash and gas erupting from the southern part of the
island. Mercer watched strike after strike. On the far
side of the ridge he had teams drilling into the mountain trying to stabilize the slope. The drill trucks were
well grounded, but it was only a matter of time before
one of the men was struck.

With just one week left he considered evacuating
them. The extra support pipes they were pinning into
the rock wasn't worth the risk of one or more being
killed. He knew from the beginning that the whole
scheme had been a long shot at best. His hopes had
always lain with the nuke.

But what if each pipe prevented one ton of debris
from slamming into the ocean? And what if that one
ton meant saving a family trapped on the Bahamas,
or in the Belgian lowlands?

On his numerous inspection tours he'd talked to
enough of the roughnecks to know that they'd probably ignore his evacuation order anyway. He was pretty
sure a few of the tougher ones would even continue
to drill as the Cumbre Vieja split and slid down to
the sea.

He turned his back on the atmospheric discharges
and looked to the east. Dawn was hours away, but the
glow from the erupting Teneguia volcano painted the
sky in oranges and flickering reds. The light danced
like the mindless rage of an artillery barrage. Cracks
of thunder added to the illusion.

It would be ten o'clock on Saturday night back
home, he realized. Harry would be slouched on his
stool at Tiny's. Paul would be in his cramped office
getting tomorrow's odds for his sports book. Doobie
Lapoint would be behind the bar, the crisp towel over
his shoulder the cleanest item in the place. Mercer
desperately wanted to be a part of that normalcy, not
here making decisions that affected the lives of millions of people.

He pulled the phone from his pocket and started to dial the Arlington number when he realized he didn't have a signal. The lightning, he guessed, and turned back to appraise the island.

Mercer had a second to realize the sky had been shredded—the burst of ash had already climbed to five thousand feet—before the wall of sound rocked the *Petromax Angel* and threw him off his feet.

San Juan was erupting.

Lit from below by its own fiery heart, the top of the volcano had been blown skyward, a seething, billowing column of ash and rock that spread as it rose, a bruised purple mushroom cloud that cleaved the darkness.

The ship was a mile from shore, and the volcano was another eleven miles inland, and yet the shock wave slammed the *Angel* with hurricane force. Mercer clung to the rail as the wind ripped and tore at his precarious grip. He had to find cover. In moments the first ash and chunks of pumice would rain on the deck, yet he could not let go until the wave passed.

His head was filled with the ceaseless bellow of the explosion, a sound that seemed to shake his flesh loose from his bones. When the concussion finally dissipated, he felt like a dried husk. His fingers were bent into claws from his grip on the metal stanchion.

He staggered to his feet, his first concern for the crews working to pin the side of the mountain. He had to find a working phone or radio. He had to know how many he'd lost. At least five drill trucks were working the lower flank of San Juan. Fifty men had been within three miles of the blast, more when he considered the tanker drivers and relief workers, who rarely ventured far from their machines.

A door into the superstructure flew open. Spirit Williams was backlit against the interior lights. Her T-shirt was cropped so high that the bottom of her breasts were visible, two heavy crescents of white skin. Her panties were little more than a triangle of silk. Mercer brushed past her without a glance.

"What happened?" she cried and raced to keep pace.

"It blew. The son-of-a-bitching mountain blew." Crewmen and scientists tumbled from their cabins in various states of undress.

Mercer climbed for the bridge. Third Officer Rourke stood at the windscreen, binoculars pressed to his eyes. "Get on the radio, Seamus. See if you can get a signal. We need to know what's going on." Mercer tried his cell again but there was no signal.

"Your little girlfriend said we had two more weeks," Spirit accused.

"Go find Jim," Mercer ordered. "And your husband. We have to push up the dive."

"Dr. Mercer, I have someone onshore." The watch stander handed him the radiophone handset.

"This is Philip Mercer. Who is this and where are you?"

"Bill Farley, Doctor. I'm an assistant supervisor for the drilling crews. I'm about eight miles south of the volcano."

"What's the situation?"

"Chaos. I don't know what's happening. There were three crews up near the summit and another two farther down. I haven't heard from them and from what I can see here I don't think they made it."

That news wasn't unexpected but still hit like a body blow. "What about the fault?" Mercer asked. "Has it slipped?"

"If it had I wouldn't be here. I'm standing on it now."

"Bill, I want you to reach as many of your people as you can. Evacuate everyone. I don't know why San Juan erupted early, but you need to get everyone off the island any way you can." Mercer's cell vibrated. The atmospheric disturbances must have abated enough for the signal to reach him from the towers on the island. "Keep this line open." He passed the phone to the officer and flipped open the little Nokia. "Mercer."

"It's Ira. What the hell happened? I just got a call from the USGS. They're recording a massive eruption on La Palma."

"The San Juan volcano just lit off. I just talked to a guy in the field. He says the fault hasn't slipped so we may have time."

"It doesn't matter. As soon as the president hears about this he's going to order the evacuation."

Mercer was forced to agree. "I would too."

How had Tisa been so wrong? That question had hidden in his subconscious since the first instant of the eruption and now stood at the forefront of his mind. On Santorini she'd predicted the earthquake to the minute. How could she miss this by three weeks?

"Where's the warhead?" he asked the admiral.

"Still at Livermore Labs."

"How fast can you get it here?"

"Four hours."

Even the SR-71 Blackbird couldn't travel the thousands of miles from California to Spain that fast. Mercer suspected that the world was about to get their first look at the SR-1 Wraith, the secret hypersonic reconnaissance aircraft mistakenly called Aurora.

"Get me that bomb, Ira. There's still a chance."

"Mercer, if that mountain goes it won't matter that you're on the other side of the island. The wave's going to nail you. Maybe you should get out of there."

"I've ordered everyone off La Palma, but we're not running. I have to make a try with the nuke."

"If you're wrong, that's a death sentence for the crew with you."

"I don't need you telling me the obvious." Mercer tried to calm himself. Snapping at his friend wasn't going to help. "Ira, can you buy me twelve hours with the president? We both know if that evacuation order comes, thousands are going to die in the panic."

"And millions would be saved if the island collapses. There's no way he's going to take the chance."

"What if this wasn't the main eruption? What if we still have time? Tisa hasn't been wrong before. I don't think she's wrong now."

"Then tell me why that volcano's erupting as we speak."

"I can't," Mercer admitted. "Not until I talk to her."

"And if Tisa can't explain it either?" Mercer had no reply. "I'm sorry. He's not going to have a choice about ordering the evacuation tonight. And I think I back him on this one."

"All right, do what you have to, but get me that bomb."

"That I can promise."

"I'll be in touch." Mercer folded the phone into his pocket. Jim and Tisa stood at the back of the bridge. Tisa's face reflected anguish as she looked at the towering ash cloud spreading over the dark island. Yet her voice was resolute when she said, "This isn't the eruption from the prophecy. This is just a prelude."

"I believe you." Mercer touched her shoulder. "Unfortunately no one else does."

"They're going to try to evacuate the East Coast?" Jim asked.

"The president will probably make the announcement tonight."

"What are we going to do?"

Mercer's reply was never in doubt. "Finish what we started." Jim nodded. "The bomb will be here in four hours. We need to pull *Conseil* from the vent so we can set it as soon as it arrives. We have to implode the mountain and stabilize the ridge in the next few hours. Where are C.W. and Scott?"

"I saw Scott heading for the control van," Tisa said. "I haven't seen Charlie."

Spirit raced onto the bridge at that moment. She was nearly hysterical, sobbing and trying to catch her breath at the same time. She hadn't yet put on anything to cover her near-naked body. "C.W.'s hurt. His head is bleeding bad and he won't wake up."

The pieces fell into place. "Jim, get down to the van and prep for the dive," Mercer snapped the order. "Tisa, stay with him." He addressed Seamus Rourke. "Are there any firearms on this ship?"

"Firearms? Why?" And then Rourke had the same thought as Mercer. The saboteur. "No, nothing. I'll call the crew together and sweep the ship."

"Good. Lock up everyone who came aboard with the *Surveyor* team except Jim here and Scott Glass. Put them in the mess hall."

"What are you doing?" Jim protested.

"C.W. was attacked."

"What?!" Spirit and McKenzie cried.

"The signal to turn on the turbines when we were on the *Sea Surveyor*, the glitch in the GPS yesterday that cut the cable to the ROV and now C.W., the best diver we've got, is hurt. It's not a coincidence. Someone you brought with you has been sabotaging our work."

"It could have been . . ." Jim's voice trailed off as he made the connection, and came to the same conclusion. "Son of a bitch!"

"Tisa warned me that the Order had thousands of members and potentially millions of sympathizers. There's no way we could have known they already had an agent in place."

"I left him alone," Spirit wailed, making no attempt

to wipe at the tears pouring down her cheeks. "They could come back to attack him again."

"Come on," Mercer pulled her along as he rushed from the bridge, calling over his shoulder to Jim, "Prep both suits. Maybe C.W.'s okay."

They ran down to the second deck. Mercer threw open the door to C.W.'s cabin. The young diver lay on the floor at the foot of their bunk, wearing jeans and shoes but no shirt. Around his upper body was a pool of his own blood. His blond hair was matted to his head, and his normal tan had faded to a ghostly white.

Spirit couldn't enter the room. She stood at the door, her fist jammed against her mouth to keep from crying out. Her whole body trembled. Mercer knelt next to C.W. and felt for a pulse. It was there, but weak. Next he felt along Charlie's head until his fingers sank into a sticky dent above his temple. Bits of bone grated as he pulled his fingers from the wound.

"Is he—?"

"He's alive, but this is serious." Mercer checked Charlie's eyes. One pupil was dilated, the other just a black point. "His skull is fractured and he has a concussion. He needs medical attention." There were twenty Ph.D.'s on the ship but not one medical doctor. "I don't want to move him, but we have to cover him up. Give me a hand."

Together Mercer and Spirit stripped the bed and tucked the blankets under and around Charlie so he wasn't lying on the linoleum floor. Mercer turned up the cabin's heat and found more blankets in a storage closet.

By the time they finished, the ship's second engineer arrived with a hard plastic medical chest. "What happened?"

"It looks like someone hit him over the head," Mercer said, kneeling back to let the engineer, who obviously knew what he was doing, make his own examination. "Good job with the blankets," he said in a rich Scottish accent. "He's in shock. Hold this." He handed Mercer a plasma bag and inserted the needle into Charlie's muscled arm. "Blood loss is just as dangerous as the head trauma."

"Are you a doctor?" Spirit asked, heartened by the man's efficient manner.

"No, ma'am. I cross-trained as a corpsman in the Royal Navy." He used scissors and a razor to get rid of the hair around Charlie's wound. Then he cleared away the blood with a lavage of warm saline. "Okay, let's see here. It's deep and the bone is broken, but this part of the skull's pretty lean so that doesn't mean anything." He removed some of the bone chips with a pair of tweezers. He looked at Mercer then Spirit, noticing for the first time she was barely dressed. She quickly wrapped one of Charlie's corduroy shirts around her torso. "I'll bandage his noggin and it's just wait and see. He's young, and looks fitter than an ox, so I think he'll be okay. He'll have a hell of a headache when he wakes and will be more than a wee bit tired for a few days. Keep an eye on him and I'll check back in an hour or two."

Spirit threw her arms around the engineer. "Thank you."

"I'm going to ask if a crewman can keep watch on your door, if that's all right," Mercer said to Spirit after the engineer had left.

"Bit fucking late, isn't it? His head's already bashed in."

"I'm sorry. I didn't think it would go this far."

"Didn't think it would go this far?" she shouted back. "It went this far when someone tried to kill him on the *Sea Surveyor*. And what would have happened if he'd been in that lava tube when the ship drifted? You really are a conceited bastard, you know that?

You don't care about anyone or anything so long as you get the glory." She began to sob. "Just leave."

Mercer backed out of the cabin, knowing in his heart this wasn't about glory. Maybe Tisa had gotten her wrong.

On deck, a blizzard of ash swept the ship in unending waves. Even with all the lights ablaze, the workboat was nearly blacked out by the ashfall. A resourceful officer had ordered the vessel's water cannons to sweep the upperworks and deck, turning the ash into mud that drained from the scuppers. The rain that had begun to fall stung when it touched Mercer's skin, made acidic by sulfur belching from the volcano.

He found Jim, Scott Glass and Tisa in the control van. "How's Charlie?"

"Someone hit him over the head," Mercer said, wiping the grime from his face with the towel Tisa had handed him. "He has a concussion, but the ship's engineer was a corpsman and seems to think he'll be fine."

"What about the dive?" Scott asked. He was younger than Charlie, dark-haired and sporting a goatee and a nearly shaved head. Where C.W. was laid back and casual, Glass had an intensity and an attentiveness that Mercer appreciated. "One man can't tow the line in alone."

"Do any of the Petromax people have experience in the ADS?"

"No. There's only the one pilot for their minisub. He might be able to do it, but he's only five two. The suit's too big."

Jim added, "Most of the work Petromax does in the North Sea is done with saturation divers."

"Can we use them?"

"It would take days just to set the diving bell and allow the divers enough time for their pre-breath on gas." Jim shook his head. "*Conseil's* stuck more than five hundred feet inside the vent and we have to go even deeper to place the ~~bomb~~. It's the suits or nothing."

"I don't know if he was bragging," Scott put in, "but C.W. says that Mercer was pretty good in the suit when you were together a few weeks ago. If you're willing to risk it, I'll dive with you as my backup."

Mercer hesitated. "Look, we only made a couple of dives. I have maybe three hours in the suit. And that was in open water. Forget it. What about you, Jim?"

"It's ironic, but I've never even snorkeled." Another resounding explosion echoed across the water. "We don't have time to get someone else. We have to do this in one dive as soon as the bomb arrives."

Mercer knew this was too important to risk on his limited skills. He would jeopardize everything if he made even a simple mistake. He shouldn't do it, but what were the alternatives? He looked to Tisa. She understood how the decision tore at him. She gave him an imperceptible nod, not of consent but of compassion.

Scott would lead. Mercer's role would be support if Scott needed something. All he'd really have to do is hang back and not be in the way. He could handle that, he thought. But what if he messed up? Mercer couldn't let himself think about it. Glass needed someone to help haul the tow cable into the vent and there was no one else and no time to find someone.

"Okay. We'll go as soon as the bomb's delivered. That gives Scott four hours or so to teach me everything C.W. missed." Mercer gave Glass a lopsided smile. "I hope you know what the hell you're doing."

"I was about to say the same to you."

Before heading for the suits, Jim convinced Mercer that he needed at least one of his technicians with him to monitor the dive and personally vouched for the man.

"Just him," Mercer agreed, but not liking it. "I

don't want the others released from the mess hall until they can be vetted."

Mercer wanted an update on the bomb's ETA and tried Ira on the cell phone but couldn't get a signal again. He was able to radio Bill Farley, the supervisor over on the eastern side of the volcanic ridge.

The evacuation had been ordered, but no one was leaving their posts. In fact, Farley reported that the first- and second-shift workers were showing up by the hundreds, eager for an all-out assault to keep the Cumbre Vieja from slipping. He said the men would only leave the danger zone and head to the north of the island when the bomb was in the ground and the clock was ticking.

Mercer couldn't have been more proud.

Crossing from the amidships control van on the *Petromax Angel* to where the NewtSuits were housed in a container at the *Angel*'s stern was like a walk across a newly turned field in the middle of a cyclone. Wind and rain lashed the ship, and the best efforts of the crew couldn't keep up with the swampy mud that had grown a couple of feet thick in some areas. Layers of ash and sizzling bits of pumice blanketed the sea.

The bright yellow NewtSuits stood on their wireframe lifting cradles and were cracked open ready for the men. They resembled the discarded carapace of some science fiction insect. The technician Jim had vouched for was installing extra lights to the shoulders and forearms and a secondary battery pack.

"We'll be hauling in a tow rope to pull the ROV from the tunnel so we can't be on tethers," Scott explained. "Too much risk of getting everything tangled. You and I will be able to communicate but once we're in the tunnel we may lose the acoustical phone from the surface."

"How will they know when to pull *Conseil* back out?"

Scott patted his suit's steel claw. "Once we've got the line attached, just smack it with this. Jim can pick up the vibrations on his monitors. One tap for go, two to stop."

"That easy?"

"K-I-S-S. Now, tell me everything you did with C.W. when you were together and I'll take it from there."

Over the next three hours the men went over the suits, Mercer absorbing as much as he could of what Scott told him. He remembered a great deal of what Charlie had taught him, but Glass had a way of imparting even more. They worked for an hour inside the suits, taking power off the ship's mains so as not to drain the batteries. Although it was a dry run and would differ dramatically from when they were underwater, Mercer was grateful for the practice.

The only change they made from their original plan was that Scott would use Charlie's suit, while Mercer operated the spare, the one he'd toyed with aboard the *Sea Surveyor*. Scott felt he'd be better able to handle the idiosyncracies of Charlie's suit.

They took a break when Ira's four-hour promise approached. Mercer tried to raise the admiral on his cell phone but still couldn't get through. Jim had been able to use the ship's radiophone to contact an official on the island of Tenerife who'd been told the bomb had been delivered to Lisbon, Portugal, and was now en route to La Palma. The man didn't know how.

"There's no way they can get a chopper to us in this soup," Scott said as they looked out into the storm from the cargo container.

Dawn was just a gray promise. The San Juan volcano had stopped spewing ash several hours earlier but the sky was choked with it. It would remain the color of lead even if the rain clouds passed. There was barely enough light to see the outline of the island a mile away.

"Hey, Mercer!" Jim's shout came from the control van. "I think I have something."

Mercer dashed through the filthy rain to the van. "What have you got?"

McKenzie handed him a headset. "Hello?" Mercer said into the mouthpiece.

"That you, Snow?"

There was too much interference to recognize the voice and it took Mercer a moment to remember the nickname. "Sykes?"

"Roger that." The Delta commandos hadn't stayed in La Palma for even an hour when they flew here with Mercer. Lasko and others in Washington needed a mission debrief and Mercer hadn't been able to spare the time to give it. They'd been flown straight to Washington on the same Citation they'd borrowed to get to La Palma from Katmandu. "The Monkey Bombers have gone nuclear."

"What are you talking about?"

"I'm about ten miles up-range of your position. The warhead was loaded into an MMU in Portugal and we're about to drop it."

"Don't tell me you're coming in too."

"Sorry, not this time. I'm sitting behind the two pilots of the stealth that plopped us into Tibet. The least they could do was give me a ringside seat."

Mercer saw the logic in delivering the W-54 bomb in one of the Manned Munition Utilities. The pods were designed to accurately and gently deliver a soldier to the battlefield. They couldn't risk sending a chopper to the island until the volcanic fallout subsided. A regular parachute drop didn't have the precision to land the weapon on the deck of a ship at sea, so the monkey bomb was the sensible choice.

"I'm calling to verify your GPS coordinates," Sykes

went on. "And to let you know the trigger is a three-hour delay. Once it's set there ain't no turning back."

"Okay, Booker. I'm turning you over to Jim McKenzie—he's the master of ceremonies for this particular ring of our circus. Good to hear your voice, man."

"Same to you. Good luck down there. Sounds like you're going to need it."

"Hoo-yah!" Mercer returned the headset to Jim and went back to the deck, shouting for the crewman trying to hose mud over the side to clear the way.

The *Petromax Angel* had about forty feet of open deck between the control van and her stubby superstructure, more than enough room to land the MMU. He waited in the shelter of the bridge wing, shielding his eyes against the acid rain and swirling ash to glimpse the stealthy black pod as it fell from the cheerless sky. He mistakenly looked straight up, not realizing the MMU's onboard computers were constantly correcting the pod's descent for the brutal windshears.

The MMU actually swooped over the port side scant feet above the rail and dropped to the deck, falling lightly onto its back as the parachute was cut away. The billow of nylon vanished over the starboard rail, as fleeting as a ghost.

The seals around the lid hissed and the coffinlike door opened a crack. Mercer couldn't help the eerie feeling he got as he approached the MMU. He almost didn't want to touch it. He swung open the lid and stared in wonder at what lay nestled in the protective foam.

The bomb was white and nearly featureless, just a rectangular box that really was about the size of a large Samsonite suitcase. He placed a hand on its casing. It was cold.

Mercer shivered in the rain. Beneath the steel and

lead shielding lay a ball of explosives that would implode an even smaller sphere of plutonium. It had the power to level a city.

He prayed it had the power to save a planet.

A deckhand approached hauling a small winch on wheels. Together he and Mercer slung a cradle under the nuclear bomb and lifted it from the MMU. The weapon swung and twisted on the end of the cable in a way that reminded Mercer of an obscene piñata. The absurdity of his observation brought a smile to his face.

"What's so funny, Doctor?" the crewman asked.

"Just that it's a good thing I don't have a blindfold and a stick."

They wheeled the bomb across the slick deck to the container at the stern of the service boat. The ashfall had smothered the waves so the ship sat as solidly as if she were in drydock. Fire hoses had been directed over the fantail to open a spot in the muck so the divers could be safely lowered into the sea. Gantry lights showed the pace of the ashfall was slowing, as was the rain. The sky had even brightened to a dull pewter.

Mercer passed his side of the winch dolly to another crewman to answer his vibrating phone. The signal was the clearest it had been since the eruption four hours ago.

"You must pull some serious weight with the president," Ira said without preamble.

"What happened?"

"I've been trying to get through to tell you that he decided to wait until morning on the East Coast to make the announcement."

"I doubt it was my influence," Mercer said, overjoyed by the news. "Waiting until daylight to start the evacuation makes better sense than starting it at eleven o'clock at night."

"Either way you have five hours. If you can set off that nuke and prevent the avalanche he won't call for the evacuation. Has it arrived?"

"About two minutes ago. Good thinking using an MMU."

"Thought you'd like that," Ira said. "We'll make sure that anyone on the western sides of the other islands will be above the surge line of any wave created when that bomb goes off. The navy is pushing out their quarantine zone. An Aegis cruiser is going to remain inside the cordon if you need it."

"What about the North African coast?" Mercer asked, still amazed by the level of coordination even though he was at the center of it.

"Even more deserted than normal. The UN has done a good job there. Are the divers set to go?"

Just as Mercer didn't need to know the details of the world reaction to the crisis, he wouldn't bother Ira with the attack on Charlie Williams or how he would be making the dive. "Ready and willing." Mercer didn't know how to ask the next question. It wasn't in his nature to question success, but he had to make plans. "Listen, Ira, I'd like you to do me a favor."

"Name it."

"If this doesn't work and they call for a full evacuation I want you to look after Harry."

"Already taken care of. He and Tiny have your car gassed and loaded, and a hotel reservation near Lynchburg, Tennessee."

Their choice of destination was no surprise.

Lynchburg was the home of the Jack Daniel's distillery. "Just make sure they leave."

"I will but you shouldn't worry. I think they're going whether the president makes the announcement or not."

That brought a smile to Mercer's face. "Then tell him if his dog scratches my leather seats I'm going to reupholster them with his wrinkled hide."

"You got it. I have to go, Mercer. Keep me posted."

"I might be out of touch but I'll make sure Jim McKenzie or Tisa are available."

"Okay. Good luck."

Mercer returned the phone to the pocket of the overalls he'd been given by Scott. Glass stood by his ADS talking with Spirit. "How's C.W.?" Mercer asked.

Spirit glowered at him and said nothing.

"Still unconscious," Scott answered, not understanding the animosity. "The engineer pumped a third IV into him. Spirit says his color is better and the bleeding has stopped."

"That's good."

Tisa stepped through the open container doors. Spirit shot her a sharp glare and wheeled on Mercer. "I see you're not man enough to use Charlie's suit." Then she stormed out.

"Told you," Tisa said to Mercer.

"I'm afraid you're way off base about her. If possible she hates me even more."

She stroked his arm. "You don't know much about women. Bad for you. Good for me."

"How is that bad for me?"

"You'll never see my feminine tricks coming."

Of all the burdens and distractions Mercer was shouldering, all the directions he was being pulled in, all the demands that were draining him down, only Tisa, and the promise of their relationship, gave him sustenance and the strength to carry on. Sometimes all it took was a sly comment to make him forget everything else. He reached for her hand as he addressed Scott. "We have five hours before the president orders the evacuation of the eastern U.S. and causes a panic that will claim thousands. The bomb has a three-hour delay timer once it's set and I want at least an hour after the blast to evaluate the results."

"Leaves us an hour to pull *Conseil* out of the vent and place the bomb," Scott grunted. "Not a whole lot of time."

"All the more reason to get going. How are we going to carry the weapon?"

"My suit will take the brunt of the weight from the towline. We'll mount the bomb to yours in a quick-release harness. Onboard gyroscopes will compensate for the added weight and keep the ADS trimmed."

"Okay then." Mercer shook Scott's hand.

Two Petromax workers helped Mercer and Scott Glass climb into the NewtSuits. Before sealing the back, Mercer motioned Tisa over to him. "I'll see you soon."

"What time is it?"

"Ah, eight thirty. Oh God! Did the oracle predict something else for today?"

"No. I was just curious." She smiled and kissed his cheek. "If I hadn't lost it on the ferry, I think I'd start wearing the watch you gave me."

"I'll get you another," he promised.

Tisa stepped back and Mercer's suit was closed and the seals engaged. The ventilation fans were already working, but he needed several deep breaths to feel his lungs fill with air.

"Can you hear me, Mercer?" Scott called from his own suit.

"Loud and clear. Jim, are we on-line in the van?"

"I read you both. Everything looks good from my end. Say the word and they'll maneuver the cradle to the stern and lower you in."

"Give us a minute," Scott requested. "Mercer, do one more check of your motors. Make sure everything's okay."

Mercer rocked his feet on the large toggle switches in the base of each leg and was rewarded with the buzz of the appropriate propeller. Outside the thick faceplate, Tisa gave Mercer a thumbs-up, then pretended to be impressed with the size of his biceps by squeezing the suit's armored skin. In the air, the suit was too heavy to move so he couldn't respond other than to flash a smile she couldn't see.

"We're ready, Jim."

Mercer watched one of the technicians motion Tisa away from the heavy steel cage that would lower the divers to the tunnel entrance. Before she would allow him to vanish, Tisa stepped forward, leaning over the bomb strapped to the suit's torso, and left a lipstick kiss on Mercer's helmet. With her face inches from his there was no mistaking the words she mouthed.

"I love you."

Adrenaline surged through Mercer's heart. But before he could react the A-frame crane hanging over the stern took up the slack and the cradle rolled back on tracks embedded in the deck. The drizzling rain couldn't smear the impression of her mouth from the plastic.

He shook thoughts of her words, and his reply, from his head and concentrated on the task at hand. With a quick glance he checked the electronic monitors ringing the bottom of his helmet. Power, oxygen and coolant levels were all in the green. Condensation formed on his faceplate. Mercer used the finger controls to adjust the ventilator and concentrated on slowing his breathing. He had more than enough air for the dive, but Scott, and his scuba instructor months earlier, cautioned about taking nothing for granted.

The cradle reached the end of the track and the crane lifted the large basket into the air. Mercer and Scott stood solid as statues as the heavy-duty hydraulics raised them up and over the crane's apex and held them suspended over the scummy water. With the suits in a neutral hunched position, Mercer could just see the ocean under his feet.

"Okay, Jim, we're set," Scott radioed. "Lower away. Just keep an eye on the tow spool." The drum of thick cable was bolted just below the crane's legs.

"Here you go."

The crane unwound its line and the basket sank past the deck height. In a moment they could see where the service boat's name had been painted on her stern and then the top few inches of her rudder. Inside the armored suits there was no sensation when water began to fill the lifting basket and surge around their legs. Mercer watched it climb higher, past the bomb on his chest and up his torso. A weak wave splashed filthy water against his helmet. Tisa's kiss washed away.

And then they were submerged. The water was completely black, choked with sediment. The lights atop the cradle gave them barely two feet of visibility.

"It'll clear when we get under the layers of ash," Scott remarked.

The cradle and crane acted like an elevator, dropping the divers into the abyss without them having to rely on their suit's batteries. When the mission was over they'd be able to climb into it again for the ride to the surface.

The descent took ten minutes, but with no references it felt much longer. The water was as cloudy at this depth as it was near the surface. Mercer and Scott would have to work virtually blind.

"Jim, we're here," Scott reported after turning on

his suit's powerful halogen lamps. "I can see the vent opening. It's right in front of us. Only problem is the water temperature is up to ninety degrees."

"The suits can take it," Jim reassured.

"I know the suits can, but I just don't want to get cooked alive in this thing."

"We'll serve you like lobster with drawn butter and corn on the cob. We'll even put your picture on the little plastic bibs."

"You're one sick man."

McKenzie knew how to banter to keep his people from thinking too much about their jobs, but not too much to lose their concentration. "We've got five hundred fifty feet of cable stripped from the drum and enough floats to keep it neutrally buoyant. Proceed when you're ready."

"Roger," he replied. Then to Mercer he said, "I've got the end of the tow cable. Take your grip about ten feet back. Don't forget the thumb toggle lets you lock the pincer so you don't need to maintain pressure."

Impossible to move on the boat, the NewtSuit's joints were amazingly flexible underwater, thanks to their ingenious fluid-filled design. Mercer raised his arm and took hold of the inch-thick cable where Scott had requested then locked the mechanical claw so it wouldn't slip. "Got it."

"Let's go."

Propellers on Scott's suit burst into life and he lifted himself from the cradle before pitching the swivel nacelles back and moving off into the gloom.

Mercer applied pressure with the toes of his right foot. Like the rocket packs worn by shuttle astronauts, the NewtSuit gently skidded from the cradle and entered the realm for which it was designed, indifferent to the hundreds of pounds of pressure bearing down on its thick aluminum skin.

The water cavitated off the multiple propellers on

the back of Scott's ADS as Mercer followed him into
the volcanic conduit. The bubbles seemed sluggish as
they rose through the soupy water.

"I'm in," Scott said when the glow from his lights
was swallowed by the cave.

Mercer followed him, trailing the long tether behind
him. Scott's suit was taking the strain of dragging the
cable through the water. Mercer was there only if he
needed a bit of extra leverage.

"The temp's up to one ten."

Mercer couldn't feel the heat. His suit had an integrated meshwork of water pipes that circulated either
cold or warm water depending on the conditions. C.W.
had said it could keep a diver comfortable in temperatures up to two hundred degrees. In fact, the climate-
control system could take more than that; it was the
plastic faceplate that began to melt above two
hundred.

"How you doing, Mercer?"

"No problems." With gyroscopes keeping the ADS
upright, and Scott steering their little train, all Mercer
had to do was keep even pressure on the foot switch.
This dive was far easier than his foray into the flooded
DS-Two mine with Booker Sykes.

"We're in two hundred feet."

McKenzie's reply was garbled.

"Say again, Jim."

Static filled Mercer's helmet.

Scott wasn't concerned. "Interference from the rock.
We planned on this."

At three hundred feet from the vent opening the
temperature had climbed to one hundred thirty degrees and the cave had constricted. Scott walked Mercer through the procedure for adjusting his trim so the
NewtSuit floated at an angle to reduce its height. Before Mercer got it right he flew into the floor of the
cave, grinding the warhead against the rock.

"Takes a licking and keeps on ticking," he said.

"That thing better not be ticking."

Their pace into the volcano had slowed because of the weight and drag of the towline. Motors on Scott's suit were overheating, but rather than wait to let them cool, they switched positions on the cable so Mercer had the lead and his suit did the lion's share of the work. His steering lacked Scott's finesse, but he managed to keep the suit from scraping the side of the tunnel again.

They rounded the first gentle bend in the otherwise straight shaft and found *Conseil* resting forlornly in the dark. With its camera eyes opaque in the wavering light of their lamps, the ROV looked dead.

"And that's why we brought the tow cable." There was about three feet of clearance from the top of the robot to the cave roof, almost but not quite enough to climb over in the bulky suits. "It has to get dragged back until the cave is wide enough for us to get past."

"We've been down twenty minutes," Mercer said. "Wouldn't it be quicker if we smashed off the top struts and removed some of the gear to climb over right here."

Glass didn't answer.

"Scott, I said wouldn't it be—" Mercer stopped talking when he heard the dive leader make a wet choking sound. "Scott? Scott?"

It took a minute to swivel the suit in the tunnel so he could face his partner. Mercer beamed his lights into Scott's helmet but could not see the man's face. The suit had filled with some dense white gas.

"What the—?"

Suddenly Scott pressed his face to the thick plastic. His eyes were smeared with bloody tears and his tongue was swollen to twice its size. "Something shorted," he croaked. "I can feel wires burning."

Scott Glass's greatest fear was being realized as he

was parboiled in the suit. His skin turned red and began to blister as the fire grew at his feet. His suit jerked spastically with his frantic attempts to stamp out the flames. Mercer had to turn the volume on his underwater phone down to its minimum setting. He couldn't bear to listen to the agonizing screams, though he did not pull away from Scott's suit until the last gasping cry.

Mercer's anger built until he almost couldn't see. Something in Scott's suit hadn't shorted. It had been tampered with. The saboteur had struck again and this time he had a good idea who that person was.

Later, he seethed and turned from Scott's inert form.

Conseil was basically a strut framework around an inner body housing its cameras, sensors and propulsion nacelles. Mercer gripped the top of one cross support and tore it bodily from the ROV. He slashed and tore at the robot, scissoring wires with the pincers and using the suit's tremendous weight as leverage to rip it apart.

His frantic efforts were fueled partly by hatred but mostly by fear. He would be a fool to think his suit hadn't been tampered with. But he would not turn back. The bomb needed to be another three hundred feet deeper into the mountain in order to collapse the water-trapping dikes that threatened to split the island in half. Considering the yield of the nuclear device, a hundred yards didn't seem like much, but the explosives experts had been adamant. They were trying to implode the mountain the way demolition experts took down a building. Placement of the device was everything.

The pincers could snip through pipes up to an inch in diameter. He used them to sever *Conseil*'s bracing and literally peel the top off the ROV. He shoved the tangle of metal and wire behind him and climbed on top of the robot. The back of his suit wedged against the vent's roof, forcing him to twist violently, clawing to get past, his feet dancing on the pedals to eke out that last bit of momentum.

He popped free and drifted to the floor. His efforts had whipped up a storm of sediment and his faceplate was fogged by his heavy breathing. Uncaring, he powered up his thrusters and advanced deeper into the volcano.

An alarm in his helmet went off. He scanned the LEDs. The water temperature had shot up to a hundred and eighty degrees.

"Jesus, not now." He killed the shrill horn and pushed on, unwilling to admit he was beginning to feel heat seeping into the suit despite its cooling system.

He had no idea what had been done to Scott's suit to cause the fire. It probably wasn't on a timer or both suits would have shorted at the same time. Something else had triggered it. Mercer remembered that Scott had overheated his motors. Could that have been it? Had the strain of dragging the towline activated some device that caused the fire? He checked the status board for the six motors on his suit. All of them were green.

"No, damn it. That isn't it," he said aloud.

During their training session he and Scott had switched suits. The saboteur knew Mercer would be carrying the bomb, but couldn't have known that he'd be using Scott's suit and not the one left available by the attack on Charlie Williams. By tampering with C.W.'s ADS, the saboteur thought he would kill Mercer and prevent him from delivering the bomb. There would have been no need to damage the suit they believed Scott Glass was going to dive in.

No less pressed for time, Mercer figured he no longer had to fear immolation. He continued down the tunnel, his heart a little slower, the sweat bathing his body a little less oily.

When he was well past what he knew to be the

eight-hundred-foot mark, he shut down the suit's motors and allowed himself to settle on the bottom. The temperature outside his ADS hovered just below the two-hundred-degree mark. Inside the suit it hadn't grown uncomfortable yet, but Mercer was well aware of the heat. He was also noticing that the plastic faceplate was losing a little of its clarity.

It was awkward to unclip the bomb from the shackles on his chest, and when they finally released the weapon dropped to the floor with a dull thunk. He flipped it onto its back. A bolt had been hastily welded to the timer's access panel so he could open it with the unwieldy pincers. Scott was supposed to have done this.

Gently, Mercer snapped the claw around the bolt and tried to expose the timer. The panel flew open. He looked and saw that the timer was still sealed. It was the bolt that had snapped off. He muttered a curse and tried to grab the bead of weld still attached to the bomb, but the pincer couldn't get a tight grip. He strung his next curses into a long sentence.

He had no tools.

"Think, damn it, think."

He needed something strong and flat to wedge into the seal and pry the lid open. The folding knife he always carried in his pocket would be perfect. It had the perfect blade.

Blade, he thought. One of his suit's propeller blades.

He reached for one of the nacelles on his shoulder and came up far short. The ADS didn't have that degree of flexibility. There wasn't enough time to go back and snap a blade off of Scott's suit.

Mercer settled across the narrow shaft, braced his feet against the wall and shoved back as hard as he could. The impact rattled him in the suit and the power failed for a second as a wire jarred loose. In the momentary flash of darkness he saw a muted glow emanating from deeper inside the volcano. Molten rock was entering the vent. It couldn't have been much or the water would have boiled away by now, but it was enough. He slammed the back of his suit into the rock again and again. His head caught a sharp edge at the back of his helmet, opening a trickling wound.

The seventh time did it. He felt one of the main motor housings pop loose from the suit. It drifted on the minute current until coming up against the bundle of wires acting as an umbilical. He reached into the nacelle's throat and ripped the prop off its shaft.

Each of the three blades was about two inches long and made of tungsten steel. It was a miniature work of art in a way, its delicate curve designed for maximum thrust with minimum resistance. He unceremoniously jammed it against the timer panel and heaved open the thick lid.

Inside the small compartment was a single red button. Mercer pressed it, giving no consideration that he had just unleashed four and a half thousand tons of TNT. His suit's electronic display recorded the temperature as two hundred and ten degrees. At this depth it would need to be much higher to boil the water, but it was slowly dissolving the faceplate. Already Mercer's view had the same murky blur as trying to open his eyes in a chlorinated swimming pool.

He could also see the glow of lava even with his lights on.

Mercer closed the bomb's lid and started back the way he'd come. Even if the lava flowed over the weapon, its casing would protect it from the thermal onslaught.

With one main thruster trailing uselessly behind him, steering the NewtSuit became a challenge, especially when he realized the other primary motor had been damaged and ran out of balance. The suit wanted

to veer left, then down. He adjusted his trim so the
ADS was horizontal, allowing him to use the direc-
tional nacelles to push him forward. He felt like he
was barely creeping along the tunnel, and with his
pincers dragging along the floor he was blinded by
sediment.

Behind him magma continued to drip into the tunnel, and no matter how fast he struggled forward he
couldn't escape the envelope of scalding water. The
digital thermometer read two hundred eighteen degrees. Mercer's face mask had become a wavy prism.
The cooling system was struggling to keep pace. A hot
spot had developed at his elbow that blistered his skin.
The inside of the suit smelled of cooked meat.

His helmet clanged against *Conseil*'s ravaged car-
cass. It had taken fifteen minutes to cover the three
hundred yards. The *Petromax Angel* had a top speed
of twelve knots. He had to give them at least two
hours to get clear of the bomb blast and the inevitable
tsunami to follow.

He climbed over the ROV, snagging the detached
motor in the tangle of braces. He snipped the wires
and pulled himself free. More than anything he
wanted to take Scott's body back to the surface, but
there was no way he could do it. Without an operator
in control, the suit could easily jam in the narrow vent
and trap them both.

Mercer laid a hand on the suit's chest. "I'm sorry,"
he muttered and cut the tow cable out of Scott's grip.
He took a firm hold on the cable and tapped it with
his pincer.

Nothing happened. He rapped it again, harder, and
suddenly he was being pulled from the tunnel. He
skipped and bounced against the shaft as the topside
crane operator recovered what he thought was the
ROV.

It took a few minutes but he finally saw that he had

outpaced the temperature spike. The thermometer was down ten degrees. And not a moment too soon. It was hard to be certain, but it looked like half the thickness of his faceplate had been dissolved.

Three minutes later the cable drew him out of the vent and into cold water. The plastic gave a sickening pop as it cooled, but it did not crack. Mercer was in the clear. He allowed the cramped muscles in his back and shoulders to relax for the first time since entering the volcanic shaft.

"Jim, can you read me, over? Jim, it's Mercer, can you read me?"

"I read you. What the hell happened down there? We expected to pull out the ROV a half hour ago."

"I'll explain everything in a minute. I'm holding on to the end of the towline. That's me you're pulling up."

"What? Where's Scott?"

"He didn't make it. Please, Jim, just pull me up. I'll tell you everything."

"Ah, okay."

"And Jim. Find Spirit Williams and keep an eye on her."

"Why?"

"She wears wooden shoes." Mercer hoped McKenzie knew the apocryphal story about the origins of the word "sabotage," which supposedly came from a revolt during the Industrial Revolution in which the French workers threw their wooden shoes, or *sabots,* into factory machinery to shut it down.

He continued upward like a fish on the end of two hundred feet of line. As soon as he surfaced he'd have them recover the lifting cradle or maybe just cut the thing loose. It didn't matter.

At fifty feet the water was still as black and ominous as it had been near the vent. The blanket of ash cut all the sunlight and particles seemed to fill the sea.

When he reached thirty feet he felt the tow cable slow. The workers were preparing for the delicate operation of slinging him onto the service boat. Mercer still couldn't tell where the surface began, let alone see the *Angel*'s outline.

Finally at fifteen feet he could see the vessel's deep keel and the shadow of something next to the ship, but he lost his vantage as he was drawn ever closer to safety.

He was pulled through an eight-foot-thick layer of volcanic ash and mud, a cloying mess that slowed his progress for a moment as the crane operator adjusted to the added weight. He double-checked that the hydraulic pressure on the claw gripping the cable was at maximum. He chuckled at the irony if the suit fell free. To get this far he'd destroyed the motors, and if he did plummet back into the water he'd have no way to save himself.

His head broke the surface and mud oozed off the suit, obscuring his view entirely. Even when it cleared, he could barely see through his damaged visor. The crane pulled him higher still and started to swing him over the transom. The suit's grip on the cable felt secure.

He could just make out Jim McKenzie on the deck and Spirit and what looked like Charlie, or at least someone with their head swathed in bandages. There was no sign of Tisa.

His feet came level with the stern railing when he realized Jim, Spirit and Charlie were arguing. And then he saw that there was another boat tied up to the *Petromax Angel*. He looked down. He didn't recognize the man operating the winch.

"Mercer!" Tisa's scream burst over the communications line.

"Tisa?" he shouted back.

She burst from the control van, two men giving

chase. Both appeared armed, but Mercer couldn't tell. His faceplate was too distorted.

Jesus, the *Angel* had been hijacked. They had just been waiting for the chance. Mercer understood too that they'd recovered the ADS so they could return to the vent and remove the bomb.

One of the men reached Tisa and cut off her charge with a flying tackle. Both tumbled across the deck. The second man rushed to her side. Mercer recognized the way he moved, so much like her lithe rhythm. Luc Nguyen.

Trapped in the armored suit dangling from the crane just inside the railing, there was nothing Mercer could do as Luc helped Tisa to her feet and tenderly wiped her hair off her face.

"Come on, Jim," Mercer shouted, though he couldn't be heard. "Do something!"

And Jim did. The argument reached a fever pitch. Charlie and Spirit were screaming. From under his untucked shirt, McKenzie pulled a snub-nosed revolver and pumped three shots into Charlie's stomach. The bullets were hollow points and the spray of blood from his back was a hovering cloud of carmine mist.

Even inside the NewtSuit, Mercer could hear the triple blasts. He had no idea what he'd just witnessed. Spirit dropped to her knees next to her dead husband. Tisa appeared catatonic. Luc Nguyen left his sister's side and padded over to Jim. The two embraced like long-separated friends.

The moment their backs were to her, Spirit leapt from where she'd fallen and raced at Mercer, her face a twisted mask of anguish and determination. One of the terrorists who'd boarded the *Angel* had reactions as quick as hers. He had his rifle up to his shoulder by the time she'd covered ten of the twenty feet separating her from Mercer.

Her strides were impossibly long, like those of a

gazelle. She managed two more before the rifle cracked. The shot tore a chunk out of her shoulder and still she came.

The next bullet hit her square in the back and exploded out her stomach, carrying enough velocity to ricochet off the NewtSuit. Her mouth flew open and still she ran, born by momentum until she slammed into the ADS.

Spirit's impetus pendulumed the five-hundred-pound suit over the rail with her clinging to its body. As soon as it cleared the ship, she mouthed, "Let go."

At the apex of the swing, Mercer didn't hesitate. He released the lock holding his pincer closed and the suit plummeted from the ship. Spirit lost her grip as they plunged into the water. Mercer fell through the layer of ash and dropped like a stone into the inky blackness, leaving Spirit to die in the ooze.

He was too stunned for several seconds to do anything but ride the NewtSuit as it sank ever deeper. When he finally broke free of his daze and activated the motors to arrest his descent, he found they didn't have the power. The battered ADS was out of trim and negatively buoyant.

The fall seemed to go on forever, an endless slow-motion journey into the depths. The NewtSuit could take the pressure of a thousand feet, but Mercer knew the ruined visor would implode long before that. According to his gauge he'd already sunk five hundred feet. He hadn't forgotten that La Palma was one of the steepest islands in the world. Its submerged buttresses would likely be even sheerer. For all he knew there was a mile of water under his feet.

He passed through eight hundred feet, a tiny figure outlined in the glow of his own lamps. He had been sure Spirit was the saboteur. Her New Age philosophy fit perfectly with the Order's beliefs, and she had had the opportunity on the *Surveyor* and here. After being with C.W. for so long, she'd have known how to tinker with an ADS. But what had clinched it for him was how she'd been dressed during the eruption. Moments earlier she'd been arguing with C.W. Mercer had heard them in their cabin. She had run out as soon as she'd heard the blast. Charlie was taking his time getting dressed. He'd already put on his jeans and shoes. Mercer had been certain that was when she'd hit him, to prevent him from making the dive.

But he knew now that wasn't how it was. She really had just run out. It was Jim who'd gone in when Charlie was dressing and bashed him with something. Her comment about him not being man enough to use C.W.'s suit hadn't been made in a panic when she'd realized she'd damaged the wrong one. It was a possessive expression of love for C.W. She'd lashed out because she did have feelings for Mercer and hated herself for it.

He checked the gauge. A thousand feet. Around him was nothing but darkness.

Goddamned Jim McKenzie. He'd had more than enough opportunity and an obvious motive if he was a member of the Order. He'd done just enough to gain Mercer's confidence. He'd stayed close enough to the center of things to make himself indispensable. He'd planned this setup since his admission on the *Surveyor* about a rogue signal activating the tower.

"Damn!" Mercer shouted aloud. The suit had an emergency lift bag. C.W. had referred to it as the antichute, joking that parachutes slow your descent, the antichute reverses it.

Mercer fumbled with the control pad in his right arm, lifting the safety catch off the antichute's release button. He hit the switch and shouted with relief as the sounds of the bag inflating over his head filled the helmet. His descent came to a gradual halt.

But that was it. He didn't start rising as he should have.

"Come on." He hit the button again. The bag had

deployed as far as it would. He'd damaged the cylinder of gas when he'd smashed away the engine back in the vent. Like someone trapped in the basket of a runaway hot air balloon, he started drifting with the benthic currents.

"No. No way." Mercer put everything out of his mind. He spooled up the few working thrusters and took a compass bearing.

The *Petromax Angel* had been a mile from shore. Mercer factored in the angle of the undersea cliffs and estimated he was no more than a quarter mile from the island's submerged flank. He checked the suit's digital chronograph. He'd set the nuke thirty-two minutes ago, leaving him two hours and twenty-eight minutes before it detonated.

With the half-inflated bag acting as a sail, Mercer worked with the current as best he could and squeezed a half knot from the roughed-up ADS.

For the next thirty minutes Mercer wouldn't let himself think about anything but keeping his body as still as possible and the pressure on the foot pedal constant, although thoughts of Tisa swirled at the periphery of his concentration.

The ash had yet to penetrate this deep, leaving Mercer almost fifteen feet of visibility even with his warped visor. The cliff seemed to build itself as he approached, first just a suggestion, then a solid segment and finally a towering wall that had no end. He reached out and touched one rocky projection, reassuring himself that it was real. Making it this far was a victory, but now the real work began. He checked his depth. He'd drifted down another two hundred feet, well past the suit's limit.

The emergency bag afforded him almost neutral buoyancy, otherwise what he had in mind would have been impossible. He didn't have the strength and the suit certainly didn't have the flexibility. He jammed his foot against the cliff, searching for a toehold. Once he was reasonably stable he kicked upward, scrabbling along the rough stones for a place to grip with his pincer. His kick rose him eight feet but he fell back four until the claw found purchase.

He found another foothold and kicked upward again, gaining only six feet but losing nothing when his pincer closed around a narrow ribbon of ancient lava. Just two awkward lunges in the bulky suit already cramped his legs. Mercer checked his oxygen. He had plenty so he made the mix a bit richer, giving his muscles more of what they needed.

In short fits and starts Mercer scaled the cliff. Sometimes he'd gain ten feet with a single lurch; other times he'd lose five. It was frustrating and agonizing. His body ran with sweat and with his arms trapped in the suit he couldn't wipe the salt from his eyes. His shoulders and thighs were on fire yet he steadily gained. And as he climbed higher the pressure on the gas in the lifting bag decreased. When it expanded it increased his buoyancy, making each halting leap that much easier.

After a half hour he had to rest. He could barely fill his lungs and his heartbeat was out of control, hammering so hard it was almost arrhythmic. His feet were sodden with the sweat that had pooled in the suit's lower extremities.

Five minutes before he felt he could go on, Mercer leapt again, clambering to find a handhold for his mechanical claw. He didn't dare look at his depth gauge. He didn't want the disappointment of discovering he hadn't climbed as far as he thought or the encouragement that he'd climbed farther. He continued his measured pace, taking the good jumps with the bad but always ascending.

He checked the time again and was dismayed to see another thirty minutes had passed. The surrounding water was still black, the cliff face as featureless. He hadn't seen a single fish or aquatic plant. He couldn't stop himself from looking at his depth.

Two hundred fifty feet.

He'd climbed almost a thousand in an hour, but his pace had slowed. Those final two hundred fifty feet would take an hour all by themselves. The damaged bag had expanded as far as it would twenty minutes ago so it wasn't providing any additional lift. The rest would be up to him.

He kicked off again, gaining a dozen feet, but couldn't find anything to grab on to. He started to fall away from the cliff and punched up the motors, thrusting the suit back into the mountain. His helmet hit with an ominously soft plink. He'd scratched a deep gouge into the faceplate. Tiny fissures grew off it like crystals under a microscope.

His foot connected with the rock and even before he was sure he had solid footing Mercer thrust himself upward, grabbed an outcrop and used just his arm to keep climbing.

More cracks appeared in his visor.

He found a rhythm, an exhausting series of movements that taxed him and the suit to the extremes of their capabilities. But he did not stop. And when he found a plateau that ran along the cliff in a shallow incline he bounced along it like Neil Armstrong had bunny-hopped on the moon, his boots kicking up gouts of mud with each heavy impact. His cracking visor pinked and tinged with every step.

At fifty feet the shelf petered out and he was tempted to set the emergency release that would open the suit and let him swim free. Instead he turned back to the cliff, methodically planted his foot and kicked upward.

Mercer didn't sense daylight until he was twenty feet from the surface and his suit was being battered by wave action. It was time.

He found a secure perch on the cliff and locked the claw around a rock. He took a deep breath and in one sudden snap wrenched his left arm out of the suit's sleeve. The pain of the near dislocation was like a knife under his shoulder blade and across the top of his back.

When the agony turned into numbness, he reached into the pocket of his overalls. By feel he flipped open his cell and dialed Ira's direct line. He brought the phone as close as he could to his mouth. He was just shallow enough for the signal to bounce off one of the nearby cell towers.

"Ira, listen to me," he shouted when the ringing stopped. "It's Mercer."

"Mercer? Where are you? You sound like you're talking from the bottom of a barrel."

"Close enough. The bomb is planted. It goes off in, shit, fifty minutes, but I have a problem. Luc Nguyen has taken over the *Petromax Angel*. They boarded from another boat that either came from the island or broke the quarantine. Jim McKenzie is part of his group. He's the one that turned on the hydrate pump in the Pacific."

"Where's that ship now?"

"I assume they took off. I don't know. I jumped— well, I was pushed overboard."

"Are you on La Palma?"

"Not quite. I'm calling you from one of the diving suits. I'm about twenty feet under the surface."

"What?"

"I don't have time to explain it. Right now I'm directly above the nuke. You have to get a chopper off that Aegis cruiser you said was standing by."

"It's going to take a few minutes to coordinate."

"I'm not going anywhere. In case we lose this signal I'm going to pop to the surface in exactly thirty minutes. Tell the pilot I'll be the guy holding the cell phone. Can't be too many of them around here."

Ira smiled. "I'll tell him the model in case there are

more than one of you out there. Don't worry, Mercer. We're coming for you."

Ira kept his line open, but as Mercer suspected he lost the signal a few minutes later and couldn't get it back.

Now that he'd stopped climbing, he shivered in the suit, his sodden clothes and hair sticking to his body like a clammy skin. He played with the climate system but couldn't get heat. All his exertion had nearly drained the suit's batteries. He just stood slumped in the aluminum shell and waited for time to trickle by. He was too wasted to even worry about Tisa at the moment.

She'd said she loved him. It wasn't an ambiguous moan at the height of passion. She'd said the words to his face. Mercer knew he'd get her back, if for no other reason than for him to tell her he loved her too.

When his deadline approached, he began to hyper-extend his lungs, building up oxygen to the point he felt he was going to pass out. Then he hit the emergency release located awkwardly along his right wrist where it couldn't be accidentally activated.

The suit split along the back and filled in a rush of frigid water that momentarily pinned Mercer. He kicked free and stroked for the surface, allowing a trickle of air to escape his lips as he rose.

Ash formed a thick ceiling at the surface. He hit it and began to claw his way through, kicking frantically as mud closed in around him. It was like struggling through quicksand. He fought and twisted and was certain he was sinking. His chest burned. There was no way to know if he was one inch or ten feet from the top.

He forced himself to calm and took even, measured strokes. The ash tried to draw him back into the depths but he refused to succumb until at last he shot out of the morass. His first breath drew a mouthful of dust that he coughed and spit back into the sea. He could barely keep his head above the quagmire, but it didn't matter.

As soon as he'd surfaced, the sharp-eyed pilot of the Seahawk off the cruiser spotted him struggling in the otherwise placid curtain of debris. A few seconds later he had his chopper hovering over Mercer and a pararescue jumper ready to haul him aboard. A basket was lowered.

Mercer was able to use the undulating mass of ash and pumice as a springboard to roll himself into the basket, eliminating the need for the PJ to leap to what would have been a broken leg. Mercer was winched into the chopper even as the pilot opened the throttle. They had seventeen minutes to get clear of the blast and the electromagnetic pulse that would wreck the chopper's avionics.

The PJ threw a blanket over Mercer's shoulder. "Are you hurt?"

"No," Mercer said unconvincingly. "I'm fine."

"I think you'd better lay back until we get back to the ship."

Mercer shrugged off the blanket. "I need to speak to the pilot."

"I don't think that's a good idea, sir," the burly PJ advised. "If you don't mind my saying so, I've seen drowned rats who'd win a beauty contest over you."

Mercer grabbed a headset from the bulkhead dividing the cockpit from the cargo hold. "Any chance you noticed a ship inside the cordon on your way to get me?"

They'd come under the cover of the eruption and storm on a sleek powerboat they'd stolen in Santa Cruz. Luc had brought only three men with him, but he hadn't needed more. The *Angel* carried a skeleton complement of twenty-five, and only a handful of others were aboard, including Jim McKenzie and his assistant, Ken Bowers, both of whom were armed, both of whom were part of the Order.

Trying to reach the service boat had been a desperate gamble, a last role of the dice for Luc Nguyen. With the Order's sanctuary in ruin and the oracle destroyed, his only hope of achieving anything was to see the Cumbre Vieja destroy much of the civilized world and hope the Order's well-protected financial resources would give him power to rule in the chaos to follow.

It had taken just a few moments to hijack the *Petromax Angel*. As soon as they tied up to the rig tender, one man had gone to the bridge, another to the engine room, and the third scoured the crew accommodations, herding everyone he found to the mess hall, where technicians from the *Sea Surveyor* were already being guarded on Mercer's orders. Luc had been able to secure the deck spaces with help from Jim and Ken.

They'd been too late to prevent Mercer from diving with the weapon, although Jim had been confident the damage he'd caused to his NewtSuit would prevent him from even reaching much past where the ROV was blocking the tunnel.

So it came as a numbing surprise when Mercer had radioed that he was on the end of the towline Luc's soldier had started reeling up from the bottom. No sooner had the call come through than Charlie Williams, pale and still weak, staggered into the control van. The Order soldier who'd rounded up the crew had left him unconscious in his cabin. He raged at Ken Bowers, accusing him of attempted murder for smashing a wrench over his head. Jim had remained calm, coaxing Mercer to the surface so they could use his ADS to retrieve the bomb and at the same time trying to maintain his façade of innocence.

It all fell apart when Spirit realized that Jim had personally vouched for Bowers. They were on deck then, waiting for Mercer to be hauled over the rail. As soon as Jim knew they had the suit, he'd ended C.W.'s rants with the pistol he'd kept with him since he first left California on the *Sea Surveyor*.

Now Mercer was gone, pushed over the side by Spirit in her last act of defiance. All that remained for the surviving members of the Order was to run and hope the nuclear bomb failed to prevent the catastrophe.

Luc, Jim McKenzie and Tisa stayed in the confines of the control van as the workboat raced from the weapon's epicenter. Jim maintained contact with the navy and fed bogus updates to Admiral Lasko, buying them the time they needed. Tisa hadn't said a word since Mercer fell from the stern and made no protests when her brother tried to console her by touching her hair or her shoulder or hip. Her only movements were to gently rub the place where once she wore the watch he had given her.

"How far have we come?" Luc asked.

McKenzie checked the GPS readout on one of the multiple computer screens. "Almost twenty miles."

"Is that far enough?"

"To avoid the fallout, yes, but we need to keep going. There's going to be a pretty big wave following the blast and we're still inside the navy quarantine zone. Once we make it to the nearby island of La Gomera, we'll hide there until things calm down. We still have two weeks to make our escape if the bomb fails and the main eruption splits La Palma."

"How much more time?"

"I estimate ten or fifteen minutes."

"Do you think they will ever stop hunting you?" Tisa asked, breaking her hour-long silence.

"They don't know we're running," Jim countered. "They don't know they have to hunt us."

Luc smiled at her. "My dear sister can speak after all. I'm sorry it had to come to this."

"I doubt that. I think you feed off destruction. You need it the way others need love."

"I need love too, you know."

"And even that is something you've managed to pervert."

Jim shifted in his padded seat. He'd known of Luc Nguyen's incestuous feelings toward his sister and the thought made him uncomfortable.

"Not pervert, Tisa. Purify. Think of it. The two children of the Order's last lama. Think what we could create."

"A monster for the monstrous new world you want to build on the ashes of the old."

He looked at her sadly, but also with the knowledge that he would have what he wanted.

Out of nowhere, the thunderous roar of a helicopter shattered the relative quiet of the control van. Jim launched himself out of his chair and looked out the open container doors. A gray SH-60 Seahawk hovered over the *Angel*'s fantail. Its side door was open and a soldier covered the workboat's stern deck with an M-16. Behind him was the shadowy outline of another man. McKenzie was dumbstruck when the chopper turned slightly and the shadow passed. The other man was Philip Mercer.

Mercer saw Jim McKenzie standing just outside the container box, tapped the PJ on the shoulder and pointed. The M-16 spat and bullets sparked across the ship's steel deck.

Jim dove back into the van. "It's Mercer!"

"I told you they'd hunt you down." Tisa never doubted that Mercer would come back for her.

Luc glanced out of the container and was driven back by fire from the Seahawk. He grabbed a walkie-talkie from his shirt pocket. "Everyone, get on deck! We're under attack." He checked the holster around his waist and racked a round in the chamber of the machine pistol he'd brought. As soon as his men appeared, they'd shoot the chopper from the sky.

He looked out again. The American helicopter remained over the stern, flying sideways so the gunman in the doorframe could cover the entire aft of the service boat.

"Paul, Pran, where are you?" he radioed.

"I'm on the bridge," Paul Thierry replied. He was a boyhood friend from Paris who'd gone to Rinpoche-La with Luc when he'd returned to his father's side. "As soon as I run to the wing I will have them."

"I've just reached an exterior door on the main deck of the superstructure," Pran, a Vietnamese cousin, answered. "I'm ready."

"Gerhard?"

The young German had been recruited into the Order while in Nepal seeking life's answers among the mountains and the opium. "On the port side making my way aft. A lifeboat is blocking their view. Give me a moment longer. Ja, okay, I am ready."

"On my mark we all fire at once." Luc jacked the

slide again, mistakenly ejecting a live round. Tisa smirked at his nervousness.

"Now!"

He rounded the corner of the container again and fired as soon as his rifle barrel was clear. He'd cooked off half a magazine before realizing the helicopter had peeled off and paced the workboat fifty yards to starboard. "Damn it. Hold your fire. Wait until they return."

From cover behind the drum of tow cable Mercer watched Luc shouting into the walkie-talkie. He'd leapt from the helicopter to the *Angel* in the few seconds between Jim's frantic retreat into the container and the first time Luc Nguyen surveyed the scene. He cradled the second M-16 carried on the Seahawk and two spare magazines. He had no idea how many men Luc had brought.

When Luc gave the order to fire, Mercer counted four separate muzzle flashes: Luc's, a gunman on the bridge wing, another on the starboard-side main deck near the superstructure and the fourth one deck up hiding behind the port-side lifeboat. He called in their positions with the tactical radio the PJ had given him.

"I can take the guy on the bridge wing even if he ducks inside. The guy by the container's just going to hide again. Same with the guy at the door into the superstructure. I advise you take the one by the lifeboat. We'll come in from the bow."

"Affirmative."

"Beginning our run, now. Hot guns!"

Mercer paused a beat as the chopper dove in on the workboat. As soon as the PJ opened up and Luc vanished into the van, Mercer rose from his position and dashed forward to get a better angle on the gunman under the port-side lifeboat. The man had spun so he could watch the helo rake the opposite side of the ship, concentrating its fire on the bridge.

Just as the Seahawk shot along the length of the vessel, breaking wide in case Luc or Pran counterfired, Mercer put two rounds into the back of Gerhard's head. The German pitched over the rail, hit the top of the main deck railing and tumbled into the water. Mercer reached cover beside the container they'd used to store the NewtSuits.

"One down," Mercer reported.

"Call it two," the parajumper corrected. "And we've got six minutes."

Mercer looked at his watch. The nuke.

"Roger. Give me cover fire on the control van. I need to reach the superstructure."

"You got it."

The chopper wheeled again and came back at the *Angel*, carefully aimed shots plinking around the container, sparking off the roof and keeping those inside pinned.

Mercer raced forward, keeping to the port side of the ship, and found an open hatchway. He could see clear across the ship and hoped to have outflanked the third gunman, but the man had changed positions. Instead of hunting the soldier, Mercer went for the mess hall. The door had been secured with a chain around a standpipe. He shot off the padlock and whirled, making sure the three-round burst hadn't drawn the missing gunman.

The door to the mess flew open. The first man out was the third officer, Seamus Rourke. "Mercer! What the hell is going on?"

"No time. The bomb goes off in four minutes. The men who took over your ship stupidly headed due east. You have to turn us about. When this side of the island collapses it's going to produce some monster waves and we're right in their path. If we're not facing them, we don't have a chance."

"Okay, I understand."

"There are two men outside with machine pistols. One in the control van. I don't know where the other is. Also, Jim McKenzie is part of the hijacking and I suspect his assistant is too."

"Gawd."

"I need volunteers to distract them."

"I'll get one of the lads to handle the ship. Oy, mates," he called into the mess. "We need a hand getting this scum off our boat. Who's with me?"

A dozen voices joined in a resounding chorus of rebellion.

Mercer led them back out the way he'd come. There was still no sign of the third gunman. "Seahawk, this is Mercer. What's happening?"

"No movement," the pilot reported. "The container doors are closed. The jumper saw at least three people inside. One he swears is the woman you told us about."

Mercer wasn't surprised. Luc would want to keep his sister close. The third person was Jim, so that meant Ken Bowers was still lurking around too. "Roger. Keep them pinned. I just released the crew. A helmsman is going to turn the ship around to face the blast. The rest are with me. We have to flush out the third soldier and I believe one more hijacker who was already on the ship."

"Just so you know, we're down to our last two magazines. Then it's pistols, which are about as worthless as shooting dirty looks."

A dozen sailors crowded the hall just inside the exterior door, waiting for Mercer to give the word. All of them were facing out so none saw Paul Thierry sneak up from a stairwell leading to the engineering spaces. He laid down a scathing wall of fire, mowing down men like wheat with a scythe. It only ended when his clip ran dry.

Four sailors were dead, three wounded, and the others went after the Frenchman with the savagery of attack dogs. They caught him halfway down the metal stairs and helped him the rest of the way by pushing him headfirst into the steel decking. The blow was enough to kill the hijacker, but not enough to satisfy the crewmen. When they were finished, Thierry's corpse was a bloody ruin that was nearly unrecognizable as having been human.

Mercer stood at the top of the companionway. Seamus Rourke climbed up from the dim engine room, blood smeared across his face and dripping from his hands. "You get your woman and get yourself clear." His voice was eerily calm. "We'll look after our own on the ship."

"You'll be okay?"

"Aye. If the *Angel* can take the worst of what the North Sea serves, she can take anything."

Mercer shook his hand. "Good luck."

He retreated back outside, feeling a small measure of sympathy for what would happen to Ken Bowers when the crew caught up to him.

The control van sat squarely in the middle of the deck, a small fortress immune to fire from Mercer's M-16. He had two minutes before the blast and five before the tsunami. He also had no idea how to get Tisa out of the box.

Then he'd take the whole thing with him. "Seahawk, what's your lifting capacity?"

"Forget it," the pilot radioed. "I know what you're thinking. That container weighs a couple of tons empty. No way we can lift it if it's full."

But with the door tightly closed, Luc and Jim didn't know what was happening. "Lower your safety basket and hover directly over the container anyway."

"I told you we can't lift it."

"You don't need to."

Mercer ran for the stern and the A-frame crane that towered over the fantail. The controls were on a seat mounted a few feet up one of the steel supports. Mercer climbed into the seat and quickly recognized the function of the knobs and joystick. The diesel generator that gave the crane power chugged away softly. He increased the power and dropped the crane's arm back over the ship, paying out line as it descended. He halted the arm above the container and paid out more cable until the steel hook lay on the top of the box. With the chopper thundering overhead there was no way anyone inside could hear what he'd done.

Keeping the M-16 at the ready, Mercer reached the side of the container and climbed its integrated ladder. The top of the box was flat steel, but eyebolts had been welded to the four corners so it could be lifted on and off the ship if necessary. Mercer dragged the heavy hook to one of the lifting points at the back of the container and snapped it through.

He climbed back to the deck, cursing the seconds lost by not being able to jump. He was operating on nothing but adrenaline now. At the crane controls he brought his radio to his lips. "Okay, take yourself up a few feet, change the pitch of your rotors. Make it sound like you're working."

He pulled back on a control lever. The diesel bellowed as the crane hoisted the back corner of the container off the deck. Mercer rotated the A-frame, lifting the box even farther. He locked the controls and jumped from the crane, the M-16 pulled tight to his shoulder.

The van's door swung open, rocking in time with the roll of the ship.

The first person to stumble out was Jim McKenzie. He dove for the deck as if certain the container would be snatched off the ship at any moment. Mercer kicked him in the chest, flipping him onto his back and sending his revolver sailing. As much as Mercer wanted to put a bullet between his eyes, he didn't. He pressed himself to the side of the container and waved his hand over his head for the pilot to lower the safety basket right to the deck.

Luc Nguyen exploded from the van, firing his machine pistol in a wild spray. He vanished around a winch housing before Mercer could fire. The two traded bursts, neither able to get an angle. Ricochets filled the air. One struck McKenzie in the leg as he lay sprawled. Jim screamed as blood erupted from his severed femoral artery. He'd bleed out in minutes without treatment.

Twenty miles to the west, two hundred feet under the sea, the vent was nearly choked with lava that spurted from rents in the tunnel's walls. Enough water remained in the shaft to prevent the molten rock from flowing so the whole chamber was simply being sealed off.

None of the tremendous heat or increased pressure affected the suitcase-sized box so meticulously placed inside the mountain. The timer clicked to zero.

The trigger for the bomb was a complex ball of shaped high-explosives charges. They went off with nanosecond precision. At the center of the blast wave was a sphere of refined plutonium. There wasn't enough of the deadly material to form a critical mass and create the self-sustaining chain reaction of a nuclear blast—until the trigger charges compressed the sphere. In a burst as bright as the surface of the sun, the plutonium went critical and mass became energy according to Einstein's famous theory.

The explosion bloomed at nearly the speed of light for the first few fractions of a second, vaporizing everything in its path—rock, soil, and most importantly the western supports of the natural dikes inside La Palma.

At the surface the light pulse was a flash capable of blinding even miles away, and when it faded, a giant mushroom cloud had appeared, a glowing seething column of plasma and debris equal to the volcanic eruption the day before. At its base tens of thousands of tons of rock had been pulverized, releasing a million years' worth of trapped rain. A mile-long, mile-deep chunk of La Palma slid into the sea, washed away in a deluge of trapped water.

On the southern part of the island, the Teneguia volcano suddenly ceased spewing lava as internal pressure deep under the island shifted. Magma and boiling water poured from the tear in the island in a seemingly never-ending gush.

Ahead of this surge, a wall of seawater grew, born of the nuclear blast and nourished by the release of the dikes. While nowhere near the size of the mega-tsunami that threatened the United States had the eastern part of the island collapsed, the wave reached eighty feet in a minute and sped outward at a hundred miles per hour.

Mercer and Luc both paused as the horizon bloomed a fiery purple. And then movement on the deck broke both from their awe. They wheeled at the same time. Mercer held his fire. Luc did not. Tisa had finally freed herself from the container.

She'd come out on deck, unknowingly standing between her brother and Mercer. Luc's burst caught her in the stomach, blowing her body back against the container. Her blood trickled down the side of the steel box.

Luc dropped his weapon, wailing as he raced for his sister. Mercer tightened his grip on his M-16 and put Luc's head right in the crosshairs. He pulled the trigger on an empty magazine. Luc reached his sister's side, cradling her limp body in his arms.

Mercer's rage boiled. As he rushed to them, the safety basket skittered by as the chopper pilot fought a crosswind. Mercer grabbed the edge of the mesh litter and dragged it with him. He slammed the heavy stretcher into Luc's shoulder, spinning him away from Tisa. She fell back to the deck.

Luc held up his hands. "No. We must save her. Help me to get her out of here."

Mercer hooked the corner of the basket under the edge of the shipping container and threw three coils of the wire line around Luc's chest. Luc didn't understand; perhaps he even thought Mercer was going to save him too. Mercer didn't take his eyes off the madman as he spiraled his hand over his head, a universal sign to take up slack on a cable.

The pilot heaved back on his controls, tightening the wire around Luc's chest until he could not scream. Mercer's face was an inhuman mask as he repeated the gesture.

The chopper heaved again. The coils sliced into Luc Nguyen's chest, and as they cut through to his spine and snapped his backbone the recoil sent his legs skittering across the deck like a crab. He flopped sideways, trying to reach out for the severed limbs as they came to rest a few feet away.

His eyes swiveled to Mercer. "At least you won't have her." And he was dead.

Those words drained everything from Mercer. He could barely see through the tears as he freed the safety basket from under the container. "Hold on," he cried. "Hold on."

Tisa was alive, but barely. She'd taken three rounds, two in the abdomen and one in the chest that leaked frothy blood. A lung shot. "Mercer?" Her voice came as a soft whisper.

"I'm here, darling. Hold on."

She was so deeply in shock she hardly reacted as he rolled her into the litter. Mercer placed himself over her, keeping his weight off her body, and felt the stretcher lift from the *Petromax Angel*.

The wave bore down on the ship in an unchecked rampage, a wall of water stretching across the breadth of the sea. True to his word Seamus Rourke had gotten the ship turned so she faced the wave that towered over the ship. She started to scale the front of the tsunami as the Seahawk began to winch Mercer and Tisa from the deck. The litter remained rooted as angry black water foamed around the ship's bows and covered the deck.

Mercer and Tisa were soaked and the litter began to skid toward the stern. An instant before it slammed into the NewtSuit garage, it flew up and off the deck, lifting clear of the watery frenzy.

The *Angel* rose ever higher, her inclinometer pegged at ninety degrees as the wave's momentum kept her pinned to the wall of water. And then her bow reached the crest, cleaving a fat wedge from the wave's apex, and she vanished into the trough, dropping as fast as a runaway roller coaster. She should have been driven straight under the surface when she reached the bottom. Or at least snapped in two. But the *Angel* buried her prow deep, then fought her way back. Her deck had been scoured clean. The garage, the control van, and the cranes had all been torn away. Not a single piece of glass, from her windscreen to her smallest porthole, was left intact. But she fought it off, pouring water off her deck as though she were a surfacing submarine. The next wave was half the size of the first and she met it almost contemptuously. The ship was safe.

Tisa kept her eyes open as they were winched into the helicopter, a smile on her lips as she stared up at Mercer. "Hold on," he kept repeating, although his words were lost in the noise of the rotors and the wind that buffeted the stretcher.

When they reached the chopper, strong hands hauled the basket into the cargo hold and the side door was slammed closed. The PJ helped Mercer out and then cut away Tisa's shirt and assessed her wounds.

"How is she?" Mercer shouted.

The PJ continued to work as if he hadn't heard.

"I said how is she?"

A minute passed before the man slumped away from her. His arms were bloody to the elbows. "There's nothing I can do."

Mercer shoved him aside and knelt next to Tisa. He took her hand. It was cold, much colder than anything he'd ever felt.

"Mercer?" He put his ear close to her mouth. "Mercer, what time is it?"

That's when he finally understood. Her request was a plea, an attempt to find her place in a future she'd always known. She'd lived at a lonely crossroads between the past and inevitability. She'd been denied the promise of the unknown, the sense of wonder each new day could bring because she knew somewhere how it would end.

He'd worn the TAG Heuer for almost two decades. It was almost a part of him. He unsnapped it and fit its steel band over her wrist. "You tell me," he sobbed gently.

She touched the watch and smiled up at him again. "It's my time."

"I know."

"I wish . . ."

"So do I."

"Say it once," said Tisa. "We will never be able to experience it, but please at least let me hear it."

Mercer couldn't see her through his tears. "I love you, Tisa."

She never heard. She was already gone.

AUTHOR'S NOTE

Of course *Deep Fire Rising* is a work of fiction. However, I have based its premise on scientific fact. Quantum teleportation has been carried out in a dozen experiments around the globe involving clouds of atoms that are "zapped," for lack of a better word, across a room in an instant. The ability to transport a submarine into a mountain is beyond our capabilities. For now. But as Dr. Marie points out, tomorrow's breakthroughs are made by people inspired by some of today's scientific speculation. Methane hydrate, methane gas trapped in ice crystals, is very real and will likely become the next great source of fossil fuel energy once the technology to develop it becomes available. The story of Admiral He and the Chinese treasure fleets is a true one. I recommend Louise Levathes's book *When China Ruled the Seas* to anyone wanting to know more about this little-known time in China's history.

As for the Canary Island La Palma—well, this is where I started working my imagination. If the island stays true to its history of eruptions, the Cumbre Vieja volcano will become active again in the next two hundred years or so. The eruption will further fracture the island's western flank and it is probable that the trillion-ton slab of rock will crash into the Atlantic. The devastation to the United States, Europe and Africa described by Mercer will occur. The truly fictional element of *Deep Fire Rising* is that there is something that can be done to stop it. There isn't.